'Funny, dark, insightful and unique, this beautifully written novel is a story and a magpie you will NEVER forget.'—Jennie Godfrey, author of *The List of Suspicious Things*

'Gripping, dark, funny and touching, Chidgey's magpie hero is a brilliant creation.'—Sofka Zinovieff, author of *Putney*

'A remarkable and original writer, whose novels have the golden combination of being both riveting and superbly written.'—Lissa Evans, author of *V for Victory*

'*The Axeman's Carnival* is both tense and disconcertingly charming. The story is filled with delightful moments but tightens with frightening inevitability to a shocking conclusion.'—Lulu Allison, author of *Salt Lick*

'I didn't think it was possible to fall in love with a magpie, but from the opening chapter, which is a masterclass in prose, to the final scene, I was spellbound by the foul-mouthed, wisecracking Tama and his quest to save gentle Marnie from unspeakable violence. Another tour-de-force from Catherine Chidgey.'—Karen Powell, author of *Fifteen Wild Decembers*

'Chidgey/Tama hop through the depths of toxic masculinity, environmental collapse, the perils of anthropomorphism and the dark side of social media with a sureness of touch that will guarantee the book's status as a classic. It bristles with subversive Angela Carter-like energy.'—John Mitchinson, judge at the 2023 Ockham NZ Book Awards

'*The Axeman's Carnival* is remarkable, brilliant, a classic in the making.'—Rachael King, *Newsroom*

'A compulsive read and flat-out brilliant.'—Elizabeth Knox, author of *The Absolute Book*

'This is a brilliant book. Tama's view of the world is a fantastic way into making modern human society strange and showing us to ourselves anew. Absorbing, fascinating, funny and thrilling.'—Ann Morgan, author of *Crossing Over*

ALSO BY

CATHERINE CHIDGEY

In a Fishbone Church
Golden Deeds
(*The Strength of the Sun* in the United States)
The Transformation
The Wish Child
The Beat of the Pendulum
Remote Sympathy
Pet

FOR CHILDREN
Jiffy, Cat Detective
Jiffy's Greatest Hits

THE AXEMAN'S
CARNIVAL

Catherine Chidgey

THE AXEMAN'S
CARNIVAL

Europa
editions

Europa Editions
27 Union Square West, Suite 302
New York, NY 10003
www.europaeditions.com
info@europaeditions.com

Library of Congress Cataloging in Publication Data is available
ISBN 979-8-88966-022-4

Chidgey, Catherine
The Axeman's Carnival

Lines from James K. Baxter, 'High Country Weather', reprinted by
kind permission of the James K. Baxter Trust.
Lines from 'A Bushel and a Peck' from *Guys and Dolls* by Frank
Loesser © 1950 (Renewed) Frank Music Corp. Rights Reserved.
Reprinted by kind permission of Hal Leonard LLC.

Cover design and illustration by Ginevra Rapisardi

Prepress by Grafica Punto Print – Rome

Printed in the USA

For Alan,
who gave me Wilderness Road

and for Alice,
my little chick

CONTENTS

Surrender to the sky
Your heart of anger.
—James K. Baxter, 'High Country Weather'

THE AXEMAN'S
CARNIVAL

PART ONE
HIGH COUNTRY

CHAPTER ONE

A long long time ago, when I was a little chick, not even a chick but a pink and naked thing, a scar a scrap a scrape fallen on roots and wriggling, when I was catching my death and all I knew of sky was the feel of feathers above me, the belly of black as warm as a cloud above me, when I was blind, my eyes unsprouted seeds, my eyes dots of gravel stuck under skin, when I was a beak opening for nothing nothing nothing, she lifted me into her pillowed palm. My siblings cried out as she carried me away, calling from our nest high in the spiny branches: *Father! Father! Where are you? Come back!* My mother called for him too, her voice frantic and afraid – but he, hunting for food, had left us all unguarded.

That first day she sang me a strange human song as she packed me into a slippery box punched with holes for air. *I love you, a bushel and a peck, you bet your pretty neck I do . . .*

Then came another voice, deeper than hers, and it was a voice I knew already, a voice I remembered chopping its way up our tree and into our nest of sticks and wire and wool. Shaking us in our shells. *Come away*, and *Get in behind*, and *Dutchie, Dutchie, ya mongrel*. She stopped singing to me about pretty necks then and said, 'You're not to touch him.'

'Haven't you learned your lesson, babe?'

'I said you're not to touch him.'

The box tilted and bumped and I was all claws in search of something to hold.

'I'm just looking.'

Their breaths on my bareness, raising featherless bumps. A snort that I felt as a shock, a shove.

'It's got no chance.'

'Give me the lid. He needs to rest.'

'Well, for Christ's sake, don't name it. And don't come crying to me.'

I wanted the membranous press of the egg; I wanted back in my shell. In my shell I understood my own dimensions, how I curled leg to breast and beak to wing, how I filled the wide world. There I heard my mother talking about the sun and the wind, which could parch us and pummel us, and I felt her tidying the nest, cushioning every corner, pushing away sharpnesses that might hurt a hatchling. I heard the songs of my flock, too, and when they all sang at once I felt the notes blood-deep. At the tip of my beak, a bony spike: an egg tooth, aimed at the blunt end of the shell. My sister and my brothers spoke to me from within their speckled planets, telling me to let in the air, to take my first breath in the soft close dark so that I would be ready. I listened to their hammering, all three of them breaking stars in the sky. 'Now?' I asked. 'Now,' they answered, and I began to shift my body, to move as they too were moving.

In the slippery box I lay like a stone, and she touched me to check if I had died. Then she cupped me under her hand, and when I was warm again I began to beg. Whatever she brought in her little syringes, minced and mashed and measured, I swallowed. I was a hole of hunger and I shouldn't have survived, but she stroked my spine with a single fingertip and said, 'What shall we call you?' Back then I did not know light and could not know light and I thought, when I opened my eyes, that her hand was my mother. A day or two later, I saw her hair as feathers, black against the white of her temples and shoulders and neck, and I knew that she loved me.

'Oreo?' she said. 'Sushi? Domino? Or are you a Panda? Or

a Puffin? No, that's confusing.' She picked up the lid of the box. 'Vanilla Choc Chip?'

He peered in at me too, his riverstone eyes red-rimmed, scratched with broken veins. Hair a dirty yellow. His face tanned but the squint lines white. 'You know if it keeps me awake I'll have to wring its neck.'

'It's just until he's old enough,' she said. 'Then I'll let him go.'

'And what about the mess?'

'I'll housetrain him.'

'Marnie, it's wild. You can't housetrain it.'

'Yes you can, kind of, when he's a bit older. I've been reading online.'

'It won't be staying that long, though.'

'Mmm.'

'If you keep it that long its parents won't take it back.'

'If I return him during nesting season they'll swoop me.'

Tufts of downy feathers grew as soft as dandelion fluff, and spiky pinfeathers, spiky blood feathers. Oh, I was a scruff of a thing, patchy and mismatched, a little branchling only a mother could love. I perched on her finger as if it were my home, and she held me to her chest and hummed, and I felt myself taking shape, shuddering into life. I started to flap my wings. To realise what they were for.

The slippery box was in the hot-water cupboard and the hot-water cupboard was in the laundry with its shelves of sprays and poisons and its white deep-freeze. Beyond the window, the paddocks of sheep, hundreds of them, thousands, chewing and shitting and turning themselves into meat, and the single eucalyptus trees and the stands of poplar, and the vast dark pines on the hillside that stretched their branches full of needles and blocked the sun and the wind and cut black shapes from the air. Higher still, the mountains where no trees grew. And inside the cupboard the old towels ragged at the edges, and the flannelette sheets worn smooth from the rub of bodies, and the hot-water cylinder that whooshed and ticked, a hot heart. She left the cupboard door open a crack when she put me to bed, so I wouldn't feel too cooped up, but I wasn't to make a break for it, did I understand? I was still small. It was still dangerous.

One night I saw him through the crack. I saw him. He opened the deep-freeze and shouted, 'I'll get it, babe. Do you want Boysenberry Ripple?' He chipped away ice. Shifted frozen sheep legs. The hot-water cylinder heaved and hissed. In the distance another voice: *Any lingering showers will clear by late morning, with a high of sixteen.* Then he had a box, a slippery blue box just like the one she'd kept me in, and he was pulling off the lid and scooping out something bloody, a mess of veins. I saw him. Dropping it into two white bowls. Thud. Thud. Licking his monstrous fingers. I must have called to my siblings to save me, I don't remember, I saw him with his box of dead birds, slippery and dark red, and the pine trees huge in the evening. Then the crack opened and she said, 'What's all this racket?' and I must have kept calling to my siblings, *Help me, find me, save me,* and I fluttered to the bare-board floor and hid behind the cylinder in the downy dust.

She said, 'It's all right, it's me. It's Marnie. Marnie's here.'

And I understood that the sounds she was making were not just sounds: they held a meaning, the way my own tongue held meaning.

And when she lifted me and held me I saw that the box of dead birds was not a box of dead birds, but still I did not trust him, and again she said, 'Marnie's here. Marnie's here.'

And I knew what she meant.

From the windowsill I could see my flock in the distance, and hear them, and I tried to tell which birds were my magpie mother and father: little bits of black and white, dark and light, too far away. One day I thought I heard them singing for their lost chick, but every family lost half their chicks, and all parents sang for them, and the voices might have been the voices of someone else's parents.

I saw the new lambs through the window as well, shaky on their new legs, tails fluttering as they drank from their mothers. And I saw him collecting the dead lambs and throwing them into the cage on the back of his quad bike, and the dead mothers too.

'Isn't it old enough yet, Mar?' he said.

'Not yet,' she said.

I walked before I flew, lurching left right left across the waxy floor.

'Just like a drunk,' he said.

'Just like a toddler,' she said. 'Baby steps, baby steps, little boy.'

I flapped my way to the seat of a steel stool, and then to the top of the slick deep-freeze. Put together all wrong for this smooth world, I skidded and slid. When I came to a stop at the windowsill I thought I could step through the glass, that mysterious slice of nothing, that trick of the light. He let me crash into it not once but three times, though she held her hand to her mouth, because I had to learn, didn't I, and the best way to learn was by making a painful mistake.

'Told you,' he said as I staggered back from the thing I couldn't see. 'Just like a drunk.'

He put shapes on the windowpane for me, though: bird silhouettes that looked as distant as the sky. I watched her peg the washing to the clothesline, watched it turn in the hot nor'west wind, scree, scree, scree.

I knew he would make her take me back to the pines on the hillside when I was old enough, and I wanted to leave and I wanted to stay. She picked me up and zipped me into the front of her jacket where it was warm and dark as love, and I began to warble against her, trying out my voice.

She said, 'A bit longer.'

He said, 'It's not natural.'

She said, 'You owe me.'

He said, 'Don't start that again.'

And perhaps I played at helplessness. Perhaps I trembled my wings and begged open-beaked when she came with her syringes and her soft voice. When she scratched me behind my head. When she folded a jersey into a feather-soft nest that smelled like wool and like grass and like bark and like her. She was so beautiful. *I love you, a bushel and a peck . . .*

They kept the laundry door closed but I knew the house had other doors. That was how houses worked. I heard their footfalls in those shut-off places, their questions and their pleas: *Are we out of kindling?* and *Have you seen my lighter?* and *Make us a cuppa, there's a good girl.* At night their whimpers and sighs, and every morning and evening, in the room on the other side of the wall, downpours that started from nothing and pelted and gushed in time with the hot-water cylinder until they stopped just like that. And now and then, moving from room to room, the suck and howl of a storm that I thought must surely snatch me and cast me away and away like a seed. I screamed for her when the storm came, and kept screaming until it stopped – again, just like that – and then I lay on my back in her arms and she rocked me and sang to me, *you bet your pretty neck*, and I closed my eyes and recalled the dark of the nest when I was still blind and bare, and the rocking of the branches, and my mother's song.

He said, 'It's not a baby. I'm worried that you think it's a baby.'

She said, 'I know it's not a baby. Babies don't have feathers. Babies don't have claws. Babies don't eat raw meat.' She cooed to me, held out her pinky finger for me to nibble.

He said, 'If I could undo it I would. You know I'd never hurt you, not on purpose. I'm no monster.'

She said, 'Who's a good boy? Who's the best boy?'

And I was not the only animal they brought into the house: I heard the orphan lambs that bleated for their mothers, and I saw Marnie mixing up milk for them at the laundry tub, then scrubbing the bottles and the rubbery pink teats.

Little by little she began to let me into other rooms – the kitchen, the hall, the living room – following me round with the slippery blue box that I had long since outgrown. 'Do you know how crazy you look?' he said, but she held it under my tail and kept repeating, 'Use your box,' and whenever I shat in it she fed me a treat because she loved me.

He was always watching her: I remember that. He'd watch her pull off her muddy clothes or brush her long black hair. He'd watch her pick up the feathers I shed, watch her tuck them into her pockets. Now and then he'd sit on the steel stool and watch as she bent into the deep-freeze. 'How lucky am I?' he'd say, slapping her flank and smacking his lips. And sometimes she shooed him away, and sometimes she laughed and perched on his knee, then put her mouth to his mouth and fed. And then, laughing, they disappeared down the hall and I heard him: *Marnie, Marnie, Mar Mar Mar.*

That was my first human word, and though I collected countless more it remained my favourite. When the house was quiet and I was alone I practised: *Mar Mar Mar Mar.* I felt the air moving in and out of me, the thrum of the syrinx deep in my breast as I tried to copy the sound. How strange the shape of their language, how blocky and thick. How stunted it still feels compared to my own. I tightened different muscles, vibrated different membranes, flexed my chest and my throat and even my tongue until I got that first word right. Then I collected another, and another.

I was perched in the fake pine tree he'd put together in their living room; it glittered with fake icicles and fake pine cones as I sang my morning song. I could see the real trees through the window, a crack in the glass bending the hillside in two.

He said, 'I don't care where you let it go, babe, just do it today. *Today*, Marnie. It's been over three months and I've been reasonable, anyone would agree I've been reasonable, but I'm at the end of my rope. It's not normal to keep a wild bird inside. It's not kind. I bet it can't wait to escape – and I for one would appreciate a bit of peace and bloody quiet. I've got the carnival coming up, and I need my sleep, and that thing is noisier by the day. I've had a gutsful. Did you know they can get as loud as a jackhammer? I looked it up online. A jackhammer, Marnie. I don't think we want that. I don't think it's reasonable to have to put up with that. I've let it go on this long because I love you and, yes, I owe you, but there's crap on the face cloths, Mar. There's crap on the *tea towels*. It's not healthy.'

I stopped singing and hopped from the fake pine tree onto her finger, and I did not trust him and I was right not to trust him.

'He still has the occasional accident,' she said. 'But hardly ever now.'

'All the same,' he said.

She zipped me into the front of her jacket where I could feel the rush and beat of her.

He said, 'See, that's exactly what I mean.'

'All right,' she said. 'God. All right.'

Then we were outside, just the two of us, because he had work to do, but he'd shoot into town that night and get Chinese for tea, would she like that?

Beyond the yolk-yellow house the wind thrilled through my feathers, fluttered Marnie's hair. Every sound carried. The squeal of the turning clothesline, the buzz of breeze in the pines on the hillside. The clatter of eucalyptus bark that hung dry and dead. A black-and-tan dog whining on its chain. The cough of the quad bike or the old two-wheeler, fading and fading. The sheep, swivel-mouthed and dissonant. And everywhere the birds: chittering sparrows and skylarks and thrushes, the click and gurgle of starlings, the chiming bellbirds. Fantails on the wing, snapping at insects mid-air. Pipits flicking their tails, stuck on a single phrase. And above all these and louder, the magpies. The songs I'd heard from the house everywhere around me now, tumbling down on me, each bird leaping octaves, whirring, bubbling, fluting, sounding two notes at once. I made out distress calls, alarm calls, food calls, open-necked carolling. *We are here and this is our tree and we're staying and it is ours and you need to leave and now.* I listened for my parents and my siblings, turning my head to every new voice.

'This is the place,' said Marnie, and she set me down in the shade of the pines, among the rippled roots. 'Stay away from the dogs,' she told me. 'And the broken fence wires. And especially the cherry orchard. They have traps down there.'

From a little bag in her pocket she took some fresh mincemeat, and I remembered how my parents brought me and my siblings our food, how we begged fit to shatter stone when we felt them alight on the nest with something caught and quivering. How they fed each of us in turn, no favourites. I opened my mouth and waited for Marnie to feed me, but with her hand, the hand I had thought was my mother, she scattered the mincemeat on the ground. Pointed at it. Nudged me in its direction. Further down the hill, the lambs were filing from one paddock to another. The dogs forcing them through the gate. Rob whistling to the dogs. And where was Marnie going? Why was she backing away? Why the choke choke choke in her throat?

Then, high above, a cawing and a screeching, and wide black wings that flashed with white, and rust eyes that fixed on Marnie, and *Get out of here, get out get out get out, I'll pierce your eyes and drink your blood and clean your bones.* Down he swooped like a gale, like a god: my father. At the end of his rope.

CHAPTER TWO

People tell bad stories about magpies. That we hold the souls of gossips. That we carry a drop of the devil's blood in our mouths. That to meet a single magpie brings bad luck, or sorrow, or death. We refused to take shelter in the Ark, people say; instead we sat on its roof and laughed at the drowned world. We were the only bird not to sing at the crucifixion. Magpies bore into cattle and sheep and eat them from the inside out. Magpies steal anything that shines. Witches ride to their seething sabbaths on magpies' tails. To make a magpie talk, cut its tongue with a crooked sixpence.

When I hid unsure and shaking in the pines that day, I knew none of those stories, but I knew I was not good. I had fled when the person who saved me came under attack. I took cover and left her to my father's beak and claws. I kept my mouth shut. High on a branch I huddled, thinking he might not find me, that I might disappear into the dappled air. I watched him slash at her, and her face bled and her arms bled, and small and foreshortened she cried *Rob Rob Rob*, and when at last he let her go he carried a strand of black hair that whipped along behind him, twice his length. He landed at the foot of my tree and stalked around in the dead needles, and his eyes were as red as the dead needles, even redder, and he called of conquest to his audience, and they cackled.

Another magpie with markings like mine – still wearing the mottled grey feathers of a juvenile – sidled along my branch.

'Are you my brother?' she asked, and I knew that I was.

She said, 'Nobody ever comes back. Death by cold. Death by hunger. Death by wire. Death by disease. Death by poison. Death by dog. Death by powerline. Death by car. Death by trap. Death by gun. Death by fall. You fell and you came back. Nobody comes back.' She looked at me and did not blink.

'Don't tell him,' I whispered.

'What?' she said. 'What what what?'

'What what what?' chorused the branches around us.

And he looked up and saw me, and I thought he would pierce my eyes and drink my blood and clean my bones, because hadn't he said so? But he was no monster, and he called *There is my son. My son has come back from the dead. He fell from the nest and he did not die. My son is alive. Come to me. Come come come.*

My sister leapt from the branch and skittered down to him, stumbling a little when she landed, then righting herself. I had never flown from such a height – only fallen – but as I followed my sister I felt the air holding me like glass hands. On the ground I too careened through the needles, and once I came to a stop my father was pecking up the last of the mincemeat. I gaped my mouth and called my begging call, ready for him to feed me, his son back from the dead, and he strode over to me, the meat pink and perfect, and I opened my mouth even wider and called even louder, shrieking *My turn my turn*, my sister at my back, except she wasn't begging. She was laughing.

Gulp and it was gone, the last of the meat from home, down my father's gullet.

'You're getting too old to beg, boy,' he said, and pecked me in my side.

Snagged on the trunk behind him, the strand of Marnie's hair.

'Where is my mother?' I said.

'Death by car,' said my sister.

'And my brothers?'

'Death by cold.'

'Quiet now,' my father told her, and the two of them took a few slow steps onto the grass, scanning it all the while. They stopped and stared, and my sister turned her left ear to the ground, holding her breath, listening for something. Then she plunged in her beak and pulled out a twisting white grub.

And I belonged and did not belong, and I was bird and not-bird. I learned how the wild worked: where to take shelter, and what voice the adults used when another flock tried to invade. I learned to behave. I learned my place. I learned to leap octaves and to sing two notes at once. Certainly, I could talk to my bird family: the sounds came so naturally I barely had to think, and if I tried to form human words they stuck somewhere inside me like sad memories. My sister taught me to land on a branch or a fencepost or even a single wire without losing my footing. I lay with her in a sun-trance, staring at nothing, beak open, head twisted and feathers spread to let the heat touch my skin. She showed me the shape of the harrier hawk high against the blue, and how to tell berries from poison, how to smash open a snail. How to balance on the back of a sheep, claws hooked in the wool, scanning the ground for cicadas and moths, and how to rub the sting from a wasp so it was safe to eat. I flew for food, spying mice and lizards from the air, but I flew for the joy of it too, for the feel of every feather stroked flat. And I saw that black is not just black, but green-black, purple-black, blue-black. My father took me down to where the cherry trees grew, and explained that the birds who stared with shining eyes from the branches were dummy birds, not real: a trick to scare us. He showed me how to strip the flesh from the cherry stones, but I must never go near the cages, no matter the succulent bait inside, because every cage was a trap. I must never go near the reeking pit on the hill, either – not unless I wanted to see all the things the humans poisoned and shot and killed and threw away to rot. Even their own dogs, he said, if they wouldn't work.

I could feel him watching me as we flew past the yolk-yellow house, and I did not look at the place, I did not slow the beat of my wings to glimpse Marnie through the windows, nor try to make the sound that was her name. My sister and I played games, fetching a eucalyptus leaf or a poplar leaf and passing it back and forth: *You keep it, no I don't want it, you keep it.* We flew up past the pines to where there were no trees, and we hid from each other behind the matagouri bushes and the fluttery tufts of tussock and the rocks that held the heat, picked our way around the patches of speargrass with their knife-edge leaves and their savage flowers. We pulled on each other's wings and tails, bumped breasts, pretended to fight, and when our father came to scold us we rolled on our backs and showed him our soft bellies. My sister taught me to listen for grubs in the paddocks too, and I waited for a bit of peace and bloody quiet, then tilted my head and tried to follow their swish and gnaw. And yes, there it was, down deep, biting at the roots of the grass, and I took one slow step and then another until a grub was right underneath me, and then I stabbed for it. And when one of my uncles died – death by powerline – I went to the vigil with everyone else and cawed and keened for him, and nudged at his cold wing.

And yet.

My father kept his eye on me, waiting for me to betray myself. Every day he told me another bad story about humans: they wrung our necks, they ran us down, they shot us, they poisoned us.

'Doesn't that bother you?' he said.

'Yes, Father,' I said.

'I don't think it bothers you. I don't think you believe me.'

'I believe you, Father.'

'You still reek of her.'

And I did not perch with the other birds high in the pines; I took my place on a scraggy lower branch that offered little shelter. But below the trees, down at the foot of the hill, I could see the yolk-yellow house, and hear the scree, scree, scree of the clothesline as it turned in the wind, all the dresses and shirts alive.

CHAPTER THREE

Two voices. Two human voices, singing. The notes climbing above the infinite cicadas, curling one around the other like feathers. *I love you, a bushel and a peck, a bushel and a peck though you make my heart a wreck* . . . And then, two Marnies, black-haired and white-throated, walking through the pines. *A doodle oodle oodle ooh doo*, they sang, which made no sense. One of them warming a baby against her chest like an egg.

'You need to think about diversifying. Alpacas. Organic honey. Elk.'

'As in venison?'

'And velvet. It heals wounds, boosts immunity. Helps in the bedroom. They can't get enough of it in China.'

'Yeah, but Rob's good at sheep. He knows sheep.'

'The sheep aren't making you any money.'

'It's just a bit of a downturn. We're in it for the long haul.'

'Nick's been looking into peacharines. Or there's saffron – what about that? Thirty thousand dollars a kilo, apparently.'

'I think Rob wants to stick with what we've got.'

'Has he . . . how's he been?'

'Fine. Happy about his win at this year's carnival. Busy training for the South Island champs.'

'Only whenever I see him he doesn't look very happy.'

'Oh, he's just worried about the farm – you know. Still not sleeping well.'

'But he hasn't done it again.'

'It was an accident. He was drunk.'

'Right, so because he'd had a skinful—'

'It was an accident. He doesn't know his own strength.'

'Marnie.'

'No, Ange. He hasn't done it again. He's no monster.'

'Because we're just next door.'

'I know. And it was an accident.'

'Okay. All right. Hey, you could milk the sheep. Hawk the stuff to all the people who've gone off cow's milk. Make boutique cheeses.'

'Can you really see Rob milking sheep?'

'Well, I imagine they have machines. He wouldn't be out there with a stool and a bucket.' The Marnie who was called Ange – the Marnie who warmed the baby like an egg – rummaged in her pocket. 'Cherry?'

'You've had a dream first season.'

'The birds took their share. We need the nets.'

'Still, though – no major disasters.'

'Pray the rain holds off for one more week.'

'Hmm.'

'Sorry. I know you guys could do with some.'

'Rob's obsessed with it. Checks the gauge every morning even though the ground's bone dry. We have to watch the forecast for the whole country in silence.'

'That's a bit extreme.' She looked up then, and I saw that her face was different, the eyes darker, the cheeks thinner. A sister. 'Someone's watching us,' she whispered.

'What?'

'There.' Tilting her head at me.

Marnie looked up too, and I thought she would smile and would know me and hold out her hand as a perch, the hand I had thought was my mother, but she froze. Death by cold.

'What's wrong, Mar?'

'I think that's the one that attacked me.'

Cold, cold, despite the great hot eye of the sun.

'They remember faces. I read that. They remember enemies.'

'I'm not an enemy.'

'You took its baby.'

'I *saved* its baby.'

'Don't break eye contact. Eyes intimidate them. And don't flap your arms. See? It's fine. We're fine.'

'Promise me you won't tell Rob. He'll be out here with his rifle.'

'You're joking.'

I didn't hear Marnie's reply – they were too far away by then, so I didn't hear if she was joking. Away they walked, spitting a path of cherry stones all the way back to the house.

Only after they'd gone did I realise I'd made a mistake. Only then did I realise what I should have done, what I should have said.

'I'm going home,' I told my sister that evening. That was my second mistake.

'You are home,' she said.

'I'm leaving the pines.'

She grabbed at my wing, pinned it to the ground with her claws. 'We are your blood. You belong with your blood. We're teaching you that. All the bird things you should have learned when she took you prisoner.'

'I miss her.'

'What? What what what? How did our mother die?'

'Death by car.'

'Who kills with cars?'

'Humans.'

'What is she?'

'Human.'

'Our father will die for the shame of it. His last son, leaving to live in a house with a human. Death by shame.'

'I don't belong here. And I miss her.'

'You know he'll blame me. He'll pierce my eyes and drink my blood and clean my bones for the shame of it.'

'He loves you. He loves you best.'

'I could scream for him right now.'

'And I could peck out your throat.'

'See, you are bird.'

'I miss her. She loves me.'

My sister's claws slipped a little. 'Who will play the leaf game with me?'

'All the leaves are yours.'

'I don't want them.'

'When my eyes opened, I thought her hand was my mother.'

'We have no mother.'

'No, we have no mother.'

'Death by car.'

'Death by car.'

'No more brothers, either, who spoke to us from their shells. Death by cold.'

'Death by cold.'

'And you, the last son, leaving the pines to live in a house with a human.'

But she let go of my wing.

At dusk, when the day birds were calling and carolling and the night birds rehearsed their hollow hoots, and the sheep glimmered in the falling light and the cherries hung black in black trees, I flew home. Straight to the ledge of the laundry window I flew, and I tapped three times on the glass. It still held the shapes of the bird silhouettes they'd fixed there so I would not hurt myself, and I saw another bird in it too, life-size, that tapped when I tapped – but I was quite alone. Again I tapped, and again, and then she came and peered from the unlit room, hair wet and eyes as black as black cherries.

'Oh!' she said when she saw me, and I heard it through the glass, a soft single note. 'It's you, isn't it?'

And through the glass I said what I should have said in the pines: 'Mar Mar Mar Mar.' My first word. My first human word.

'What?' she said, and then, 'Rob!'

She opened the window and I repeated it: 'Mar Mar. Mar Mar.'

'Did you hear that?'

'Yeah.'

'What did it sound like to you?'

'Like it's asking for its mother.'

'He said my name, Rob.'

They stared at me and I stared back.

'That's crazy,' he said.

'So is a bird asking for its mother.'

'Yeah. Well, yeah. Both scenarios are crazy.'

I said, 'Crazy.' The word a wet cherry-skin in my mouth.

'Holy fucking shit.'

'Don't swear in front of him.'

'Jesus fucking Christ.'

I stepped from the ledge to the windowsill. From the windowsill to the deep-freeze. My right eye saw the gathering night and my left eye saw Marnie, and she was not going to wring my neck, or run me down, or shoot me, or poison me. That was not how houses worked. I threw myself on my back and waited for her to scratch my belly because she loved me.

'This time we're keeping him,' she said.

Then she scratched my belly.

CHAPTER FOUR

Rob said, 'Could it be hormones? Since she lost the baby? Since all that?'

Marnie's mother, who lived next door with Marnie's sister and Marnie's sister's husband, said, 'Perhaps she's gone light in the head – I have no idea what she's thinking. She's her own worst enemy.'

'People will talk,' said Rob. 'People will gossip.'

'You just have to rise above.'

'It mimics the bloody alarm clock. On Sunday I reached over to switch it off but the sound kept going, and there's the bloody bird at the end of the bed, beeping away. Watching us.'

'You could build it some kind of outdoor enclosure, perhaps.'

'She wants it to live inside. In the house.'

Marnie's mother eyed me sitting on the kitchen table and said, 'That's a bit much. They carry parasites.'

'And they're pests.'

'Mmm,' said Marnie's mother. 'They also eat pests.'

'Mmm,' said Rob.

'I know what Nick and Ange think.'

'That she's crazy. That *I'm* crazy.'

'I'm crazy,' I said.

Marnie's mother said, 'My goodness.'

Rob said, 'I told you.'

'Do you think it . . . understands us?'

'Now who's crazy?'

'Jesus fucking Christ,' I said.

Marnie's mother said, 'My *goodness*.'

Rob said, 'It didn't get that from me.'

Marnie's mother said, '. . . so they've taken on a dozen Filipinos, because they tend to be quick and clean.'

'Hello,' said Marnie. 'What are you talking about?'

'Fruit pickers,' said Marnie's mother. 'Nick and Ange need to stay ahead of the rain.'

'What bloody rain?'

'It's a touchy subject. I shouldn't have said anything. Have you had a good day?'

'Yeah, all right. I did a window display of the new autumn casualwear, and I steered a mother of the bride away from white.'

'Autumn!' said Marnie's mother. 'So early!'

Rob said, 'Your mum agrees the bird would be happier outside. I can fix up the old chook house, how about that? Add a few perches, a feeding table. A spa pool. I'm kidding about the spa pool. But definitely some kind of water feature.'

'We have the spare room,' said Marnie. 'Or the nursery. Nobody's using that.'

Marnie's mother said, 'The thing is, he's not a human.'

'He thinks he is.'

'But he's not.'

'Have you had a good day?' I said.

Marnie's mother said, 'How is he *doing* that?'

I felt the words I'd learned to speak chafing inside me like swallowed grit.

Rob said, 'He's just parroting.'

'I missed you,' said Marnie. 'Are you hungry?'

Rob said, 'It's the night time that's the problem. You're lying there sound asleep, dead to the world, and then *Get in behind!* and *See how much you'll save!* and *Here are the headlines!* He's for the stew pot if he can't learn to shut his trap.'

Marnie's mother said, 'Magpie pie.'

'He's a very special bird,' said Marnie. 'He's a pet. We don't eat our pets.'

'Much as I'd love to stay and talk,' said Marnie's mother, 'Nick and Ange will be starving. It's risotto night.'

Marnie spooned some diced heart into my dish because she loved me. 'Remember those things we had when we were kids, Mum? Those Tamagotchi things. Little plastic eggs. You had to feed them and look after them, and if they got sick you had to give them medicine.'

'Beep beep beep, all night long,' said Marnie's mother.

'And if they died you gave them medicine too, and they came back to life.'

'I had to hide the batteries.'

'I'm calling him Tamagotchi.'

'That's a Japanese name.'

'Tama for short.'

'That's a Māori name.'

'Yes.'

'He's not a Māori bird.'

'No, Mum, he's not a Māori bird.'

Rob said, 'They're introduced. They're bloody Australian.'

Marnie's mother said, 'Not Māori and not Japanese. Well, it's none of my business.'

In the nursery I slept in a wooden bed that looked like a cage but wasn't a trap. Clouds and stars hung from the ceiling, pinned around a puffy crescent moon and a puffy sun, and along the walls swam a border of ducks painted by someone who had never seen a duck.

'You can have my ferris wheel,' said Marnie, and she put it on the shelf at the end of my cagey bed: a plastic machine that held pairs of plastic people, and when she wound a key they began to turn, rising and falling, around and around, as the machine sang its tinkly song. 'It was mine when I was little,' she said. 'It helped me go to sleep.' One of the plastic people had no head.

Each night when it was time for lights out she tucked me under a yellow blanket alongside a bear that was not real. It cost her an arm and a leg, she said, but I might as well have it now. If I tipped it I could hear the clunk of its heart, and it growled when I sat it back up again. *Clunk-grrrr. Clunk-grrrr.* Through the bars of my bed I pecked at the striped wallpaper, peeling it away in patches to see what was underneath, but I found only more wallpaper: yellow wicker baskets bursting with roses. I pecked at the bear, too, opening a few of the stitches in its stomach and pulling out its silky white insides. At the top of the windows a row of smaller windows glittered with pieces of coloured glass that looked like leaves or eyes or cherry stones or berries, and when the sun – the real sun – shone on them, they threw their colour onto the floor. Tiny holes spattered the window frames and floorboards, the wardrobe door and bedroom door, and wood dust fell from these holes and gathered in pale piles. All the wood in the house was the same, eaten by borer beetles too small and secret to see, and one day the entire place would turn to dust.

Marnie and Rob slept in the room next to mine, in a bed covered with cushions she'd sewn herself. There were cushions trimmed with ribbons tied into tiny bows, and cushions fat with ruffles and lace. Cushions in the shape of hearts, pink and red and satiny, cool to the touch. Cushions stitched with daisies and hollyhocks, cushions stitched with cats. One cushion had a little net pocket on the front, filled with old lavender that smelled of nothing any more. Another showed a patchwork house with a black-and-tan dog lying on the porch, and another a paddock dotted with sheep, each one a knot of real sheepswool. But the cushions weren't for comfort; they weren't for lying on. Every night Marnie stacked them on the window seat, and every morning, when she made the bed, she put them back again in exactly the same order. All the little soft things. That was how houses worked.

I wasn't allowed in that bed. It was strictly out of bounds. No go. Hanging on the wall above it, Rob's trophies: a row of nine golden axes.

There was a spare room too, for guests, but we never had any guests, and at the heart of the house sat the dark hall where the floorboards sloped and the walls bulged with the weight of the place. Down the far end, near the kitchen and the nursery, the bathroom huddled cold and cramped, not enough room to swing a cat. It had a rusty heater and a broken tile floor, and speckles of mould that crept across the ceiling and down the peeling paintwork, and a lightshade that looked like the moon if the moon were filled with moths. Below the frosted window, the hollow white scoop of the bath. The cold claw feet.

'I'm having a shower now,' said Marnie. Water began to fall from above, though I could not see the sky – in those early days, I remember, I wondered at it every time, the way she conjured rain with a single hand. She fluttered her fingers through the drops and said, 'Not too hot, not too cold. Right then, off you go.'

I remained on the floor, pulling at an unravelled tassel on the edge of a spongy pink mat.

'Tama,' she said, which was my name, 'Tama, I'm having a shower now. Off you go.'

I peered under the bath, squeezed myself past one of its feet. The cold, the mould. My claws made patterns in the dust, and above me the water thudded and drummed. There in the shadows I found things: a face cloth hard and dry, a cardboard tube with nothing at one end and nothing at the other, a barbed toenail. Another bit of tassel. A candle stump. A spider, which I ate. And far, far back, against the gurgling pipe that vanished into the ground, a little silver butterfly with holes punched in its wings.

'Tama,' Marnie was saying at the end of her rope. 'You're being very naughty.'

Out I came, and I shook the dust from my feathers, and she peeled a cobweb from my back, and I hoped the spider I had eaten was not a special spider, not a pet, because we did not eat our pets. I dropped the silver butterfly at her feet.

'My earring! I thought it was gone for good! Rob gave me these, for our first anniversary. Chose them himself and everything. Stuck them through the petals of a rose so it looked like they'd just landed there – how sweet was he? Though to be honest, they're not really to my taste. Don't you tell him that.'

She lifted me onto the vanity, and then I saw it: the other bird. The bird whose shadow I'd seen in the window when I first returned home. I stepped away, and the bird stepped away. I stepped closer, and the bird stepped closer. I watched him with my left eye and waited for him to speak. When he simply stared at me, I threw back my head and opened my throat: *This is my bathroom and this is my house and she is my Marnie and now you should leave.* But when I looked at him again he was still standing his ground.

'That's you,' Marnie said. 'That's Tama.'

'That's Tama,' I said in my human voice. The other bird moved his beak.

'You're Tama,' Marnie said.

'You're Tama,' I said. Again the bird moved his beak, and behind him the rain fell and fell, and clouds of steam were starting to rise, and then another Marnie appeared, and she pointed at my Marnie and said, 'That's me. It's a mirror. See? Just a piece of glass. This is my hairbrush. This is my concealer. This is my lost earring. You are my Tama. See?'

And I pecked the glass, and it was only glass, and there was no rival.

Though I was starting to look like my father.

'All right, we've wasted enough water. Just . . . avert your eyes. Good boy.'

She took off her clothes, all of them, until she was bare as an egg, and I shivered for her bareness, and puffed up my feathers as if I might be able to keep her warm.

Down her white back, black. Green-black. Purple-black. Blue-black. Black-black. She looked over her shoulder at the strange markings in the mirror, and the mirror Marnie looked at them too, until the steam covered them up. Then she climbed under the water and pulled the clattering curtain around herself, and from behind the curtain, from under the water, she spoke.

'We got together five years ago – Nick and Ange had just planted the cherry orchard, and they said come and have a look. Come and see what we're sinking our life savings into. Wilderness Road: you can't miss it. And he waved when I drove past, Rob I mean, all muscles and tan, and then there he was on the doorstep. Thought I should introduce myself to my new neighbours, he said. Mum loved him right from the start – He seems very dependable, Marnie, and you could do a lot worse than a farmer, and goodness he's handsome with his blond hair and his physique, and if I were ten years younger . . . I told her not to be creepy. He took me to mini golf and the movies, and that was pretty much that. Mum said when you know you know. Nick and Ange offered us the orchard for the wedding, though the trees were still saplings, and it was January and hotter than hot, and I forgot to wear sunscreen. My own stupid fault. When I took off my gown you could see the pattern of the lace burned all over my arms. Mum had made the dress and she couldn't stop laughing – she didn't realise how deep the burn was. Rob brought me cold face cloths and laid them down as gently as he could, but I thought it would never stop stinging. We went to Melbourne for our honeymoon and spent it looking for shade, and I came back a farmer's wife. I'd hardly set foot on a farm before then, let alone a high-country station, and I'd never lived so far inland, as far from the water as you could get. I don't know what I wanted to be when I was little – an air hostess, I think, and then a Spice Girl. I always liked singing. Me and Ange, we used to put on shows for Mum, and she'd choose the winner. Excellent engagement with the audience, she'd say, or a refreshing interpretation, or I feel you're holding back. Rob can't sing to save himself but he likes listening to me. I could have really made it, he says, if I wanted to. He's just being nice. Anyway, I love being a farmer's wife. I do. All that space. All that sky. And I get to work at the shop one day a week as well. Best of both worlds. It's been on the main street forever – Lynette's Gowns and Casualwear. The kind of place I'd like for myself one day, I think. Lynette must be in her seventies but she's always so beautifully turned out. Rings and scarves and hairspray. One of those women. I'm good with the customers, she says. I have an eye for it. A feel. They come into the shop and they say make me look beautiful, and I do. I know how to cover up their worst bits. The bits they don't want anyone to see. How to layer, how to drape.'

I crept around the side of the curtain. Hopped under the water with her.

I hated the days when Marnie was at work. All that space. All that sky. Rob watching me with his riverstone eyes like he was planning something, like he wanted to drive me up to the killing house where he drove the dog-tucker sheep. Marnie put one of her cushions on a kitchen chair for me – it felt like fur but wasn't fur – and she turned on the radio on the kitchen table so I would have some company. And the radio said *Here's one from the Beach Boys to get your toes tapping.* And it said *Get down to Cameron's Flooring for ten percent off – terms and conditions apply.* And it said *The Maoris want it both ways. They want the land back, but they want to keep the electricity and the flushing toilets and all the things we brought with us.* Before she left she kissed me on the head and said, 'Be a good boy,' and then she belted herself into her silver car with its yellow eyes at the front and its red eyes at the back and its hot oily breath. I wouldn't go anywhere near the car. I watched from the front window as she drove away, the gravel crackling under the black wheels. Then I went back to the kitchen to listen to the radio.

The Eye was Marnie's idea too. She sat it on the shelf at the end of my bed that wasn't a trap, next to the ferris wheel, so it could watch over me while I napped. Black and unblinking it watched, and I knew that she loved me. On her work days, when I pulled the guts from my growling bear or peeled the striped wallpaper away to show the roses underneath, it spoke to me in her voice. *Stop that, Tama*, it said. *Put that down. Use your box. Be a good boy.* I learned to listen for it at noon, and I told it my new human words, pushing the choppy sounds from my breast and up past my throat, and it laughed Marnie's laugh. I said them to her in person, too, when she came home to me and nuzzled me with her lovely hand. I suppose I sounded like a child, the words clumsy in my bird mouth. Yet Marnie told me every time that I was such a clever boy for learning how to copy them, the cleverest boy in the world. So I kept doing it.

And at night the ghosts of my brothers came in the peace and bloody quiet, and the ghost of my mother too, and they sang to me through the glass, their voices the wind in the pine trees, their voices the rain, their voices the swish and gnaw of something underground. And the ghosts of my brothers were only feathers, and the ghost of my mother was only bones. *Death by car*, they sang. *Death by cold.*

CHAPTER FIVE

U nderstand this: I was no prisoner. Marnie, who loved me, showed me the cat door and taught me to say meow whenever I used it, and I could let myself out to forage for worms and grubs and beetles and moths, and hunt the mice that nested at the dank foot of the compost pile. Next to the haybarn I discovered the grain silo: a great steel tower filled with barley, and always a scattering of kernels at the base. One day I found the lid left off, and I plunged in and ate my fill, and when I could eat no more I lay back on my barley mountain like a king. 'You're being very naughty,' I said in my human voice, and the words shivered and rang inside my silvery vault, the sky a blue coin above me.

Sometimes I perched on the sagging porch and watched the dogs mustering the sheep, herding them into the yards or into the next paddock when they'd bitten the grass down to the dirt. A dog could tackle a lamb or even a full-grown sheep if Rob told it to, holding it down with an open mouth, ignoring the instinct to bite. The dogs ruled the sheep but Rob ruled the dogs, urging them on with his whistles and commands. How obedient they were, moving fast and lithe and full tilt, almost flying as they encircled the mob. Smoke was the black-and-white heading dog raised by Rob from a pup. She could eyeball a sheep at close range, standing her ground while it stamped its hoof, waiting stone-still and staring until it backed down. Some old rivalry in the blood: she crept along like a predator, stalking the stock without needing to make a sound.

Dutchie, Night and Help – who was named as a joke but it stuck – were the huntaways, the noisy black-and-tan dogs who forced the sheep from the holding pens through the narrow passageway of the race. Sometimes Dutchie, the smallest and lightest, leapt up on top of them and barked, and danced across their backs to keep them moving forwards. My sister had told me that magpies could die a death by dog, but I was no sheep to be stared down or herded, and the dogs took little interest in me. I pecked the marrow from the bones Rob threw to them, and found feasts in the dirt Help loosened when he dug his holes. Every few days he started another one, attacking it as if he'd scented something he needed to unearth – but the holes never led anywhere. He never found anything. Only beetles and worms and grubs, which I began to peck at as he walked away, defeated.

It didn't take me long to learn Rob's whistles: odd songs, to my ears, but when I mimicked them I could make the dogs stop dead and look around for their master. I'd let out a cackle after a moment or two – I couldn't help it – and they'd realise that there was no Rob, that I was Rob. I learned his commands, too, and shouted them at the top of my voice: *Come away* when he wanted a dog to move to the right, and *Come bye* when he wanted it to move to the left. *Keep out* to get it to take a wider cast, and *Go back* to gather more sheep, and *Wayleggo* to return to him, and *Get in behind* to walk or sit at his back. *Hold 'em* when he wanted it to pin a sheep down with its mouth – but no biting, no biting. *Speak up* when he wanted it to talk, to tell the sheep something important, except that never worked, because hard as they tried the dogs could only bark, poor dumb animals.

'Speak up! Speak up!' I yelled from the porch.

High in the pine trees, the rattle and chortle of the magpies.

The days were blue and blazing and the gorse pods popped, scattering their seeds as the sun squashed every shadow. Rob shifted the ewes to higher country to ease the pressure on the lower blocks, and a hot and rasping wind blew from the north-west, and the sweet briar flowers fell away and left behind glossy rosehips that hung from the brambles like red eggs.

'At least it's dry for cutting the hay,' said Marnie.

'I've left it too late,' said Rob. 'The grass is dead on its feet – there's no goodness in it now.'

He tore through the paddocks on the tractor, slashing every stalk, making the grass into great shining wheels, but it wasn't enough; it wouldn't be enough.

By the end of summer the sun had baked the earth so hard it could let in no rain even if the rain came. Some days I thought my beak would break when I tried to peck for food. Even Help stopped his digging. The sheep tore at the dead brown ground, and you could see their bones. Rob and Marnie fed out the hay and baleage they should have been saving for winter, and what would they bloody feed them then – and the swede crop was showing signs of dry rot, which didn't bloody bode well, did it. Rob kept going up to the haybarn to count the number of bales left, and to check the level of barley in the silo, and to mutter fuck fuck fuck. He killed any wilding pine seedlings he found marching up the hills, but they kept on marching. He hacked at the patches of gorse and sweet briar that spread across the paddocks and turned the farm to thorns, and then he sprayed the stumps with poison, but still they grew back. He hacked at the shelterbelts of pines and poplars and the single eucalypts, too, sawing off branches, sometimes felling an entire rotten tree. As I watched him through the cracked window that cut the hillside in two, I could feel every blow. And once, I remember, I was sunning myself in the back yard, sprawled on the hot ground, wings spread, feathers splayed, head twisted to the side so the heat could reach my neck. I'd fallen into my usual sun-trance, and my beak hung open and my eyes stared at nothing. I didn't notice Rob until he nudged me with his boot – and then I sprang back to life, and he let out a yell, and I barked like a dog.

In the evenings he lay in his TV chair and watched the weather, hoisting up the footstool and leaning back so the joints of the thing clicked and creaked. 'Shh!' he said when the weather woman appeared on screen to tell him the future, except every night she repeated the same thing: *dry, punishing, no relief in sight.*

I liked to poke around in the dark space under the chair, where I found toast crumbs and a teaspoon and an entire untouched peanut. One night Marnie spotted me and she said, 'No Tama, dangerous,' and I tried to scuttle away. 'He could have mangled you,' she whispered into my feathers. 'You must be careful.' I knew I'd done something wrong, but I tingled at the touch of her voice. 'You must be *careful*,' she repeated.

Death by TV chair.

Unlikely.

I started to whistle Total Eclipse of the Heart.

'Shh!' said Rob, jabbing at the screen. 'We'll miss the fore-cast!'

But you only had to go outside. You only had to feel the hot dry breath of the place on every leaf, every rock, every wire of every fence, every crackled plank of the yolk-yellow house.

The weather woman put on her sad face when she men-tioned the poor farmers. She said she knew they were crying out for rain, especially down Central Otago way, especially in the high country, and she'd do her best to bring them some soon.

'She bloody better,' said Rob. 'You should see how much they're asking for grain. An arm and a leg and then some.' But he wouldn't let his animals starve the way some farmers did; he'd cull the ones that had to be culled, and buy in extra feed for the rest, and hope for a break in the weather.

Later he watched his crime show about beautiful dead

women found in alleyways, all rucked up and staring. The man who came to look at the beautiful dead women wore a gun strapped to his side and sunglasses that were also mirrors, and he said things like *This was no suicide, Trent. See the spatter patterns?* and *The perp's taunting us. He's dangling the victims as bait, and we're biting.* We could never guess who the perp was, but the man with the gun always caught him and put him behind bars, and then the TV went off and it was time for lights out.

I heard Rob pacing while Marnie slept, and once, through the wall, I heard her drowsy voice ask, 'Aren't you tired?' And I imagined I was lying next to her, just the two of us dropping off to sleep.

'I'm listening for the rain,' said Rob.

CHAPTER SIX

T hrough the kitchen window Marnie and I watched the axemen setting up. They lugged lengths of pine into place, lying them down in metal cradles or clamping them upright, chalking marks on their sides so they'd know where to cut. Then they took out their axes, the silver heads flashing like mirrors. Marnie said, 'That guy on the left almost beat Rob to the trophy last month. Rob wins every year – nobody expects any different – and then this new guy turns up at the carnival, more than a decade younger, and just about takes it. Ethan bloody McKay, Rob calls him. Can you imagine? If Rob had come home without the Golden Axe? Without the prize money? Actually let's not. Let's not imagine. He's playing so nice now. Giving his rival some tips so they can win the team relay at the South Island champs, but what he really wants is to make the South Island team. He reckons there's big money in it if he gets to the States – oh, that was fast. He's broken his own record, I'd say. And the guy doing the Standing Chop – the one with the big scar on his chin? Rob doesn't like me talking to him because he's single. As if I'd ever do anything. Look at them, scrutinising the wood for clues. It's serious business, Tama. Serious men's business. Still, it's an outlet, isn't it. As long as he's pouring himself into that . . .' She broke off, smiled at Rob through the glass. Held up the kettle.

I could hardly believe how quickly the axemen demolished the pine. They'd had a gutsful. They stood next to the logs and chopped sideways; they climbed on top and chopped between their feet. They attacked with saws, too – sharp-toothed lengths of steel that turned the wood to dust.

'Strange,' said Marnie, 'how you can see the blows a split second before you hear them. You know they're coming but you don't quite believe it.'

When they stopped cutting I fluttered outside: chips of trunk littered the back yard, the hacked-off stumps still sprawled where they had fallen. I couldn't look, though it smelled like home.

'I reckon we're in with a chance,' said Rob, and the other axemen agreed – a smooth operation, a tight unit. Rob was in the best form of his life, too, anyone could see that. Why not Australia? Why not America?

After they'd gone, he asked Marnie to look at his practice axe and tell him if she noticed anything wrong with it. No, she said, it looked fine to her – it looked perfect. Ah, he said, but run the honing stone over the edge – now did she feel it? The bump? Yes, she said, now she felt it. He'd hit a knot, he told her, and the blade wasn't true. He took to it with a file first, then a stone to get rid of the feather edge, and little bits of steel drifted free, tiny specks of feather edge that lodged in the weave of his clothes, the grain of his skin. That night, in front of his crime show about attractive dead women with evidence under their nails and leaves in their throats, he stropped the blade back and forth over the palm of his hand to pull away the last feathery burrs: hush, hush, hush, until it was true. Then, to test the sharpness, he ran it down his forearm, slicing away the fine blond hair.

Marnie waved him off when he left in his beetle-black car for the South Island champs. 'A whole weekend to ourselves, Tama!' she said. 'Just you and me.'

I slept in the master bedroom while he was away, as if we were married, but I wasn't to let on. I wasn't to say a word. Marnie made a shadow bird on the wall as I snuggled down on

Rob's side of the bed. She fluttered her fingers and the shadow bird fluttered his wings; she bent her thumbs and the shadow bird bent his neck. Then she sang me a lullaby about the wind in the treetops, and I went to sleep.

As soon as I heard him inside Marnie's phone, I could tell he wasn't happy.

'You look disappointed,' she said, staring into the screen as if it were a mirror.

'We lost.'

'I'm sorry, Rob. Where did you come?'

'Second.'

'That's not losing.'

'Yeah it is, and it was my fault. And the rest was an abortion too. I won't make the South Island team, that's for sure.'

'I'm listening for the rain,' I said. I couldn't help myself.

'Someone there with you?' said Rob.

Marnie glanced over at me so I kept my trap shut.

'Just Tama.'

'Show me.'

'Rob.'

'*Show* me.'

Marnie turned the phone to me – I was tugging at the braid on the living-room couch at the time – and there was Rob's face, as small as the palm of her hand. My size. I looked at him with my left eye, looked at him with my right eye. I said, 'As if I'd ever do anything.'

'Fucking poplar,' said Rob. 'It sucks the silt into its heart. Blunts the blade. Would've been a different story with pine.'

'So that's America off the table, then?'

'It was never on the table. Not really.'

'I'm sorry.'

'Yeah, the money would've come in handy.'

'You're still king of the local chop, though,' said Marnie. 'Nobody can take that away.'

'Too bloody right,' he said.

The next day I made the sound of Marnie's phone ringing, and she ran to pick it up, then frowned at the screen.

'Hello?' I said.

'Hello,' she said, smiling.

Rob and the dogs brought the ewes down from the hills to the covered yards for the night in preparation for the next day. They spiralled and swirled across the ground like clouds, and later in my bed I heard them bleating for the open space they knew, their voices carrying through the cool quiet air. I heard a possum, too, creeping around on the roof, and until I recognised its raspy breaths I thought Rob was somewhere nearby, dragging a file across the edge of his axe. In the morning he herded the ewes into the woolshed that sat musty and musky and half falling down the hard hillside. Up the ramp they went, and then into the cramped catching pen, and from there they could only go forwards. Chin Scar the axeman was back to help him, and one by one they hauled the ewes out to crutch their backsides so they would be ready for the rams. I watched Rob hold each one still between his knees, squeezing on her neck, pushing his fist into her hip. The handpieces buzzed and bit, and Marnie swept up the dirty wool, deft with her broom, careful not to get in the way.

'You're a lucky man,' said Chin Scar. 'Where do I find one like that?'

'Not here, mate, that's for fucking sure,' said Rob.

From the rafters I saw him flip a ewe on her back, clamp her with his knees and shave her, then shove her through a door and grab the next one. Every few minutes he stopped and wiped his face with a torn blue towel that hung on a nail, and after the ewes were finished he and Chin Scar sat on the broken couch in the breeze by the woolshed door and drank. They talked about keeping on top of parasites; they talked about terminal lambs and sacrifice paddocks and kill value and smothers. They watched for the rain, and the rain never came.

One day a truck turned into our driveway and crunched its way up the gravel to the yards, and a man jumped out and shook hands with Rob. Then he backed up to the loading ramp, and Rob and the huntaways pushed the lambs through the yards, but gently, gently, so as not to bruise them – so as not to bruise the meat. 'Night, come away,' shouted Rob. 'Come away! Speak up! That'll do! Wayleggo!'

The lambs trotted up the ramp, one after the other, each with a smudge of blue chalk on its head that meant Rob had chosen it.

Then the truck drove away to the works, tufts of white wool bursting through the gaps in its sides.

The sound of the engine faded.

They shouldn't have climbed in there. They shouldn't have trusted him.

When the cool weather came Rob lit the fire and fed it with chunks of pine that he split with his axe. They whistled and hissed as they burned, and behind the guard they spat out sparks redder than a father's eye, and I lay belly to the flames then back to the flames, and Rob said, 'Look at it cooking both sides. DIY rotisserie.'

Marnie tried to light the fire once, but she did it all wrong, he said: she didn't take the time to twist the paper and stack the pinecones, didn't lay the kindling crisscross, crisscross. She didn't leave gaps for the air to get in.

'What would you do without me?' he said.

'I'd freeze to death,' she said.

He was allowed to light the fire inside the house, but he wasn't allowed to light cigarettes because those things would kill him. That was how houses worked. If he wanted a smoke he went outside to the back porch, or to his beetle-black car, or to the chook run with all the coppery chickens that could not sing. Sometimes he went way up past the gut hole – the reeking pit that my father had told me about – where he took all the dead things and threw them away to rot, even his own dogs if they wouldn't work. I'd peered inside once and once only: a bloated sheep, a chicken head. Mostly, though, if Rob wanted a smoke, he went to the woolshed and sat on the broken couch and looked out to the hills, waiting for the rain to come, and when it failed to come he drank, and when it came only in trickles he drank too, filling himself to the brim.

Marnie's mother joined him for a smoke on the porch whenever she visited.

'You're a dreadful influence, Rob,' she said. 'I gave up years ago.'

'No one's forcing you, Mum,' said Marnie.

'But who can say no to him? I mean, look at the man.'

'Let me get that for you, Barbara,' he said, lighting the end of her cigarette as she sucked before they were even out the door.

Afterwards they came inside stinking of it.

'Something smells good,' said Barbara.

'Shepherd's pie,' said Marnie.

'Can we tempt you to stay for a bite?'

'Anyone would think you're trying to fatten me up.'

'A few mouthfuls won't hurt. Shall I set a place?'

'If you insist.'

Rob was full of jokes and stories and best behaviour. 'This'll make you laugh,' he said. 'One time in the school holidays, when we went to stay with my uncle on the West Coast—'

'I don't think Mum wants to hear that,' said Marnie. 'I know I don't.'

'I know I don't,' I said, tugging at the braid on the couch, waiting for Marnie to smile at the way I copied her and to call me a good boy, the cleverest boy.

'Well, now you have to tell me,' said Barbara.

Rob said, 'One time in the school holidays, when we went to stay with my uncle on the West Coast, me and my brothers thought we'd go exploring on his farm. It's different country over there, different from home, and we took his BB gun and aimed at a few rabbits and let out a few war cries. Then when we were deep in the scrub we found this massive sinkhole. It just crept up on us and I nearly fell in, but Adam grabbed me, and Lachie grabbed Adam, and there we were, right on the edge of it. We threw a few stones down inside and we couldn't hear them hit the bottom, so we got some bigger stones, some rocks, and we couldn't hear them hit the bottom either. Lachie said it probably went down forever. We looked around and Lachie found this huge log, though Adam thinks he found it and I can't remember, but it doesn't matter. We dragged it to the sinkhole – we had to crouch down and grab it from under-neath, and I could feel my fingernails digging into the rot, and we could only go a few steps at a time. And we pushed it over the edge bit by bit, and it teetered in mid-air, and then we gave it one final nudge, just a touch was all it took, and it heaved into the hole and disappeared. We listened, and for a moment there was nothing, and then we hear this tink tink tink tink, and then a terrible scream, and something comes rushing and crashing through the undergrowth, straight for us. Lachie tries to lift the BB gun but he's shaking too hard. And out of the scrub bursts this goat, flying along on the end of a chain, and the chain's connected to the log, and the goat whips past us, yellow eyes bulging, and straight down the hole and gone.'

Barbara laughed until she cried. 'Oh! Oh my goodness! I did not see that coming!'

'Neither did the goat,' said Rob.

'Stop it! Stop it!' choked Barbara. 'Let me catch my breath.' She was beside herself, she said – but clearly that was untrue.

'It's a horrible story,' said Marnie, and she shuddered. 'Imagine the ground swallowing you up.'

'It was just a goat,' said Barbara.

'You have to watch your step round here too,' said Rob. 'My father lost a dozen sheep down a mine shaft once. When I was little, I remember, Mum tied me to a rope to explore the gold workings.'

'Makes you wonder what's still down there,' said Barbara. 'You could be sitting on a fortune.'

'There's no gold these days,' said Marnie.

CHAPTER SEVEN

S trewth she's dry,' said Nick, kicking at the cracked paddock. 'Did you just say strewth?' said Rob.
'Yeah.'

'Thought so.'

Nick gave the ground another kick. 'I don't want to pressure you,' he said, 'but we need to make a decision about the water. Whether we're applying to Council separately or together.'

'You know it's just to keep their paper-pushers busy.'

'Okay, but the thing is, mate, the law's changing whether we like it or not. We'll have to come up with a rationing plan. Prepare an assessment of environmental effects.' He cocked his head at the glittering ribbon that wound down the hillside, through the tussock and the speargrass: the old water race cut by gold miners, though there was no gold these days. 'You can't rely on wild flooding any more.'

'It's worked all right for a hundred and forty years.'

'Like I said, I don't want to pressure you, but you know you'll have to install irrigation. Why not start pricing it out, at least? So you can talk to the bank?'

'How much did it cost you?'

Nick sucked in his breath. 'Thirty-five, forty thousand per hectare, from memory. But yours might not be that much.'

'I better start digging for gold.'

'It's an investment, for sure. All I'm saying is, don't leave it too late.'

Rob unhooked the gate to the rams' paddock and let Nick

in, then shut it again behind them. The rams paused in their chewing.

'You can't let them see the ewes till it's time for them to do the business,' said Rob. 'Otherwise they get too hot under the collar. Try to bash through the fence.'

'We've all been there, mate,' said Nick. 'They're good-looking girls, eh?'

Rob ignored him and strapped a harness on each animal.

'Whoa,' said Nick. 'Whatever you're into.' He bent down for a closer look at one of them. Leaned in to peer at its chest. 'What's with the block of red crayon?'

'It rubs against the ewe when he serves her, so we can see where he's been and what he's done. Different colour for each ram.'

'Romantic,' said Nick.

'I'd stand up if I were you, mate,' said Rob.

The rain started as I followed them down to the house – true rain, lasting rain, whipping against my wings – and Rob threw back his head and howled at the sky.

'It's been rough on you, mate,' said Nick, but Rob just laughed.

'That's what I call irrigation,' he said. 'And it's all free.'

The first time I saw him hit her was not the first time he hit her. So I learned, so I gleaned. That was also how houses worked. One night in the dead of winter he came in from the farm and drank and drank and drank. He sat with his head in his hands. He said, 'We're so far in the red we'll never get out. We can't keep making a loss. You chose the wrong man. You married a loser.' Marnie fluttered around him, no no no, and don't be silly, and it's just a bit of a downturn, and we're in it for the long haul. Then he drank some more and then he staggered to the dining table and said, 'Are those oven fries? How much did they cost? Can't you cut up a fucking potato?' His hand a rock against her jaw. His face a monster's face. Plates upside down on the floorboards, tomato sauce spattering the table leg, the pepper grinder rolling all the way to the hall where I watched with my left eye and did nothing. Was it some kind of mating dance? Some kind of male display? But I knew. I knew. She lay on the floor and made no sound. That's what I remember. He lay in his TV chair and turned on the TV, and the TV said *Thirty percent off all pots and pans and twenty percent off everything storewide, but only till Sunday. Rush in now and save.*

The next day was a Lynette's Gowns and Casualwear day, and Marnie's jaw was purple-black, red-black, and I could see where Rob had been and what he'd done.

Rob said, 'There's a dead ewe in the haybarn paddock. Nick's going to help me chuck her in the gut hole. Bit of a taste of real farm life for him.'

'Don't be cruel,' said Marnie.

The rain started to rattle down on the roof and Rob gulped his coffee and said, 'I better get going or she'll be twice as heavy.' He pressed out two white pills from a silver sheet and gulped them too. Touched the plate of honey toast he'd made for Marnie. 'Aren't you hungry, babe?'

'Hurts to chew.'

'Shit, I'm sorry. Do you want some yoghurt instead? Or some porridge? I'll make you some porridge, eh?'

'No thanks.'

'Or scrambled eggs? What about scrambled eggs? Marnie?'

'Hurts to talk.'

'Shit. Sorry. Shit.'

'Rush in now and save,' I said, but they paid me no attention.

'I don't even remember doing it,' said Rob. He held his hand above Marnie's head, to stroke her, to strike her. 'It's like I turn into someone else.'

In the cramped bathroom the water trickled down the walls and windowpane, pooled on the rotting sill, and the rusty heater breathed out its rusty breath. I sat on the lip of the bath and preened a wing, and Marnie wiped the mirror until she could see herself. She made a space among the bottles and tubes for her phone and found a young woman inside it whose eye was purple-black, red-black. Then she tapped the phone and the woman began to talk, and the woman said, 'Hi there beautiful people! So, you have a black eye, or a bruise in a really like obvious place. Maybe you've had some injectables, like some fillers, or maybe you've had a nose job, and you're left with some discoloration, and you don't want to stay cooped up at home until it heals, right? Okay, so stick around and I'll show you how to make it disappear like magic. So the first thing I'm going to say is that most girls rely on just one product and expect it to fix everything. Big mistake. You need like a whole range of ammo for this kind of problem, so don't be afraid to use more than one corrector. Okay. To start with you need to figure out the right shade to neutralise the bruise. I'm going to go ahead and add a little orangeish-yellow eyeshadow on top of mine. This is the Urban Decay palette I'm using here. If it's more purple then you want to choose yellow, if it's more blue then you want to go with orange. Make sure you use a light touch. Like a feather touch. You might want to try your pinky finger, or a beauty bullet which you wear like a finger. I prefer the Beautyblender sponge, because it's aqua-activated and non-toxic and gives an airbrushed look. Now I'm going to take some Eve Pearl Dual Salmon Concealer, the lighter colour, and I'm going to dab it over the affected area to neutralise it even further. Okay. See how it's starting to like disappear? Okay. Now I'm taking Hard Candy's Full Coverage Concealer, and this time I'm going in with like a really small dense brush, and I'm really packing it into the bruise now, but remember, not too much pressure. Watch out for ashiness – if you're starting to look ashy, go a little darker. Now I'm taking some powder, just like whatever from the drugstore is fine if that's all you have, but I'm using Kat Von D Beauty Lock-It Setting Powder to give the best result, which is cruelty-free. I'm going to go ahead and brush it on, lightly, lightly, and this will set everything in place so it doesn't budge, and it also uses micro-blurring technology. And there you have it: invisible. Gone. Like it never happened. So now you can just go ahead and apply your normal makeup over the top and no one will be any the wiser. Oh and I should say to all my gorgeous subscribers, in case you're worrying, no, Parker did not hit me! Ha ha. The true story is, I had one or two Moscow mules and a dirty Girl Scout, and me and my friends were like twerking, and according to them I just like lost control. So now you know. Don't tell anyone. Oh, but I'm over the drinking age, so I wasn't like doing anything illegal, so you don't need to call my mom or anything ha ha. But if someone is hurting you, remember, you're not alone. And if you want to buy any of the amazing products I've used today, check out the links down there. Personally I'm so glad I invested in an awesome concealer like the Eve Pearl Dual Salmon Concealer and Hard Candy's Full Coverage Concealer, and don't forget the incredible Kat Von D Beauty Lock-It Setting Powder. Okay, love you, bye.'

Marnie stopped and started the woman, made her say certain parts again. She dabbed with her pinky finger, feather touch, feather touch. She blended and smoothed and layered. The bruise still showed through.

'It's better though, right?' she said. 'I mean, I'll get away with it.'

'Watch out for ashiness,' I said, and she laughed. Then sucked in her breath through her teeth.

When she climbed into her car and pulled the belt across her chest she winced, and she sat there for a moment, eyes closed tight. I watched from the front steps. Though I could see the car was hurting her, I wouldn't go anywhere near it.

At noon I went to my bed to listen for the Eye.

CHAPTER EIGHT

Ange's baby was dead to the world and all wrapped up in wool, lamb's ears on its head and a lamb's tail on its rump. Ange set it down on the double bed, pillows either side to keep it there, no falling in its future.

'And Tama's okay?' said Ange. 'I mean, he won't do anything?'

I walked along the edge of the mattress, watching the baby as it twisted its face and frowned at its own little dreams.

'He's curious, that's all,' said Marnie. 'He won't do anything.'

'Sure?'

'Of course I'm sure. Anyway, he's just had breakfast.'

'Shit it's cold in here,' said Ange. She went to the window, tried to pull it shut, but it kept jamming. Borer-beetle dust fell from the sill. 'Is that ice on the inside of the glass?' she said. 'Actual ice?'

'You get used to it,' said Marnie.

'And look at this!' She displayed the back of the curtain. 'Covered in mould! I thought I could smell something.'

'It's an old house,' said Marnie. 'It has its problems.'

'Can't be good for you.'

The two of them stood in front of the mirror that went all the way to the floor. They considered themselves from every angle, pinching their waists and lifting their breasts, pulling tight their throats.

'So foul.'

'So disgusting.'

'At least you have a collarbone.'

'At least you have ankles.'

Ange peered at her forehead. 'When I was in Auckland I went to a skin place. They take a UV photo of you and it shows all the damage you normally don't see. Right down through the layers.'

'Why would you even want to know?'

'Well, it was free. And they have these special machines that can fix the damage. And special lotions. And then they show you what you'll look like if you don't fix it.'

'I think I'd prefer not to know.'

'Red?' said Ange. 'Or baby blue?' She held up two pieces of patterned fabric. 'I can't decide. I keep changing my mind.'

'Are we really wearing dresses covered in pistols?'

'*Yes*. Sexy cowgirl, remember. Sexy Doris Day.'

'You said cute cowgirl. Cute Doris Day. I didn't agree to sexy.'

'Cute, sexy, whatever.'

'You owe me.'

'Red's sexier, but blue makes our eyes pop.'

'Blue, then.'

'Really?'

'Ange.'

'Okay, blue. I'll get it next time I'm in town. Mum can do the machine sewing at your place when Rob's not there – Nick hangs around ours too much. You haven't said anything to them?'

'I haven't said anything.'

'I don't want you ruining the surprise.'

'I won't say a word.'

They sang the song then, in front of the bedroom mirror, each watching the other. *I love you, a bushel and a peck, a bushel and a peck and a hug around the neck, a hug around the neck and a barrel and a heap, a barrel and a heap and I'm talking in my sleep . . .*

'What do you think?' said Ange. 'Maybe we should go with something more modern. Beyoncé. Rihanna. Something with a bit of spice.'

'No thank you,' said Marnie.

'Hmm. I suppose it's retro. Retro is modern.'

'It suits our voices. And it works a cappella.'

'We'll need an act. A routine.' Ange sang the first line again, *I love you*, hands over her heart, then pointed at her reflection. 'Leave it with me and I'll come up with some moves.'

'Nothing too raunchy.'

'We won't be taking our clothes off, Mar.'

'It's a family event, remember.'

'Family. Okay.'

'How much is a peck, anyway?' said Marnie.

'It's little. A little kiss on the cheek.'

'But in the song, I mean – how much is a peck?'

'You mean, what does it cost? What's the price of a kiss?'

'It's a unit of measurement, Ange. She's talking about how much she loves him. But how much is it?' Marnie began to tap on her phone. 'Here we are – a peck is a quarter of a bushel, and a bushel is thirty-two dry quarts. So a peck is eight dry quarts.'

'And also a kiss. Oh hello – someone's awake.' Ange lifted the baby from the nest of pillows and changed its nappy, and underneath its lamb's clothes it was white and bare, and it might have been candle wax, it might have been soap, it might have been mutton fat. 'There we are, little lamb,' she said, and it knew its part, and it bleated and cried until she pulled up her top and attached it to one of her teats – but it did not know what happened to little lambs. 'We'll need to make my costume big enough for these,' she said, nodding at her breasts.

'You look amazing, Ange.'

'Well, I'm hardly ready for my post-baby bikini-body shoot. They wreck you, Mar, they *wreck* you.'

'I'll have to take your word for that.'

'God. Sorry. I'm an idiot.'

'Yeah.'

'Sorry.'

'Anyway, the carnival's ages away.'

'I know I know. I just want it to be perfect. A proper dance routine and everything. It shouldn't be all about the men and their muscles.'

When the baby had finished feeding Ange put it face down on the floor, and it picked up bits of fluff and tried to eat them, and lifted its arms and legs and tried to fly. Outside, Rob was heaving lengths of pine trunk into the foggy back yard and Help was digging one of his holes to nowhere, scratching away at the wet dirt. I preened myself on the bed and a breast feather drifted down to the baby; it opened and closed its milky mouth, opened and closed, and then it grabbed at the breast feather and shoved it in, and nobody saw. And perhaps it would become part bird: perhaps it would sprout bones on its back, pliant and light, and the bones would grow into wings, and it would know how to fly when the truck came to take the lambs to the works. Rob dropped the last length of pine on the ground, thud-thud. He looked at it for a moment, walked around it, gave it a kick. Then he fitted it into the steel cradle, cut away a slice of wood from each end and climbed on top, placing his feet on the flat spots. Then he began to chop.

'He's practising too, eh?' said Ange.

'Every day. Even when it snows.'

'I thought Nick should have a go this time.'

Marnie laughed. 'That city boy?'

'In the novice class. Just for fun. You know.'

'Fun?' said Marnie. 'Fun?'

'Fun?' I said.

Sleet began to fall. The trees in the shelterbelts began to flail their arms. The wood, white as chicken meat, shattered and flew under Rob's blows, and when he'd opened up the heart he turned around and started to cut the other side.

'He's not coming home without the trophy,' said Marnie.

'You've decided that, have you?'

She pointed at the nine golden axes that hung on the wall above the bed. 'He wants ten in a row. Ten unbroken wins for best overall competitor. Failure is not an option.'

Ange looked back out the window at Marnie's vegetable patch. The shrivelled spinach, the rotting cauliflower. The leaves burnt black by the frost, as if someone had set them on fire. 'You never learn, Mar,' she said. 'You just can't have that sort of garden here.'

'Remember the capsicums Dad used to grow? The beef-steak tomatoes? Massive things.'

'Different soil,' said Ange. 'Different climate.'

Rob aimed one final blow and the log split beneath him, and as it toppled he did not topple but jumped neatly to the ground.

'Aren't you ever worried he'll chop off his foot?'

'There's an art to it. He knows exactly what he's doing.'

When I think about what happened later, I remember that day. Rob's breath turning to smoke in the freezing air. Shreds of pine all over him. The way he cut clean through the log he was standing on.

CHAPTER NINE

It started with a single photo: me in my human bed, my cage cot which was not a trap. Tucked under the yellow blanket with my clunk-hearted bear that said *Grrrr*, and the yellow ducks swimming round the striped walls, and above me the sun moon stars clouds hanging on their threads. Marnie showed it to me on the internet, which was on her phone, which was not a mirror – though there I was inside it.

'Oh my God,' she said. 'I only just tweeted it and it's up to forty likes. Look – see the numbers ticking over next to the heart? You're a star.'

'You're a star,' I said, hoping she would reward me.

'A retweet! And another retweet! Someone wants to knit you a bonnet. Someone says you need a dummy. Someone says Tamagotchi you are so sweet I would like to gobble you up.'

'I would like to gobble you up,' I said, and she scratched the back of my neck.

'Great,' said Rob, sprawling next to us in his TV chair and opening another bottle of beer. 'Now the world knows you've lost it.'

'Not the world,' said Marnie. She took a sip from his bottle. 'Just . . . fifty-three people. Fifty-six. Fifty-seven.'

'Lunatics,' he said.

Marnie sniffed the air. 'Have you been smoking inside?'

'No,' he said.

'I can smell it, Rob.'

'I might have had a sneaky smoke when you were in the shower.'

'I wish you'd give up. Those things will kill you.'

'The odd one doesn't hurt, Mar.'

He watched his crime show about beautiful naked dead women strangled in secluded forests, and the man with the sunglasses and the gun combed the scene for any clues, for any evidence the perp had left behind, because even the tiniest thing could break the case wide open. *He'll strike again, Trent. This guy's a monster, but sooner or later he'll slip up.* Afterwards he lifted the phone away from Marnie and put it on the coffee table and leaned in to her, sniffing her neck, licking her earlobe. 'It's a good thing you're beautiful,' he said. 'Beautiful people get away with all kinds of crazy. Beautiful people get away with murder.' Then he pressed her down onto the couch, and then he mounted her.

'You've lost it,' I said. I nibbled at their leftover lasagne.

Over Rob's shoulder, Marnie watched the phone screen. The numbers ticking over next to the heart.

Marnie's mother ran a measuring tape round Marnie's hips and tsked her tongue. She said, 'The thing is, you've never been slender. You have your father's Irish blood to thank for that. Your cells remember the famine, I think is how it works, so you're always in a state of hunger. Always on the lookout for the next potato. There might be potatoes today but will there be potatoes tomorrow? I'd better eat all the potatoes today. But it's about moderation, Marnie. It's about sensible choices. I was eight and a half stone when I got married, and I'm eight and a half stone now. I've never let myself go. Look at me in my skinny jeans.'

'I'm still carrying some of the . . .' said Marnie. 'Some of the . . .'

'Some of the . . .' I said.

The measuring tape lay coiled on the coffee table. A twitch.

Another twitch. Slowly it began to unwind itself. I watched it with my left eye.

'I'm still carrying some of the baby weight,' said Marnie.

'Darling, that was a year ago,' said Barbara. She folded a length of fabric in two – little pistols pointing this way and that on a blue background – and flicked it up into the air, then let it settle on the floorboards.

'Baby weight's the hardest weight to shift, Mum.'

Barbara said, 'It was so early though, wasn't it. You can't really call it a baby. I think if you stopped calling it that you might feel a bit brighter. It's very common, you know. Lots of pregnancies just aren't viable, just aren't meant to take, and they flush themselves out of their own accord. Nothing to go to pieces over. I lost two before I had Angela and I didn't plunge into despair. I didn't stop washing for weeks and neglect to clean the house. I just got on with things. And then Angela came along, and then you. Goodness but you were a whopping one. Almost tore me in half.'

She took a cushion from the couch and knelt on it, then spotted something that made her mouth turn down. 'What,' she said, 'is that?'

A lizard that I'd tucked behind the cushion for later.

Well, half a lizard.

The tape measure kept twitching at me.

'One of Tama's snacks,' said Marnie, whisking it away on the coal shovel.

'Don't you think you've let things get a bit out of hand?'

'How's it any different from Snow bringing his catches inside?'

'Snow was a cat. A domesticated cat.'

Twitch. Twitch. The tape's golden head hanging over the edge of the coffee table now. The little black lines running right down its body like the filaments of a feather. I snatched at it and dashed for my room and it whipped along behind me, and nobody saw. I would hide it under my yellow blanket I would hide it behind the curtains I would bury it in the dirty washing – but there was Marnie's mother flying down the hall, letting herself go, all coral lipstick and dark roots, and she yanked the end of the tape hard enough to snap my neck and said, 'I don't think so.'

'Tama, you're a very bad boy,' said Marnie. 'Yes you are. Yes you are.' She fed me a sunflower seed from between her teeth, and I knew that she loved me.

Barbara said, 'That's a dangerous road. Rewarding bad behaviour. When you and Angela misbehaved we ignored you.'

'Look at me in my skinny jeans,' I said, which made Marnie smile.

Another sunflower seed.

'Is that sanitary? Don't they carry parasites? I say this out of concern.'

'Everyone carries parasites, Mum. I saw pictures online – the things that live on your skin. Under your fingernails. In your eyes.'

'I don't want to know.'

'Little goblins, little monsters, feeding on your sweat. Eating your dead cells.'

'Don't be repulsive.'

'I can send you the link.'

'No thank you.' She smoothed the fabric out on the floor, and I wanted to scuttle underneath the way I scuttled underneath my yellow blanket when Marnie made my bed, but I didn't think Barbara would laugh and pretend she had lost me and look all around for me, saying where's that naughty boy, he was here a moment ago and now I can't find him, oh, what's that lump under there, I must smooth it out, I must flatten it.

'Where are my pins, darling?'

A rattle and a clatter. A little tin full of berries, tiny dots of green blue yellow white red, each on a sharp silver stem.

'And the pattern?'

Wisps of paper cut into wings, cut into crescent moons, filmy, flimsy. Barbara pinned them to the fabric and snipped around the edges, the scissors a ruthless beak in her hands. Then she sat at a black machine with a needle that moved too fast to see, and the needle began to join the pieces together.

'I must say I'm pleased you girls are singing again,' she said. 'Is one allowed to know, is one permitted to inquire, what song you've chosen? Or am I just the workhorse? The hired help?'

'It's a secret,' said Marnie. 'A surprise for Rob and Nick.' She checked over her shoulder, but Rob was ages away, driving into town in his beetle-black car.

'You know how I feel about secrets.'

'Sorry. Nothing I can do. You'll just have to wait till the carnival.'

'I'm the hired help, then.'

'Well, we're not paying you.'

'Home on the Range?' said Barbara. 'The Tennessee Waltz?'

'I'm not telling.'

'Jolene? Stand By Your Man? Whiskey Lullaby?'

'Mum.'

'Mum,' I said.

'A Bushel and a Peck?'

'What?'

'Is it?'

'What makes you think that?'

'You two always used to sing it.'

'So?'

'It is, isn't it.'

'I'm not telling you.'

Barbara looked at the ceiling and blinked several times. 'Your father kept things from me too, you know,' she said. 'Dinners at Il Pozzo with Janice the Whore. A weekend in Queenstown with Janice the Whore.'

'I know, Mum. But this is different. It's not really a secret—'

'You just said it was a secret.'

'It's more of a surprise. Okay? Let's call it that.'

Barbara sniffed. 'Have it your way,' she said, and held up the beginnings of a dress. 'Come on, slip it on for size.'

Marnie turned her back and took off her clothes, then poked her arms through the ragged holes. 'And we thought some tassels along here and here,' she said. 'And some sequins. Maybe some embroidery? We're thinking cute cowgirl.'

Her mother, mouth full of pins, arranged the dress on her body, tugging and straightening, standing back to look.

'Don't make it too short,' said Marnie. 'Or too tight.'

'We can always adjust if you haven't lost the extra weight by January.'

'Or you could just make it to fit me.'

'A little incentive.'

When she pulled at the fabric around the waist, Marnie let out a cry.

'I didn't prick you, did I?' said Barbara, her voice bitten flat with pins. She opened the dress, and there it was on Marnie's trunk, on her soft white stomach, green-black, purple-black, blue-black, black-black, the size of a fist. 'Darling, what did you do?'

'Door handle,' said Marnie. 'Bringing in the groceries. My own stupid fault.'

'It looks painful.'

'It's nothing.'

I nudged at the scissors with my foot and they were glassy cold. I remember thinking: what an instrument. What a tool. If I had a beak like that I could uproot the deepest morsels, drag them fat and squirming from their burrows. I could snip the cherries from the trees. Plunge straight into the heart of an enemy. *I'll see you in court or I'll see you in hell.*

'I think he wants to help,' said Marnie. 'Tailor Tama Helping His Mum. That's a good caption.'

She looped the measuring tape round my neck and sat me on top of the black machine with the needle that moved too fast to see. Then she took a picture of me. And then she put me on the internet.

When Barbara went home Marnie packed away the machine and picked up the scraps of fabric with all the little pistols pointing this way and that. She sucked up the bits of thread with the vacuum cleaner that was just a vacuum cleaner and not a storm that would snatch me and cast me away and away like a seed. She looked at me looking at her.

'What?' she said. 'I *have* done that with the door handle before. I have. And he didn't mean to. He just works so hard, and the farm's not making any money, or not making enough, and I don't bring in much from Lynette's – one day I'd love a little shop of my own, but at the moment I really don't pull my weight, and if we lose this place then where will we be? And maybe I was flirting with Nick without thinking it through, just the way you flirt with family, but Ange didn't have a problem with it, and when she said Nick could keep it up for hours if he had to, meaning his rowing on their new rowing machine, all I said was I bet you could, Nick. That's all. Except Rob'd had a few beers and took it the wrong way. He didn't say anything at their place, but he had a few more beers, and when we got home and you were tucked up in bed, Tama, his voice went all quiet and low and I knew I'd made some kind of mistake.

'He's your brother-in-law, Marnie, he said. Your sister's husband. Classic whore move, babe. But hey, be my guest, if that's what floats your boat. That walking wank with his commerce degree and his granite kitchen. Maybe you should have married him instead, he said. And in the morning he didn't even remember – he swore he didn't remember. He was looking for the painkillers and whimpering to himself like a little boy, and then he asked me why I was all hunched over, and I told him. And he didn't believe me till I pulled up my pyjamas, and then he went white, totally white, and then he started to cry. To *cry*. He's no monster. He knelt on the kitchen floor and sobbed, wrapped himself around my legs and said he was sorry, so so sorry, and if he could undo it he would, and he begged me not to leave him. And I said sorry too, because of the way I behaved with Nick, and everything's good now, I think. It looks worse than it is. Honest.'

She tapped on her phone and found the picture of me with the measuring tape round my neck. 'Two hundred and sixty-seven likes!' she said. 'And twenty-four retweets! They love us, Tama. Someone thinks you're very dapper in your suit. Someone wants you to make her wedding dress but she has to find a husband first. Someone says marry Tama! Someone's posted a shot of their corgi wearing a measuring tape.'

I hopped onto her lap and she stroked my back, and I tilted my head and gazed right at her, purring a quiet purr, fluffing my feathers under my beak so I looked like a nestling again. 'My baby,' she said. 'My little boy.'

When she headed to the kitchen to start on lunch I pushed my way through the cat door – meow – and went looking for Rob. I found him loading two of the dog-tucker sheep onto the trailer while Smoke the heading dog hung around, eyeballing them, skulking along on her belly and then freezing. The pair of ewes stamped their hooves but Rob paid no attention; they were too old to have any more lambs, too old to make him any more money. Up the hill he drove them.

The killing house was an old water tank just behind the woolshed, its flanks spotted with lichen and its windows covered with mesh to keep the flies out. Rob opened the door cut in its side, and I saw the round room, the concrete trunk, hollow at the heart and hung with a hook. Before I knew it he'd grabbed a ewe and slit her throat with his butcher's knife. The blade dripped in his hands, and the blood ran down the sloping floor and into the drain, into the ground, and her legs moved in a gentle running motion. He broke her neck to make it quick. I didn't say a word. A dark shape passed overhead, tilting so I could see the pattern on his back: my father, watching me watching Rob.

Marnie kept putting me on the internet, tweeting a new photo every day: me playing with the clothes pegs, me sitting on her head. Me perched on the edge of the toilet seat. Me as a DIY rotisserie. Me stealing one of her hair clips, me eating a sunflower seed from between her teeth, me giving her a soft peck on the cheek. Me rolling in the snow. Me climbing up the floor lamp's slender trunk, poking my head out the top of the pleated shade. Me pitying the coppery chickens that could not sing. Me in the bath, underneath the showerhead, wearing a tiny shower cap made from a plastic shopping bag. Me spread out in a sun-trance on the back porch, warming myself under the low winter rays. Me hanging upside down from the clothesline, waiting for Marnie to give me a ride. Me wearing a pirate hat, a top hat, a nurse's hat. Me wearing bunny ears. Me dressed as Batman.

'They love us,' said Marnie. 'They *adore* us. Someone says Tama you can have all my hair clips even the sparkly ones. Someone says OMG I want a bird on my head. Someone says you need a little dressing gown and slippers for after your shower. Someone says don't do that to me, I thought he was dead – oh, that was the porch shot. We've hit seventeen thousand followers, Tama. Seventeen *thousand*.'

And she showed me all the faces, the tiny pictures of faces, piling up underneath me.

CHAPTER TEN

Now and then the dark was so dark that it swallowed the house. Now and then, if I headed for home after sundown, with all the lights out and no moon to show me the shape of the place, I couldn't find it. I couldn't see the shelterbelts of poplar sucking the silt into their hearts, nor the papery eucalypts, nor the pines that cut black shapes from the air: no house and no trees, no Marnie and no magpies. Only the ghosts of my brothers brushing against me like cobwebs while the hoarfrost grew on the tussock. Only the maze of thousands of sheep. *This is the way*, my brothers sang, leading me nowhere I wanted to go: to the musty musky woolshed, to the gut hole with its dead stink. To the kennels, where Night and Dutchie and Smoke and Help twitched and whined in their sleep as if they were awake. *This is the way, this is the way.* Taking me further and further from home. Up to the snow drifts that buried sheep, and the only way to rescue them was to look for steam from vent holes melted by their breath, and when you dug them out they'd have eaten the wool from each other's backs. *Stay with us*, sang my brothers. *Stay out here with us. We are so cold.*

One blind night I walked in circles in the snow and thought I might have to bed down with the animals, take shelter in one of Help's holes. I sang my best songs, fluting up and down octaves, sounding two notes at once, but nobody answered. I whistled I Think We're Alone Now. Then I heard someone stumbling, and wood scraping against wood. The click and fizz of a bottle of beer. I moved in the direction of the sound. *So cold. So cold.* Ahead of me a red dot that glowed and shifted and blinked like a father's eye, and the smell of smoke – and then the dark unswallowed the house, and I made out the dim windows and porch and something else too.

'What time do you call this?' said the dark, and laughed, and I jumped out of my skin. Rob with a cigarette, crouched on the top step. Rob with his axeman's arms right between me and the cat door. I flew to the wooden railing and watched him with my left eye, and I did not trust him and I was right not to trust him.

'She wanted me to go look for you,' he said. 'I told her you'd find your own way back. Can't get rid of you, can we?' His voice baggy with beer.

I edged further away along the railing. A blister of paint cracked under my foot. Rob breathed out great rags of smoke.

He said, 'You hear that? Tick. Tick. Tick. Bit of grass somewhere, touching the wire. Dad put all the electric fences in, and the place was even bigger then, before he started carving it up. You're supposed to test the wire by holding a blade of grass to it so you feel the current but you don't get a shock. Rather than just putting your hand on. I grabbed it once and I didn't feel anything – see, I said to Dad, didn't even hurt, and he said you stupid little shit, you just grabbed it in between the pulses. You just fluked it. And he made me hold onto it, and *whack*. When I was a kid I used to sit out here, riding my rocking horse. I used to watch the big fertiliser trucks come in and spread superphosphate around. One day I was wearing my cowboy outfit with my two six-shooters which were plastic and tin but I thought they were real. And I took aim at the fertiliser man when he drove past in his truck, and I shot him, and he threw his arms back and threw his head back and slumped in his seat, and I thought I'd killed him. I ran inside and I didn't say anything, but I hid my guns because if the fertiliser man was dead then the grass wouldn't grow, and if the grass didn't grow then the sheep would die. I remember I woke up one night and looked out the window and the sky was on fire, but it was just Dad burning off bracken and matagouri on the hill blocks so he could oversow. And for years, whenever he ploughed the front paddocks on Wilderness Road, he kept bringing up stones – it was an old riverbed along there and the grass seed wouldn't take. Can't feed them stones, he said. He lost his best land down on the flat when they flooded it for the dam. They drowned orchards and farms and the two bridges as well. The damn dam, he used to say – and they built it on a fault, the bloody idiots, the bloody mongrels. I was only three and I don't remember the old homestead, the one we lost to the water, but sometimes I get a flash of a fireplace or some steps so maybe I remember bits of it. Anyway, Dad had this massive trailer that he hooked up to the tractor, and he parked it in the lower paddocks and went round picking up all the stones by hand and throwing them on the trailer, and then he drove it over to the shelterbelts and up to the woolshed and stacked them into huge piles. His burial mounds, Mum called them. And he did that for years on end, and now those lowland paddocks grow the lushest grass. Grass and bloody cherry trees. I remember when I came home from uni on the bus and it stopped at Wilderness Road and I walked that long walk past the front paddocks, up the gravel driveway to the farmhouse. The smell of the pines and the eucalypts, and everything green, green, green, and I didn't give a shit about failing Principles of Farm Management, or Soil Science 1, and I never went back. *Explain what is meant by the principle of diminishing returns. Explain opportunity cost (when the supply of an input is limited). Define the term "permanent wilting point." Define the term "stress point."* Bunch of cunts.'

He was lying on his back by then, eyes closed, cigarette a

finger of ash. I crept past him and through the cat door – meow – and straight down the hall to Marnie.

'Rob?' she said, her voice full of sleep.

'I thought I'd killed him,' I said like a husband. 'Can't feed them stones.'

'Tama, there you are.'

As the ice spread across the windows I pushed my way under the blankets and she said, 'You know that's not allowed. He'll have your guts for garters.'

But when Rob stumbled inside he stumbled only as far as the living-room couch. Marnie hugged me to her chest, held me close and perfect the way the egg had held me, and I knew that she loved me, and all night I felt the current of her. Tick. Tick. Tick.

The following evening I climbed through the pile of cushions that weren't for comfort, that weren't for lying on, and I slipped into their bed again. I burrowed around for a bit, trying out Rob's side, discovering where the warm ended at the edges of the electric blanket, then settling in on Marnie's side to wait for her. But Rob got there first. He'd been bringing the sheep to the yards all day to treat them for lice – an emergency treatment which wouldn't even kill the bastards, but he'd scrimped on it in summer time and now he was paying. He didn't notice me on the bed to begin with – I lay quiet between the dead-lavender cushion and the slippery red heart cushion – and he pulled off his clothes and dropped them on the floor, and the thing between his legs hung like a hairless mouse. He stood in front of the mirror and looked at himself as he raised an invisible axe, and then he started chopping an invisible log, one foot balanced on each invisible end. His biceps leapt and flexed. I could hear Marnie cleaning her teeth in the bathroom, and in the distance the dogs barked at something only they could see.

'He'll have your guts for garters,' I said, and Rob stumbled off his log and dropped his axe.

'Mar,' he called. 'Mar! What the fuck's that doing here?' Beer on his breath, bitter.

She came running. 'Tama,' she said, 'we've talked about this. You need to sleep in your own room.'

I nestled down a little further. The pillow smelled of her hair.

'Out of bounds,' said Rob. 'No go.'

'Could I just . . .' said Marnie, scanning his face, gauging him. 'Could I just take one quick photo?'

'For fuck's sake,' said Rob. 'I've been out there with infested ewes in the freezing fucking cold for the last ten hours. When I come home I just want to have a few quiet beers and then crawl into my bed, with my wife, and try to grab some sleep before I have to wake up and go out there and attack the bloody lice again so the fuckers don't wreck every fleece.' He sighed, looked at her.

'Please?' she said.

He sighed again. 'Get your phone.'

And she was gone.

Rob watched me and I watched Rob. He took his pyjamas from underneath his pillow where Marnie had left them folded that morning and he started to pull them on, still watching me, but he missed the leg hole the first time, and the second time. 'Fucking loser,' he mumbled, and fell onto the bed, and the weight of him shuddered through the springs. He shook out the pyjamas and tried again: 'Right rabbit in the right hole, left rabbit in the left hole,' he said. 'What are you staring at?' Then he sat on the window seat and clipped his toenails, and the clippings sprayed across the carpet, and when Marnie came back she said, 'A little piece of me dies every time you do that.'

'Hurry up and take your bloody photo,' he said, and I did not trust him and I was right not to trust him.

'Okay, keep still,' said Marnie, aiming her phone at me, and then it flashed in my eyes and I was as blind as the day she brought me home, and I hid under the blankets in case Rob tried to grab me when I couldn't see. 'Oh, sorry, Tama. You didn't like that, did you? I'm sorry. I'm sorry. Tell you what, I'll do a video instead. No more flash, okay?'

'I just want to get into my bed,' I said from under the blankets.

'Fuck's sake,' said Rob. 'He's really winding me up. He's doing it on purpose.'

'He's a bird,' said Marnie.

I felt her lifting off all the cushions, and she folded back the covers on her side of the bed and aimed the phone at me once more. I closed my eyes.

'You've got one minute,' said Rob. 'Tick tick tick.'

'Shhh, I'm doing a video. Tama, shall I tuck you in? Say something. Say something.' She reached for me with her free hand and I dived under the covers on Rob's side.

'Get him out of there,' said Rob, 'and don't you dare let him back. Don't you dare.'

'Okay,' said Marnie. 'Sorry. Okay.'

'Don't you dare,' I said, and climbed out onto Rob's pillow.

'Tama, that's naughty. Come on,' said Marnie.

I stepped away from her hand. 'Don't you dare.'

She shouldn't have laughed, but she laughed. I loved the sound of it, loved that I was the reason for it. 'Come on now, Tama,' she said. 'Be a good boy. An obedient boy.'

She reached for me again and I darted away again. 'Don't you dare,' I said. 'Don't you dare.'

'Sleepy time, Tama. Time to go nigh-nighs. Shall I scratch your belly?'

I jumped onto her pillow. 'Don't you dare, don't you dare, don't you dare.'

She laughed again, and she shouldn't have laughed.

At the side of the bed Rob staggered, steadied himself against the wall. The row of golden axes trembled. Marnie shot him a look, then said, 'I'll tell you a bedtime story, okay? Snuggle down.' Another look at Rob. 'Don't worry, this'll settle him, and then it'll be a piece of cake.'

I let her lift the blankets over me, and I gave her a gentle peck on the cheek. In a soft voice she said, 'Once upon a time there was a very clever bird, a very handsome bird, who wanted to be a human. He came to live in a human house, and he slept in a human bed, and he even learned to talk like a human. People all over the world started following the human things he did, and they told him every day that they loved him, and this made him very happy. The end.'

'The *end*,' said Rob.

Marnie nodded her head at him but kept the phone on me, and still in her soft voice she said, 'Night night, sleep tight, now it's time to turn out the light.'

'Don't you dare,' I said.

She turned out the light. Then she turned it on again and smiled and put down her phone. 'Tama, that was brilliant! You're such a star!'

But Rob had pulled back the blankets on his side, and he wasn't smiling. 'What's that?' he said, pointing at the sheet.

'It looks like he's had a little accident,' said Marnie.

'He's crapped the bed, Mar. There is crap in the bed, and it's on my side.'

'It must have been an accident. He's very good about using his box, you know that. You must have frightened him when you yelled.'

'Right,' said Rob. 'I get it. The crap in the bed's my fault.'

'I . . . I didn't mean that. It was just an accident,' she said, pleading.

'Sleep tight,' I said.

'He didn't have an accident on your side,' said Rob.

'No,' Marnie said, and glanced at him. 'That's how accidents work. They're accidental.'

The wrong thing to say, and she knew it as soon as she said it.

'Seems kind of deliberate to me.'

'He's a bird,' said Marnie. 'A *bird*.' Her pleading voice again.

I said, 'You must have frightened him.'

'Know what, Mar?' said Rob, walking round to her side of the bed and standing very close, his body touching her body, his voice too slow, too quiet. 'I'm a bit fucking sick of sharing a house with a wild fucking animal that can't control itself. I'm a bit fucking fed up to the back teeth, Mar.'

He was swaying from side to side, shifting his weight, finding his balance, his chest brushing her chest, and I thought he would mount her. That's what I thought. That was how houses worked – wasn't it? She moved half a step back and he moved half a step forwards, and there was no room between them, and I thought he would put his mouth to her mouth, but instead he put his hands to her neck.

'Ever since you lost the baby—' he began, and Marnie said, '*I* lost it? *I* lost the baby?'

'Ever since then,' he said, 'I've been trying to go easy on you. But you make it bloody hard, Marnie, and there's only so much I can take.' He tightened his hands. His voice grew and grew.

'I'm sorry,' she whispered. 'I know.'

'That's how accidents work,' I said.

Rob looked over at me and growled a low growl.

'Get in behind,' I said.

Another growl. Another step back and another step forwards. No room between them. No gaps for the air to get in.

'I really need you to shut that thing up,' he said. 'All day every day blah blah blah. It digs in my head and I can't think straight.' He tightened his hands.

'I can't think straight,' I said.

'Tama, get out of here,' whispered Marnie. 'Go to bed.'

'I can't think straight,' I said.

He tightened his hands.

I should have gone for him then, straight for his riverstone eyes that were locked on me. I should have swooped him like a real bird swooped, like my father swooped.

'Get out,' whispered Marnie, and didn't she know best? Wasn't I a good boy, an obedient boy?

I flew to the hall and then to my bed and I lay under the sun moon stars clouds and pulled the guts from my bear and peeled away the striped wallpaper to show the baskets of roses underneath.

'That wasn't me last night,' said Rob, scraping the black off his toast. 'That was the beer.'

But it had looked like him.

'I'm under a lot of pressure, Mar,' he went on. 'You know that.'

She handed him his headache pills. 'Lots of people are under a lot of pressure.'

All across the kitchen window, feathery patterns of ice. I couldn't see outside.

'I don't know how it happened,' he said. 'Honest. It was the beer, and the lice all through the flock, and then the bird crap in the bed . . . I just lost it. I could have kicked myself this morning.'

She handed him a glass of water. 'You need to start work on the Council application,' she said. 'The water rights.'

'Not today.'

'We're running out of time.'

'You won't . . .' he said. 'You won't leave me. You can't leave me.'

'No?' she said.

'I don't know what I'd do if you left me, Mar. Something stupid. Something terrible.'

'What does that mean?'

'Don't make me say it. Something terrible.'

'You shouldn't talk like that.'

'You shouldn't let me drink so much.'

'I can't stop you. I'm not your mother.'

'That's how accidents work,' I said, waiting for Marnie to laugh, to scratch me behind my neck.

'Not now, Tama,' she said.

'Not now, Tama,' I said.

Rob bit at his scraped toast. 'Tastes like wood. I can hardly get it down me.'

'Serves you right,' said Marnie.

'Yeah,' said Rob. 'It won't happen again.'

'No,' said Marnie.

'I better get back out there.'

'Yeah,' she said.

'You're not going to say anything, right? To Ange. Or to your mum.'

'What would I say?'

'I don't know. I don't know what you'd say.'

'I don't know.'

'Because it should be something we keep to ourselves. It's nobody else's business.'

Marnie touched her fingers to her neck where I could see the blue marks of other fingers.

'You know it was all talk,' said Rob. 'That's all it was.'

'Yeah,' she said.

'So we're good,' he said.

'Yeah,' she said.

Out on the sagging porch he lit a cigarette, and then he headed off on the quad bike to attack the lice so the fuckers didn't wreck every fleece. Marnie clicked her phone to life and showed me the video of her hand chasing me round the bed, and it was definitely me and not another bird, and definitely Marnie's hand and not another hand, and definitely our house and not another house, because there was Marnie's pillow that smelled like her hair, and there were the nine golden axes hanging on the wall. We watched the previous evening happen all over again, only inside the screen, just as if I were on TV, just as if I were a beautiful dead woman found stripped of my clothes and stuffed into a rubbish bag. We couldn't see Rob but we knew he was there too, off to one side like a ghost, and we heard him stagger, steady himself against the wall, and we heard him say *Tick tick tick* and *Don't you dare let him back* and *The end.*

'What shall we call it?' said Marnie. 'Bedtime for Tama? Storytime for Tama? Bedtime, I think.' She tapped on her phone and put me on the internet. Then she shifted the break-fast plates to the sink and wiped up Rob's black toast crumbs that sprinkled the table like soot, like mould. And then, in the master bedroom, she searched through her drawers until she found a particular jersey, and it was the jersey she'd folded into a feather-soft nest for me back when she first brought me home, and I don't know why but the sight of it made me gape my mouth and tremble my wings just as if I were a helpless lit-tle chick again. 'You *remember* this,' she said, and stroked my breast. 'You really are the cleverest boy in the world.' But she didn't make it into a feather-soft nest for me, because I was no longer a helpless little chick; she pulled it over her head and rolled up the collar so it reached all the way to her chin. So it covered the blue marks on her throat. Then she dressed me in my sheriff's costume.

Back in the kitchen, the phone was flashing with likes.

'That can't be right,' said Marnie. 'Over four hundred? Already? And thirty-eight retweets! Tama!' She flicked her fin-ger over the screen. Flicked it again. And again. 'Look at them all!' she said. 'Someone says I want to cuddle up with Tama. Someone says uh-oh, Dad doesn't sound too happy. Someone says funniest thing ever. Someone says Tama and Mama. Someone says just let him sleep in the bed with you guys because clearly he loves you and he's lonely. Someone says awwww, he gave you a kiss. Someone says more Tama, we need more Tama . . . don't let them catch you, Tama . . . ha ha, he's copying his dad . . . run Tama run . . . Tama don't you dare stop being so adorable . . . Tama don't you dare make me snort coffee through my nose at work LOL . . .'

She pulled on her jacket and her boots and went to feed out barley to the sheep from the ancient truck and grain trailer. 'Be good,' she said.

'Be good,' I said.

After that people started making their own don't-you-dare pictures of me from bits of the video and my other posts, adding their own captions. Marnie read them out when Rob wasn't there: Don't you dare eat the last Tim Tam, don't you dare agree my bum looks big in this, don't you dare leave the toilet seat up, don't you dare suggest we stop and ask for directions, don't you dare tell me it tastes like chicken, don't you dare use the marge knife in the Vegemite . . . I was a meme, she told me, I was a gif. I was trending. I was an influencer. I had gone viral.

'I love you so much,' she said, so I repeated it back to her, because that was what you did.

'You're not putting anything else on there about me,' Rob said one night, turning on the TV. 'Right?'

'What else would I put about you?' said Marnie. 'It was just that one video. You're hardly in it.'

'Home life should be private,' he said.

He settled down in front of his crime show about pretty young dead women all waterlogged and naked, sand in their mouths and rope marks at their wrists. The man wearing the gun strapped to his side took off his sunglasses that were also mirrors, and knocked back a bourbon, straight. *You have to stay one step ahead of the perp, Trent. Figure out his MO, then beat him at his own game.*

I crept to the master bedroom and found one of Rob's socks discarded and deflating by the wardrobe. I dragged it down the hall like something I'd killed and I hid it under the bath, against the gurgling pipe that vanished into the floor.

CHAPTER ELEVEN

Rob wasn't sleeping and it was my fault. I kept hearing things on the TV and the radio and Marnie's phone, and I kept wanting to practise them for her, and sometimes I practised them at night. They croaked and rattled out of me, those unwieldy human words; I couldn't keep my trap shut. 'That's cocaine all right, Trent. Book him,' and 'How can I love you if you won't let me in?' and 'Watch the weight melt away before your very eyes,' and 'I will take you *down*, motherfucker.' I said them in my bed, tucked under my yellow blanket, my bear unravelling next to me and the Eye watching us both.

'Tama, Tama,' whispered Marnie, and she was a shadow above me as the sun moon stars clouds turned on their threads. 'You need to be quiet. You'll wake him. *Please.*'

But I knew she loved to hear me speak in her language.

'You have the right to remain silent,' I said. 'Anything you say can and will be used against you.'

In the morning Rob crashed around the kitchen and I kept my distance, jumping at every loud noise. He snatched at the radio to turn it off, then banged his coffee cup down next to it, stabbed his knife into the cold-hearted butter like a monster. 'I swear to God, Marnie, one more night like that and I will lose it.'

I adjusted my Superman costume.

'He can't help himself, Rob. He's just following his instincts.'

'My instinct is to wring his neck. All right with you if I follow it?'

'To be fair, you weren't sleeping that well before he arrived.'

'He's got to go, Marnie. If you won't get rid of him, I will.'

'We tried taking him back to the pines, remember? He wants to live here.'

'Well, you made sure he can't survive in the wild.'

'This is his home.'

'*His* home?'

'Ours. It's our home. And what about all his followers? They'd be gutted.'

'It's not natural.'

'In news just to hand,' I said, 'a serious crash at the Takanini off-ramp has closed State Highway 1.'

'Jesus fucking Christ, shut *up*!' said Rob.

I started to whistle There's Nae Luck aboot the Hoose, and he roared.

I suppose I should have tried to behave myself – and I was wary of him, don't get me wrong. I saw the strength in his hard hands, and I knew it could lead nowhere good. I knew he'd had a gutsful. But I couldn't keep quiet; I was my own worst enemy.

'Me and my friends were like twerking,' I said.

He came for me then, lurching through the air, flailing and flightless.

'Meow,' I said as I dived for the cat door, and then I was out and soaring into the brittle white day, my Superman cape flaring out behind me. My father, I thought – my father could tell me how to take on Rob. Where to find his weak spots. My father understood humans. Hadn't I seen him swooping Marnie like a gale, like a god, driving her away though she was twenty times his size?

Over the paddocks of louse-bitten sheep all ringed in wire I flew, scraps of wool scratched onto every fencepost. Over the gorse thorns and the sweet-briar brambles and up past the woolshed, up past the killing house, up into the hills where the gold miners' water race carved its glittering channel though there was no gold these days, and the gut hole breathed its rotten breath and the icy tussock tinkled at its edge. Before I knew it I'd reached the pines – and there was my sister, pecking at the hard ground, coming up with nothing.

'You again,' she said. 'Can't you make up your mind? Bird or not. Bird or not.'

And though this was the place of my birth, and though she was my blood and I could talk to her in my own tongue, I stood a little distance from her, my claws not quite touching the border between farm and flock.

'I wanted to see you,' I said. 'And to ask Father's advice.'

'Have they tried to kill you?' she said. 'Wring your neck, run you down, shoot you, poison you?'

'No,' I said. 'No no no.'

She looked at me with her right eye. Came one step closer. 'What's it like down there?'

'In the house?'

'Yes, in the house, the house.'

'She feeds me from her own mouth.'

'Are you still a nestling? A naked little nestling?'

'Not naked,' I said, turning to show her my Superman cape. 'I'm faster than a speeding bullet. More powerful than a locomotive.'

'What?'

'I don't know.'

'What things does she feed you from her own mouth?'

'Bits of apricot. Bits of apple. Grapes and nuts and cherries.'

'Cherries. Cherries. I could live on cherries. What else is it like?'

'I'm allowed to lie in front of the fire. Belly to the flames, back to the flames.'

'What is fire? What are flames?'

'Your own private sun, close enough to touch.'

'I want my own private sun. I want cherries served from the mouth of a slave.'

'And she watches over me even when I'm alone.'

'Nobody can see you when you're alone.'

'She put an Eye at the end of my bed.'

'What eye? Whose eye?'

'She can see me but I can't see her. I know that she's watching, though. I know that she loves me.'

'I don't like the sound of that.'

'Sometimes she talks to me through the Eye. Tama, put that down. Tama, don't eat that. Tama, use your box.'

'Who is Tama?'

'I'm Tama.'

'No you're not.'

'Tama is my name.'

'Your name.'

'My name. And she says other things. Who's the cleverest boy in the world? Who's the best boy ever?'

'Who is? Who is?'

'I am.'

'Says who?'

'Says she. Says the Eye. And she takes pictures of me with her phone and puts me on the internet, and people in America and Japan and Germany and Wales say I'm the best boy ever too.'

'People in whales?'

'Everywhere. All over the world. I'm a meme. I'm a gif. I'm trending. I'm an influencer. I've gone viral.'

My sister backed away then, and I could have kicked myself, and I said, 'Not that sort of viral,' but she was looking at me with her left eye, and a noise was bubbling up in her throat, and the noise was *Stay away from us, keep out keep out keep out, this is our land and you are not welcome here.*

Some of the others saw me and came to join her, lining up along the border, pacing back and forth. Ruffling their flank feathers to look bigger than they were. Snapping their beaks, arching their necks, splaying their wings. That was how the wild worked. *Sick sick sick*, she called. *Don't touch him and don't let him in.* Then the rest of the flock descended, my family, my blood, and they threw back their heads and expanded their breasts and carolled *Who is this sick stranger? Who is this invader bringing his disease? We don't know him and we don't want to know him and we won't let him in.*

'I'm not sick,' I said. 'Look at me.'

My father pushed his way to the front of the flock. 'He's not sick,' he said. 'Look at him. Bright eyes. Glossy feathers. Well fed.'

'That'll be the grapes and nuts and cherries,' said my sister. 'Bits of apple. Bits of apricot. Served to him from the mouth of his slave.'

'What stories have you told her?' said my father, strutting along the border.

'She asked me,' I said.

He fixed me with one red eye and then the other. 'You do not speak to her. You do not come to the top of our hill, wearing human clothes, and fill her head with stories of slaves and cherries. We have forgotten you. Understand? You are not even a memory. Not even a ghost.'

And they all turned their backs.

I remember that the house seemed smaller when I returned. I meowed as I entered through the cat door, the sound unnatural in my throat after talking with my family, but Marnie was down in the front paddock, feeding out to the sheep. She was a black-haired queen on her truck throne, and barley poured from the trailer as she drove, a ribbon of barley that stretched from fence to fence, and the sheep all came running for it, their hooves clattering across the frozen ground, and the wheels of the truck were huge and black, and if she had wanted to crush Rob she could have crushed Rob – but he was somewhere else.

On the first day of shearing the men arrived at the woolshed early, when the mountains still cast their long shadows, and all through the morning the handpieces buzzed and the ewes groaned and the dogs ran about, tongues too big for their mouths. The shearers, wet with sweat, hummed and smoked and cursed, and took out their needles and thread to stitch up any ewe they cut too deep, and wedges of wool fell grimy from the grimy animals, and underneath they were as pink and white as babies. The rousies gathered up the fleeces and threw them across the slatted tables, tore off the necks and all the ragged edges and stains. After that Marnie classed the wool, sorting it into different bins depending on its quality and softness and strength; these things were hard to see, but she had learned to tell them by touch. The cogs of the wool press clicked as it squashed the fleeces into great greasy bales: dock dock dock dock dock thud. Dock dock dock dock dock thud. The metal plate held in tension, the cables stretched tight. One of them frayed at the base.

Out in the woolshed paddock, I remember, next to a huge mound of stones, Help started a new hole. He let out little whines and huffs as he scrabbled at the sheep-churned soil, digging in a frenzy, the dirt spraying from his paws. I could see all sorts of morsels wriggling and crawling in the fresh earth, and when Help finished his hole and lay panting beside it, I helped myself to lunch. The shearing gang had stopped for lunch too, and I noticed the way Rob looked at Marnie as she chatted to the man with the scar on his chin, laughed at the jokes told by the man with no hair and the man in the green singlet. I noticed, too, the way Rob hurled the lighter aside when it wouldn't light his cigarette, the way he swore at Help when he saw the new hole. I followed him back inside, whistling I Want to Know What Love Is, and roosted in the rafters as if the woolshed were a giant tree. The handpieces started up again, and the click and thud of the wool press with its plate held in tension, its cables stretched tight. One of them frayed. Fraying.

I must have fallen asleep. The screams woke me, high and hectic, and at first I thought they were bird rather than human, though they made no sense to me. Then I saw the man in the green singlet lying beside the wool press, howling, one hand crushed, and the snapped cable dangling above, the metal plate hanging askew. The unbaled wool falling out, messy as bear guts. Marnie running to him, shouting, 'Cam, oh my God, Cam,' and Rob just standing there, looking like he wanted to scream as well.

One of the shearers drove the injured man away while the rest of the gang exchanged glances.

'The thing is,' said Chin Scar, 'you'll need to report it to WorkSafe.'

'He'll be right as rain,' said Rob. 'No need to drag them in.'

'The thing is,' Chin Scar said again, 'you failed to identify a hazard. You knew that press was half buggered and you should have fixed it or bought a new one. It's your responsibility to provide a safe work environment.'

'Yeah, I've read the manual too,' said Rob. 'And it's the contractor's responsibility to refuse unsafe work. So there's that.'

'Don't be a prick about it, mate. His hand looked pretty bad.'

'I'll sort it with him,' said Rob. 'We don't need WorkSafe crawling all over us – they could fine me six hundred grand.'

The one with no hair pointed at the wool press. 'I said to Cam just this morning, that's a bloody antique. It should be in a bloody museum, I said.'

'You know how much a new one costs, right?' said Rob. 'I'll sort it with him.'

'There was a guy in Southland,' said Chin Scar. 'Dairy farmer. One of his workers came off an unregistered quad bike and broke his leg. The guy pressured him to lie about it, so they did him for perverting the course of justice.'

'Look, I'm just trying to make a go of things,' said Rob. 'Pull ourselves out of the red. Okay?'

Chin Scar looked at him. Looked at Marnie. Sighed. 'Yeah, okay.'

They sharpened their cutters and then they returned to their work, and the fleeces piled up and up like dirty snow while Rob tried to replace the broken cable. He hissed and swore to himself as he wrestled with it until Marnie said, 'Maybe you should get someone out.'

'And how much will that cost?' he shouted.

'I don't want you to hurt yourself,' she said.

'I can do it. I can *do* it,' he said, pushing her out of the way.

'Careful, mate,' said No Hair.

'For fuck's sake, I've had a gutsful!' said Rob. 'Can everyone just get back to work and let me fix the fucking press so we can be out of here before fucking midnight?'

'Don't be a prick about it,' I said from the rafters.

'Shut your trap!' yelled Rob.

No Hair swallowed a laugh.

They were out of there before fucking midnight; Chin Scar said they had to stop working when the sun went down, for health and safety reasons.

As the men rolled their shoulders and stretched their backs, the last lot of ewes wriggled into the counting-out pens, clean and new, smaller than when they went in.

PART TWO
TALKBACK

Rob sat at the kitchen table with his laptop and his papers and his pencils and said, 'Even further in the red.'

'It's just the winter,' said Marnie. 'It's been hard on everyone.'

He grabbed at his bottle of beer, and the table wobbled on the crooked floor and I wobbled on the table. I shifted to my chair with the cushion that felt like fur but wasn't fur. I was wearing my doctor's costume, and my mini stethoscope clattered into a heap.

'Dad should never have kept this place on,' said Rob. 'When they built the dam – when they flooded us out – he should have thrown it all away.'

'Is it still there, under the water?' said Marnie, retrieving the stethoscope. 'The old house?'

Rob looked at her across the stack of paper. 'I don't know. The bridges are there, but I don't know about the houses. I think I dream about ours sometimes. Swimming through the bits of it I think I remember.'

'Nick's done the dive. Down to the drowned bridges.'

'Course he has.' Rob took another swig from his bottle. 'Anyway, we should send them all to the works and be done with it.'

'You don't mean that. There's always ups and downs. Once the weather improves—'

'It's not the weather, Mar. It's this place. It's me. We should cut our losses. Get out.'

'Things'll look better when we sell the wool – and when the lambs come. You're good with the lambs. Fattening them up.'

'I can't fatten them up if there's nothing to fatten them up with.'

'The grass will grow. It will. It always does.'

'And the ewes are aborting. I found three today.'

'We always lose some. It's normal.'

Rob hit the tabletop, and Marnie and the radio and the stethoscope and I all jumped. 'Christ alfuckingmighty, shut up!' he yelled.

'It's just the winter,' I said, and he hit the tabletop again and his bottle of beer fell to the floor and smashed.

'Perfect, fucking perfect!'

'I'll clean it up,' said Marnie in a low voice. 'Don't worry, stay where you are. I'll get the brush and shovel.'

'How much is that costing us?' Rob said when she came back, jabbing a finger at me.

'What?' she said, crouching down and sweeping around his feet.

'Your bird,' he said. 'Your famous bloody bird.'

'What do you mean? Nothing. Hardly anything.'

'You feed him, though. Bits of bacon. Bits of dried fruit. Sunflower seeds. I've seen you.'

'He mostly feeds himself. It's best for him to eat what he'd eat in the wild. I asked the vet.'

'You dress him. You heat his room.'

'It's the middle of winter, Rob. And we have no insulation.'

'You think he'd have a heater in the wild? You think he'd have *clothes*? A fucking *doctor's* outfit?' He was watching me again like he was planning something, like he wanted to drive me up to the killing house where he drove the dog-tucker sheep or load me on the truck that came to take the lambs to the works.

The pieces of glass tinkled as Marnie swept them up, sharp

sharp. She wrapped them in newspaper, and she pushed the
bundle deep down into the bin with the soggy tea bags and the
biscuit wrappers and the milk cartons. 'Good as new,' she said.

But later that night, after lights out, I heard a cry. I flew
from my bed towards the sound, and there she stood in the
cold kitchen, cradling her foot in her hand as icy feathers
spread across the window.

'What's wrong?' called Rob, and she called back, 'I think I
cut myself.'

He came to the kitchen then too, and we all looked at the
bead of blood on Marnie's foot.

'Is that it?' he said. 'I thought you'd lost a finger. Opened
an artery.'

'I must have missed a bit of glass,' she said, and cast her eye
across the floor. 'The tiniest splinter. I felt it go in.'

I tilted my head to inspect the floor but could see no pieces
of Rob's bottle, only the old linoleum with the pattern rubbed
away by the back door, and the dips and dents where the wood
was rotten underneath.

'Let's have a look,' said Rob, and we sat at the kitchen table
with all his papers and pencils, his big pile of loss, and he took
her foot onto his lap. 'Nothing there,' he said.

I bit the worm-pink end of a pencil, but it didn't taste very
nice.

'I can feel it,' she said.

He wiped away the blood, tried to turn her foot to the light.

'Ouch! It doesn't bend that way, you know.'

She shifted, and he looked again. Wiped away the blood
again.

'Marnie, there's nothing to see. Nothing there.'

'But it hurts.'

'You'll have forgotten by morning. What are you doing out
of bed, anyway? It's past one.'

'I wanted some water.'

Beside her on the table, her phone screen pulsed as the likes ticked over.

'Water,' said Rob, picking up the phone. A picture of me hanging upside down from the clothesline. 'Oh Tama,' he read, 'please fly over to Sydney to say hello, we have a spare bedroom and lots of treats. Tama come to Wellington, look at all our lovely clothes pegs. Tama you make me smile every day. Tama they've hung you out to dry. Hi Tama from Vancouver. You need to clone Tama, I want my own Tama. I'll take a Tama thanks. I'll take two, and they can talk to each other. Tama for President. Vote Tama.'

'It hurts,' I said.

Marnie was staring at Rob's hands, Rob's knuckles, and when he threw the phone to her, she flinched.

'You're bloody obsessed,' he said. 'It's not healthy.'

'They love him,' she said. 'He makes them happy. What's unhealthy about that?'

'I guess I don't really feel the need to make strangers happy.'

'They're nice people. Some of them have turned into friends.'

'Internet friends aren't real. You know that, right?'

'I have no friends here.'

'What's wrong with me?'

'You know what I mean.'

'And you have Ange and Nick.'

'They're family. You have your axemen friends – I don't have anyone.'

'Anyway,' he said, yawning, 'you should be in bed, Mar. We've got too much to do tomorrow and I can't do it on my own.'

'I was on my way. Then I stood on the glass. From your bottle.'

'Meaning?'

'Nothing.'

'Right.'

'What's wrong with me? What's wrong with me?' I said.

'Don't fucking start,' said Rob.

Marnie stroked my wing. 'He's pretty special, you know. His vocabulary. His voice.'

Rob snorted. 'It's all just nonsense. Bits of whatever he hears. Talking his head off because you feed him for it.'

'A bird scientist in Australia said we should have him tested. She's the world expert.'

'Okay, sure. You knock him out, and I'll get the scalpel.'

'That's a horrible thing to say.'

'Christ, it's a joke, Mar. A fucking *joke*.'

'If you ever touch him, I'll kill you.'

Rob snorted again, nudged me with the back of his hand. 'Look, Mar, I'm touching him, oh no, I'm touching him.'

'You're such a child.'

I backed away. On the phone the likes kept ticking over.

'These friends,' said Rob. 'These internet friends. Are they men?'

'What do you mean?' said Marnie.

'Well, are you staying up till all hours talking to men is what I mean.'

'Some of them are men, I suppose. Tama has thousands of followers.'

'We're not talking about Tama and his thousands of loser fucking followers, we're talking about these friends of yours. These male friends.'

I backed away.

'Some of them are men and some of them are women. They send me a message and I reply. I don't really keep track.'

'Oh right,' said Rob. 'So any sweaty-handed psycho can get in touch and have a good old tug while you're chatting to him. Classy, Mar.'

I backed away, and so did Marnie.

'It's way too late,' she said. 'Let's get some sleep.'

'It hurts,' I said.

'You know they're all guys, eh,' said Rob. 'The ones who message you. Even the ones who say they're called Cindy or Sandy or whatever. They're all guys, tugging away to your picture.'

'It's not like that. Anyway, most of the pictures are of Tama, not me.'

'How can you tell, though? How the fuck do you know who you're talking to? It's not safe, Mar.'

'I just know.'

'It's not safe.'

I backed away to the very edge of the table.

The phone chimed, and Rob picked it up. 'New message,' he said. 'Shall we have a look?'

'If you want,' said Marnie.

'From a Margaret Rossi,' he said. 'Hi Tama and Tama's mom – just wanted to let you know that you've kept me going over a really rough patch and I love seeing all your adventures. Oh my gosh, the bumblebee outfit LOL! Don't you dare stop tweeting. Sending you hugs from Tucson.'

'It's not safe,' I said.

'That's what most of them are like,' said Marnie. 'So I write back a quick thanks for getting in touch, it's so nice to hear from my fans, pecks and love from Tama.'

She stood up from the table, walked towards the dark hall where the walls bulged with the weight of the place.

'Love?'

'What?'

'You sign off with love?'

'Well, Tama does.'

She kept walking and I followed behind. Dots of blood on the crooked floor. Icy feathers on the window.

'So he's the one whoring around. Spraying the fucking
internet with love. Not you.'

'It's just a bit of fun, Rob.'

'You won't mind if I read the messages then.'

'Why would you want to do that?'

'Just a bit of fun.'

'Up to you.' She shrugged.

'Great.' He began tapping on the phone.

'What, now?'

'All of a sudden I'm wide awake.'

'There's hundreds of them. You'll be there all night.'

He didn't reply.

'What are you looking for, anyway?'

'I think I'll know it when I find it, won't I?'

'Rob, there's nothing to find.'

'What's wrong with me?' I said.

'Rob?'

'Night,' he said.

'Night,' she said.

'Night,' I said.

I followed her to her room and I jumped up on Rob's side
of the bed, because he'd be in the kitchen all night. It was still
warm, and I nestled under the covers. Perfect, fucking perfect.

'Not allowed, Tama. Sorry,' Marnie said, and lifted me out
again. 'Come on. We don't want to make it any worse.' She
carried me to my own bed and her hands were trembling and
I lay down like a good boy even though I wanted to stay in
the master bedroom with her. Then she wound up the ferris
wheel, and it started to move the little plastic people up and
then down, up and then down. Its song like broken glass, its
song like the tussock that tinkled with ice up by the gut hole.
Tucked under my yellow blanket, I watched for the headless
person to appear each time the wheel turned. Head head
head head head, no head. Head head head head head, no

head. Slower and slower. The ghost of my mother, who was only bones, sat on my pillow and said *What kind of lullaby is that?*

I woke to the sound of Rob shouting about kisses. He shouted, 'They're not from the fucking bird, Marnie, and don't try to tell me they are. It's your name at the bottom. You're the one who's been messaging him for weeks. How's NYC today, Ramon? I've always wanted to see the Statue of Liberty, Ramon. Is it true you can climb right up inside her, Ramon? Just send him a shot of your tits and be done with it. Maybe you already have. You probably already have. Meanwhile I'm working myself into the ground to save this place. Twelve-plus hours a day, seven days a week. I don't have time to trawl the internet and flirt with whoever tells me I look pretty in my photos. I bet he's not even called Ramon. I mean, what kind of name is that. I bet he's not even from New York. He'll be some morbidly obese old fucker holed up in his mobile home in Nowheresville, jerking off every time you message him. If you don't know that's how the internet works, you're dumber than I thought. And he's probably not the only one, right? You're probably chatting to a dozen others at the same time. Telling them how you're not really cut out for country life. How hard it is here, how cold. How lonely. Signing off kiss kiss kiss. I can keep reading for days if I have to.'

I couldn't make out Marnie's reply, but something crashed against the wall – that was how houses worked – and the little plastic people wobbled on their wheel. It let out a single glassy note.

'Oh, he's gay!' said Rob. 'Of course he's gay. Of course he has a partner named Billy.'

Another crash. I climbed out from under my yellow blanket and puffed up my feathers.

'Why don't you just fuck off to NYC then? Since you seem to hate it here so much.'

Marnie's voice lost somewhere inside the wall.

I shook myself, a bit fucking fed up to the back teeth. I would go to the master bedroom and confront him. I would stand between them, and if he tried to hurt her again I would pierce his eyes and drink his blood and clean his bones. In the black chill I trapped more air beneath my feathers: I was huge, I was strong, my beak a pair of blades. Then I saw the ghost of my mother in the doorway to the hall, and she said *He is bigger, he is stronger, he has fists of rock to crush you, he has fingers of rope to choke you.* I tried to dodge around her but she would not let me pass. When I flew for the space above her, she rose to block it, wings spread wider than my best intentions. Should I have fought my own mother? There she stayed on the threshold, singing to me until the house fell quiet and I slept.

In the morning I could see no marks on Marnie, no blue-black, no black-black, but she moved slowly and held one arm across her trunk. Opened the fridge with her left hand. Ate her cornflakes with her left hand.

'Can I have my phone please, Rob?' she said.

'Why?' he said. 'Is Ramon missing you? Crying all over his bagels?'

'I have to go to work,' she said.

'You don't need your phone to sell Lynette's shitty clothes.'

'I need to keep an eye on Tama. He's used to me talking to him through the webcam.'

Rob laughed. 'You're not serious.'

'You know I talk to him.'

'You think he sits in the cot all day waiting to hear from you? He's outside most of the time.'

'He comes in when it's my lunch break, though. He knows that's when I check on him and he's always there, staring at the webcam until I talk, and then he starts chattering away. It makes him feel safe.'

Rob laughed again. 'Right.'

She walked carefully to the sink, turned on the tap with her left hand to rinse her plate – but no water came out. Instead, a knocking sound, like something trapped in the wall. 'I think the pipe's frozen,' she said.

'Well, I'm not paying the plumber to come out,' said Rob. 'All he did last time was stare at your tits.'

'Rob,' Marnie said in a quiet voice. 'Maybe, you know, this jealousy—'

'It's not jealousy if it's real!'

'Okay,' she said. 'Okay, sorry.'

'We just need to wait for the sun to reach this side of the house.'

She nodded. 'And leave the tap dripping so it doesn't seize up again. That's what he said.'

'Total waste of water.'

'We don't want a bigger problem. He said if everything froze, it'd put the system under huge pressure – it could all just burst.'

'It never has, though. It always comes right.' He folded his arms, and she shrugged, winced.

'Okay,' she said. 'I need to get going.' She picked up her keys so she could start the car – I wouldn't go anywhere near the car – and then she waited.

'And?' said Rob.

'Can I have my phone please?'

'I'm not happy, Marnie.'

'Oh, he's gay!' I said.

'Be quiet, Tama,' she said.

'Not happy at all,' he said. 'How can I trust you?'

'You can trust me.'

'How do I know that? There's pages of messages I haven't even opened.'

'You can trust me, Rob.'

'I'll have to work my way through them one by one. You're leaving me no choice.'

'Okay. That's fine.'

'I'm not happy,' he repeated.

But he handed over the phone.

Marnie turned the radio on for me before she left, and I listened to it complaining about place names being said the Māori way, which was the wrong way, and not the way everyone in New Zealand had grown up saying them. *Toe-paw*, it said. *It's not Toe-paw. What kind of word is that? We camped there every Christmas and it was always Tau-po.* 'Toe-paw,' I said. 'Toe-paw.' *And why does the bank have to say Tēnā koe when I ring them? Why can't they just say Hello? I'm not a Māori. It's completely out of hand.* 'Tēnā koe,' I said. 'Toe-paw.' *Thanks for your call, Graham,* said the radio. *Kia pai tō rā.*

At noon I went to the bedroom to hear Marnie's voice talking to me through the Eye. My bear had worked its way down to the bottom of the bed, a soft round lump under the yellow blanket, so I dragged it out by an ear and tipped it till its heart clunked, then righted it again. *Clunk-grrr. Clunk-grrr.* I opened up a few more stitches in its stomach while I waited, listening for Marnie – but the Eye remained silent. I returned to the kitchen and pecked at the dish of walnuts and diced heart left for me; it was far too cold to look for lunch outside, though now and then I saw some of my flock in the distance, flying through the sleet, picking their way across the snow. Perhaps I was becoming soft. Forgetting how to be a real magpie. I snuggled down on my cushion that felt like fur but wasn't fur to learn some more words from the radio.

How are they any different from proper cigarettes? it said.

Well, it replied, *they don't contain as much nicotine. Some don't contain any. And no tar, no ash.*

They still get you hooked, though, it said. *The scientists don't even know how dangerous they might be. It's the nanoparticles, I read. I went into town last Friday night and all the young people were sucking away on them like there was no tomorrow.*

Isn't that better than the bad old days of secondhand smoke, Jillian? it asked.

You have to fight your way through all those fruity clouds just to get to your car, it said. *Fake apple. Fake watermelon. No thank you.*

Appreciate your call, Jillian. Back in a moment.

Then it sang about carpet – *Come home to Cameron's Flooring, you'll be glad you came home to Cameron's Flooring* – and then it said *We've got Megan on the line. What's your take on vaping, Megan?* And it started to talk in Marnie's voice.

My husband's a smoker and I'm worried the things will kill him, it said. Megan said. Marnie said. *I wish he'd try the e-cigarettes.*

I hopped onto the table and peered at the radio. Was it also an Eye? Could Marnie see me through it? Why was she mimicking Megan, or why was Megan mimicking her? I tried to look inside but the holes were too small.

He smokes in the house, does he, Megan? the radio said.

No. He's not meant to at least, said Megan. Said Marnie. *But he sneaks the odd one when I'm not there. It's only when he drinks.*

I knew the voice belonged to Marnie, my Marnie. I felt it humming through the tabletop, up through my feet and into my breast.

Ah, the sly smoker, said the radio. *Why do they think nobody'll notice?*

It reeks, said Marnie. *It gets in the curtains, the furniture. He knows I hate it.*

Any kids, Megan? Any little lungs breathing it in?

Well – no. No kids.

That's something, then. What does he say when you pull him up on it?

Oh I'd never pull him up on it. I tried that once and it was a bad idea.

What happened, Megan?

He got angry. This is my home, he said, and I decide what I can and can't do. He flew into a rage and he . . .

Silence.

He started . . .

Silence.

Are you still there, Megan?

I moved closer to the radio. Then a whisper: *He started hitting me.*

Okay, wow. What did you do?

I didn't do anything.

And this was all because of a cigarette?

It's only when he drinks.

The hitting, Megan? Or the smoking?

The hitting, I guess. Yeah.

When was the last time it happened?

The hitting or the smoking?

The hitting.

Last night.

Okay. Okay. Where are you calling from, Megan? Are you safe right now?

I'm in the tearoom at work. I'm on my lunch break.

Megan, you need to leave this guy. Trust me, it won't get any better.

I can't leave him.

Megan, I'm speaking from a place of genuine concern here. He won't stop. He might say he'll stop, but he won't.

He loves me. He doesn't mean it.

And I bet he says he's sorry, and he has no idea what comes over him when he's had a skinful, and it won't happen again . . .

We're just under a lot of pressure at the moment. Money's very tight, and . . . and I have a pet that really gets on his nerves.

My fault. My fault.

There's no excuse for domestic violence, Megan, said the radio. *I've heard this story so many times. You need to leave as soon as possible.*

We're trying for a family.

Even more reason. I'm telling you, Megan, do not have kids with him.

I almost did. I was pregnant last year, but I lost it. He was so angry with me.

Is that love, Megan? Getting angry with your partner for losing a baby?

He wasn't angry after it happened. He was angry before.

What are you saying, Megan?

What was she saying?

Well . . . Well, that's why I lost it.

He hit you, and you miscarried?

It was so early. You can't really call it a baby.

Megan. Listen to me. He killed your unborn child, no two ways about it. He killed your baby.

He killed her baby.

He knows what he did. He knows he needs to make it up to me.

The radio let out a sigh. *I guess I'm just stumped, Megan. I'm wondering why you're still with a monster like him. I know our listeners will be wondering too.*

He says he'll do something dumb if I leave. Something terrible.

That's emotional blackmail. You are not responsible for this man's happiness. Do you have family you can go to?

They live next door. Well, just down the hill.

That's too close, Megan. You need to get away from him. Trust me, I know how this plays out. If you make contact with the shelter, the refuge, they can—

My boss is coming.

Megan? Megan, are you there? We've lost Megan. We'll try to get her back. What an extraordinary call, eh? You think you're talking about one thing and bam, you're talking about something else. I did not see that coming and I'm sure none of you did either – but that's talkback for you. It's unscripted. It's raw. It's real. You're listening to 97.1 The Works, and stay with us for more surprises. Can we get her back? No, no, we've lost her.

When Marnie came home she looked in every room of the house. 'Rob?' she called. 'Rob?'

But he'd gone up to the haybarn to count the number of bales left, and to check the level of barley in the silo, and to mutter fuck fuck fuck.

Marnie unzipped a suitcase and laid it on her bed. She pulled an old label from the handle, glanced at it. 'Melbourne,' she said, and crumpled it in her good fist. Then she opened the wardrobe, and then she just stood there, right hand held to her chest. She said, 'What do I even take, Tama? What do I even need? How cold will it be? The same as here, I suppose. Stupid. Of course the same as here. Enough for a week, do you think? Two weeks? I don't know what Mum's going to say. Actually I do: Have you lost your mind, Marnie? Every marriage has its ups and downs. You need to admit your own faults and failings instead of constantly picking away at the other person. By golly, if I had a man looking at me the way Rob looks at you – if I had a man who loved me enough to get jealous – I'd be thanking my lucky stars. Even before your father ran off with Janice the Whore he was always ogling other women. We'd be driving to the supermarket or the rugby or the food court and he'd be turning to ogle every female we passed. He was a traffic hazard, really. I used to say to him, Phil, I'm sitting right here. And he'd say, what have I done now? And I'd say, if you don't know, I'm not going to tell you. And he'd say, I was only looking, I wasn't touching. Except then he was. And apparently the touching went on for six months before I even found out about it. You don't know how lucky you are, Marnie. You don't know you're alive. You'd be mad to throw away a good man like Rob because of a few little hiccups.'

She pulled an armload of clothes from the wardrobe and stuffed them in the suitcase, hangers and all, then three more armloads from the drawers. I fiddled with the end of the zip – a little silver tongue – and then I jumped inside and nestled down into the socks. She lifted me out. I jumped in again and she lifted me out again. 'Tama, we don't have time for this. We need to get away.' A distress call rising in her voice. She dragged the suitcase to the front steps and looked all around, then dragged it to her car. Why had she parked so close to the house? Why was the door on the driver's side hanging open like a hurt wing? She came up the steps for me, and her face was a stone and her eyes were stones and for the first time in my life I backed away from her. When she grabbed me I felt each one of her fingers digging in, and I sounded my own distress call: not human words but the magpie tune I remembered, the notes that sometimes reached me from the pines, only I wasn't sure I remembered them in the right order. No one answered. No one came. Just the ghost of my mother, just the ghosts of my brothers, and they could not help me, they could not save me. Feathers and bones, they sat on the eaves and sang their shadowy song: *Death by car, death by car, death by car*. Marnie's fingers, pressing hard, stones in my side. The car, waiting to swallow me whole. She shoved me onto the passenger seat, then jumped in, slammed the door and turned the key with her bad hand – and everything began to move. I lurched to the side, and my claws caught in the fabric of the seat. Through the glass I could see bits of sky sliding past, bits of tree, the grey eucalypts, the leafless poplars sucking the silt into their hearts, no shelter in the shelterbelts and no way out. Down the hill the bare cherry orchard, the icicles dripping from the branches, the dead grass showing through the snow, the wire fences – they all began to hurtle past like there was no tomorrow, and the roof so low above me, and the engine juddering my spine. The air gushing from the black vents, hot and hotter, hot enough to cook me where I sat. Behind us the house slipped away and the car breathed out its poison. And though I knew there was no way out – though I understood how glass worked – I flew at the windows all the same, bashing myself against them in the hope they might break, calling my jumbled distress call.

'Tama, what are you doing?' Marnie yelled. 'Stop it, stop it!' The car started to swerve, and I felt myself yanked this way and that. I would be pulled in two; I would break my neck. A fence veered towards us and she screamed and I screamed and it was coming for me, death by car, and she stamped down her foot and we were thrown forwards and backwards and then everything stopped. Straight away I tried to push my beak in between the window and the door to see if I could get out. A truck thundered past, sounding its horn.

Marnie rested her head on the steering wheel for a moment, her breaths a gust, and watched me scrabbling at the glass. 'I guess you're not leaving, then,' she said. 'Eh, Tama?' She leaned over and opened my door, and I shot out, thanking my lucky stars, and I flew back along Wilderness Road and straight up the gravel and home to the yolk-yellow house.

She sat in the car for a while, and I thought she might not come back. I watched from the front steps as another truck went by and sounded its horn, and another, and surely she would shift herself out of harm's way – and yes, at last she turned round and followed me, returned home to me. Unpacked her suitcase. Took some meat from the deep-freeze. Made dinner. Listened and nodded when Rob said it was just because he loved her so much, and she could see that, couldn't she?

So I suppose everything that happened afterwards was my fault.

CHAPTER THIRTEEN

C hin Scar took one last swing, and the pine block split in two, the severed top tumbling to the ground. He and Rob were practising their chopping in the back yard, timing each other, urging each other on – *Go hard, go hard* – and when they'd gone hard enough they began to clean their blades on the porch.

'How's Cam doing?' said Rob.

'Yeah, you know,' said Chin Scar. 'He reckons it won't slow him down.'

'He wanted twenty grand,' said Rob. 'For a pinky finger.'

'Yeah,' said Chin Scar.

'So there goes my new wool press.'

They each opened a bottle of beer and took a sip.

'Had to ask my rich prick of a brother-in-law for a loan,' said Rob. 'And even then he could only lend me ten. They're saving up for bird nets for their designer fucking cherries.'

'Cam said you bargained him down.'

'I mean, it was only the pinky.'

Chin Scar took another sip of beer.

'But he's happy now, right?' said Rob. 'He's not taking things any further?'

'He's not taking things any further,' said Chin Scar.

Rob let out a long slow breath. Drank his beer. Watched the sky.

And I did not trust him and I was right not to trust him.

I began to keep a very close eye on Rob. I crept under the bath and examined the sock that looked like a thing I'd killed, and I started to take more of his things too: the pinch-edged top from a bottle of beer, a coin that he spun on the kitchen table till it turned to a golden blur, a box of cigarettes with a picture of a baby breathing through a tube, a box of cigarettes with a picture of a man dying in a bed, a slice of toast thick with butter, a green plastic lighter, a blue plastic lighter, a coffee mug with a splodgy flower on it, a toenail clipping, his headache pills in their sheets of silver foil, a page of newspaper he'd twisted into a fake twig to burn, an egg cup shaped like a chicken with a hole in its back for the egg, a chicken bone he'd sucked clean, the chapstick he said wasn't gay, the rind of an orange he'd peeled in one unbroken strip. Under the bath they went, into the shadows, stowed against the gurgling pipe where no one would find them, all my clues, all my evidence – only one day, when Marnie came home from Lynette's Gowns and Casualwear, she caught me making off with the matted mate of the first sock.

'Now then, sneaky sneaky,' she said, aiming her phone at me and starting to video, 'you mustn't go rummaging about in Rob's things if I'm not here. Well, not if I *am* here, either. You mustn't touch his things at all.'

But I remember that she was smiling because of what I'd done, and she put the video of me taking the sock on the internet all the same. And ten thousand people liked me, and over three thousand shared me.

Did I miss my own family? My own blood? Of course, of course. I did not dare return to the pines, but I watched my flock digging for worms and grubs in the paddocks, or lying sprawled in their sun-trances, or perching on the fenceposts and powerlines to carol together with one great shimmering voice. I watched them pass above me as passing thoughts, black bodies with flashes of white. I watched the shape of my father, the shape of my sister. They did not acknowledge me, and when I tried to call to them, no answer came. Just as my father had said, I was not even a memory, not even a ghost.

The trees were alive with magpies trying to make new magpies, each male mounting his female, beak shoved flat against her head for balance, beating his wings to stay in place until the pines shook with gusts of love. That was how the wild worked. I saw birds making their nests, collecting bits of this and that and taking them back to the spot they had chosen at the fork of a downwind branch. How beautiful they were, those bowls of twig and vine, wire and twine, no two alike. Each mother began with a stack of sticks, and on top of those she built an outer nest strong enough to protect her eggs, strong enough to hold her hatchlings. I spied all kinds of things woven into them: scraps of sacking, lengths of rope, silver foil, strips of plastic, nylon thread, pieces of china, pieces of glass, a handkerchief, a spoon, a matchbox and three of Marnie's clothes pegs. Was that how the wild worked too? I did not know, I could not tell, I could only watch from a distance as the magpies went about their magpie business. When the outer nest was finished, all hooked together so the wind would not pummel it apart, the mother made a lining from the soft things she had gathered: grasses and feathers, tufts of wool, ribbons of eucalyptus bark – and sometimes her mate brought her soft things to weave in as well. Little offerings, little gifts. These inner nests I could not see, but I remembered the feel of my own before I fell from it. I remembered the feather-soft home my mother had woven, how she had shaded me with her wings when the rain came or when I started to pant in the sun.

And I remembered Marnie's jersey, feather-soft, that she had folded into a nest for me.

And I remember this: my father passing above the yolk-yellow house one day, and in his beak a strand of tussock as long as the strand of hair he'd torn from Marnie's head. The wiry grass fluttered along behind him as he flew home to the pines, home to a new mate. I knew, I knew. And she would take it from him, this new mate who was not my mother, and she would weave it into the new nest she was building for their new family.

'This is delicious, Marnie,' said Nick as he sliced through the meat.

'Practically still bleating,' said Rob. 'One of the dry ewes.'

'All right, all right,' said Marnie. She was wearing the silver butterfly earrings Rob had given her. They weren't really to her taste, but I didn't tell him that.

'They want to know more about farming, babe,' he said. 'I'm just obliging them.'

'Bleating?' said Nick. 'Or bleeding? Ha ha.' He pushed a carrot round his plate. Fiddled with a roast potato. 'I hate to bring it up again,' he said, 'but have you talked to the bank about irrigation?'

'Yeah, we're still good with wild flooding,' said Rob.

'Except you can't use the water race forever,' said Nick. 'Sooner or later Council will force your hand. If we make an application together—'

'Yeah, we're good, mate,' said Rob.

'So we've decided on peacharines,' said Ange. 'We'll plant them east of the cherries, where they'll get the best sun.'

'That's the spot where Dad used to grow the lucerne,' said Rob. 'Till he carved it off and sold it to a couple of pricks from Auckland. They wanted to be winemakers but only on the weekend. Never planted a single vine.'

'I'm from Auckland,' said Nick.

'Yep.' Rob helped himself to more meat.

'Ha ha.'

'He picked stones out of the ground for years, till it was

good enough for grass,' said Rob. 'Made piles of them all over the place.'

'We wondered what they were, didn't we, Ange. Took ages to clear them when we ploughed for the cherries.'

'Old riverstones,' said Rob. 'From a dry riverbed.'

I flew to Marnie's shoulder, and she fed me a morsel of meat because she loved me.

'At the dinner table, babe?'

'Nick and Ange don't mind.'

'Bleating or bleeding, ha ha,' I said. 'You don't know you're alive.' I shook my feathers; I'd just been sitting in the kitchen sink, under the dripping tap.

'You see what I have to put up with?' said Rob.

'Extraordinary,' said Nick.

'It could be worse,' said Marnie. 'You could be living with your mother-in-law.' The silver butterflies trembled as she spoke.

Nick said, 'You girls are so cruel about Barbara. She's the nicest woman.'

Marnie looked at Ange and Ange looked at Marnie.

'We're lucky to have the help,' said Nick. 'She's great with the baby.'

'Of course she is,' said Marnie. 'He's a boy.'

'It's not natural,' I said, and ate another morsel of meat.

'Extraordinary!'

'Mum called them his burial mounds,' said Rob. 'The piles of stones. They just kept working their way up through the soil, and he kept picking them out.'

'We still have one up by the woolshed,' said Marnie. 'Massive thing.'

Rob said, 'What the fuck's a peacharine?'

'It has the taste and juice of a peach, and the skin and fragrance of a nectarine,' said Nick. 'It's the hot new hybrid.'

Rob snorted. 'If you say so.'

'We've done our homework, mate. People want something new. That's where the real money is.'

'Look at avocados,' said Ange. 'Look at kiwifruit. This could be the next kiwifruit.'

Nick said, 'You should think about diversifying. It pulls the risk out of the volatility of different markets. If one crashes, you still have other options. Even if your margins are pushed, you'll have built resilience in your operations. You're in a low-return industry, a low-return asset class, and traditionally it produces commodity products that can't be easily differentiated. Sure, you can try to rely on good old-fashioned productivity gains, but you can also create gains by undertaking land-use change. That would be one approach. Or you could look to develop a farm-to-consumer supply chain based on internet selling. That's where the action is. That's the future. You want to shift from commodity fluctuations into price certainty and connect to your end market.'

'Yeah, we're good,' said Rob.

'Seriously, though. Why wouldn't you want multiple revenue streams?'

'We already have them. Meat and wool.'

'But beyond that. Beyond the sheep.'

'We could think about it, couldn't we?' said Marnie. 'I mean, there's less and less money in wool, once we've paid the shearers.'

'See, that doesn't make any sense,' said Nick. 'You need to position your product at the top end of the value chain. Get it made into carpet for private jets. Maseratis. That'd pay for the irrigation all right.'

'There's still money in wool,' said Rob, 'and there's money in meat.' He took a long gulp of beer. 'If they'd stop aborting, that is. I found four more today.'

'It doesn't mean anything,' said Marnie.

'It might mean campylobacter,' said Rob. 'An abortion storm is what it might mean.'

'We always lose a few, though.'

He glanced at me. 'You know it's spread by birds, right?'

'You could add a different breed,' said Nick. 'I saw this guy in the *National Business Review* who imported embryos from overseas. The ones with the black faces and knees, and the fluffy hairdos . . .'

'The black-nosed Swiss Valais,' said Rob.

'Yes! Aka the cutest sheep in the world.'

'I don't need them to be cute.'

'But then you could host farmstays. The Asians go crazy for them.'

'Farmstays.'

'Why not? Nice little money-spinner, with the Asians.' Nick looked around at the slumped furniture, the curtains hanging off their tracks. 'Fix the place up a bit. Charge what you like.'

'Mmm,' said Rob. He opened another bottle of beer, swallowed half of it. He said, 'Dad used to run merinos. And then prices for fine wool tanked, so he switched to crossbreds for the meat. Fuck knows why – the high country's too delicate for them. They eat it right down, make it vulnerable, unstable. In poured the rabbits. The nor'west wind stripped away the top-soil, and on the worst days you couldn't see two steps in front of you for all the dust in the air. The only thing holding the place together was the scabweed. So then he switched to half-breds, but the damage was done, and I've been paying for it ever since. And now merino wool's getting top dollar again, and TV did a story on our neighbour who's signed a contract with an Italian suitmaker, and they filmed him parading round the paddock in his Italian suit and gumboots like a twat, but I guess that's what you do when the big money comes calling. I tried to tell Dad we should switch back to merinos, but he'd never admit he made a mistake. Then he blew his brains out.'

Everyone fell silent.

I said, 'Nice little money-spinner.'

More silence.

I started to whistle Lady in Red.

'Well,' said Nick, 'you could capitalise on the by-products. They're using lambs' stomachs to make wound dressings – did you know that? The human body can't tell the difference between the lamb tissue and its own skin. Helps it to heal faster.'

'I read that they used alpaca hair for the *Lord of the Rings* costumes,' said Marnie. 'There'd have to be money in that.'

'She's got the right idea,' said Nick. 'Get yourself some alpacas.'

'Mate, we already have three and a half thousand ewes, and I like a day off every year or two.'

'So what you need to be aiming for is less input and more production. A hands-off operation, ideally.'

'Hands off,' said Rob.

'Hands off,' I said, fluttering to the edge of the table.

Nick stretched out his finger and prodded my belly. 'That is one intelligent bird.'

'Gives me the creeps,' said Rob. 'Bloody pests.'

'Hands off,' I said.

'We've never caught a single one in the traps,' said Ange. 'The occasional possum, the occasional ferret, but never a magpie.'

'You can borrow my twenty-two if you like,' said Rob. 'Pop pop pop. Much quicker.'

'Shh!' said Marnie, pointing at me.

'You need to cover your face, though – they remember faces.'

'That's okay, thanks,' said Nick. He gave me another prod.

'I'll throw in a few lessons, no charge. You'll be away laughing.'

'No thanks, mate.'

'Yeah, didn't think so. You don't want to get your hands dirty.'

'There's dirt and there's blood,' said Nick.

Rob laughed. 'What do you do when you catch something, then?'

'Humane release,' said Ange.

'Beg your pardon?'

'We drive way up into the hills and let it go.'

Rob threw back his head and roared. 'Brilliant! Bloody brilliant!'

'Not everyone has your stomach,' said Marnie.

'That's why we need the nets,' said Ange. 'We lost fourteen percent of the first crop – that was with the traps and the dummy birds. With nets, we'll lose nothing. Not to birds.'

'You could put mirrors in the traps,' said Rob.

'Really? They fall for mirrors?'

'That's what Dad used to say. Or just swerve to hit them. Easy.'

'Shh!' Marnie said again, covering my ears.

Ange laughed. 'You know, when we were little, she held a funeral for a squashed hedgehog. Made us all sing Nearer My God to Thee for roadkill.'

'Too soft,' Rob said, and planted a beery kiss on Marnie's cheek. 'Always bringing home injured this and that. They never survive.'

'Hands off,' I said.

'Almost never,' he said.

'Seventy grand per hectare,' said Nick. 'That's what we need to borrow, for the nets. But looking at the returns from the first crop, and the projections for the next, the bank should come to the party in two years.'

'And then, all going as planned, the peacharines after that,' said Ange.

'Good for you,' said Rob.

'Yeah, good for you,' said Marnie. She was staring at her plate. 'If they do trap one with a mirror, though, what happens then?'

'They take care of it,' said Rob. 'Or they ask me to.'

'What does that mean?'

'Jesus, Marnie, you know what that means.'

'Anyway,' said Nick, prodding me again, 'you hire more workers, increase production, then sit back and watch the cash roll in.'

'And I pay them in wool, do I?' said Rob.

Nick was still prodding me. 'You should look into vertical integration.'

'Is that where you do it standing up?' said Rob.

'Ha ha, yeah.' Prod. 'I'm planning on retiring by forty.' Prod. Prod.

I pecked his finger.

'Fuck!'

'Oh my God, are you okay?'

'Tama! Bad boy! Naughty boy!'

'It's fine. I'm fine. Look, no blood. Ha ha.'

'Put him outside, Mar.'

'It's freezing out there.'

'He has to learn.'

'He'll freeze.'

'Really, I don't mind. There's no blood.'

'To be fair, you were annoying him.'

'At least put him in his room.'

'He has a room?' Nick was staring at me again.

'Oh sure,' said Rob. 'She's even trained him to crap on command.'

'They love us on Twitter,' said Marnie. 'Him. They love him. He's a meme.'

'You should read the messages they send,' said Rob. 'They're obsessed with him.'

I hopped back onto Marnie's shoulder and gave her a little peck on the cheek, started to preen her hair.

'Is that so?' said Nick. 'Maybe they should talk to Lakshmi, eh Ange?'

'Who's Lakshmi?' said Marnie.

'She studied business with us. She's super-sharp. Specialises in viral marketing.'

'How many followers does he have?' said Nick.

'About a hundred thousand,' said Marnie.

'A hundred *thousand*?' He stopped rubbing his finger and pointed it right at me. 'There's your money-spinner.'

CHAPTER FOURTEEN

There were things living in the roof. Scurrying above us in the dark. They scratched and scraped and thudded and knocked and they were not birds.

'Can't you smell them?' said Marnie. 'Especially in the bathroom, by the vanity?'

'Not really,' said Rob, dumping an armful of pine next to the fireplace.

'I'm not imagining it.'

'I never said you were.' He started building the fire, twisting newspaper into fake twigs, stacking it over the pinecones in the grate.

'Go into the bathroom and stand in front of the vanity and tell me you can't smell them.'

'What do you want me to do, Mar? I've put down traps. I've stopped up every hole I can see. They'll always find a way in.'

'We should get a pest-control place to have a look – Lynette gave me the number of a guy in town. We need to get it sorted before Lakshmi comes.'

'Bleating or bleeding, ha ha,' I said.

'Lakshmi can take us as she finds us,' said Rob. 'I don't want some strange guy rummaging round the house. Opening every cupboard.' He lay kindling over the newspaper and pinecones, crisscross, crisscross, leaving gaps for the air to get in, and then he flicked a flame from a yellow lighter, because I had stolen the green lighter and the blue lighter, and the flame started to take, and I saw the burning edges of the paper, bright ragged lines like the line between the mountains and the sky when the sun disappears. And I saw the black shapes that the flames made on the paper, the shapes of trees on a hillside, and those shapes turned to fire too, and the flames ate their own shadows. Rob balanced two pieces of pine on top, each holding up the other.

'Lynette said he's very good. He'll come and quote for free.'

'I bet he will,' said Rob. 'Quick look through your underwear drawer while he's at it.'

'Do you know how you sound?'

'Happens all the time. They caught a guy like that last year – busted him with a hidden camera. They blurred his face but you could tell exactly what he was up to.'

In the roof something scuttled and scuffed. Something skittered and thumped.

Marnie said, 'It sounds like they're going to crash right through. Land in our laps.'

'I'll get the poison myself,' said Rob. 'A broad-spectrum one, eh Tama?' He nudged me with the poker. 'Yum yum yum.'

'Yum yum yum,' I said.

He stood the fire guard in front of the fire, and then he turned on the TV to watch his crime show about young lovers stumbling across the corpse of a beautiful unclothed woman in the park. *One partial print on the barrel. Run it through the database, Trent.*

'They deal with this kind of thing all the time,' said Marnie. 'We need professional help.'

'You just have to know how to think like a rat,' said Rob, levering up the footrest on his TV chair.

'She's been dead for at least twelve hours,' I said.

Marnie held her hands out to the heat. 'They can start fires, you know. Chew through electrical cables.'

'Those are defensive wounds,' I said.

'I'll do it myself,' said Rob. 'Save some money for a change.'

Rustle, scuttle, scuffle, thud.

A few days later he came home with a pail of poison. He waited outside the bathroom with a ladder while Marnie finished her shower, and as soon as the water stopped he opened the door and the steam came billowing out like rainclouds, and Marnie pulled a towel round herself and said, 'Give me a chance.'

He turned off the rusty heater, then stood in front of the vanity and sniffed.

'Well?' said Marnie, who was still standing in the bath because there wasn't enough room to swing a cat. 'Can you smell it?'

'I suppose so,' he said, peering at the ceiling. 'I'll need to lay it all through the house as well, though. If they're up there, they'll be down here.' He was casting his eye around, looking for hiding places. Looking at the space under the bath.

'What the fuck's a peacharine?' I said.

'No. It's too dangerous for Tama,' said Marnie. 'And I've never seen them in the house. Not a single one.'

He put the pail down on the vanity and took off the lid, and the smell was delicious, like berries, like cherries, and I could have dived in and eaten my fill. I flew towards it, and I was nothing more than a smudge in the foggy mirror, and Rob and Marnie were smudges too, and the ghosts of my brothers were smudges of smudges and sat on the smudged curtain rail and sang *Eat the berries. Eat the cherries.* I looked behind me, and Marnie was drying herself, her black hair, her white skin, so beautiful, and Rob was steering the ladder into the bathroom, chipping bits off walls that had already been chipped before, and Marnie said, 'Be careful!' because he almost crashed it into the lightshade that looked like the moon if the moon were filled with moths. I moved a little closer to the pail while he balanced two feet of the ladder on the floor and two feet in the wet bath.

'Do you think that's safe?' said Marnie. Then she noticed me making my way across the vanity, baby steps, baby steps, and she said, 'Rob! The lid!'

'Ah well, worth a shot,' he said, and sealed the pail shut.

'That's not funny,' said Marnie.

'That's not funny,' I said.

'Hold it steady,' he said, and started to climb the ladder, but it slipped and lurched and he almost lost his footing halfway up. 'Do you *want* me to fall?' he said. 'Do you *want* me to break my neck?'

Marnie tucked her towel in around herself, and Rob started climbing again, all the way to the ceiling, where he paused and hooked the pail over his arm like a handbag. I had never noticed the little trapdoor up there, right above the vanity, painted white and speckled with mould the same as the rest of the ceiling. Rob pushed it open and shone his torch inside the high dark hole, and then he vanished into it just like that.

'Be careful,' called Marnie. 'You're invading their space – they could turn on you.'

'I'm invading theirs?'

'Well,' said Marnie. 'Well, I'm thinking like a rat.'

The stench tumbled down from the open hole: old straw; something unburied. Rob thudded round above our heads, and the pellets of poison rattled like rain, and one of them bounced down the ladder and landed at my feet, sky-blue. Marnie was drying the mirror and studying herself, looking with her left eye, looking with her right eye. Digging her fists into her waist to make it smaller.

I sniffed the sky-blue pellet. Delicious. Pushed it a little way along the chilly floor. Delicious, delicious. I could hide it under the bath with all the other things I'd taken from Rob. All the clues, all the evidence I'd saved to stay one step ahead. His headache pills, his gold coin, his sucked-clean bone. His cigarettes with the picture of the dying man. His egg cup in the shape of a chicken with a hole in its back for the egg. His chapstick that wasn't gay. His twisting orange peel, dried and shrunk to leather. I could push the pellet under there too, all the way to the back.

Or I could gobble it down in one bite. I sniffed it again. Like berries, like cherries.

'Tama! No!' said Marnie, and she grabbed it and threw it in the washbasin, then grabbed me. 'Did you eat any? Tama? Tama?'

I didn't know what she wanted me to say, but she was waiting white-eyed for me to answer. I said, 'This is not the scene of the crime.'

She prised open my beak and looked in my mouth like there was no tomorrow. 'Did you eat any?'

'Yum yum yum.'

'Rob! Rob!' she called.

His face appeared in the hole.

'Tama got hold of one of the pellets. I don't know if he's eaten any. How the hell did he get it? Did you give it to him?'

'Don't be stupid.'

'Do you think he's all right?'

'Looks all right.'

'What if he's eaten it?'

'You'll know in an hour or two.'

'Do you *want* me to break my neck?' I said.

'I'm calling the vet.'

Rob lowered himself back through the hole, and he was dirty, he was filthy, and when he closed the trapdoor his hands left black marks.

'Is that it?' he said, picking up the pellet, and I should have hidden it when I'd had the chance, because it was a clue about him that belonged with my other clues about him, and I could have kicked myself. 'He hasn't touched it,' he said. 'Look. Completely intact.'

Marnie squeezed around the side of the ladder and studied the pellet, holding it close to her face and inspecting every edge. Couldn't she smell it? The berries, the cherries, right under her nose? I fluttered my wings, gaped my mouth for it like a chick, the way I had gaped my mouth for her little syringes, minced and mashed and measured, back when she saved me.

'Not for birds,' she said, and she dropped it in the pail and shut the lid tight.

But for hours afterwards she sat with her phone and looked at pictures of sick cockatiels, and budgerigars with tubes fed down their throats, and canaries' eyes held under running water.

Snow fell the week the lambs started coming, and surely they were coming too early, and surely it was too cold. Sometimes twins, sometimes triplets, all wobbly legs and fluttery tails. I could smell the blood.

'You keep that bird the fuck away from them,' said Rob.

'Have you ever seen a magpie attack a lamb?' said Marnie.

'It happens. I've heard of it.'

'But you've never actually seen it.'

'I've heard of it. They zero in on the weak ones. Tear them open. Peck out their eyes. '

Another bad story about magpies.

'I don't believe a word,' said Marnie, feeding me a pumpkin seed from her mouth. 'You'd never do anything like that, would you, Tama? You're a good boy, the best boy.'

I knew that she loved me.

But I could smell the blood.

And I saw Rob climbing on the old two-wheeler motorbike to head up the hill with his rifle, up towards the pines, and he was pulling on a black balaclava, covering his face like a perp, and soon I heard the magpies calling their alarm calls, and when the shots sounded I looked at Marnie and she looked at me and she said, 'Rabbits. Just rabbits. They're pests.' And I believed her.

It's true that Rob always helped the mismothered lambs: the ones who pushed their way through the fence into another paddock and could not get back, or the ones born to bad mothers who simply walked away from their babies. And he righted any sheep that were cast – he'd find them stranded on their backs, legs in the air, and if they stayed like that they suffocated. Sometimes he failed to reach a cast sheep in time, or he missed one hidden in the tussock for a few days all bloated and rank, and that was four hundred and fifty dollars down the fucking gut hole – a hundred and thirty for the dead ewe and a hundred and sixty each for her dead lambs, and by Christ they were stupid animals.

'Plenty of farmers don't even bother,' Marnie said to Ange, pegging out the wet washing. 'They just let them die. Rob saves every single one he can. That's the kind of farmer he is.'

I hung upside down from the clothesline, waited for her to push me. She gave it a shove and made a video of me spinning around: Tama Online. Twenty-two thousand likes.

As soon as a lamb was born, its mother dried it off with her tongue so it would not freeze to death, and then it stood up on its shaky new legs and drank from her. If a lamb was born dead, it didn't stand up. Sometimes its mother tried to lick it into life, this little warm thing that smelled like her baby, until finally she turned away and left it for Rob to throw in the trailer on the back of his quad bike. Thud. Thud. He loaded the mother onto the trailer as well, so he could take her to the woolshed, grabbing her before she could run, but if she really bolted he used Smoke the heading dog to steer her back. Smoke never barked; she didn't need to. She crept along beside the ewe, fixed her with a look, crept along, fixed her with a look, while Rob whistled and called *Walk up, Smoke. Sit down, Smoke. Walk up! Hold 'em!* If a mother died giving birth, Rob took her to the gut hole, and any dead lambs found without mothers he collected up too, but they weren't for the gut hole because they could be sold for money. He left them out at the main gate on Wilderness Road, all the little slinkskins, and the slinkskins man came for them in his truck to make them into gloves and jackets and the insides of shoes. Motherless lambs and lambless mothers: it was a dangerous time, full of blood, and I could smell the blood. But I never touched a lamb. I never touched a live lamb. Not that anybody saw.

Rob brought the weak ones, the orphaned ones, inside. He kept them in cardboard boxes in the living room, which was no place for animals, and I could hardly push my way through them to my usual spot where I lay belly to the flames then back to the flames. Marnie held the lambs up by their chins so their throats stretched straight and open, and then she pushed a length of pink tube down and down inside them and fed them something that looked like their mothers' milk but wasn't. When they were stronger they drank from the bottles with the rubbery pink teats, sucking so hard at them that Marnie had to hold on with both hands. I tried fluttering my wings at her again, gaping my mouth, but the lambs were her babies now. All day they bleated from their boxes, loud enough to bring down the crooked house. Marnie sat me on the back of one of them and tucked my yellow blanket over the top of us: Tama's New Friend. Twenty-nine thousand likes.

'How is that keeping him away from them?' said Rob, staring at me with his riverstone eyes.

'Yes, look at him going in for the kill,' said Marnie. 'Look at him tearing it limb from limb.'

'We can't afford to lose any,' said Rob. 'We had enough abortions.'

'Not campylobacter, though,' said Marnie. 'Not total disaster.'

'One of these days he'll take a chunk out of a lamb, and once they get the taste for it there's no going back. This is our livelihood at stake.'

'Tama might be our new livelihood.'

'That's nowhere near a done deal.'

I flew up to the woolshed to get a bit of peace and bloody quiet, but the lambless mothers were penned in there and they were bleating too, calling from their cages for what they had lost. The haybarn, then, I decided – or the grain silo next to the haybarn. Perhaps someone would have left the lid off, and I could dive inside and bury myself in the barley and thank my lucky stars. Have a little nap and then eat my way out. Except before I could leave the woolshed Rob came with his butcher's knife, and he began to cut at something over in the corner, and I saw that he was cutting at a dead lamb. I perched in the rafters to watch. He chopped off the head and legs, sliced straight down the dead belly and peeled the little yellow fleece free. Then he spread it out and cut a hole in each corner, and after that he went back to the house.

I took a sniff of the skinned lamb. Just a tiny sniff. Just a tiny nibble. The mothers who were no longer mothers bleated from their pens.

When Rob returned he was carrying one of Marnie's lambs. He stood it on the table where a moment earlier he'd been busy cutting and skinning – that's the kind of farmer he was – and he took the pelt and poked the lamb's left legs through the two holes on the left, then pulled it across its back and poked its right legs through the two holes on the right. A lamb in lamb's clothing. He lifted it into one of the pens, and the lambless mother stamped her hoof and let out a long, low moan. Gently he pushed it closer – closer, closer, until the lamb could smell the milk and the mother could smell a miracle: her baby, her own baby, back from the dead.

The next day he shifted all the new pairs to the home paddock, where the snow had disappeared and the grass had started to grow and the poplars sheltered them from the worst of the wind. He drove stakes into the ground and chained the mothers to them by their hind legs to make sure they would not leave their new babies, would not change their minds. And even when the grass around each stake was bitten bald and he released the mothers from their chains and removed the yellow pelts from the lambs' backs, they stayed together, these false little families. They never noticed how he had tricked them.

Around that same time I dreamed of Rob telling every bad story about magpies. We killed new lambs, we held the souls of gossips, we carried the devil's blood in our mouths, we brought bad luck and sorrow and death, we laughed at the drowned world, we stayed silent at the crucifixion. On and on he talked, his black balaclava covering his face, but I knew it was him. With his axe he cut off my legs, and with his butcher's knife he peeled away my skin to lay across the back of a lamb, and the lamb slept with Marnie in its cloak of bloody feathers and she fed it from her own mouth. I woke shivering. Then I heard a click-click, a tap-tap, a click-click. The ghost of my mother sat on my yellow blanket and watched me, though she was only bones.

'Is it true my father has taken a new mate?' I said.

She sighed a bony sigh. *Have you not heard her?*

'I don't know. Have I?'

She pulled apart a rival's nest. Destroyed the eggs, shrieking all the while.

'Is that how the wild works?'

That is how the wild works.

'And are they true?' I said. 'The stories people tell about magpies?'

Those stories are not about us, she said. *They are stories about other magpies half a world away.*

I wriggled further down into my bed. 'Where did I come from?' I asked.

The egg, she said.

'But before the egg.'

You were not before the egg.

'Where did magpies come from, then?'

And she told me a different story from all the other stories. We came from just across the water, she said: *Victoria, Tasmania, Australia.* Her voice sang the names.

'Victoria, Tasmania, Australia,' I sang.

They called us pipers, bell magpies, flute birds, organ birds. They called us booroogong, garoogong, warndurla, koorlbardi.

'Booroogong, garoogong, warndurla, koorlbardi,' I sang.

'Shut up!' Rob yelled through the wall.

The ghost of my mother lay on my pillow, right next to my ear. She said *Long ago, in the Dreamtime, there was no daylight. The sky pressed itself to the earth, and all the people had to crawl, and all the animals hunched and hobbled. The kangaroos could not jump. The emus could not straighten their necks. None of the birds could fly. Even the trees could not grow. Cold, cold, cold. We had to creep around on our bellies to search for food in the darkness, feeling for the shapes of fruits and berries, and some days we found nothing, and nothing was the shape that filled us. The wombats dug themselves deep into the ground and slept. Only the snakes were happy. So the magpies, the clever magpies, called a meeting. How shall we fix this? they said. We shall prop up the sky, they said. They gathered all the sticks they could find and began to push the sky away from the earth, levering it first onto the boulders and then onto the low hills . . . but the sky was too heavy, and the magpies, the clever magpies, knew the sticks could not hold it, and soon it would collapse on everyone. How shall we fix this? they said. We shall take the longest stick to higher ground, they said. So up they climbed, up the high hills, the longest stick in their beaks, pushing at the sky as they went, until they came to the highest mountain. There on the peak they raised the stick and shoved and heaved against the sky, and with one last push it flew up into the air, and as it rose it split open, and the light and warmth of the Sun-Woman poured down onto the heads of the clever magpies and all the land below. The animals and people wondered at the high sky awash with red and yellow and orange and pink: the first dawn. And as the magpies burst into joyous song, the last of the darkness broke apart and skittered away to make the clouds, and the Sun-Woman began her journey to the west, her bark torch in her hand. And now, every morning, when she wakes and prepares her fire and touches her torch to the flames, the magpies sing to greet her, and as she daubs herself with paint, the dust from the crushed red ochre tints the morning clouds. She sets out across the sky, carrying her bright bark torch, only snuffing it out when she reaches the western edge of the world. Then she paints herself once more in her brilliant colours and begins her underground journey back to her camp in the east, where the magpies will sing to greet her again, and everyone hearing their song will remember their clever thinking.*

CHAPTER FIFTEEN

M arnie kept tweeting photos and videos – me and a lamb asleep in front of the fire, me and a lamb out in the snow with matching scarves around our necks, me and a lamb inspecting the gold miners' water race though there was no gold these days, me perched on a lamb's back and talking my head off, me and a lamb hiding in the basket of clean washing – and the people on the internet loved us. They adored us.

'OMG can you stop?' read Marnie. 'My ovaries can't take it any more! That's it I'm moving to New Zealand and marrying a farmer. I'm dying here, DYING. Tama don't you dare let me catch you with the mint sauce LOL.'

'Three hundred thousand followers?' said Ange, peering at Marnie's phone screen. 'How did that happen?'

'I have no idea,' said Marnie.

'I have no idea,' I said.

'Well, you must be doing something right.'

We were sitting on the back porch one warm morning, watching Rob train for the axeman's carnival. He was practising on an upright length of trunk as thick as a person, and he chopped into its middle on one side, the cut gaping like an open mouth, then ran round to start on the other. Soon only the narrowest waist remained, and with one last blow he sent the top half thumping to the ground. Marnie stopped the timer.

'How long?' he called.

'Twenty-nine,' she called back.

He cursed, kicked the felled trunk.

'He's worried he's past his prime,' Marnie whispered. 'There's a younger, stronger guy who's going to topple him.'

'This one, you mean?' said Ange, scratching me on the back of my head. 'So strong and handsome. Aren't you? Aren't you?'

I closed my eyes, warbled a wordless song.

'Look at him,' said Marnie. 'He loves his Aunty Ange.' She picked up a fallen feather and held it to the light to see all the tiny branches, all the little barbs.

'Mum doesn't get it,' said Ange. 'The thousands of followers. She can understand people wanting to see the lambs – very cute when they're that size, all soft and helpless. But a magpie, Angela? she says in that voice of hers. There's just something evil about them.'

The drop of devil's blood in my mouth. The bad luck, the sorrow, the death.

'Pay no attention, Tama,' said Marnie, holding out her arm to me like a branch.

I climbed up to her shoulder. Nuzzled her cheek. 'I'm touching him, oh no, I'm touching him,' I said.

She smiled. 'See, such a good boy. Mum doesn't know the real you.'

'She'll change her mind once the money starts rolling in,' said Ange. 'When's Lakshmi coming? I bet she can't wait to get her teeth into him.'

Which couldn't mean what I thought it meant. Could it?

'End of next week,' said Marnie.

'She's super-sharp. The sharpest in our year.'

'Her emails are very . . . decisive.'

'She ate our tutors alive.'

'Shit, really?'

'Got one of them fired for making a comment about her

chest – but everyone knew she dressed for the attention. Fed on it.'

'Shit,' said Marnie.

'Shit,' I said.

'Oh, she'll be fine with you. You're the client.'

Rob turned his gaze to an entire trunk that stretched up above his head, twice his height. A tree stripped of its branches, metal roots securing it to the ground. He looked over at Marnie, axe poised.

'And . . . go!' she called, starting the timer.

He cut a notch into the side of the trunk, jammed in a board and sprang up onto it.

'What the fuck's he doing?' said Ange.

'It's the Tree Felling Event,' said Marnie. 'They have to climb the trunk by way of the boards, cut halfway through the block at the top, then climb back down and repeat the process on the other side.'

'How can he even balance on that thing?' said Ange, watching the second board flex under Rob's feet. 'Has he ever fallen off?'

'Not since I've known him.'

'No way is he past his prime,' said Ange. 'He's a bloody machine.'

'A bloody machine,' I said.

Marnie was stroking my back in time with Rob's blows, and I closed my eyes again for a moment, breathed in the smell of her. 'Are you sure we're doing the right thing?' she said. 'Taking on Lakshmi?'

'She's very, very good at her job,' said Ange. 'You should see her house. Her car.'

'No, but I mean – making money out of Tama.'

'A bloody machine,' I said.

'Why the hell not? It's fallen from the sky right into your lap. You'd be crazy not to exploit it.'

'I suppose so.'

'And you keep telling me the farm's not making any money and Rob's under so much pressure.'

'He is. He is.'

'But he hasn't done it again, right?' Ange glanced over at him swinging his axe on the uppermost board, shattering the wood's soft heart. She lowered her voice. 'He hasn't hit you again?'

'I wish you'd stop asking me that. It was only ever the one time. He doesn't know his own strength.'

I said nothing.

'And it was an accident,' she added. 'Because he was drunk, and under pressure.'

I said nothing.

'Remember you can come to us,' said Ange. 'Day or night.'

'He loves me,' said Marnie. 'He'd do anything for me. Everyone deserves a second chance, don't they?'

I said nothing.

'Okay, okay, just looking out for you. I like the guy, you know that.' Ange flicked through the latest photos of me with the lambs. 'Is that one in your *washing* machine?' she said.

'Yeah. With Tama about to press the Woollens and Delicates button.'

'That's kind of twisted.'

'We didn't actually start it! It was all staged!'

'But what if some sick copycat out there decides to have a go?'

Marnie sighed. 'I've had some horrible messages from animal rights people. He belongs in the wild, who are you to play God, we know where you live, we will come for your children, what kind of monster, et cetera. What they're forgetting is that he wouldn't have survived without me.'

'You see? You have to be careful. Lakshmi can help you with that.'

'I'd never hurt an animal. Never. Tama has a great life with us. And Rob looks out for every single lamb. Beats himself up for days if he loses one.'

The block split in two, and Marnie stopped the timer. 'Two thirty-nine!' she called, and Rob nodded and wiped his hand over his face.

'That was two forty-seven, though,' said Ange.

'Shh,' said Marnie.

I saw a black shape passing above us, and flashes of white under its wings and tail: my father patrolling his territory, protecting his new family. Watching us with his red eye. I knew he could swoop like a gale, like a god, and it was swooping season.

'Okay, I've worked out our act,' said Ange. 'Can we go inside now?'

They shut themselves in the master bedroom and stood in front of the mirror, Ange on the left to showcase her good side.

'What about my good side?' said Marnie, examining her reflection.

'Both sides are your good side,' said Ange. She began to sing their song, putting different actions to each line, and Marnie copied her. Soon they were both smiling and pointing and nodding at their reflections and at each other, bending and turning, hands on hips, hands on knees. Blowing kisses.

'G-rated enough for you?' said Ange.

'It's sweet,' said Marnie. 'Thanks.'

'Don't say I never listen to you.'

'How's Mum going with our costumes?'

'They're looking amazing. She can only work on them when Nick's not around, but they'll definitely be ready in time for the carnival.'

'Mar?' I called, and they both jumped. 'Are you there?'

'It's just Tama,' said Marnie. 'Up to his tricks.'

One day soon after, we were in the kitchen, having lunch – Marnie was getting the tomato relish from the pantry, and Rob and I were sitting at the table – when two faces appeared at the window: a pair of young men carrying backpacks taller than their heads. They wore puffy black jackets that made them look like car tyres come to life, monstrous living car tyres aimed at the house, and as soon as I saw them I ducked down onto my furry cushion. They waved through the glass at Rob.

'What the hell?' he said, halfway through his cheese and chicken sandwich. He opened the back door.

'Hello,' said the one with the blue backpack, 'we are Klaus and Volker from Hamburg. We would like now to meet the bird who thinks he is a person.' He held out his hand.

'Yeah, piss off, mate,' said Rob.

'What's this about?' said Marnie, coming over to the door. 'Are you lost?'

'Hello,' said Blue Backpack, holding out his hand again, 'we are Klaus and Volker from Hamburg. We would like now to meet the bird who thinks he is a person.'

'Ah,' said Marnie.

'Mate, this is a private house,' said Rob.

'Is the bird who thinks he is a person at this time unavailable?' said Blue Backpack.

'Well . . .' said Marnie.

'No idea what you're on about,' said Rob.

'But this is the bird, I think,' said Green Backpack, peering around him.

'There's no bloody bird,' said Rob.

'Look at him going in for the kill,' I said.

'This is him! This is Tama!' said Green Backpack. 'I see him on the chair underneath the table. Volker, do you see him?'

'Yes, yes, this is the bird!' said Blue Backpack. 'This is his favourite cushion! He is wearing his wizard costume!'

'We're not fucking Hobbiton,' said Rob. He tried to close the door, but they had already stepped inside.

Death by car, sang the ghosts of my brothers. *Death by car.*

'They've come all this way,' said Marnie.

'Do you know them?' said Rob. 'Have you been messaging them?'

'No,' she said.

'Has she been messaging you?' he asked.

'No,' they said.

He looked them up and down. 'Are you gay?'

'Yes,' said Blue Backpack, 'we are German homosexuals.'

Green Backpack nodded. 'Tama is enormous with German homosexuals.'

'They've come all this way,' said Marnie.

Rob threw his hands in the air. 'Apparently I have no say in my own house. Perfect.'

Marnie was smiling and bending down to me, saying it's all right, Tama, they're our friends, you don't need to be scared. I hopped onto the floor and walked over to the visitors, who had come all this way, and they were German homosexuals, not living car tyres, and Marnie was right and my brothers were wrong. I pecked at the wormy bootlace trailing from Green Backpack's boot, thanking my lucky stars.

'Volker, get out your phone!' he said. 'Quick, quick!'

'Oh my goodness, he thinks it is a worm,' said Blue Backpack.

I kept pecking at it until they had their video.

'You have no idea what this means,' said Green Backpack.

'No idea at all,' said Rob.

'Look at him tearing it limb from limb,' I said.

'He sounds exactly like a human!' said Green Backpack.

'You knock him out, and I'll get the scalpel,' I said.

'This is very astonishing,' said Blue Backpack, and he began unzipping the many zips on Green Backpack's bag. 'Does he like to eat muesli bars?' he said. 'Klaus, where are the muesli bars?'

'They are just there, in the top pocket.'

'They are not in the top pocket.'

'I know I stored them in the top pocket.'

'Perhaps you stored them in your fat stomach. Like the last banana.'

'You don't like to eat bananas when they are very ripe. This banana was very ripe.'

'It was the last banana. You could have shared it with me like a normal polite person.'

'I am a normal polite person, and also—'

'You gobbled it all up when I was making a photo of the Hundertwasser toilets.'

'—and also, my stomach is not fat.'

'It's a bit fat. Ah, here are the muesli bars, in the middle pocket and not as you said in the top pocket.'

'So it appears I did not eat the muesli bars.'

'Just the last banana.'

When Blue Backpack tore open the wrapping I could smell oats and brazil nuts and almonds and honey.

'Is it allowed?' Green Backpack asked Marnie.

'We try not to let him have too much human food,' she said.

I fluttered up to sit on Blue Backpack's shoulder and leaned in close to the bar.

'Klaus! Klaus! Make a picture!'

'I am a normal polite person,' I said.

'Oh my goodness!' said Blue Backpack. 'He copied you! He copied you!'

I hopped onto his arm and began to whistle Wild Thing. I could have snatched the whole bar then and there.

'Just a small piece?' he said to Marnie. 'It's gluten free. Very low GI.'

'Jesus fucking Christ,' said Rob.

'Okay,' said Marnie.

'And will you please now make several photos of us feeding Tama?'

'Okay.'

'Klaus, pull your stomach in.'

I took little bites of the bar: oats and brazil nuts and almonds and honey, and dates and raisins too, and chunks of a sweet yellow fruit that tasted like the sun.

'Don't you dare make a blurry photo, ha ha,' said Green Backpack.

'Stop moving your mouth then,' said Blue Backpack.

'I am a normal polite person,' I said.

Later that day, when Marnie was feeding the motherless lambs in their boxes, Rob came into the living room and lay in his TV chair. 'The thing I'm wondering, Mar,' he said, 'is how they found our house.'

'I don't know,' she said.

'How could anyone possibly find us, unless they had the address?'

'I really don't know,' she said.

'I mean, do you think they just wandered round the country, peering in windows, looking for a magpie?'

'No,' she said.

'No,' he said.

'No,' I said.

'Well, did you put the address online?'

'Why would I do that?'

'Beats me.'

'Beats me,' I said.

Marnie dragged one of the lambs a bit further away from the fire so it wouldn't cook. She picked at a soft spot in the floorboards. 'I might . . .' she began. 'I might have mentioned Wilderness Road in one of the photo captions.'

'Right,' said Rob. 'Which is, you know, our address.'

'Yeah,' said Marnie.

'Yeah,' he said.

'Yeah,' I said.

The lambs were bleating for their bottles, snatching at the teats.

'There must be hundreds of Wilderness Roads out there, though,' she said. 'All over the country. There must be.'

'Mmm. Except I had a bit of a look at your posts, and you talk about Central Otago weather, and high-country weather, and the cherry orchard just down the hill . . . you don't have to be a detective.'

'That's cocaine all right, Trent,' I said. 'Book him.'

'I guess I didn't really think it through.'

'Marnie, you show the *house* in some of the shots.'

'People wanted to see him sitting on the porch. Using the cat door. Lakshmi says we should be connecting with his followers.' She looked over at Rob, and the teat popped out of the mouth of the lamb she was feeding.

'So you just post pictures of whatever they want to see. *Show us your bedroom, Marnie. Show us your shower, Marnie. Show us your bush, Marnie.*'

'You know it's not like that.'

'No I don't. I still have hundreds of messages to read. New ones every day.'

'I'm telling you, there's nothing to find. There's nothing to be jealous of.'

'Have they all figured out where we live? Are we going to get busloads of tourists showing up?'

'I'll delete those posts.'

'The horse has already bolted, Mar! It's three towns away by now, charging down the main street, trampling pedestrians!'

'Klaus and Volker were nice, though.'

'The thing is, I should be able to eat a cheese and fucking chicken sandwich at my own kitchen table without gay Germans barging in.'

'They were harmless. Lakshmi says—'

'You know, I'm a bit fucking sick of Lakshmi.'

'We haven't even met her yet.'

'Exactly.'

'She says she has high hopes for Tama. She says he ticks all the boxes. She's already getting nibbles from advertisers. A garden-sprinkler place. A new brand of corn chips. Even, she hinted, Air New *Zealand*. This could be our chance to turn things round, Rob. Don't you want to make some money?'

'Of course I want to make some money, Marnie. That's why I'm going along with it. Just watch your step, is all I'm saying.'

'Money Marnie, money Marnie,' I sang.

The lamb followed her hand and latched back onto the teat, frantic for the milk. Drinking for its life.

PART THREE
BIRD BUSINESS

C ome in, come in,' I heard Marnie say. 'Thanks so much for flying all the way down here.'

'My absolute pleasure,' said the woman.

In the living room I leapt to the sill under the cracked window that bent the hillside in two, my feet leaving tracks in the borer-beetle dust. Rob was working in the front paddock, churning it up to sow grass seed. From behind the curtain I watched the woman take a seat in his TV chair, though she didn't turn on the TV. Her hair was cut so short that I could see the bones of her skull, and a black beetle clung to the back of her neck – just a drawing, I realised, not an actual beetle. In her nose she wore a tiny red stone that glittered whenever she moved.

'Sorry about the lambs,' said Marnie, waving a hand at the orphans in their cardboard boxes.

'Clearly you're people with big hearts,' said the woman. 'We can use that. Now, where's the star of the show?'

Don't trust her, sang the ghosts of my brothers. I stepped further back behind the curtain.

'He was here a moment ago,' said Marnie. 'Tama! Tama! Come and meet Lakshmi!'

'Lak, please,' said the woman.

'Tama! Don't be naughty. She's flown down from Auckland.'

I doubted that, but I didn't say anything.

'I'll check his room,' said Marnie. 'He can't be far away.'

'Of course, please,' said Lakshmi. 'I'm in no hurry. I'm on no particular schedule. Free and easy.'

After Marnie had left she ran a hand over the sticky coffee table, looked inside the good china cabinet. Over by the cracked window she examined the singlets and shirts and bras and underpants drooping on the drying frame, and she came so close to me I could have snatched the peacock feather that hung from her left ear. *Don't trust her*, sang the ghosts of my brothers, but they would not tell me why. She took some pictures of the room with her phone, then bent down and poked at one of the lambs, and it latched on to her finger and started to suck. Free and easy, she wiped the finger on another lamb, then on a damp singlet. I puffed up my feathers, opened my mouth. *Don't trust her*, sang the ghosts of my brothers, but still they would not tell me why. Was she going to wring my neck, run me down, shoot me, poison me? They fell silent, blurred into wisps of smoke. Hadn't I trusted Marnie? Hadn't I trusted the German homosexuals? And she had saved my life, and they had fed me bits of muesli bar that tasted like the sun.

'What time do you call this?' I said.

'Hello?' she said, whirling around.

'Hi,' said Marnie. 'Sorry, I can't find him. Little shit.'

'I thought I heard someone just then. I thought it was your partner.'

'Get in behind,' I said.

Marnie pushed back the curtain. 'Lak, meet Tama,' she said.

I bleated like a lamb.

'Marnie, my friend,' said Lakshmi, 'that bird is going to make you a mountain of money.'

'He's one of the family,' said Rob when he came inside. 'Simple as that.'

'So you're his mum and dad,' said Lakshmi.

'Exactly,' said Marnie.

'Yeah,' said Rob. He was fiddling with a pink plastic lighter – I'd stolen the green lighter and the blue lighter and the yellow lighter – and he tapped it on his palm and turned it over, tapped it and turned it over.

'And you did all this –' Lakshmi gestured at my room – 'for him?'

'Not exactly,' said Marnie.

'I did it,' said Rob. 'It was already done when he arrived.'

'You're trying for a family.' Lakshmi set the puffy sun swinging on its thread. 'Perfect. A baby would seriously up the engagements.'

'Yeah, I'm not sure that's something we want to go public with,' said Rob.

'Oh sure sure sure,' said Lakshmi. 'You two are totally driving this, don't worry.'

I picked my way along the rail of my cot bed, then hung upside down from the blinds.

'Does he ever snuggle up with you? In your bed? I'm just thinking about angles. Pitches. We'll be wanting to monetise your presence, obviously.'

'He's tried it a few times,' said Rob. 'Haven't you, eh? Little rascal.' He scratched my belly.

'We made it a rule that he's not allowed in with us,' said Marnie. 'Rob suffers from insomnia.'

'I'm so sorry to hear that,' said Lakshmi.

'Little shit,' I said, and did a forward roll across my yellow blanket.

'Someone's showing off,' said Rob.

'Let's talk advertisers,' said Lakshmi. 'I'm not making any promises, but we now have an energy drink pretty keen to get in on the ground floor with Tama, and Air New Zealand are giving him their full consideration.'

'Oh my God!' said Marnie.

I did another forward roll.

'I could watch him all day, really I could,' said Lakshmi, peering at the Eye, the beetle on her neck squashing as she bent. She tapped the slick black eyeball with a fingernail, and I blinked. 'Which reminds me – the team wondered about investing in something a bit more powerful.'

'That cost eighty dollars,' said Rob.

'And it's served you well till now. It's a good entry-level model, don't get me wrong, but imagine what we could do with 4K resolution and remote pan and tilt, for instance. Imagine what we could do with night vision in colour. Live streaming would be a game changer – a few units spread throughout the house so we don't miss anything. Though you'd have to disincentivise the profanities, obviously. Just have a think. Have a chat. I'm happy to leave you alone for ten to fifteen if that's what you need.'

'Why would we want night vision in colour?' said Rob.

Lakshmi said, 'It's all about reach. Tama has followers right across the planet, so a woman in Barcelona, say, might want to see him in the middle of our night, but she probably won't watch for long if the image is grainy black and white. There's something very potent about high-quality live footage – knowing that you're watching the events as they unfold. It makes users feel included, like members of a special club. Party to a secret, even. But reach is only as good as impressions, and impressions are only as good as engagement. I can see you're confused. I can see I've lost you. Engagement is the likes, the follows, the replies, the retweets, the click-throughs, including any hashtags and links in your original tweet. Engagement *rate* is engagement divided by impressions, with impressions being the number of timelines your tweet appears on. But the impressions metric doesn't take into account how, or even if, a user engages with your tweet, which is why we don't rely on impressions alone as our key performance indicator. Which brings us to reach. The difference between reach and impressions is that reach indicates potential – so it includes users who don't follow you but follow one of your followers. Reach is usually higher than impressions. Say you have a thousand followers, and seven hundred and eighty of them see your tweet: your impressions are seven hundred and eighty, and your reach – the number of followers who could *potentially* see your tweet – is a thousand. But say you have a thousand followers, and seven hundred and eighty of them see your tweet, and one of them retweets your tweet to their thousand followers, and two hundred and ten of them see the retweet – then your impressions are nine hundred and ninety but your reach is two thousand.'

I think that's what she said.

'And the website?' said Marnie. 'The little shop?'

'We'll need to rush the merchandise through pretty smartly,' said Lakshmi. 'We're thinking coffee mugs, of course. T-shirts, hoodies, novelty underwear, shot glasses, phone cases, laptop sleeves, calendars, greeting cards. Costumes were another idea we had. People can dress their dogs as Tama. Dress their cats as Tama. Hilarious. And our big hitter –' she paused, smiled a huge smile – 'a talking plush toy.'

'Like a stuffed toy?' said Rob.

'We prefer to say plush.'

'Plush,' I said. 'Plush.'

'We'll record a few key phrases,' Lakshmi went on, 'and he'll speak them when the user presses his wing. Batteries included, so he's ready to go as soon as he arrives at his new home. If you're happy to sign today, after you've had a bit of a think, a bit of a chat, we can fast-track the design process. We can prioritise you as clients, and get the samples to you within the month. Sound good? And then, once the site's up and running, we'll be pulling out all the stops to make sure your social signals keep rising, which will improve your SEO. You're sure you want to handle the distribution yourselves?'

'Yes,' said Marnie. 'We need to keep the cost as low as possible. We'll store everything in the spare room, and I'll do the packing and posting. It'll be like my own shop.'

I was their little gold mine, their money spinner, their cash cow, their sure thing, their meal ticket, their golden ticket, their golden goose. I was their retirement plan.

Barbara stood in the hall with her hands on her hips and said, 'Now, would you like me to help with a bit of a spring clean before they come to do the calendar photos and what have you?'

'Oh, I don't think—' began Marnie, but her mother was already making her way through to the living room, pulling on a pair of rubber gloves.

'I'm not saying I agree with all this bird business,' she said, 'but you'll need the place looking its best. Nobody will want to stare at your filthy floor for the whole of the month of June, will they. Nobody will want to see your sagging wallpaper. Your mouldy shower curtain.'

'It's not mouldy,' said Marnie. 'Not very.'

'I mean, I can't do much about the borer holes and the rot – I can't promise *House and Garden*,' Barbara went on, 'but we'll at least try to improve on the current situation. Do you know, they stage houses before they sell them these days? It's big business.'

'How do you stage a house?' said Marnie. 'What does that mean?'

'They clear out all the owners' junk,' said Barbara, picking up a giant ceramic snail from the mantelpiece and grimacing at it, 'all their rubbishy furniture and knick-knacks and photos, and they replace it with tasteful things. Pieces that really say something. A chaise longue here, a Venetian mirror there. I think I'd be good at that. Helping people. Like that Japanese lady who makes you get rid of everything. I think I could take the Hiroshima approach. Oh for goodness' sake, it's just an expression.'

'We're fine, Mum. Really,' said Marnie, taking the snail from her and returning it to the mantelpiece.

'I don't know if the owners stay living there and try not to touch anything,' Barbara said. 'Possibly they move out for the duration so it stays nice and tidy. That would be simpler all round. At the very least, I can lend you some throw rugs. Some matching towels. You'd be surprised what a difference they make. No?'

CHAPTER SEVENTEEN

W e'll start shooting in here,' said Lakshmi, striding into the living room.

I had not seen her gun – no Glock registered to a suspended cop, no pearl-handled pistol bought at the mall with a stolen ID – but I dashed under the couch all the same.

'We can use backdrops, or shoot around anything problematic,' she went on. 'And we'll be cleaning it up post-production – you'll hardly recognise the place. The main goal is to have the merchandise out in plenty of time for Christmas. Wait, where did he go?'

'Come on, Tama,' said Marnie, dragging me out. 'No silly games.'

Something scuffled overhead. Rob glanced at the ceiling.

'Let's start with the greeting cards,' said Lakshmi, 'and then we'll do the calendar. Scott?'

A young man with a gigantic beard began assembling a camera.

That sort of shoot.

They put me on top of a birthday cake; they put me inside a ribboned box. They dressed me in reindeer antlers, an elf hat, a Santa hat, a halo. They tied a balloon round my leg and a bow tie round my neck. I held a diamond ring in my beak; I held a baby's rattle. I held a red rose. I ripped the wrapping paper from a pair of socks and I lay on my back next to a bottle of champagne and I peeled the foil from chocolate eggs that were empty inside. I bowed my head next to a single white lily.

'Let's throw him in the bath,' said Lakshmi. 'He loves water, right? With the shower cap? And then some in his cot, naturally. Does he have any jammies? No? Well that's a shame. That's an oversight. Will he sit in a saucepan? Will he read the newspaper? We need him to take up the space in an interesting way. Someone bring me a lamb or two. And what about one of the dogs? People love dogs. We'll get him sitting on a dog. Stealing its food. I don't suppose you have a cat?'

'Just a cat door,' said Marnie.

'Right, so no actual cat. What about the chickens? That could be funny. We'll grab a chicken.'

When they'd finished the photo shoot Marnie offered them a cup of tea, but Lakshmi said they should press on with the voice.

'I think he's a bit tired,' said Marnie. 'He might need a rest.'

'Five minutes,' said Lakshmi. 'We have to make our flight.'

Marnie fed me some slivered almonds and told me what a good boy I was, what an obedient and clever boy. Rob broke open a chocolate egg and ate it. Then we pressed on with the voice.

'So Marnie, if you can get him talking away while Scott records him. Just let Tama go for it but make sure he says the catchphrase, preferably a few times, and then later on we can choose the rest of the lines we want for the plush toy. All good?'

'I think so,' said Marnie.

Something pitter-pattered and scratched overhead. Rob glanced at the ceiling again.

'And . . . action!' said Lakshmi.

'You don't need to say action,' said Scott.

'I'll say action if I want to say action,' said Lakshmi.

'Shall I just start?' said Marnie.

'Of course, please,' said Lakshmi. 'Whenever you're ready. Action.'

'Who's the best boy ever?' said Marnie. 'Who's the cleverest boy in the world?'

'Don't come crying to me,' I said. 'You're not to touch him. OMG I want a bird on my head. I'm thinking like a rat.'

'Tama,' said Marnie, 'what did you have for breakfast?'

'Dutchie, Dutchie, ya mongrel,' I said. 'Babies don't have feathers.'

'Mmm,' said Lakshmi. 'Okay.' Something scurried and rustled. She looked up at the ceiling. 'What *is* that?'

'Sorry,' said Marnie. 'Rob thought he got them all.'

'Yeah, sorry,' said Rob.

'Is it a problem, Scott?' said Lakshmi.

'I can clean it up later.'

'Let's just keep going, then. Action.'

'Tama, how are you feeling today?' said Marnie.

'Get yourself some alpacas,' I said. 'Get yourself some alpacas. Bleating or bleeding, ha ha. Get yourself some alpacas.' I barked Night's bark.

'Mmm,' Lakshmi said again. 'Not much to work with so far.'

'Here are the headlines,' I said. 'You know I'd never hurt you, not on purpose. Wayleggo! Wayleggo! Are you a panda? Or a puffin?'

'Maybe if you asked him some more interesting questions,' said Lakshmi.

'Tama,' said Marnie, 'are you still hungry? Do you want another snack? Shall I get you another snack?'

'Open-ended questions,' said Lakshmi.

'Tell me what snack you'd like,' said Marnie.

'I'm at the end of my rope,' I said.

'Ask him about Christmas,' said Lakshmi. 'Ask him what he wants for Christmas.'

'I know how to cover up their worst bits,' I said.

'Tama,' said Marnie, 'what do you want for Christmas?'

'Yum yum yum,' I said. 'Good morning and welcome. I'm Tama. Blue makes our eyes pop.'

'What do you want for Christmas?'

'You married a loser.'

'What do you want for Christmas?'

'Watch out for ashiness.'

'What do you want for Christmas?'

'Your cells remember the famine.'

'What do you want for Christmas?'

'Bunch of cunts.'

'Okay! Just say the catchphrase,' said Lakshmi.

'Do you mean me or Tama?' said Marnie.

Lakshmi looked at her and spoke very slowly. 'I want Tama to say it, so you need to say it to him and get him to repeat it.'

'I can't make any promises,' said Marnie.

'I can't make any promises,' I said.

'Don't you dare,' said Marnie.

'I would like to gobble you up,' I said.

'Don't you dare. Don't you dare.'

'Can't feed them stones. He'll chop off his foot.'

'Don't you dare. Tama. Tama. Don't you dare.'

'It's like I turn into someone else.'

'Tama. Don't you dare.'

'Maybe you've had a nose job. Classic whore move, babe. What the fuck's a peacharine? Can't you cut up a fucking potato? I'm not an enemy. This was no suicide, Trent. See the spatter patterns? Do you think it's hormones? Am I just the workhorse?'

'Obviously we can't use profanities,' said Lakshmi.

'We can't use profanities,' I said.

'He's being a dick on purpose,' said Rob.

'He's being a dick on purpose,' I said.

'Tama. Don't you dare,' said Marnie.

'We can't use profanities,' I said.

'Don't you dare,' said Lakshmi.

'Rob suffers from insomnia,' I said.

'Don't you dare,' said Lakshmi.

'I could take the Hiroshima approach,' I said.

'Don't you dare, don't you dare,' said Lakshmi.

'That's not funny,' I said. 'Rob suffers from insomnia.'

'Can we leave me out of this?' said Rob.

'Leave me out of this,' I said.

'Tama,' said Marnie. 'Tama. Don't you dare.'

'I'm on no particular schedule,' I said.

'Don't you dare, Tama,' said Marnie.

'Sorry about the lambs,' I said.

'You're being a very naughty boy,' said Marnie.

'Swerve to hit them. Easy,' I said.

'Are you going to behave?' she said. 'Are you going to be a good boy for Marnie?'

'Mar Mar Mar Mar Mar,' I said. 'Meow.'

'Cut,' said Lakshmi. 'You'll have to do it, Rob.'

'Sorry?' he said.

'You'll have to do the catchphrase, and we'll use that.'

'But then it won't be Tama,' said Marnie.

'Scott can manipulate it later,' said Lakshmi. 'Nobody will know.'

'The Tama toy has to be Tama,' said Marnie. 'That's what people are paying for.'

I made a sound like an ambulance on its way to the scene of the crime. I made a sound like a squad car chasing a perp.

'We need the catchphrase,' said Lakshmi. 'And we need to make our flight. Do you have any other suggestions?'

'We could take it from the video clip,' said Marnie. 'That's what kicked it all off.'

'The quality's not good enough,' said Lakshmi. 'At this point, Rob's our only option.'

'It looks worse than it is,' I said.

'Rob?' said Marnie.

'Whatever,' he said. 'Don't you dare.'

'Speak up,' I said, and tugged at my favourite bit of braid on the couch.

'Hold on,' said Lakshmi. 'Are you ready to go, Scott?'

'I'm still recording.'

'But I said cut.'

'Yeah.'

'We'll talk about it later. All right. And . . . action.'

'Don't you dare,' said Rob.

'Yes, but like Tama,' said Lakshmi.

'Don't you dare,' said Rob.

'Like Tama. Imagine you're a bird. Close your eyes if it helps.'

'Don't you dare,' said Rob. He sounded like my father.

'Better. Again.'

'Don't you dare.'

'Squeakier. Again.'

'Don't you dare.'

'Throatier. Again.'

'Don't you dare.'

'Bit more conviction.'

'Don't you dare. Don't you dare.'

'Angrier.'

'Don't you dare, don't you dare, don't you dare.'

'Okay. Okay. I think we have it – that's a wrap.'

'Can I stop recording?' said Scott.

'Yes, Scott, you can stop recording.'

'Only you didn't say cut.'

'Cut.'

Scott pressed a button.

'Don't you dare,' I said.

CHAPTER EIGHTEEN

O h, you brought the bird,' said Barbara. 'Is it normal, do you think, to bring a bird to Sunday lunch?'

'He followed us, Mum,' said Marnie. 'We didn't bring him.'

'Perhaps he can wait outside.'

I perched on the deck, next to the dining-room window, which Marnie opened a crack – not wide enough for me to squeeze through but wide enough for her to slip me some sun-flower seeds.

'For heaven's sake!' said Barbara. 'Go and wash your hands. God knows where the creature's been.'

'You don't know the half of it,' said Rob. 'She feeds him with her mouth sometimes.'

'I've seen it,' said Barbara. 'I've told her.'

'Where's the harm?' said Marnie.

'You know they peck through sheep shit, right?' said Rob.

'Tama doesn't do that.'

I turned my head away, began to preen myself.

'Whatever you say, Mar.'

I peered in at them as they took their places around a large dining table. Ange strapped the baby into a high chair and put a dish of slop in front of it.

'Something smells fantastic,' said Marnie.

'Individual salmon soufflés,' said Ange. 'Nick's quite the chef when he wants to be.'

'Is he going to sit out there and stare at us for the entire meal?' said Barbara.

'He thinks he's a human,' said Nick. 'Part of the family. That's the narrative, right? That's the hook.'

'The narrative?' said Barbara. 'The *narrative*? Goodness me, it's just a bird – but then, I haven't been to university. What does Ba-ba know, eh Kaden?'

The baby produced an unintelligible sound and rubbed mashed banana through its hair. I started to whistle When Doves Cry.

'Lak says Tama's going to make us a mountain of money,' said Marnie.

'Don't be vulgar,' said Barbara.

'You reckon she's the real deal?' said Rob. 'I mean, she knows what she's talking about?'

'Lakshmi could turn dishwater into cold hard cash,' said Ange.

'I'd be careful if I were you,' said Barbara. 'It sounds very risky.'

'It's a calculated risk,' said Marnie. 'A chance for us to drag ourselves out of debt.'

'And when it all falls over? And you're left with hundreds of underpants and coffee mugs nobody wants?'

'Mum, we have to try something. We can't keep making losses – we're going under.'

'Yeah, all right, Marnie,' said Rob.

'What? It's no secret.'

'Maybe we don't need to bring it up at the dinner table, though.'

'It's on the news every week. Falling meat prices, falling wool prices, another drought likely this summer . . .'

'They're all turning vegetarian, aren't they,' said Barbara.

'And now the overseas supermarkets are complaining about the meat.'

'What's wrong with it?' said Ange.

'Nothing,' said Rob. 'Nothing's wrong with it. But their customers have decided they're a bit upset about tailing.'

'They don't want to buy meat from docked animals,' said Marnie.

'Why on earth not?' said Barbara.

'Apparently it's cruel,' said Rob. 'Apparently we're monsters. They'd prefer to eat lambs slaughtered with their tails still attached.'

Barbara laughed. 'Ludicrous!'

'There's a lot of pressure,' said Marnie.

'Well,' said Nick, 'it's important to listen to the voice of the consumer.'

'You know what's cruel?' said Rob. 'Leaving a lamb with a tail so long it gets caked in shit, and then the blowflies come and lay their eggs, and then the maggots hatch and eat the animal alive.'

Barbara shuddered, pushed away her bread roll.

'Sorry,' he said. 'It gets me worked up.'

He looked at me through the glass and I looked at him.

'No worries, mate,' said Nick. 'But you know, if you ever want to free up some capital, we'd be interested in buying another patch of dirt.'

'We're good thanks, mate.'

'Will you stop, though?' said Ange. 'Cutting the tails off?'

'No bloody way,' said Rob. 'We'd lose half the flock to flystrike. And the thing is, it doesn't even hurt them.'

'No?' said Ange.

'They run back to their mothers, right as rain. Come and see if you like – next weekend.'

'Am I invited too?' said Barbara.

'You're all invited. We could do with the extra help.'

'Meaning he won't have to pay so many casuals,' said Marnie.

Something started to beep, and Nick said, 'Let's get those babies out of the oven.'

But I think it was just an expression.

The wild thyme was in bloom and the haze of the mauve-white flowers seemed to hover just above the hills. Rob whistled and called, and the dogs traced great arcs across the grass, mustering the ewes and lambs, forcing them towards the pens in the corner of the paddock. Night headed off any stragglers, catching the most persistent and holding them down with his open mouth, taking not so much as the tiniest nibble, while Marnie and the casual trapped the panicking mob inside movable fences. Gradually they made the space smaller and smaller, and then they separated the mothers from the babies.

'So basically it's a production line,' said Rob. 'Ears, B12 jab, balls, tails.'

'Balls?' said Nick.

'Balls?' I said.

'Can't have the little girls running round with the little boys if they're still intact,' said Rob.

'Right, sure,' said Nick.

'Balls?' I said.

'The meat doesn't taste as nice either,' said Marnie. 'And they can get aggressive.'

'You're looking a bit unwell, Nick,' said Barbara. 'Shall I get the smelling salts?'

'Ha ha,' said Nick.

'Don't worry, I won't put you on balls,' said Rob. 'You'll be at the other end.' He showed Nick how to lift the lambs into the tailing cradle by grabbing them around their middles and hoisting them onto their backs. 'Most of them shouldn't struggle, but bend from your knees. Workplace safety and all that. Oh and nobody touch the tailing iron – it'll take your skin off.'

He connected it to a gas bottle and turned it on, and in a moment I could feel the heat hissing from its scissory tip.

Barbara and Marnie made the baby a little pen of its own. 'That'll keep you out of mischief,' said Barbara. She gave it some wooden blocks, but it failed to build anything useful.

Rob was showing Ange how to use the ear markers: a notch on the right for the males and a notch on the left for the females, along with an age mark on the other ear.

'Sure you're up for it?' said Nick, eyeing the trickle of blood.

'Absolutely,' said Ange, taking her place at the cradle. 'Just like bus tickets, really.'

Marnie stood opposite her with the needle and injected each lamb in the neck, and then the casual took over with his pliers, attaching tiny rubber rings between the legs of the males.

'Easy as that?' said Ange.

'Easy as that,' said the casual. 'After a week and a half they'll shrivel up and fall off.'

Barbara watched him as he worked, one finger held to her coral-coloured lips. 'Where were you twenty years ago,' she said, 'when my former husband was sniffing round Janice the Whore?'

Rob waited at the foot of the cradle, grasping each tail and severing it with the hot iron. A cloud of steam formed at the moment of contact, as if from his very hands. *Whoooooooooo*, said the gas bottle. I could smell cooked meat, burnt wool. Blood.

'But surely it hurts them,' said Barbara.

Rob shook his head, pushing another one off the end of the cradle: the lambs were too young to feel pain, and anyway, it was for their own good. 'Over before they know it,' he said, and grabbed the next one.

'I can't look,' said Barbara, looking.

Yes, for their own good, though the mothers cried and

bunted the sides of the pen, and some lambs tried to climb across other lambs to get out, but they couldn't, they couldn't.

The air was warm and thick with the scent of wild thyme. I lay in a sun-trance for a while, dozing, dreaming, and at one point I think I heard Marnie say, 'He's not dead. It's just something they do.'

Soon enough the tails covered the grass at Rob's feet like a pile of dirty socks, and Barbara gathered them into a sack.

'What happens to all these?' she said.

'Don't you worry,' said Rob, 'they'll be put to good use.'

She was watching the casual again, so deft with his tiny rubber rings.

'Do you want a turn?' he said.

'Oh goodness me no!' said Barbara.

Over in its pen, the baby was eating grass.

'I'll have a turn,' said Ange.

'Is that a good idea?' said Nick.

'What could possibly go wrong?'

Rob said, 'You're gamer than my wife, that's for sure.'

Everyone watched Ange fit the rubber ring to the pliers and then transfer it to her first lamb – and wasn't she a natural? Wasn't she born to the job? Look out, Nick, they said. Look out.

While they laughed and the lamb bleated I scuttled over to the sack of severed tails. Jumped inside for a little taste. Delicious, delicious. A freshly amputated lamb trotted past, looking for its mother, right as rain. I pushed a tail out of the sack and dragged it over to the grass-eating baby. Nudged it under the bars of the pen. A bit closer. A bit closer . . . and into its pudgy grip. It picked up the woolly scrap, rubbed it over its face. Started to suck.

Marnie noticed first. 'What's that he's got?' she said.

'He's cut himself!' said Barbara, dashing to the pen with Ange and Nick close behind. 'He's bleeding! He's bleeding!'

'Oh my God, it's everywhere!' said Ange.

The baby smiled up at her and offered her the soggy tail. They all stared at it for a moment.

'Ah,' said Ange. 'False alarm. Where did you find that, eh?'

'Tama,' said Marnie in a voice I did not like, 'did you give Kaden the tail?'

'Balls?' I said.

'Naughty boy! Bad boy! No!'

I threw myself on my back like a cast sheep and made soft warbling sounds, but Marnie did not scratch my belly and she did not scoop me up into her arms and she did not take my photo and put me on the internet.

They had to finish before dark so the lambs could still find their way back to their mothers. The mountains turned to violet and the last of the sun glittered on the water that snaked down the hill in the gold miners' water race, though there was no gold these days. I remember that the shadow of the shelterbelt stretched the length of the paddock as everyone helped to dismantle the pens, tie up the sacks stuffed with tails, turn off the gush of the gas. Then they headed for the yolk-yellow house. I remember the magpies heading home to roost, too; I remember a parent flying under a tired child, carrying it to a tree. That was how the wild worked.

Ange buttered bread while Marnie took plates from the cupboard and potato salad and coleslaw from the fridge. Every time I tried to catch her eye, she held up a finger and said, 'Bad boy,' and perhaps she did not love me any more.

I slunk out through the cat door – meow – and down the steps.

In the twilight Rob was stoking the barbecue, his face reflecting the glow of the flames.

'Can I tempt you?' said Barbara, wiggling a packet of cigarettes at him. On the box a picture of rotting teeth.

'Always,' he said.

'Bit chilly yet for al fresco.'

'It's tradition.'

'What is?' she said, lighting his cigarette with a purple lighter. I didn't have a purple one.

'What do you think?' He stirred the coals, then tore open a sack of tails and scattered them on the grill.

'We're *eating* them?' said Barbara.

'Compulsory,' he said.

'I might just have a bit of coleslaw.'

'You'll change your tune once they're cooked.'

They both sucked on their cigarettes, which would kill them.

'I was in town the other day,' said Barbara. 'I had a coffee in the old Post Office building. You'd never know they rebuilt it – that it's not the real thing.'

'Yeah, it looks the part,' said Rob.

'You'll have to show me where your old place was.'

'Can't remember. I was only three when they flooded us out for the damn dam. You know they built it on a faultline? Bloody idiots. Bloody mongrels. So one day . . .'

'When he did the dive, Nick said he saw a car down there, still parked on the bridge. Windows gone, door open, covered in muck. Who'd leave a car behind like that?'

'Dunno.' Rob poked at the fire and Barbara exhaled smoke.

'You're on board with all this bird business, are you?' she said.

He shrugged. 'They tell me it's a sure thing. Or as close as.'

'But I mean . . . she dresses it up.'

'Yeah. The fans go crazy for that.'

'Not that it's anything to do with me,' she said, 'but I'd be trying for another baby quick smart.'

Rob breathed out a cloud of smoke. 'We are. We are. I want someone to hand this place down to. But so far, nothing.'

'You just need to let nature take its course.'

The smoke from the burning wool began to rise and spread; it grew so thick that Rob disappeared, and I could see only his feet in their muddy boots. On the back porch the dogs sniffed the acrid air and whined. Then the noise started: a frenzied buzz and crackle like a swarm of blowflies. Barbara waved her arms about.

'All the lanolin,' shouted invisible Rob.

I could hardly hear myself think.

The tails were charred to black by the time he piled them onto a platter. He threw the dogs their share and took the rest inside.

At the dining table everyone helped themselves, even Barbara. They peeled off the charred skin as best they could, though bits of it still clung to the meat, and soon their fingers were covered in the stuff, and their mouths too.

'Not bad,' said Nick, sprinkling another tail with salt.

'Some people boil them up and eat them bones and all,' said Marnie. 'They just crumble away.'

'Oh I don't like the sound of that,' said Barbara.

'False alarm. False alarm,' I said, tugging at the hem of Marnie's jeans like there was no tomorrow, but she ignored me. It was Rob who slipped me a morsel of meat, dropping it under the table when nobody was looking.

Outside I could hear magpies finishing their evening songs, laying claim to their territory. I settled on the windowsill, and my right eye saw the black pines, and my left eye saw the people around the dining table, their fingers black, their mouths black. I did not know how to make Marnie love me again.

That night, when the ghost of my mother came to me, she said *Gigantic birds lived here once. Great flightless plant-eaters who stood twice the height of a man, and a vast eagle who preyed on the plant-eaters. His talons were as big as a tiger's claws, and he could rip open a man, he could dig deep into bone, he could*

carry off a child. The humans knew to fear the rush of his mighty
wings. How foolish they were, walking about in feather cloaks,
looking for all the world like prey. But now they are only bones,
the great plant-eaters, the vast eagles. Now they are only draw-
ings on rock. Now they are only eggs found in a thousand pieces.

I dreamed I crept to the master bedroom where Rob lay
dead to the world. I pulled back the blankets and perched on
his thigh, and he breathed out a cloud of smoke but he did not
wake. In my dream I watched the smoke rise and vanish. Then,
with my beak, I opened a rubber ring and stretched it over the
pouch between his legs.

One day soon afterwards, I saw Marnie walking up the
gravel holding a new bird. A new magpie. In one hand the letters from the letterbox, and in the other this pretender, this
rival. She must have rescued it: she must have found it down
on Wilderness Road, clipped by a car, perhaps, or attacked by
a cat – though it was no juvenile, no helpless fledgling. It was
my size. She nuzzled it with her cheek, tucked it in close to her
neck, and it stayed there quite still and obedient, a good boy.
Not the type of boy to steal a lamb's severed tail and give it to
a baby.

'Rob!' she called. 'Come and see!'

She sat the bird on the kitchen table, which was not very
sanitary – God knows where the creature had been – and they
both looked at it, heads tilted.

'I think they've caught him,' said Rob.

'I love him,' said Marnie.

She loved him. She loved him.

Rob clapped his hands as if killing a mosquito. 'Perfect!' he
said. 'Let's keep this one and get rid of the other, and I'll be
able to sleep.'

'Very funny,' said Marnie.

But I did not laugh.

She noticed me by the back door then, skulking, sulking. 'Tama,' she said, 'meet Tama.'

Even my name.

'I'm Tama,' I tried to say. 'I'm Tama.' Except it didn't come out as human words. I felt an old territorial call surge up inside me and boil in my throat, and although I thought I did not remember it I threw back my head and carolled *We are here and this is our tree and we're staying and it is ours and you need to leave and now.*

It was as if Marnie hadn't heard me at all. She sat down at the kitchen table and pressed the new bird's wing, and on her command – a good boy, the best boy – he spoke. And he spoke with my voice.

'Good morning and welcome,' he said. 'I'm Tama.'

'Not bad, eh?' said Marnie.

'It's like he's in the room with us,' said Rob.

'I'm Tama!' I said. 'I'm Tama!' But again the territorial call I didn't remember remembering. *We are here and this is our tree . . .*

'Shh,' Marnie said to me over her shoulder. She pressed the trespasser's wing again, and again he spoke with my voice.

'I would like to gobble you up.'

Press.

'Yum yum yum.'

Press.

'That's not funny.'

Press.

'Meow.'

'Just like the real one,' said Marnie.

But there was something not quite right about this bird. He was too still, and he spoke without opening his beak. I wasn't even sure his feathers were real; they had no sheen, no oily lustre.

I flew to the table, landed right beside him. He didn't look right and he didn't smell right. I aimed a peck at his dull black belly – and over he toppled, legs in the air, past his prime. Death by Tama.

Rob let out a laugh. 'It's *you*, birdbrain.'

'It's a toy, Tama,' said Marnie. 'A toy Tama.'

'A toy, Tama,' I said. 'A toy Tama.'

I tipped it upside down and listened for the clunk, but it had no heart.

Marnie pressed its wing once more.

'Don't you dare,' it said – and this time I did not hear myself. No, not myself, just a toy faking Rob's voice faking my voice faking Rob's voice.

'What do you think?' said Marnie.

'Can't even tell,' said Rob.

'But I mean,' said Barbara, 'why does a bird say meow?'

'It's funny,' said Marnie. 'It makes people laugh.'

'How is it funny?'

'Well, because he's a bird.'

Ange said, 'Save your breath. I tried explaining to her on the way over.' She set the baby down on the master bedroom floor and it started to crawl straight for me, soft and plump, little lamb.

Barbara hung a long flat bag on the wardrobe door and unhooked two dresses. 'Never again,' she said, shaking away the wrinkles. 'We are talking months of my life, Marnie. *Months*. See these sequins? Every one of them a drop of my blood. Don't get me started on the embroidery. I have no words.'

'Seriously, don't,' said Ange.

'Torture,' said Barbara. 'I just about lost my sight. The appliqué horses alone—'

'You do have a few words, then,' said Ange.

'They look amazing, Mum. You're so clever.' Marnie kissed her cheek.

'Well, try them on, and we'll match up the hems.'

The baby made a grab for me, but I hopped to the side. It laughed. Dribbled on the floor. Babbled its nothing sounds.

The replica me, the toy, which was not real, sat on the bed like one of Marnie's decorative cushions. While she and Ange put on the dresses with all the little pistols pointing this way and that, Barbara picked it up. She eyed the label sewn into its backside, checked the quality of its seams. Almost pulled it apart. 'Thirty-nine ninety-five?' she said. 'Each?'

'Plus postage and handling,' said Marnie from somewhere inside the tassels and sequins and embroidery and pistols.

'That seems a bit pricey. It's not even washable. *Wipe with damp sponge.* No thank you.'

'We have hundreds of pre-orders already, Mum. Everyone wants their own Tama.'

'They could buy a budgie for that sort of money. And you can wash a budgie.'

'Mother,' said Ange, smearing the baby's dribble away with her bare hand, 'as per fucking usual, you're missing the point.'

'Don't use that kind of language, Angela. Do you want Kaden to pick it up?'

'It's just a word. Fuck is just a word.'

'Fuck,' I said. 'Fuck.'

Barbara put her hands over the baby's ears. 'I used to run your toys through a hot wash once a week. You can't be too careful.'

'And that's why Foxy Loxy's fur fell out and his eyes rusted,' said Ange.

The baby grabbed for me again and I hopped away again.

'Is this what you want, darling?' said Barbara, holding out the replica me. 'Here's the birdie. Ba-ba has the birdie.' She waddled it towards the baby, making it look like an idiot, then pressed its wing.

'Good morning and welcome,' it said. 'I'm Tama.'

'Fuck. Fuck,' I said.

'Marnie, tell him to stop that!' said Barbara. 'Don't listen, darling.' She pressed the replica's wing again.

'I would like to gobble you up,' it said.

'Fuh,' said the baby. 'Fuh.' It grabbed the replica me and started to gnaw on a leg.

'What did he just say?' said Ange.

'Fuck,' I said.

'I don't know,' said Marnie.

'He said a word. He said his first word.'

'Fuh,' said the baby.

'Shit,' said Marnie.

'That is quite enough!' said Barbara. 'Let's not react. Let's pretend we never even heard him. Angela, stop laughing. Now, where are the pins?'

Marnie studied her reflection. 'It's very tight,' she said. 'Very low-cut.'

'Your sister's orders,' said Barbara.

'Sexy cowgirl,' said Ange. 'Sexy Doris Day. That's our act.' She was looking at herself in the mirror too, pushing her lips forward, jutting her chest.

'I thought we agreed on cute,' said Marnie.

'Same thing, really.'

'No it's not.'

The dresses wriggled with tassels across the front, and below each shoulder a horse silhouette looked across bare skin to its mirror image. On the back, red sequins picked out the shape of roses made from Barbara's blood.

'Mmm,' she said, looking Marnie up and down.

'What?' said Marnie.

'Nothing. Nothing.'

'*What?*' said Marnie.

'I just thought you might have shed the extra weight by now,' said Barbara. 'I just thought I might be able to take in the side seams.'

'Give it a rest, Mum,' said Marnie.

Barbara said, 'I popped in to Lynette's last week. I saw the nicest pair of slacks – the lemon ones with the white topstitching – but the smallest size she had was a ten. She said to me why don't you spoil yourself and get them, Barbara? You could easily take them in. But I said Lynette, if I buy something too big for me, it's just an excuse to pig out. Just an excuse to stuff myself silly. I was eight and a half stone when I got married, and I'm eight and a half stone now. And she said I was quite right. So I suppose I'm wondering about your choices, Marnie. Where you might be going wrong. We definitely can't call it baby weight any more, can we. If we ever could in the first place.'

'Mum,' said Ange. 'Can you not?'

'Well,' said Barbara, poised with her pins, 'these things need saying. How short am I doing the hems?'

Marnie said, 'Knee-length,' and Ange said, 'Arse-length.'

'Shall we split the difference?' Barbara said, and folded Marnie's dress up to mid-thigh. 'What do you think?'

'I'm showing a lot more than I want to,' said Marnie.

'It's high time the carnival acknowledged female strength,' said Ange. 'You're empowering yourself. You're taking control.' She folded the dress up even higher.

'Mmm,' said Barbara. 'We don't want to see what you've had for lunch, though.'

'I'd really prefer the knee,' said Marnie. 'Doris Day would want the knee.'

Barbara folded it back to mid-thigh. 'A compromise,' she said, and started to pin. 'When do I get to see your act?'

'Not till the carnival,' said Ange. 'You know that.'

'Oh I forgot – I'm just the workhorse. The nearly blind workhorse.'

'I'm not sure about it,' said Marnie.

'Just you wait,' said Ange. 'We'll be the main event. Never mind the manly men chopping the wood.'

'Did you talk Nick into competing?' said Marnie.

Ange waved a hand. 'He's more of an ideas man.'

'I saw Rob out there training the other day,' said Barbara. 'My goodness but he's in superb shape. Men like him appreciate a trim wife. I'm telling you this because I love you.' She looked up at the golden axes above the bed. 'Ten in a row. What an achievement.'

'He hasn't won number ten yet,' said Marnie, and Barbara said, 'Have you seen the muscles on the man? The pure animal strength? There's no way he can lose.'

'I hope not,' said Marnie.

She and Ange rehearsed their act after Barbara left. *I love you, a bushel and a peck . . .* The tassels swung as the two of them danced, Ange on the left to showcase her good side, and the red sequins speckled the walls and floor with dots of light that the baby tried to catch.

'What's wrong?' said Ange. 'You keep stopping.'

'The pins,' said Marnie. 'They're jabbing me every time I move.'

'Rob's right, little sis. You're way too soft.'

But it was hurting her, the dress was hurting her, and as they began to sing and dance again I flew to her shoulder. Gave her a little peck on the cheek.

'Oh my God,' said Marnie.

Had I hurt her too? Did I not know my own strength?

'What?' said Ange.

'Did you see that?'

No blood, no bruise. No blue-black, no black-black. I was a good boy, the best boy. I loved her.

'See what?'

'Tama pecked me right when we sang the word *peck*.'

'He did not.'

'Honest.'

'*If* he did,' said Ange, '*if* he did, because I saw nothing of the sort, it's just a coincidence.'

The next time they sang *peck*, with Ange watching me in the mirror, I pecked Marnie's cheek again. Soft as a kiss, feather-soft. No blood.

'Now do you believe me?' said Marnie. She stroked my back, and she loved me again – she had forgiven me the way she forgave Rob.

'Okay, wow,' said Ange. 'Let's try the whole thing from the top.'

There was no special trick to it; I'd heard the song over and over, ever since Marnie had brought me home, and I knew when the word was coming. Right on cue, I pecked her cheek. *I love you, a bushel and a peck* (peck)*, a bushel and a peck* (peck) *and it beats me all to heck, it beats me all to heck how I'll ever tend the farm, ever tend the farm when I want to keep my arm about you . . .*

'Two things,' said Ange when they'd finished. 'Number one: he's part of the act now, obviously. Number two: he's going to need a bandanna.'

Rob was readying himself for the carnival too, training every few days, keeping his racing axes in shining shape, sharp enough to shave the hair off his arm. He cleaned and dried them after each use, and inspected their blades for flaws, and oiled their handles and their heads. I learned the parts of an axe, which sounded like the parts of a body: the toe, the eye, the heel, the shoulder, the beard, the belly, the cheek, the throat. His practice axes weren't so precious; if he nicked a blade on frozen wood or on a knot he took it to the woolshed to fix, reshaping the edge on the bench grinder. It had belonged to his father, who had used it on his own knives and axes, and it sang at the touch of the steel as the sparks burst and fell like bright seeds. Every so often Rob cooled the head with water so the edge wouldn't lose its temper.

On the weekends he trained with the axemen. Sometimes they drove to our house, and sometimes he loaded his case of axes into his beetle-black car and drove to theirs. Sometimes, too, he put on his white trousers and his black singlet and drove to other towns to compete against other axemen, coming home with ribbons which he hung in the living room and the hall and the master bedroom – wherever there was space left on the cockeyed walls. 'Superb bloody effort,' the axemen said on those days, drinking to Rob, to the logs, to the axes and to themselves. They were giants, every one of them, as solid as the trunks they split open, and if they weren't cutting, they talked about cutting: how to read the wood; how to estimate the soft spots by looking to see where the chainsaw had fluffed the end grain. How best to prevent a block from slabbing; the proper angle for filing a blade depending on the type of timber; the proper honing stone to keep the edge true. How to cut when you found something bad hidden in the wood. The advantages of pine over beech, which required harder hits, or poplar, which sucked the silt into its heart and blunted the blade. It had to be young pine; dry old radiata could wreck a man's chances because there was too little sap in it, and too little sap meant too much cork, and if you hit a patch of cork the axe could just stick there. They talked about their odds in the team relay; they talked about fair timekeepers, crooked referees, the calculation of handicaps. Men who ran dead for a few events in a row to get a better number, then pulled out the big guns to claim the prize money. A beginner who'd hacked into his shin because he was watching the axe, not the spot where he wanted the axe to land, and an old hand who'd sliced his toes off when he'd had a skinful, and a fine young cutter, nicest bloody bloke in the business, whose axe head had flown into the crowd one day and opened a man's artery. They talked about who would win the Tree Felling (Rob), who would win the Single Saw (Chin Scar), who would win the Underhand (Ethan bloody McKay or Rob), who would win the Hard Hit (Rob). They talked about protein powders and red meat and raw eggs to make themselves even bigger so they could hit even harder, and they talked about Consolation Events for men who failed to win any prizes – weaker men. It wasn't like it used to be, they said. One old-school axeman had whacked a block in half with the handle when the head fell off, and another cut an underhand block blindfolded, and another felled the entire Canterbury Plains in a weekend – so the stories went. But Rob was a sure thing for the overall win: the Golden Axe and the big prize money. He had it all sewn up. Foregone bloody conclusion.

Chapter Nineteen

There'll be very few dead spots,' said the man in the cap. 'It should pick up movement almost anywhere in the room.'

I was watching from the hall, and when he stepped back I saw a new Eye sitting on the bookshelves by the fireplace. I stretched and wriggled inside my T-Rex costume. Rob and Marnie waited next to the coffee table, looking unsure of what to do.

'Is it just for security?' said the man in the cap.

'It's not for security at all,' said Marnie. 'We want a live feed, for our website.'

'Easy as.'

'Is it . . . can it see me now?' said Rob.

'Yep,' said the man in the cap. 'You can set it to live feed only, or you can record. It'll store any videos in the cloud.'

I peered out the window at the sky.

'It's not recording all the time, then?' said Rob.

The man in the cap shook his head. 'That'd take way too much memory. The live feed is just what's happening in real time.'

'And when it's gone, it's gone.'

'Correct.' He checked the view on his phone screen, adjusted the Eye a little. 'Trust me, in a few days you'll forget it's even there.'

'I don't know about that,' said Rob.

'And you can always turn it off when you want some privacy,

then on again later.' He showed them a black box behind the Eye, pointed at a button on it. 'Just here, see? Or remotely. Now, there's one to install in the baby's room too?'

'And the kitchen and the back porch,' said Marnie.

'Have you seen the muscles on him?' I said from the hall.

'Beg your pardon?' said the man in the cap.

'Have you seen the muscles on him?' I said again.

'Ah . . .'

'Sorry,' said Marnie. 'That's our pet bird.'

I strolled in, hopped up on the couch. 'Let's not react,' I said. 'Let's pretend we never even heard him.'

'Oh it's you!' said the man in the cap. 'My girlfriend loves you! Can I get a selfie?'

I turned my good side to his phone, started to whistle Touch Me Jesus.

'She will not believe this! Oh my God, the dinosaur suit! Crack up!'

After he'd left, Rob peered at the Eye. His face filled Marnie's phone screen, all misshapen and strange. His forehead as big as the moon.

'Now, Tama,' said Marnie. 'There are some words you can't say in front of the cameras. Do you understand?'

'Do you understand?' I said.

'No fuck,' she said. 'No fucking. No cock, no cunt, no wanker.'

'No fuck,' I said. 'No fucking. No cock, no cunt, no wanker.'

'Marnie, what the hell?' said Rob.

'I'm teaching him.'

'You think he understands you.'

'I know he does.'

'No fuck,' I said. 'No fucking. No cock, no cunt, no wanker.'

'Congratulations,' said Rob. 'Now he won't fucking shut up.'

'No fucking,' I said.

'See, he does understand.'

'Hmm.'

'You stay here,' she said, taking her phone, 'and I'll go to our bedroom, and we'll test the camera. But don't get so close. You look weird.'

I followed her down the hall and made myself comfortable on their bed, nestling between the cushion with the patchwork house and the cushion with the sheep made from real sheepswool.

'Okay, I can see you,' she said. 'Now say something.'

'I don't know what to say.'

I could hear him right there in the master bedroom with us, but also in the distance, speaking from the living room. As if there were two Robs.

'Anything,' she said. 'It doesn't matter.'

'This feels stupid.'

'Count to ten. Sing the alphabet.'

He groaned.

'Okay. What's your favourite colour?'

'Green, I suppose. I don't know.'

'Good boy!' she laughed.

I didn't like her calling him that.

'You're having fun with this, aren't you,' he said.

'Walk around the room a bit. Like Tama does. Keep talking.'

'I can't think of anything.'

'For goodness' sake. Don't make me come down there and smack you about.'

They were both silent for a moment. Marnie stared into her screen and Rob stared into the Eye. I nibbled at one of my T-Rex claws.

He said, 'I'm not thrilled about the camera. Yes, I get why there's one in his bedroom. His fans or followers or whatever want to see him. But this one? The one on the porch, and in the *kitchen*? Tracking everything we say? Everything we do? It's creepy, Mar. All very well for Lakshmi to announce we need them. All very well for her to decide we should let the world look in our living room. But who knows how safe they are? Who knows if they're really off when they're off? They could still be recording us, sending out the footage. I've read about that. Weaknesses in people's systems. Huge security holes. There are websites where you can access cameras all over the world. Watch a woman in Hong Kong paint her toenails. Watch a woman in Madrid do yoga. Watch empty houses. Watch sleeping babies – thousands of those. I'd just like some certainty. To know that it's safe, and that we're doing the right thing.'

Marnie left her phone on the bed and returned to the living room. On the screen I saw her put her arms around Rob, and they stood there in front of the fireplace, holding each other, swaying together in a small and songless dance.

'This is just us, right?' he said into her hair. 'Nobody else can see?'

'Nobody else,' she said.

I knew I could never hold her like that.

'I want us to get back on our feet again,' he said. 'All our debt – sometimes I feel like I can't breathe.'

'Let's try with Tama,' she said. 'See what happens.'

He nodded and led her to their bedroom, where I waited on the bed.

'Sorry mate,' he said. 'Out you go.' And gently he picked me up and carried me to my own room, my own bed, though it was still the middle of the afternoon and I was not tired.

Through the wall I heard the animal noises they made – his grunts and yelps, her high cries. Not a thing I could do about it. From the shelf the new Eye watched me. I dragged out the guts of my bear in long white strands that smelled of dead grass, pecking deep and deeper until I hit the heart. I dragged that out too, and I saw that it was a hard little canister with holes at one end and a rattling stone inside. Nothing more.

But the heart was also the voice, and the bear wouldn't talk without it.

The next day there was a knock at the door.

'Hope you don't mind,' said the man in the cap who wasn't wearing his cap, 'but I brought Chrissie over to see the bird. It's her birthday soon.'

'Well, I suppose—' said Marnie.

'Next month,' Chrissie said. 'Oh my God, there he is! Tama! Hi Tama! I don't even know what to say. I'm all tongue-tied. Like when Ben saw Reese Witherspoon at the Super Value and she asked him if he knew where the batteries were – she must have thought he worked there – and he just about crapped himself. Tama! Tama! Over here!'

I sidled up to the front doorstep. Allowed her to stroke me. Perhaps she was a German homosexual; perhaps she would feed me bits of muesli bar that tasted like the sun.

'He's so silky. God, look at his eyes. An old soul for sure. Ben, are you getting all this?'

'Yep,' said Ben from behind his phone.

'Tama! Tama, say something! Are you going to talk to me? Happy birthday Chrissie! Happy birthday Chrissie!'

'What's all this?' said Rob.

'Gidday,' said Ben. 'Hope you don't mind.'

'It's fine, honestly,' said Marnie.

When Chrissie failed to produce any muesli bars I turned to the handbag hitched over her shoulder.

'Oh!' she said. 'He wants to come home with us! He's climbing right in! Ben, you're still getting this, right?'

'Yep,' said Ben.

No treats in the handbag either. Clearly she was not a

German homosexual, and neither was Ben. 'Who knows how safe it is?' I said.

More and more followers made their way to Wilderness Road: honeymooners from Tokyo; retired teachers from Seattle; two police officers on their lunch break; a vanload of real-estate agents; the neighbours from one farm over. Backpackers came from France, Denmark, Canada, Switzerland. A woman in a velour tracksuit held me to her chest and cried. A linguist from Adelaide said he was lost for words. Whole families came with their grabby children; one boy begged his parents for a photo of me sitting on his shoulder, but as soon as Marnie put me there he started to shake in terror. 'Hold still, Jacob!' said his father. 'Hold *still*! Do you want the photo or not?' I shat down his back; I don't think they noticed. Another child yanked out one of my feathers and said she'd found it on the ground and could she keep it please? Then zipped it into a plastic bag her mother had at the ready. Sometimes the followers fed me treats, if Marnie let them; she said it was important for my continuing development that I eat mostly what I would eat in the wild. I have seen pictures, she said, horrible pictures of twisted beaks and bowed legs. Right, sure, said the followers, but a few bits of cheese scone won't hurt.

One couple drove up in a whole house on wheels. They'd done the North Island first, they said, but the South was even more beautiful, and did we know how lucky we were?

'I suppose you stop seeing it if you see it all the time,' said Marnie.

'Oh, hi sweetie!' said the woman when I hopped down the front steps. 'My goodness, you're so handsome!' I peered around Marnie's legs. 'You don't need to hide behind Mommy! We won't bite!'

'Incredible,' said the man as he climbed down from the driver's side. He stood with his hands on his hips, looking around.

'No guards. No metal detectors. We can't believe how little security you have here.'

'Out you come, darling. Peekaboo. Peekaboo.' I'd thought the woman wanted to catch a glimpse of me, but she kept covering her eyes.

'We could be anyone,' said the man. 'I mean, we're not – we're Frank and Judy from Phoenix – but we *could* be anyone.'

'Is it true your police officers don't even carry guns?' said the woman.

'I think so,' said Marnie.

'Incredible,' said the man again.

'We never want to go home,' said the woman. 'We'd stay on the road forever if we could.' She closed her eyes, took in a deep breath.

'I've thought about that,' said Marnie. 'Getting away for a while. A different place every night.' She eyed the house on wheels. 'How roomy is it?'

'Would you like to take a look?'

The woman opened the door and I saw a tiny kitchen fitted with a skinny oven and a half-size fridge, and a trapdoor in the roof like the trapdoor in our bathroom ceiling, only I could see the sky through it. Marnie stepped inside and the woman bent down to me and said, 'Well hi there, little guy.'

'You're being very naughty,' I said, and she laughed a low, smoky laugh.

'Delightful! Absolutely delightful!'

I edged closer to the house on wheels. My left eye saw the tiny kitchen and my right eye saw our front porch.

'I think he wants to come in too,' said the woman.

'He's scared of cars,' called Marnie.

The woman stretched her hand out to me as if she had food. 'It's not a car, honey.'

'Come and have a look, Tama,' said Marnie, and she scooped me up and carried me inside. 'See, there's a Tama-sized dining table and a Tama-sized washbasin. A nice soft bed where we can watch TV. Each cushion made to just the right shape. And all these little cupboards to hold all our little treasures – everything safe behind its own door.'

We could have been happy there, she and I.

When the truck came rumbling up the gravel, shaking the house to its bones, I thought it was coming for the lambs – only it was the wrong time of year, and they were too young, and Rob hadn't mustered them out of the paddock, herding them into the yards with the dogs barking at their backs, crowding them in tight to wait huge-eyed for the man who would take them to the works. No, the lambs remained in the open, flicking the nubs of their tails, ripping up the grass, fattening themselves for a different day, and the truck – which had no slits in the sides for air, I saw then, and was not a truck for lambs – stopped at the house.

'It's here, Tama! It's here!' said Marnie, and she pulled the plug from the kitchen sink and dried her hands and ran outside.

Rob was already at the front steps, and he and the driver began to unload boxes and carry them down the hall to the spare room. I watched them from the kitchen, and then, when the truck had rumbled back down the gravel to Wilderness Road, rattling the windowpanes and pushing the wood dust from the borer-beetle holes, I went to have a look.

The boxes were stacked so high they blocked the light from outside. Rob was slicing them open with his butcher's knife, and Marnie was unpacking them and arranging the contents on the new set of shelves that ran right around the room.

'Careful with that thing,' said Marnie. 'Don't cut too deep.'

Everywhere I saw myself: on T-shirts and underwear and coffee mugs and key rings and cushion covers, on greeting cards and calendars and shopping bags and other things I didn't even recognise. When Rob moved the empty boxes away from the shelves by the wardrobe, I saw the birds themselves: rows and rows of pretend Tamas staring out at me from their glass eyes, and inside each one of them my voice, my words. Mine and Rob's.

I thought: if my father would just come to the window – if he would just look inside. You see? I would say to him. You see how they respect me, how they worship me? How they love me? That is how houses work.

But he never came.

I kept Marnie company each day in the spare room, which we called the stockroom, because it was important to be professional. She hummed as she packed up all the orders, and I warbled along with her. When she tweeted a photo of me poking my head inside a Tama tote bag, we sold out of Tama tote bags. When she tweeted a photo of me drinking water from a Tama shot glass, we sold out of Tama shot glasses.

'Look,' she said, pointing at the computer screen, 'it tells you who's bought what and where. Someone in Toronto just bought a phone case. Someone in Stuttgart just bought two T-shirts. Oh, Moscow! Someone in Moscow bought a laptop sleeve! The whole world wants you, Tama.'

I unspooled the roll of plastic wrap and began to pop the little bubbles trapped inside. Pop pop pop pop pop with the tip of my beak.

'Naughty boy. Naughty boy,' said Marnie, but she was laughing, and I pulled the plastic over me like a blanket and rolled myself up. She grabbed her phone – it was never far away – and I did it all again for her, the popping and the rolling, and she put me on the internet. Straight away the numbers next to the heart started flashing and the followers started talking their heads off, the pictures of their faces piling up and up. 'You're so helpful Tama,' Marnie read. 'OMG Tama please ship yourself to me! Wow those toys are lifelike LOL. @Beckys_Nana this is the bird I was telling you about. Sorry but I think that's irresponsible. He could suffocate. Lighten up lady it's just a joke. @GhostSausage you should teach Sweetie to do this!' Marnie lifted me away from the plastic. 'You're not going to suffocate, are you?' she said. 'You're a clever boy, the cleverest boy.'

The toy Tamas sold the best of all. The truck brought more and more of them, so many that Rob had to clear a space in the woolshed to store the extra units. I perched outside on the mound of stones his father had made and watched him stack the cartons next to the broken couch. Boxes and boxes of Tamas.

'I'll need to quit Lynette's at this rate,' said Marnie, but Rob said she shouldn't get ahead of herself.

Lakshmi called every few days, and Marnie put her on speaker phone so both she and Rob could listen, though neither of them understood what she was saying.

'We're maintaining good top-of-mind awareness,' she told them, 'and your KPIs indicate excellent conversion. Some older followers disengage with the content when he swears, but that's compensated by the eighteen to twenty-nine demographic who love it. We're generating qualified leads rather than basic traffic to the website – the bounce rate could always be lower, of course, so we'll have another look at your landing pages and your calls to action. And if we want to maximise customer lifetime value, we need to invest in retention, so I'll get the team to put together some ideas there. Remember that the algorithm loves rich media when ranking content because users are more likely to engage with it, yes?'

They both nodded, and when Lakshmi had gone – 'Right then my darlings, bye you gorgeous things' – they looked at each other and Rob said, 'What the hell does all that mean?'

'Money,' said Marnie. 'It means money.'

'It means money,' I said.

One afternoon I was napping in the stockroom, up on the top shelf among the toy Tamas, when Rob walked in with Ange and Nick.

'Hello hello,' said Nick. 'Thought we might stop by and see the engine room.'

'Vroom vroom,' said Rob, pretending to be a car, which fooled no one.

'Quite the set-up,' said Ange.

'She basically lives in here these days,' said Rob. 'I never see her.'

'You have to admit,' said Marnie, stuffing another toy Tama into a mailer bag, 'it was a good thing I saved him and brought him home.'

'Good morning and welcome. I'm Tama,' said the bag as she squashed out the air.

'I don't have to admit anything,' said Rob.

'Come on, mate,' said Nick. 'Credit where credit's due.' He took one of the Tama T-shirts from the shelves and held it up to himself. 'What do you think?'

'Keep it,' said Marnie. 'Here, Ange, you too.'

'Steady on,' said Rob.

'We've Nick to thank for all this, remember.'

'Nothing to do with me,' said Nick. 'You're the one generating the content. Building your brand. You and Lakshmi.'

'Have you thought about charging the tourists?' said Ange. 'You could make a killing from them alone, surely.'

'She's got a point,' said Nick. 'We see them coming and going just about every day.'

'Marnie told the world where we live,' said Rob. 'And there's cameras all over the show now. We're live fucking feed.'

'We can turn them on and off,' said Marnie. 'It's not all the time.'

Ange didn't unfold her T-shirt. 'It's sweet of you,' she said, 'but to be honest, I'm not sure a magpie top is the best look for an orchardist, no matter how much we might love him.'

'Think about it, though,' said Nick. 'We could align our brand with a viral sensation. Who knows what doors might open?'

'We should be charging you,' said Rob.

'It *was* Nick's idea,' said Ange, eyeing the stacks of address labels, the new printer. The key rings, the calendars, the mouse mats, the diaries, the fridge magnets, the underpants. The in-tray where Marnie had taken my photo: Keeping on Top of the Paperwork. Ange said, 'My little sis. Who would've thought? She was such a funny kid, Rob. Followed me round like a dog. Remember flying lessons? Yes you do, Mar. I made up this story – told her I could fly. I didn't expect her to believe me, but she kept pestering me to teach her. I said if she made my bed for a week, I'd take her out to the deck and we'd have our first lesson – I'd show her how to jump off the edge and fly to the ground. Then we'd go higher and higher each time – the apple tree, the top of the garden shed, the roof of the house – till we were soaring over the whole neighbourhood. At the end of the week I told her she hadn't been making my bed the way I liked it and she'd have to do something else: bring me toasted sandwiches after school, let me borrow her felt pens. Whatever I ordered her to do, she did. And it was never enough. One day I said she had to prove how much she wanted to fly. I ordered her to lie down on the road and to stay there even if she heard a car coming. I decide when you can get up, I told her. I decide if you've earned the first lesson. Then I went inside and watched from my bedroom window. She didn't move a muscle. Stayed there staring at the sky, waiting for me to say she'd passed the test. I don't actually remember going and getting her – I must have got bored watching – but of course in the end she ran off and told Mum. And Mum said how could you be so stupid? Meaning Marnie.'

'Nothing to do with me,' I said from among the toy Tamas, and Ange almost jumped out of her skin.

'Jesus! I didn't see him there.'

'He's a cunning little fucker,' said Rob.

Marnie took my photo. Put me on the internet.

'That's the way to do it,' said Nick. 'You've always got to be ready. Always on alert.'

Rob grabbed Marnie by the shoulders and steered her out of the stockroom. 'Time for a tea break,' he said. 'I'll put the jug on.'

Nick followed, but Ange stayed behind for a moment. She plucked at the end of the giant roll of bubble wrap. Started to pop a row.

CHAPTER TWENTY

To begin with there were two different Robs. Old Rob still watched me like he was planning something, like he wanted to drive me up to the killing house where he drove the dog-tucker sheep, or load me on the truck that came to take the lambs to the works. Old Rob still bashed the wall of the master bedroom when I talked at night. He still checked the level of grain in the grain silo and said there was not enough, and still checked the level of rain in the rain gauge and said there was not enough. He still tallied up the losses and glared at the spreading sweet briar and gorse. He still headed to the pines with his rifle, pulling on his balaclava, covering his face like a perp, and despite hearing alarm calls I still believed what Marnie told me: that he was shooting rabbits, which were pests.

But in the living room and the kitchen and on the back porch, when the Eyes were watching, new Rob appeared. He made sure I had my favourite clothes pegs to play with on the couch, and he brought me little bits of bacon and dried apricot. Laughed as I tore my way up the shredded curtains or pecked at the blistered paint. He helped with my costumes, nudging my beret to a dapper angle when Marnie dressed me as an artist, arranging my eight spindly legs when she dressed me as a spider. He agreed with everything I said – sure, Tama; whatever you say, Tama. He still watched his crime show about attractive dead women stabbed through their unfaithful hearts and necks and eyes, but during the ad breaks he jumped up for tea rather than beer, scratching me on the back as he passed.

'Whodunnit, Tama?' he said. 'Don't you dare tell me! Don't you dare!' The followers ate it up, gobbled it down. What a gorgeous family, they said. Tama you are lucky to have such a caring mum and dad. Men take note: this is how you treat the ones you love. This is a real man.

I knew he was just playing a part, waiting for the mountain of money to mount up – but then I realised I couldn't remember the last time he'd hit Marnie. And so I kept playing my part too, posing for the photos, performing for the videos. Showing myself when the followers came. Talking my head off. For Marnie. For money. I hardly ever thought of what she'd said on the radio that day when she was pretending her name was Megan: that Rob had killed her baby before it was even born. Perhaps that was just a bad story. And perhaps it wasn't even Marnie who told it.

One day I heard Rob whistling as he took off his boots at the back door. I was used to his tuneless calls when he worked the dogs, telling Smoke to keep out, Help to go back, but this was different: an entire song, sweet and lilting, the dogs nowhere in sight. The music filled the back porch, followed him into the kitchen where Marnie was cooking dinner while I lay on my furry cushion in my fireman costume.

'Are we live?' he said, pointing at the Eye on the windowsill.

Marnie shook her head.

'How much money have we made today?'

'Millions,' she said. 'Billions.'

'That's my girl.'

He brought his laptop to the kitchen table and said, 'Look at that balance. I can't quite believe it, but there it is.'

When I hopped onto the table to look as well, he didn't shove me away.

'I mean, how has that even happened?' he said. 'How are we heading into the black so fast?'

I hopped onto the top of the laptop screen, and he just laughed.

'It's partly the merchandise,' said Marnie, 'but mainly the advertising.'

'Tama, you little beauty,' he said.

I thought he was going to kiss me. I scrambled back down to my cushion.

'We could replace the tractor,' he said. 'Fix the woolshed. Fix the house. Fix everything.'

'I think I need to quit Lynette's,' said Marnie.

'Sure,' said Rob. 'Good idea.'

'I'll hand in my notice this week.'

'Sure.'

She stroked his shoulder, but he said, 'Don't touch me. I'm filthy.' And she laughed and said that was fine by her.

After he'd headed to the bathroom for a shower, Marnie slid the lamb chops under the grill. Then she crossed her arms and tilted her head and looked at me looking at her and said, 'How on earth should I know, Tama? But let's not question it, all right? It's like I have him back again – the Rob I married. He's even giving up smoking, he said.'

So new Rob was old Rob, which meant old Rob must be new Rob, and I was not to question it and I didn't question it.

Perhaps I should have questioned it.

I don't suppose it matters now.

She took some more photos of me in my fireman costume and she said, 'People can change. I truly believe that. And it's not as if he doesn't regret his actions. You've seen him cry. You've seen him kneel at my feet and beg. This is our second chance, Tama. *You're* our second chance. Our little boy. I know we've turned a corner. And I'm not sure if you're quieter at night or if he's just not hearing you, but he's even sleeping better. Why shouldn't it be our turn? My sweet boy.'

Rob came back from the shower all clean and pink. He ate

his chops with his fingers, biting the meat from the bone while I nibbled at my dish of diced heart. He said, 'I used to be allergic to this place. When I was little I used to hide in the pines so Dad couldn't find me, but they gave me asthma. I couldn't breathe – and one time I nearly died. Mum said we'd have to sell up, shift away, but Dad said we didn't sell up when they built the damn dam and we weren't selling up now just because I had a bit of a cough, so we stayed. And I got used to it. My brothers never loved the place like me. I remember one weekend the three of us climbed up into the mountains as far as we could go, up to the top of this craggy outcrop that we called the chimney. Tall and sharp and thin, and hardly enough room to hold us, but you could see the whole wide world. I took a photo of Lachie and Adam clinging to it, and years later I showed it to Lachie and asked him if he remembered us climbing up there. And he said oh, did you come on that trip? I said who do you think took the photo? Jesus fuck, do I even exist? You fell over when we were climbing down, I said, and smashed your knee open, and I laughed, and you threw a rock at me. Don't remember that at all, he said.'

Later, when they had finished their dinner, Rob gave me his chop bone so I could peck out the marrow.

Through my bedroom window, just after dawn, I heard someone talking to me in my own tongue: my sister, calling from somewhere in the distance.

'Brother! Brother! Come and try! Come and taste!'

Before I was fully awake I thought I was back in the pines, a fledgling again, and she was teaching me how to hit a snail against the ground until it smashed, and how to tilt my head to listen for the movement of the grubs that burrowed under the earth and bit at the roots of the grass. I opened my eyes, shook myself awake, and then I left my bed, my yellow blanket, my spinning sun moon stars clouds, and I wandered down the hall past all the woodchopping ribbons, and I pushed through the cat door – meow – and followed her voice, the voice of my blood. Why was she calling me now? Was I forgiven at last for leaving? Was that how the wild worked? But her voice was not coming from the pines. Down the gravel I flew, down to the cherry orchard where the trees were almost in full fruit, soft and rippling and brightly green in the low morning light. The dummy birds watched from the branches with their shining eyes, and I knew they were not real; I knew they were a trick. Perhaps we would play our games again, my sister and I, passing leaves back and forth, *you keep it, no I don't want it, you keep it*, and rolling on our backs when our father came, showing him our soft bellies. And when the flock threw back their heads to carol together, one great swell of magpie song to shake the blue sky, I would know the words.

'Brother,' she called, 'you must taste! Over here – I'm over here!'

I found a morsel of bacon fat, a morsel of mutton fat, and I paused to snatch them up.

'This way,' she called. 'Nearly there.'

I saw her then, on the grass by the far fence, inside a wire box. 'Are you trapped?' I said.

'No.'

'Isn't this a trap?'

'No trap. No trap.'

The box had two compartments, each with a mirror against the dividing wall, and the empty side gaped open and offered a feast on the glittering lid of a tin, and I should have known, I should have suspected.

'Mutton fat, bacon fat, cat food, butter,' said my sister. 'Wouldn't you like to try? There for the taking. There for the guzzling.'

The low morning sun glared in the mirror, and the mirror glared in my eyes, and I should have known, I should have suspected, but it was all there for the taking, the glittering feast, and my sister was calling, my blood was calling, and I stepped inside. And the door snapped shut.

'Now we're both stuck,' said my sister.

'Why did you do that?' I said.

'I was lonely.' She peered round the side of the mirror at me.

'I will take you *down*, motherfucker,' I said.

'What does that mean?'

'I don't know.'

'You don't talk like a bird any more.'

'No?'

'No.'

'But they made a bird who talks like me.'

'Who?'

'Rob and Marnie. The people at the house.'

'People don't make birds. People make people. They must have stolen an egg.'

'It didn't come out of an egg.'

'Impossible. You can't make a bird without an egg. What did it come out of?'

'A cardboard box.'

'What's a cardboard box?'

'Like a square egg.'

'Ouch.'

'It has my voice inside it, the bird. My human voice. It says *Good morning and welcome, I'm Tama* and *I would like to gobble you up* and *That's not funny* and *Meow.*'

'Not a real bird, then.'

'A replica. A copy.'

'Speaking of other birds,' she whispered through the wire, 'there's someone in here with me.'

'Where?'

'In the cage.' She tilted her head to the side. 'She came in when I came in, from the opposite end.'

'I thought you said you were lonely.'

'So lonely.'

'But you had company.'

'She won't talk to me. She just copies me.' She lowered her voice even further. 'She's copying me now.'

'Is she a magpie?' I said.

'Yes.'

'And she copies everything you do. Every single move.'

'Yes.'

'At exactly the same time.'

'Yes! Yes!'

'That's a mirror. That's you.'

'Me?'

'It's your reflection. A trick of the light.'

She stood back and gazed at the glass. Lifted one leg. Lifted the other. Stretched a wing. 'Look at her. She's gorgeous. Do you have a reflection too?'

'Yes.'

'Show me.'

'I can't.'

'I don't think you have one at all.' She turned and pecked at the remains of her cat food, looking back at the mirror between every bite. 'So,' she said when she'd finished, 'are you going to let me out now?'

'How would I do that?'

'I don't know. You're the cleverest boy in the world.'

'We're trapped,' I said. 'This is a trap. Our father told us about them so many times.'

'Yes. He'll kill us. It's all your fault.'

'He can't kill us if we never get out.'

'How do we get out, then?'

'I suppose we call for help.'

'Our father will kill us.'

I scanned the orchard: row after row of trees to the left, and the fence along the main road to the right. Up the gravel a glimpse of the yolk-yellow house, and the woolshed and the haybarn and the grain silo, and then in the distance the pines that cut black shapes from the air. No Marnie to save me. I heard the quad bike kick into life, and Rob's voice calling the dogs to follow him: 'Here, Dutchie. Get in behind, ya mongrel. Here, Night. Smoke! Here! Help! Help!'

'Hello?' my sister was saying. 'Hey. Hey. Hello?'

'What?'

'Can I have your cat food?'

I don't know how much time passed – most of the morning, I think. Marnie drove by on her way to Lynette's Gowns and Casualwear, and two backpackers walked up to the house, then left again when they found nobody home.

'Do you think that's him?' I heard one of them say.

'That's a starling,' said the other.

'What about that, then?'

'Also a starling.'

A fantail flitted about the cage for a while, squeaking at the sight of the mutton fat.

'The *door*,' my sister told him, pointing her whole body in a line at the latch. 'Get the *door*.'

'He's far too small,' I said.

'Small small,' squeaked the fantail.

'And far too stupid,' said my sister.

'Stupid stupid,' he squeaked. He sat on top of the cage and looked at us, tail feathers spread like a white hand. 'Stupid stupid.'

'Who's inside and who's outside, though?' I said.

'Shut up,' said my sister. 'And anyway, mutton fat, bacon fat, cat food, butter.'

'Fat fat fat fat fat,' said the fantail.

My sister picked up a scrap of mutton fat and waved it at him. 'Is this what you want, little friend?'

'Fat fat fat fat fat,' he said.

My sister gulped it down, then shoved her beak through the wire roof and tried to jostle him off, but he just hopped to another rung and kept up his one-note song.

'Can't you catch him and eat him?' she said to me. 'Drag him through the holes shred by shred?'

Rob and the dogs were bringing the lambs into the yards, and we watched as they all did what they were told.

'Hot now, isn't it,' said my sister.

'Hot,' I agreed, my mouth dry. Where was the devil's blood to wet my tongue?

My sister was admiring herself in the mirror again, preening her breast feathers. 'Hey!' she said, looking up.

'What?'

'Our little friend just took a shit on my *head*.'

'You can't see it,' I said. 'It blends in with the white on your nape.'

She threw herself against the walls of the cage, and it bumped like a branch in high winds, but the fantail simply hopped over to my side of the roof. 'Fat?' he said. 'Fat?'

Then I heard Barbara's voice: 'Don't eat that, my little lamb, you've no idea where it's been.' She and Ange's baby appeared in our row of trees, and the baby was a walking baby now, and it stumbled along on the end of Barbara's hand. 'Dirty. Dirty,' said Barbara, prising a stick from its lips and tossing it into the grass.

The walking baby stared up at her, then closed its eyes and opened its mouth and screamed.

'Oh my goodness me,' said Barbara. 'That's a very big noise for a very little man.' She offered it a toy crocodile, swooping the creature through the air and saying, 'Here's Crocky. Snappity snap. Snappity snap.'

The baby flung itself down on the grass, screaming and kicking and turning red, and Barbara stood there and watched. She said, 'We do not tolerate this sort of behaviour. We do not reward it with attention. When you're *quite* finished, Kaden, you may have a Vegemite cracker to eat instead. In the meantime I'm going to pretend this is not happening. I'm going to pretend you're a nice lovely boy who behaves properly for his Ba-ba. Not a boy who acts like a wild animal. The thing is, Kaden, nobody wants to be friends with boys who can't control themselves, and the sooner you learn that the better. Do you think Sir Jonah Lomu ever lay on the rugby field and screamed when he didn't get his own way? Of course not. He carried himself with dignity at all times, and what a fine figure of a man he was. What a splendid physique. He signed my Ayers Rock sweatshirt once, Kaden, when I was wearing it, and I could feel the enormous strength of him as he wrote his name across my chest, the power in those huge Polynesian hands, and I said I'm never washing this, Jonah, and he said cool, and I said if I were twenty years younger, and he said cheers. And I could probably make a lot of money if I sold that sweatshirt, especially now he's dead, but I have kept it as a tribute to that magnificent New Zealander, and I have never washed it, and on very special occasions like my birthday or Waitangi Day I take it out of its pillowcase and I wear it, and if you behave yourself, Kaden – if you prove you can control these outbursts – I may well leave it to you.'

The baby had stopped screaming by then and was grabbing fistfuls of grass.

'Shall we go a bit further?' said Barbara. 'Let's tire you out so you can have a nice long nap with Crocky, and Ba-ba can watch her programme. Let's completely exhaust you so you sleep till tea time. Here's your Vegemite cracker. Come on.'

As they approached, my sister and I froze. I looked at her through the wire wall and she looked at me.

'Fat?' said the fantail. 'Fat?'

Neither of us moved.

'Fat? Fat fat fat?'

The baby saw us then. It pointed at the cage and said, 'Bir. Bir.'

'Oh!' said Barbara. 'Clever boy. Yes. Bir-*d*. Bir-*d*.'

'Bir,' said the baby.

'Bir-*d*. Careful of fingers.'

'Fat? Fat?'

I said, 'I will take you *down*, motherfucker.'

'I beg your pardon?' said Barbara. 'Is that any way to talk in front of a child?'

I said, 'I'm going to pretend this is not happening.'

'What are you saying?' asked my sister.

Barbara crouched down, tucked the crocodile under her armpit and narrowed her eyes at me. 'Is it you?' she said.

I said, 'Let's completely exhaust you.'

'What are you *saying*?' repeated my sister.

The baby dropped its Vegemite cracker and the fantail leapt on it and the baby started to scream again.

'We'll get another one at home,' said Barbara. 'Come on, darling, we have to go home and find Mummy and Daddy. Kaden. Kaden.'

The baby kept screaming.

'It's not the end of the world,' said Barbara. 'Things like this happen every day, and you need to get used to them happening. You need to prepare yourself for frequent disappointment.' She grabbed the baby and strode off in the direction of Nick and Ange's house.

My sister and I watched the fantail chipping at the Vegemite cracker.

'What do they do with the birds they trap?' she said.

'I don't know,' I said.

'Every father in our flock warns his children not to go near the traps, but nobody knows what happens to the birds who end up in the traps.'

I didn't reply.

'So maybe they'll take us to a place with no sickness no hunger no cats no cars, no powerlines no poison no cold, and we can live there forever.'

'Maybe.'

'It's the one right down the end,' said Ange.

'Oh Christ,' said Nick. 'She wasn't lying. A pair. Now what?'

'Does either of them look like Tama to you?'

'I don't know. They're birds. Black-and-white birds. How are we supposed to tell?'

'Tama?' said Ange, peering in at us. 'Tama?'

'Tamagotchi?' said Nick.

We both stared at them in their matching Tama T-shirts, our feathers puffed.

'I don't think it's him,' said Ange. 'He's smaller than these ones. And he's always prattling away. Can't shut the bloody thing up.'

'So now what?' said Nick.

'Well, we take care of them.'

'Humane release?'

'Rob says it doesn't work. I think we need something more permanent.'

'We?'

'Do you want to toss a coin?'

'I don't know if I can.'

'It's easy,' said Ange. 'You just flip it in the air and call heads or tails.'

'Don't be funny. Christ. Okay. What do we do?'

'We read the instructions.'

'Okay. Good. The instructions.'

'They're on the top of the cage.'

'Right. Set the trap on open ground where magpies congregate to feed—'

'Done that.'

'Right. Yeah. Lure them in with fresh food such as—'

'Done that too. Shall I take over the reading?'

'Yeah,' said Nick.

'What's wrong with you?

'They're . . . watching us.'

'So?' said Ange.

'Like they know.'

'They're birds. They're animals.'

'Are you sure one of them's not Marnie's?'

'Trust me, he would have spoken up by now.'

'Barbara said she heard one talking.'

Ange shrugged. 'They're all mimics.'

'Because Marnie would be crushed. And she'd never forgive us.'

'I'm sure,' said Ange. 'These birds are bigger, from eating
our bloody cherries. Okay? To avoid magpies becoming trap-
shy, always kill captured birds out of view of the remaining
flock. Kill in the evening, or if during the day cover the trap
with an old sheet to quieten the birds and then kill them under
the cover.'

I threw back my head and opened my throat to sound a distress call, but all that came out was, 'We do not tolerate this
sort of behaviour.'

'What was that?' said my sister.

'Magpies may be handled with bare hands,' said Ange.

'Wait, what?' said Nick.

'Magpies may be handled with bare hands, but—'

'No, wait. That one said something.'

'Did it?'

'I think so.'

'I didn't hear anything. Magpies may be handled with bare
hands, but wear a light pair of gloves when starting out. Slide
open the top hatch by pressing down on the locking tab.

When the magpie is facing away from you, grab with your hand around the body and its neck between your forefingers.' She was gesturing in mid-air, sliding and pressing and grabbing. 'For a quick and certain kill, wring the neck with a sharp twist – concentrating the twist on a single part of the neck.'

Again I opened my throat. 'We do not tolerate this sort of behaviour. What a fine figure of a man.'

'What?' said my sister. 'What what what?'

'Okay, you must have heard that,' said Nick. 'It's definitely him.'

'Mmm,' said Ange. 'But you know, maybe it would be kinder. It's taken over her entire life. They *shower* together. It's not healthy. It's not natural.'

'He's making them an awful lot of money.'

'Rob can't stand the thing. He's said to me more than once, on the quiet, that he'd love to put a bullet through its brain.'

'You know that's just how he talks. It's just an expression. He'd break Marnie's heart.'

'But it's causing friction between her and Rob. He's always had a short fuse, and the bird situation isn't helping. I never told you this, but he hit her once, a while ago.'

'I don't believe that. He can be a bit abrupt sometimes, but I don't believe that.'

'Remember last time we visited? He was complaining about the camera in the living room. Marnie told the world where they live, he said. They're live fucking feed, he said.'

'He was kind of joking, though.'

'He's basically a good guy,' said Ange. 'I'm just a bit concerned about what might happen if all the attention continues. The invasion of privacy. Tourists peering in their windows.'

'I don't know,' said Nick.

'Trust me, it's kinder. We don't even need to tell her. She'll just think he's decided to return to the wild. He's flown off to find a mate and is living happily ever after.' She covered the cage with a sheet.

'What what what?' said my sister, jumping from foot to foot.

'It's not natural,' I said.

'What what?'

'It's talking to us,' said Nick.

'It's just mimicking,' said Ange.

Silence for a moment.

'I'll do it,' said Nick.

'I think he's going to kill us,' I said. 'Nick is going to kill us.'

'Death by Nick?'

'Death by Nick.'

We sat still as stones under the sheet, and we couldn't see Nick so he couldn't see us, and dots of daylight shone through a handful of holes, and I heard the breaths leaving my body. Then Nick slid open the hatch on my side of the cage, and before I knew it he'd reached in and grabbed me, pressing his forefingers into my neck. And I was a stone and my sister was a stone and I did not struggle and she did not speak. And then he was lifting me out, out through the hatch and out past the sheet that was to cover us while he killed us, and I was a stone but he was shouting and waving his arms around, *Get off me you little shit* – and then he let me go. And I knew he let me go on purpose.

'What the *hell*, Nick!' said Ange as I flew to the top of a cherry tree.

'Sorry,' he said, examining a finger I know I did not peck. 'He started to struggle and I couldn't hold him.'

'Jesus. If you want a job done right . . .'

'Fat fat fat fat fat,' chirped the fantail, and he abandoned the Vegemite cracker and darted in the open hatch. Without even landing, he snatched the food I'd left and flew off.

'Swoop them!' my sister called to me. 'Pierce their eyes and drink their blood and clean their bones!'

'No need,' I called back. 'No need. See, he let me go.'

'But not me. What about me? You have to swoop! Eyes blood bones!'

'Perfect,' said Ange. 'The other one's onto you now. God that's loud. I can see where Rob's coming from.'

'Go on, get out of here,' Nick yelled to me. 'And let that be a lesson to you!'

'As I mentioned,' said Ange, 'it is a *bird*. It is an *animal*.'

'I'm aware of that,' said Nick.

'Just pass me the bloody sheet.'

'Brother!' called my sister. 'Swoop! Swoop! We lay in our eggs shell to shell, and I heard you before you hatched and I told you to let in the air, to take your first breath, to break open the sky and move as I was moving. Brother! I am your blood! Swoop!'

And Ange was covering the cage and sliding open the hatch, and I could not look, and the yolk-yellow house was just up the gravel, so close, so close, and my sister was screaming for me, and then Nick said, 'Maybe we should keep it.' He pointed at the instructions. 'If your magpies have no obvious feeding ground, use a call-bird to lure them in.'

'What?' said Ange. 'How does that work? Do they have an obvious feeding ground?'

'I've seen them all over,' said Nick. 'Bait the trap as usual and keep the captive magpie in another cage set hard up against the magpie trap.'

Ange removed the sheet again and my sister kept calling to me.

'Everything is fine,' I called back.

'What what?'

'It has a decent pair of lungs, I suppose,' said Ange.

'They're keeping you,' I called. 'Everything is fine.'

'Slaves?' called my sister. 'To feed me from their own mouths?'

'Yes,' I called. 'Yes. They'll feed you.' And there was the devil's blood.

I left her then, and I flew back up to the yolk-yellow house where Marnie had turned the radio on for me so I would not be lonely. *We're going to go to Keith now. Keith, what's your position on 'Happy Holidays' versus 'Happy Christmas?'*

A bullet through my brain, I thought. A bullet through my brain that would break Marnie's heart.

Just an expression.

CHAPTER TWENTY-ONE

The followers were coming every day, and whenever they tweeted their photos and videos of me even more of them came. They pushed open the gate if it was closed. They let themselves into the house if nobody answered the door. There was no stopping them. 'Hello?' they called. 'Anyone home?' One day Marnie returned from the supermarket to find a Norwegian couple feeding me honey-roasted peanuts on the coffee table. 'It's not what it looks like,' they said, but it was. Marnie marched over to the black box behind the Eye and pressed the button to turn it off.

'You need to start locking the place when you're out,' Rob told her that evening, which was not how houses worked – not how houses in Wilderness Road worked.

'Except the locks are as good as broken,' said Marnie. 'And none of the windows shut properly.'

'Hvem er en flink gutt?' I said.

'What?' said Rob.

'Hvem er en flink gutt?'

'I think . . . I think it's Norwegian,' said Marnie.

'These are completely legitimate concerns,' said Lakshmi when they called her on Rob's laptop. 'I hear what you're telling me.' Her face took up the whole screen, life-size.

'We need some security,' said Marnie. 'A padlock on the gate, at least.'

'Sure sure. Your privacy is important.'

'Pepper spray,' said Rob. 'Tasers.'

'I know you're joking,' said Lakshmi, 'but we mustn't alienate our followers. They're our bread and butter.'

Marnie ran a hand through her hair. 'We're not getting our work done. There's a huge backlog of orders I need to pack up.'

'I did wonder about you taking on the distribution yourself.'

The house creaked and ticked as it cooled in the evening air.

'Rob wants a sign at the gate,' said Marnie. 'Trespassers will be—'

'Shot on sight,' he said.

'Asked to leave,' she said.

The little red stone at the side of Lakshmi's nose glinted. 'Leave it with me.'

A few days later the sign arrived: pictures of me down one side, and a row of boxes down the other. Each morning Rob was to tick a box to show where I was, and why I was unavailable. Marnie read me the big red heading: *Tama Requests Privacy. He Is Currently* . . . I don't know where Lakshmi found the pictures, because they showed me doing things I'd never done. Sitting in a spa pool, up to my neck in water. Lying back under a white towel, slices of cucumber over my eyes. Being fed lobster by women in gold bikinis. It felt strange to see those Tamas – as if there were stories about me I didn't know, memories I couldn't remember.

At first the followers liked it. They tweeted photos of themselves next to the sign, and photos of me sitting on the sign when clearly I was supposed to be somewhere else: having a pedicure, working on my screenplay. They brought me all kinds of treats, which I ate out of their hands, and Rob and Marnie kept reminding them that too much human food was dangerous for me, and could they please consider my welfare?

And it was true, I was starting to feel sick, and one morning I barely sniffed the morsels of cake and pizza they pushed at me. As soon as they'd all had a chance for a selfie I headed off in the other direction – up towards the woolshed, where Rob had made space for all the extra toy Tamas. Up towards the gut hole, where he disposed of the pests he shot. Up towards the pines, where I found my father showing his three new children how to listen for buried grubs. They stood there in a row, heads tilted, listening, listening, one eye on the ground and one on the sky. I think he spied me lurking at the edges of his territory, because all of a sudden he said to his three new children, 'Who kills with cars?'

'Humans,' they chorused.

'Who kills with bullets?'

'Humans.'

'Who kills with hands?'

'Humans.'

'Who kills with poison?'

'Humans.'

'Who kills with traps?'

'Humans.'

'If a human threatens you,' he said, 'they are threatening the whole family – the whole flock. You must swoop. Go for the hair, the scalp, the face. Pierce their eyes, drink their blood, clean their bones.' He paused, paced. 'Your older brother and sister have disgraced themselves with humans. They have gone to them of their own free will. Things do not end well for birds who go to humans of their own free will.'

'Yes, Father, yes,' said his three new children standing all in a row.

'We have no memory of your older brother and sister,' he said. 'If you hear their voices, close your ears. We have forgotten them. They are not even ghosts.'

'Not even ghosts,' they said.

He never so much as looked in my direction.

On my way back to the house I recalled Ange's words: that Rob would love to put a bullet through my brain. I crept under the bath and examined the clues I'd gathered about him. *You have to stay one step ahead of the perp, Trent. Figure out his MO, then beat him at his own game.* I pushed the evidence around the dusty floor, trying to read the story it told. Bottle top. Coin. Chicken bone. Box of cigarettes with dying man. Box of cigarettes with breathless baby. All day I thought about what it might mean, but there was no escaping the absence of bullets, the lack of a single bullet. And wasn't Rob bringing me clothes pegs to play with? And bits of bacon and dried apricot? Wasn't he scratching my back, sometimes when the Eye couldn't even see him? That very night, wasn't he building me a pine tree in the living room, pushing the wire branches into the plastic trunk so it looked just like a real one? Weren't he and Marnie decorating it with silver pine cones, golden birds? Wasn't I their little boy?

Then one evening Lakshmi called to tell us we needed to address the access issue. She said, 'Not to put too fine a point on it, but the followers are getting pissy. They've seen the footage of people in Tama's kitchen, in Tama's bedroom, and so they go to the trouble of making the trip themselves, only they can't even get their hands on him at the gate. What a joke, they're saying. What a scam. They should be booted off the internet. Fuckin fags – and so on. You'll have read the comments. The thing is, you have to give them what they want. You have to give them a piece of him, or at least the belief that they're in with a chance to grab a piece of him. So, this is the strategy: once a week or so, you let in a select few. Like a bouncer who has his VIP list and only admits normal people if they're super attractive. A nine at the very least. Except in your case you'll be letting in the influencers, whether they're attractive or not. They're usually attractive. Any press, naturally. And the kids with the wheelchairs and the leukaemia and what have you – they're allowed in too. Decrease supply, increase demand. Tama can still make appearances at the gate to greet the others. He's still free to do that, like the Pope. Let the great unwashed kiss the hem of his garment, et cetera.'

Rob said he'd choose which followers to let in, because he didn't want Marnie in the firing line. I had no choice but to fly down to the gate every few days as well, and walk along the fence, and hang upside down, and pose for selfies. My right eye saw all the followers waving their treats, holding up their phones, but my left eye saw the orchard where the early cherries were red and ready. My left eye saw the glint of my sister's trap through the trees.

I turned my back on her. I turned my back on my blood. I kept my distance from my sister, just as my father had commanded. Rob and Marnie were my family now.

CHAPTER TWENTY-TWO

Barbara said, 'You know how I feel about secrets, Marnie. People sneaking around.'

'What's she done now?' said Ange, all normal, all innocent. She covered her face with her hands and said, 'Where's Mummy? Where's Mummy hiding?' and the baby laughed and laughed. No mention of *the bird situation*. No mention of *kill in the evening*. She helped herself to a chocolate biscuit. All unconcerned.

'I don't know what you're talking about, Mum,' said Marnie, rinsing three coffee mugs in the sink and shaking them dry.

'Maybe you should get a dishwasher,' said Ange. 'You'd be able to afford one now, wouldn't you?'

'I suppose,' said Marnie, washing a teaspoon. 'We've been thinking of renovating. We still need to be careful, though.'

'Anyway,' said Ange, 'who's been sneaking around?'

'Just pass me the bloody sheet,' I said.

'Do you mind not letting him swear in front of the baby?' said Barbara.

Ange glanced at me, then hid behind her hands again. 'Where's Mummy? Where's she gone?' No mention of *kill captured birds out of view*.

Barbara said, 'I was in at Lynette's this morning. She's not a happy woman, Marnie. Not happy at all. She told me you've handed in your notice. Well, I said, I haven't heard anything about that. Well, she said, it happened last week. I'll be honest with you, Barbara, she said, I feel very let down. Betrayed is the

word, in fact, Barbara. I feel betrayed. My goodness, I said, has
she had her hand in the till? I almost would have preferred
that, she said. I would have understood that. This just came
out of nowhere, and in December, too, when everyone's wanting their summer casualwear and their wedding outfits. I can
only apologise, Lynette, I said, I thought I'd raised her to
behave better than that. She hasn't breathed a word about it to
me, I said. I am literally speechless. Four years you've been
there, Marnie, and maybe it's not Esprit, but it's a good little
job for someone of limited ambitions. A generous staff dis-
count and a full ham every Christmas. I just wonder what you
think you're doing, Marnie, throwing it in to sell calendars and
stuffed toys.'

'Plush toys,' said Ange.

'Plush,' I said. 'Plush.'

'I haven't been sneaking around,' said Marnie. 'It's not a
secret.'

'Did you know, Angela?'

'Sure.'

'I see. And *you* didn't tell me either.'

'Mum, no one's been keeping things from you,' said
Marnie. 'It's just been out of control here. I'm making more
money in a week than I do in a year at Lynette's.'

'Well, she's very upset you've never mentioned the shop to
all your bird people. Imagine the business you could have gen-
erated, she said.'

'Just pass me the bloody sheet,' I said.

'Do you mind!' said Barbara, pointing at the baby.

'You must be raking it in,' said Ange. 'I'm happy for you.'

'It's ticking over, all right,' said Marnie. 'I can hardly keep
up with the orders. And Lakshmi says new advertisers are con-
tacting her every day.'

'You deserve it. You've been struggling for so long – it's
about time things started to go your way.'

No mention of *a quick and certain kill*. No mention of *wring the neck with a sharp twist*.

'I will take you *down*, motherfucker,' I said.

'Unacceptable,' Barbara said, and led the baby outside to see the coppery chickens that could not sing. 'Let's find some nicer birdies,' she said. 'Some better birdies.'

'Do I, though? Deserve it?' said Marnie when they were out of earshot. She scratched at a bit of rust on the leg of the kitchen table.

'That's off, right?' said Ange, pointing at the Eye, and Marnie nodded. 'Anyway, what do you mean? Of course you deserve it. Both of you.'

'Everything's changed so fast. It was just a bit of fun to start with – a bit of a distraction – and now the world wants to see our every move. Demands to see it. Rob's a very private person . . .'

'He's okay with it, though, isn't he? I mean, all the extra income – does he know how lucky he is?'

'I thought the money would take the pressure off,' said Marnie. 'I don't know. I shouldn't complain.'

'No, you shouldn't,' said Ange.

I heard the front door open, and then Rob's voice called down the hall: 'Mar? Mar?'

'In the kitchen!'

He showed in the latest lot of followers: an influencer named Tamrah With An H; a deaf boy who held his hand to my breast as I warbled.

That night, after she brushed her teeth, Marnie stood and looked at herself in the bathroom mirror while Rob waited for her in bed. She started doing the actions to the song she and Ange were practising, moving her mouth as if she wanted to say something, to sing something, but no words came out. She pointed at her reflection, bent and turned, bent and turned. Blew herself a kiss. Up above, something crept about in the roof, and a moth battered itself against the lightshade that looked like the moon if the moon were filled with moths.

The builder came the next day. He brushed away a pile of borer-beetle dust, dug his knife blade into a rotten windowsill.

'I grew up here,' said Rob, watching him.

'I grew up here,' I said.

'These wooden villas,' said the builder, shaking his head. 'She was relocated?'

'In bits, when they built the damn dam,' said Rob. 'We lost the original stone homestead.'

'They're grand old girls, but if you don't keep on top of the maintenance they give you all kinds of trouble.' From his pocket the builder took a glass marble with a tiny orange flame caught inside and placed it on the kitchen floor: it rolled all the way into the dark hall, where the walls bulged with the weight of the place, and then it thudded into the skirting board and kept rolling. He said to Rob, 'Her foundation piles are decaying, mate – they start to sink into the ground and throw everything out of plumb. And her framing's undersized, so her floor joists are sagging, her ceiling joists are sagging, hence the cracks all over the show. Her pipes are most likely corroded. The chimney's dirty and hasn't been put together properly, meaning it could just collapse – if it doesn't catch fire first. The old wiring and the scrim walls are a fire hazard as well, and the roof needs replacing, the guttering's falling off, the downpipes have rusted right through, the windows are jammed – and then there's the borer. You've got an active infestation, mate – one of the worst I've ever seen. Water's seeped in through the holes, which has let in the mould and the rot, and at this point so much timber would need to be cut out that you'd be left with no house at all.'

'No house at all?' said Rob.

'No house at all?' I said.

The builder pointed at me with his knife. 'Does he do that a lot? Copy what you say?'

'A bit,' said Marnie. 'It's his party trick.'

How proud of me she was.

'I've heard about him, haven't I? He's shorter in real life.'

'Most people say that.'

'My brother used to copy everything I said. Drove me nuts. One day I just walloped him. Broke his arm.'

'No house at all?' I said.

'He'd keep you entertained all right,' laughed the builder.

'The thing is,' said Marnie, 'we thought we could fix things. Make it secure. We wouldn't mind a bit of mess for a while. You see it on TV, don't you – couples fixing up old villas. Putting chandeliers in the bathroom. Taking out walls to let in the light.'

'You need good bones for that kind of result,' said the builder.

'So if we don't have good bones,' said Rob, 'what are our options?'

The builder showed him the borer-beetle holes in the kitchen door. 'The ones you can see are just the tip of the iceberg, mate – the larvae will have been burrowing inside the wood for years, eating it into labyrinths underneath the surface, and not just the sapwood but the heartwood too. The structural timber. Once the heartwood's compromised, the whole place is unsound. If you'd treated all this much earlier . . . As things stand, she's well beyond repair. Better to knock her down and start again from scratch.'

He retrieved his glass marble with the tiny orange flame caught inside and returned it to his pocket.

After he'd gone, Rob sank onto the couch.

'It might not be as bad as he thinks,' said Marnie. She went to the black box, double-checked that the Eye was turned off. 'We should get a second opinion. Some of the ones on TV have been just about falling over and they've still restored them.'

'I always thought we'd fix it once we had the money,' said Rob. 'And now we're making all this money but we can't fix it.' He opened his case of axes, began honing a blade with his honing stone. Smoothing away the burrs, the feather edge.

'We don't know that for sure,' said Marnie. She made a space for me in between them on the couch.

'We don't know that for sure,' I said.

Rob said, 'When I was a kid, I thought I'd be rich. That was my plan. I was going to buy the farms on either side of us, then buy the whole of Wilderness Road. Dad raised this place up out of the dirt, out of the stones of the dry riverbed. He burnt off the matagouri and the bracken, and he oversowed and fenced. And in the good years, the merino years, he'd get a lamb to every ewe, and the clover grew so high and so thick I could hide myself inside it and never be found. Mum said I shouldn't follow in his footsteps – that even the good years were hard years and they made hard men. But I wasn't like him; I knew I wasn't like him. In the summer holidays I picked mint for money when the mint man came in his caravan. He showed me and my brothers how to look for it in among the willows by the river. I always found the best patches. I sniffed them out like a dog. You'd walk downstream, and sometimes the banks were so densely packed with willow trees and gorse that it was easier to go through the water. You'd wade for a couple of hundred metres, chest-high, and then climb up onto a bank you couldn't get to any other way. You might find nothing, but other times you'd reach a clearing and find a crop the size of this house. That was like gold. Mint up to your waist and the ground covered all over with it, and you could stay picking in one place for a whole day. I had my own butcher's knife, and I'd grab the top of a mint stalk and chop it off near the base, lay it down, grab the next stalk. I made massive piles of them, all the heads at one end. After that I sat down and started stripping the leaves, dragging my thumb and forefinger down the plant, then twisting off the head. My fingers turned black with the stuff. I couldn't wash it away, couldn't shake the smell of it, sharp and cold even in the blazing sun. I was so obsessed with finding it, searching and searching through the bushes and trees, looking for the shape of it, that when I closed my eyes at night I saw nothing but mint leaves. I drew maps of where I'd already looked and where I wanted to look – I found one years later and saw how tiny I'd made our house. How tiny I'd made Wilderness Road. But the patches of mint – the patches of money – I'd made those huge.'

'You could have drowned,' said Marnie. 'You could have been swept away.'

'But I wasn't.'

'Didn't your parents worry?'

'Not that I remember.'

'Not that I remember,' I said.

'What did you do with it? The money.'

Rob said, 'I was saving up for a Game Boy, and I bought one, too, but my brothers spent theirs on chips and comics and then I had to share the Game Boy with them. They never worked as hard as I did. Never cared as much. We packed all the leaves into muslin bags, so they could breathe, and the mint man weighed them and paid us I think five dollars a kilo in cash, less seven percent for evaporation, which seemed unfair to me, like my money was disappearing into thin air. The bags went up to Christchurch first thing the next morning on the Intercity buses. One time a story did the rounds: a boy tried to get a better price by pouring water into his bags, but the mint fermented in the heat and caught fire on the bus. I don't know if it was true – I don't think it was true – but Dad went crazy at us. Said if we ever tried anything like that we'd know all about it and he'd make us pay for the damage. I remember the last year I picked – we had a party at the end of the season. A bonfire. It was the first party I ever went to.

When Dad came down to collect me he nabbed me with a beer in my hand, and he said really quietly, so no one else could hear, I'd put that down if I were you. And I knew I was in for it later. Then he started talking to people and making jokes and laughing just like the other kids' fathers.'

Rob stopped circling his honing stone across the blade and looked at his fingers, as if he could still see the black there – but trapped in his clothes, trapped in his skin, were the glittering specks of axe.

'How old were you?' said Marnie. 'Wading through the river like that on your own.'

'Ten, I guess, that last year.'

'Ten.'

'Yeah.'

'I'd never let a child of ours . . .' she began, then stopped. They both fell silent.

I couldn't think of anything to say either.

I heard Help whining out in the back yard. He'd be digging one of his holes, frantic to find something that wasn't there.

'Shall I make us a cup of tea?' said Rob.

'No,' said Marnie.

'A coffee?'

She shook her head.

'What can I get you? A water? A beer?'

'Nothing. Nothing.'

PART FOUR
LIVE FEED

I could smell something delicious drifting up the gravel. We'd just seen the last of the followers off, and Rob had driven away in his beetle-black car, and Marnie was in the stockroom sealing the toy Tamas into their mailer bags, and I was dozing in a sun-trance in the front paddock. The aroma crept up on me, rich and bloody, and I stood and shook my feathers. Returned to the gate.

On a fencepost, a bowl of meat.

Rich, bloody.

I edged my way towards it.

My sister was calling from the orchard: I remember that. And I remember sniffing the food, and it was diced heart, and when I plunged in my beak the meat was not cold from the fridge but warm as fresh flesh, warm as something just killed. I began to eat. Delicious, delicious, and I kept wolfing it down as my sister called from the orchard. Then, from behind a parked car, a woman's voice: 'Are you ready?'

'Ready,' said a man's voice.

Slowly they approached me with their soft words, little coos and warbles. Balaclavas covering their faces, though they sounded nothing like perps, and perhaps they were going to shoot pests. Then she was stroking me, good boy, sweet boy, and then she was holding me down, and my right eye saw the bowl of food and my left eye saw his hand coming straight for me, the thin silver needle coming straight for me. A sting in my breast, and I let out a cry because I had never felt such a sting and I did not know what it meant.

'All done now,' she murmured. 'All over.' But she did not take her hands away.

My sister called and called. What was she saying? I was so tired. So very sleepy.

'Almost . . . almost . . .' said the man's voice.

My right eye saw the blurry bowl of food and my left eye saw the blurry box. The woman's voice said, 'Gently now,' and I felt both eyes droop and droop and close.

When I woke the world had turned to black and I did not know where I was, but I knew it was far from Wilderness Road. I could not hear the wind in the shelterbelts. I could not hear Rob shouting to the dogs: *Smoke, hold 'em! Night, come away!* I could not hear the groaning sheep and I could not hear the groaning house. I could not hear the clothesline turning, scree, scree, scree. I could not hear my sister's silvery calls, summoning magpies to the open-mouthed trap. And I could not hear Marnie, my Marnie, singing as she packed the orders: *I love you, a bushel and a peck . . .*

I blinked. Black-black. As black as inside the egg. As black as the blind days when my eyes were unsprouted seeds, dots of gravel stuck under skin. I tried out my voice: a nonsense warble, a wobble. My whole body heavy and slow.

A door opened. A bright wedge.

'He's awake,' said the man's voice.

'Oh thank God,' said the woman's voice.

'Put it on. They remember faces.'

'I still don't think we need—'

'Put it on. And don't stare at him – they interpret it as a threat.'

The click of a light switch, the low whirr of a fan. I blinked again and saw right next to me a mirror the width of a wall. A shower. A toilet. And closer than all of those, and on every side, the bars of a cage.

Looking in at me, two giant magpies.

Was I a chick once more? Were they my parents?

'Thank God, thank you God,' one of the magpies said in the woman's voice.

'I did know what I was doing. I did research it,' said the other one in the man's voice.

'Can you imagine, though? We don't need that kind of bad press.'

'He's fine. Nothing wrong with him.'

Through holes in the heads of the giant magpies I could make out human eyes. Human mouths.

Magpie masks. Make-believe.

'Tama, my darling,' said the woman, 'are you hungry? You must be starving. And you must be scared. Are you scared? We're your friends, Tama. God has sent us to save you.'

She poked a piece of carrot through the bars, and it plopped to the floor of the cage. I was not her darling. I just looked at the carrot. Lifted my foot. Put it down again. Too heavy, too slow. I closed my eyes and tried to call up the ghost of my mother, the ghosts of my brothers, but they would not come.

'I think he's still a bit dopey,' said the woman.

'He'll be fine,' said the man. 'I researched it.'

The woman poked through another piece of carrot. 'Look at you,' she said. 'You're glorious. God's glorious creation. Good boy. Good boy.'

They turned the light off, which turned the fan off, but they left the door open. On the vanity next to me, a row of miniature cakes of soap, a row of miniature bottles of shampoo. Bird-sized. I thought of the shower cap Marnie had made me from a plastic shopping bag. One of our first photos.

'No mention on the Twitter feed yet,' the woman said from the next room.

'Give it time,' said the man. 'It's been, what, all of an hour?'

'Closer to two.'

'You never could wait. Always tearing little holes in the Christmas presents. Flicking to the last page of a book. Remember that time we made fudge for the school fair, and Mum said we had to leave it to set, only you sneaked off to cut it up after about five minutes? And it looked like big splats of shit, and Mum made us take it to school anyway?'

'Mmm. Still nothing on Twitter.'

'Jesus, put down the phone and help me with the sheet. Here, do you reckon? Or here?'

'Over by the curtains. Otherwise you'll get the minibar in shot.'

I shook my feathers. Stretched my wings, one at a time. I could hardly turn around, and when I did I kept hitting my head on a little perch and a little bell that dangled from the roof of the cage. The orchard trap was roomier. I let out another warble, as if it were morning, though the bathroom had no windows and I couldn't tell the time of day. It had no mould on the walls, either, as far as I could make out. No mould on the shower curtain or on the ceiling. No borer-beetle dust, no mushroomy smell of rot.

I said, 'There'll be very few dead spots.'

I said, 'Didn't your parents worry?'

I said, 'Don't be a prick about it.'

The man and woman appeared at the bathroom door, pulling their rubber masks back into place.

'That's my boy!' said the woman, but I was not her boy.

'Stop encouraging him,' said the man.

'Get yourself some alpacas,' I said.

'You're quite extraordinary, aren't you?' said the woman.

'Don't offer him positive reinforcement for speaking the language of his oppressors,' said the man.

'I know, I know,' said the woman, 'but it's pretty astonishing.'

'He has been colonised,' said the man. 'No two ways about it.'

'Right. Yes,' said the woman. She poked another piece of

carrot through the bars, though I hadn't touched the last one. 'Num num?' she said. 'Good boy num num?'

The man sighed through his mask. 'At any rate, clearly he's recovered from the injection.'

'Toe-paw,' I said. 'Toe-paw.'

'Did he just say Taupō?'

'I think so. And like, the proper way.'

'Tēnā koe,' I said. 'Toe-paw. Kia pai tō rā.'

'Holy shit,' said the man. 'He knows Māori. That's amazing. Tama, you're amazing.'

'I thought we weren't meant to offer him positive reinforcement for speaking the language of his oppressors.'

'Is he, though?'

'Hvem er en flink gutt?'

'Holy shit! What was that?'

'Danish?'

'Yeah, it sounded like Danish.'

'How would he know Danish?'

'Netflix, maybe?'

'What, like *The Killing*?'

'Why not?'

'The killing?' I said. 'The killing?'

'That final episode was a total betrayal. She never would have shot a man in cold blood, then disappeared into the wilds of Iceland.'

'But that was the sacrifice she made. Shooting him was a moral act, for the greater good.'

'We don't even have Sky here. You realise that, don't you.'

I thought if I used my human voice they would let me out of the cage. They would let me go. I started to talk my head off, summoning all the words I could remember, and I kept talking even when they had returned to the next room. I said, 'You know I'd never hurt you, not on purpose. I'm worried that you think it's a baby. It digs in my head and I can't think straight.

I'm under a lot of pressure. Something dumb. Something terrible. I'm at the end of my rope. Tastes like wood. Well, it's none of my business. You're being very naughty. Out of bounds. No go. I'm kidding about the spa pool. Right rabbit in the right hole. They carry parasites, I think. I'm a bit fucking fed up to the back teeth. Wilderness Road – you can't miss it. How much is that costing us? How's NYC today, Ramon? It's like I turn into someone else. Where's Mummy hiding? Blue makes our eyes pop. He'll chop off his foot. Do you *want* me to break my neck? Goodness but you were a whopping one. Little goblins, little monsters. You're dumber than I thought. The horse has already bolted. Meow.'

After a while I heard the man say, 'Go get him,' and the woman came and picked up the cage and carried me out to the next room. There was a fish-pink double bed and a soundless TV tuned to a news channel and a half-size fridge like the one Marnie had shown me in the house on wheels. On a shelf above it, a kettle and a basket of snacks: biscuits, muesli bars, chocolate bars, crumpled bags of chips and nuts. A picture of a stag in a clearing hung on one wall, and a picture of a frothy waterfall on another. The man was balancing on a chair, tucking a bedsheet over the curtain rail and trying to smooth it flat against the drawn curtains. I still couldn't tell the time of day.

The woman put me down on a table just in front of him and checked her phone.

'Nothing yet,' she said.

'They won't even have noticed he's gone. They'll be too busy selling their sweatshop merchandise.'

'Bastards.'

'Pass me the selfie stick. And the phone. The *phone*, Rena.'

'No names.'

'Just give me the phone.'

'Maybe you could use yours? Oh wait, that's right, you dropped it in the bath.'

'Don't start.'

'Watching Japanese girls again – was that it?'

'I said don't start.'

They sat either side of me at the table and the man extended the stick. I'd seen my followers use them at the gate plenty of times, so I shouldn't have been surprised when the three of us appeared on the screen, but at the sight of my abductors in their magpie masks, flanking me like parents, I found myself saying, 'We do not tolerate this sort of behaviour. We do not reward it with attention.'

Where was my mother, the ghost of my mother? Where was Marnie?

Nowhere, nowhere.

'Quiet now, Tama,' said the woman in the mother mask.

The man looked into the screen and pressed a button on the stick. Then he said, 'We are free as a bird. We come to you today—'

'Wait,' said the woman. 'You can see a bit of curtain.' She pulled at the edge of the bedsheet behind us, and the man started again.

'We are free as a bird,' he said. 'We come—'

'Hold on. Hair.' The woman tucked a light-brown strand back up underneath her mask.

'Okay now?' said the man.

She nodded.

'Sure?'

'Just start talking.'

'We are free as a bird. We come to you today from a secret location—'

'We agreed on undisclosed, not secret,' said the woman.

'Does it matter?' said the man.

'Of course it matters. Undisclosed is more authoritative. We agreed on that. We're not the Famous Five.'

'We need to have the clip ready to go, Rena.'

'No names!'

'We need to have the clip ready to go, Comrade. If you keep interrupting—'

'To be fair, the curtain wasn't my fault.'

The man took a deep breath in and out, the rubber making a plap plap plap sound as the air left his mouth. 'We are free as a bird,' he said again. 'We come to you today from an undisclosed location—'

'We're not the Famous Five,' I said.

'Tama! Naughty little sausage!' said the woman, but she laughed.

'It's not funny,' said the man. 'And don't infantilise him.'

'It's not funny,' I said.

'Shh, Tama,' she said. When she tried to hold a finger to her lips she squashed her rubber beak first to one side and then the other, pulling her face into terrible shapes.

The man said, 'We are free—'

'We're live fucking feed,' I said.

'Shall we just do it without him?' said the woman.

'Why would we do it without him?' shouted the man. 'He is the whole fucking point!'

'We could just show him at the end. You know, as proof.'

The man's eyes stared at her from the holes in his mask. 'Comrade,' he said, 'I'm beginning to question your commitment to the cause.'

'*My* commitment?' she said. 'Who found out the address? Who went all the way to Timaru – *Timaru* – to buy the budgie cage? Who sourced the drugs and the masks? Who wrote ninety percent of the script? And yet you get to be the voice of the whole operation!'

'Naughty little sausage,' I said.

'You're welcome to be the voice,' said the man. 'Be my fucking guest. If you can get a word in edgewise.'

'I haven't learned it,' she muttered.

'What's that?'

'I haven't learned the script.'

'I guess that means I'm the voice, then,' he said.

They sat there in silence.

I said, 'Pass me the selfie stick.'

'Could we wait till he goes to sleep?' said the woman.

'We should have done the pet shop in Hamilton,' said the man. 'Smashed a window, opened the cages, taken some pictures, the end.'

'No,' she said. 'No, I want global attention.'

'Excuse me?'

'The cause. The cause wants it.'

'Right,' he said, eyeing her through his mask. 'The cause.'

'We could give him something to eat,' she said. 'To keep him quiet.'

'He hasn't touched a bite. I don't think he's hungry.'

'He loves cashews. They've posted pictures of him eating them.' She went to the basket above the fridge and found a little bag. 'Here we are.'

'Jesus, do you know how much they cost?'

She leafed through a plastic folder next to the basket. 'Twelve dollars.'

'So that's, what, two dollars a nut.'

'Brian, now's—'

'Names!'

'Comrade, now's not the time to be penny-pinching.' She ripped open the bag.

'I didn't say you could do that!'

'Who made you the boss?'

'I'm the voice, which means I'm the boss!'

'Calm your tits,' she said, and poked some cashews through the bars.

Delicious, delicious.

'See?' she said.

I whistled Wrecking Ball.

'I'm the voice,' he said. 'I'm the boss.' He held up the selfie stick again and placed his other hand on my cage. He said, 'We are free as a bird. We come to you today from an undisclosed location following our liberation of the magpie many of you know as Tamagotchi or Tama. Tama has been exploited by his captors for well over a year. He has been removed from his natural habitat and forced to sleep in an infant's cot. Forced to wear degrading costumes in photo and video shoots for the titillation of an international audience. Perhaps most damaging to his core sense of birdness has been the erosion of his mother tongue. His captors have trained him to speak for their amusement, and this deviant vocabulary includes a range of obscenities. It is clear that Tama does not know what these vile expressions mean, nor how they demean him when he uses them in place of his melodious and God-given voice. Free as a bird opposes all forms of avian domestication. We believe that Tama should be allowed to live as a magpie and not someone's pet, someone's plaything. We urge you to unfollow his captors' social-media posts, and to stop sharing the abusive images of Tama that revictimise him with every click of the mouse. Most of all we urge you to stop funding his captors by buying their exploitative merchandise. At a time and place of our choosing, we will release Tama back into the wild so that he can fly free as a bird. Hashtag free as a bird.'

He stopped recording and punched the air. 'Yes!' he shouted. 'Fucking *yes*!'

The woman shrugged. 'I could have done that.'

'But I fucking *nailed* it, right?'

She shrugged again.

'Did you hear the bit I added? About the obscenities?'

'Of course I heard it. I was sitting right here. Wordless.'

'Fucking ad fucking lib. Fucking *theatresports*.' Another air punch.

'Let's check the Twitter feed,' she said, but he was already tapping away on the phone, playing the clip of himself. I could see his lips moving through the hole in the mask, mouthing every word.

They weren't going to kill me, then. They weren't going to shoot me or poison me or run me down. They weren't going to wring my neck.

The woman carried me back to the bathroom and gave me the rest of the cashews and a few strips of ham. I suppose the day must have turned to dusk, because I began to sing some old song in my old voice: *Now it is time to return . . . come home, come home to your flock . . .* I couldn't remember the rest. I pecked at the ham. Too watery. The cheap stuff.

Some time later I heard the woman: 'Finally! They've finally noticed he's gone!'

'Let's get this party started,' said the man.

'Oh my God, listen to yourself.'

'Is this the way it's going to be? Pick pick pick till you make me do something I'll regret?'

'What does *that* mean?'

No response.

'Brian?'

'Names!'

'What does that mean, Comrade?'

'Nothing. Nothing. Just tell me what they said.'

'Has anyone local seen Tama? He's been gone all day and we're starting to worry.'

'That's it?'

'That's it. But the followers are chiming in: OMG, Tama's missing? I hope nothing horrible has happened. I'm praying for you Tama. Have you checked under the beds? My daughter hid under our bed for two hours when we said she couldn't watch Spongebob. Please Lord Jesus shine your light to show him the way home. I hope he hasn't been hit by a car. Maybe a dog attack? What about lightning. Is it mating season? I wonder if he has a corkscrew penis. Ducks have corkscrew penises. Go get 'em, Tama! Wait, birds have dicks? I've never seen a bird dick. Sometimes they have barbs on them too. I don't think it's mating season, it's snowing? Tama lives in New Zealand you moron. OMG I was there this morning and I saw him eat a blueberry! They don't mate till they're older. My kids aren't allowed Spongebob either. Hashtag find Tama. Hashtag bring Tama home.'

'Okay, let's post the clip,' said the man.

'Hmm,' said the woman.

'Hmm *what*, Rena?'

'Jesus, names! Anyway, I think we should wait. Create more of a buzz.'

'The clip is the buzz, Renatard.'

'Don't call me that.'

'Renatard. Renatard.'

'He'll hear you.'

'He's asleep, Renatard.'

'Let's try to be grown-ups, shall we?'

'Maybe you could start by posting the clip, as we agreed.'

'Hmm,' she said again. 'I think God will tell us when to post it.'

'What the fuck, Comrade?' he said. 'Is this a jealousy thing?'

'Of course not.'

'Like when Mum let me drive the Honda Prelude?'

'I didn't give a shit about the Honda Prelude then and I don't give a shit about the Honda Prelude now.'

'That's not what you wrote in your diary.'

'Cunt.'

'Where are you going?'

'The shower. I assume I don't need your permission.'

'Leave me the phone.'

'Sure. Put your mask on.'

'What for?'

'I need to bring him out here. I'm not showering in a mask, am I.'

Renatard carried me to the main room and set me down on the table, then headed back to the bathroom. The man was lying on the fish-pink bed, jabbing at the phone.

'Hey,' he called. 'Hey, it's locked. What's the code?'

'Sorry. Can't hear you.'

The bathroom door clicked shut.

'Bitch,' he said. He jabbed at the phone a few more times before dropping it on the bed. Scratching his neck underneath his mask, he browsed the channels on the soundless TV until he found one with a naked woman sliced straight down her dead belly and stitched back together again. He turned up the sound.

A different woman – alive and clothed – said *What I can tell you, Detective, is that she was around eight weeks pregnant.*

The man from Rob's crime show, gun strapped to his side, leaned in close to the body. *You see these marks, Trent? Same as on our Jane Doe.*

Typical defensive wounds, Detective, said the clothed woman.

With all due respect, Doctor, said the man with the gun, *there's nothing typical about this homicide.*

The brother was devastated. You saw how he wept when he IDed the remains.

Crocodile tears, said the man with the gun. *You learn to recognise them, Trent.*

'Snappity snap,' I said.

When the ads came on, the man climbed off the bed and flicked through the plastic folder on top of the fridge. He picked up the locked phone, discarded it again and picked up the big one that sat on the bedside table. 'Brian Holmes here,' he said. 'Room 33. Can I get two orders of spicy wings and a tiramisu?'

Then he hung up.

Then he realised.

Not the wings.

The name.

'Shit,' he muttered, looking over at me. 'Shit shit shit shit shit.'

In two steps he was at the cage. 'It's just an alias,' he said. 'Not my real name. Okay? Okay?'

I began to preen my tail.

'We won't mention it to her, right?' Sneaky sneaky.

A trickle of sweat ran out the bottom of his mask and disappeared under his T-shirt. I kept preening my tail.

'Do you want more cashews? Eh? Yummy cashews?'

'You've changed your tune,' said Renatard.

'Oh – yeah,' said Brian Holmes. 'Yeah, well, he's been such a good boy, hasn't he.' He poked a finger through the cage and stroked me. 'Such a good, good boy.'

I wanted to see the man with the gun catch the perp – tackle him at a charity dinner, corner him in an abandoned factory, *hands where I can see them, asshole* – but Renatard returned me to the bathroom, switched off the light and closed the door. In the black-black I imagined away my cage, imagined away the perch and bell that hit me in the head whenever I moved, and the cheap ham that smelled like soap, and the people pretending to be magpies. I thought of the Sun-Woman passing through her underground passage on her way back to the east, her bark torch snuffed out, and the magpies – the real magpies – waiting to greet her when she lit her fire to make the dawn. I was in my own room, my own bed, pushing all the insides back into my bear, its rattling heart restored. I was dozing beneath the puffy sun moon stars clouds while the ferris wheel sang its broken-glass song and turned and turned, head head head head head, no head, and the Eye watched over me, catching my every shudder and stretch, even in the dark. Just through the wall Rob and Marnie slept, and if I walked down the hall to their room and hopped up onto their bed they would roll apart and let me lie in the warm space between them.

The electric light woke me, bright as noon, and the fan began to hum. I squinted and blinked – and then I saw Renatard, pale in her pyjamas, stumbling to the toilet. Wispy light-brown hair, a high forehead, a sharp little chin. No mask. She sat down, stared at the unfamiliar floor for a moment, looked around at the unfamiliar walls. Noticed the cage. Noticed me inside the cage.

'Ducks have corkscrew penises,' I said.

She opened her mouth, closed it again.

'Is this a jealousy thing?' I said.

'Tama, my darling,' she whispered all in a rush, flushing the toilet and washing her hands with one of the tiny soaps, 'this didn't happen, okay? You never saw me.'

'You never saw me,' I said.

'Right, right,' she whispered. 'Our little secret, okay? Just between you, me and God. Good boy. Good boy.'

And she turned out the light.

In the morning – I suppose it was in the morning – Brian Holmes came and unlatched the cage door so he could reach in with a bit of raw mince on a plastic lid. Lamb. Reasonable quality. He started to clean his teeth with his mask on, then sighed, plap plap plap plap. He looked at me, hesitated, then folded the rubber up above his thin mouth and started brushing again. His face neither human nor bird.

'What are they saying?' he called. He wiped his mouth, folded his mask back down and left the room.

248 - CATHERINE CHIDGEY

'Worried sick . . . missing for twenty-four hours . . . not like him at all . . . reward for safe return . . .'

'How much?'

'Ten thousand dollars.'

'Wow. They really want him back.'

'That's nothing compared to what he's earning them.'

'Okay, so now we post the clip.'

'No, now we let them stew. Let them think he's dead.'

'How long are you going to delay posting it? Are you enjoying yourself? Your tragic little power play?'

'God will tell us when it's time,' said Renatard.

I fiddled with the latch on the cage door. Lifted it, let it go. Lifted it, let it go. Lifted it, pushed, let it go. Out I hopped.

In the main room the two of them were still bickering about the clip, so I fluttered up to the snack basket above the fridge and helped myself to a fresh bag of cashews. Brian Holmes wore his mask but Renatard's lay deflated and empty-eyed on the bed.

'I'm taking the greater risk,' said Brian Holmes. 'It's me they'll identify. My voice they'll recognise.'

She laughed. 'Who's going to recognise your voice? Your dole caseworker? Aunty Pam? Because we both know those are your options.'

Someone knocked on the door. They froze – and then they saw me.

'Housekeeping!' called the person just outside.

'Calm your tits,' I said.

In silence they pointed at me, at the door, at the bathroom, at each other.

'Housekeeping!' called the person again, and the door opened, and she began to step inside.

Brian Holmes leapt across the room. 'No thank you,' he said, blocking me from her sight. 'We're fine, thank you.'

She smelled something like the pines, and she had a trolley full of bottles and cloths that smelled something like the pines.

'Can I get two orders of spicy wings and a tiramisu?' I said.

'You want room service?' she said.

'No thanks,' said Brian Holmes.

'You need more minibar?'

'No, we're fine. Thanks. Thank you.' He shut the door.

'Mask,' said Renatard, and his hands flew to his face.

'Shit! Do you think she noticed I was wearing it?'

'Um, yes.'

'Shit! Shit!'

'They see all sorts,' said Renatard, waving an airy hand.

'You were meant to put out the do not disturb sign!'

'No, I asked you to.'

'I clearly remember you saying you would.'

'And I clearly remember you saying you'd reserved a twin room, yet here we are.' She gestured at the fish-pink bed. 'Anyway, she'll just assume it's some sex thing.'

'I am not having bird sex! With my sister!'

'You never saw me,' I said, pushing another cashew from the bag.

'And what the hell is Tama doing out?'

'You fed him,' said Renatard. 'You must have left the cage open.'

'Well, now he's seen you.'

'Mmm.'

'He'll be able to identify you.'

'He's a bird, Brian.'

'Names!'

'He's a bird, fuckwit.'

'You know they remember faces.'

'When will he ever see us again, though?'

'Brian Holmes here,' I said. 'Room 33.'

'Shit,' he said.

'So to recap,' said Renatard, 'you're getting all bent out of shape because he's seen my face, but in fact he knows your full name, and it appears you booked the room under that name.'

'Don't be stupid,' said Brian Holmes. 'I booked it under my alias.'

'So he's just guessed your full name?'

He looked at the ceiling. 'I might have let it slip when I rang room service.'

'Cunt,' I said.

CHAPTER TWENTY-FOUR

We must have spent another four days in the hotel. Perhaps it was five; I don't remember. They went out to buy food – singly, so that I was never alone – and ate it on the fish-pink bed: greasy things in greasy boxes, greasy things on greasy sticks. The housekeeping person brought fresh towels, and more bird-sized soaps and shampoos.

'You want shoe-shine kit?' she asked at the door.

'No thank you,' they said.

'Sewing kit?'

'No thanks.'

'Shower cap? Quite useful.'

'No.'

'You don't want room made up?'

'No.'

'Merry Christmas.'

'Okay.'

The curtains remained drawn, muffling the daylight, and when I sneaked behind them to see what I could see, all I found was a concrete patio with a spindly geranium in a pot.

Brian Holmes was getting restless, I could tell. He kept pacing back and forth, scratching underneath his mask with urgent fingers the way the farm dogs scratched behind their ears.

I wondered what they were doing, the dogs. Barking into the hot nor'west wind? Chasing wayward lambs and holding them down with soft open mouths, resisting the urge to bite? Lying with their paws in the air, footsore from mustering up on the sun-seared rocks, or prowling around the killing house while Rob slit the throat of an old and worthless ewe? I thought of Smoke fixing a sheep with her unflinching stare until it backed down. Dutchie dancing across the backs of the animals as he forced them through the race. Help digging his endless holes. Perhaps he wasn't looking for anything at all. Perhaps he was trying to escape.

'It's good for us to experience this,' said Renatard. 'God's helping us to understand captivity.'

'I just wish we had Netflix,' said Brian Holmes.

She watched him pace. 'That's quite a reward they're offering, isn't it.'

'What do you mean?'

'Nothing. Just saying.'

'Well, don't.'

Renatard sighed. 'I was just saying.' She opened the drawer next to her side of the bed and took out a book bound in red and gold. 'Remember Bible hunts?'

'Every Sunday night. *Close your eyes, open the book, God will tell you where to look.*'

'Let's do one. It'll be like Mum's here guiding us.'

'I think she'd be proud,' said Brian Holmes, picking a strand of pizza cheese from his mask.

Renatard said, 'You go first.'

Holding one hand over his eye holes, he opened the book and jabbed a finger onto the page. I listened hard, but I couldn't hear God telling him anything. 'Then Jereboam built Schechem in the hill country of Ephraim and lived there,' he read. 'Hmm. Should we – should we be releasing him in hill country?'

'Let me try.' Renatard closed her eyes, jabbed. 'No one whose testicles are crushed or whose male organ is cut off shall enter the assembly of the Lord,' she read. 'Okay, that's not so helpful either.'

'Maybe we should look more towards the New Testament end.'

'It's meant to be random. God tells you the right spot. You can't rig it.' She tried again, and I listened hard again, but I still couldn't hear God. 'I dug wells and drank foreign waters,' she read, 'and I dried up with the sole of my foot all the streams of Egypt.' She frowned. 'I'm not sure what that means. Mum would have known.'

'Here, I'll have another go.' Brian Holmes covered his eye holes once more, opened the book towards the back and jabbed. 'And I looked, and behold, a white horse! And its rider had a bow, and a crown was given to him, and he came out conquering, and to conquer.'

'Again, not sure what that means.'

'Well,' said Brian Holmes, 'well, I think I'm the rider on the white horse.'

'Do you.'

'Yeah. I think that's what Mum would have said.'

'Why can't I be the rider?'

Brian Holmes pointed at the page. 'A crown was given to *him*,' he said. '*He* came out conquering.'

'So you're the voice, and now you're the rider too. What am I?'

'Maybe you're . . . the horse?'

'Right. Cheers.'

Brian Holmes scratched underneath his mask, stretching the mouth hole all crooked and wrong. 'You know,' he said, 'I read about a guy who found ten thousand dollars in a hotel Bible.'

Renatard flipped through the pages, held the book upside down and shook it. Something fluttered out.

'What's that?'

She picked up the piece of paper, unfolded it and read, 'Tomato sauce, batteries, onions, Cheezels, oven cleaner, yoghurt (not the blue one).'

They tried to coax me back into the cage – she with her softest voice, he with a fresh dish of heart – but I wasn't falling for that again. I kept my distance.

Eventually they gave up and I made myself a bed in the shower, unspooling a roll of toilet paper and shaping it into a soft white nest. I took all the miniature cakes of soap from the vanity and tucked them around me like eggs, and whenever new soaps appeared I added them to my clutch. If my abductors approached and tried to wash themselves I shrieked at them *We are here and this is our tree and we're staying and it is ours and you need to leave and now.* If they shut the bathroom door, I shrieked too. My father's glint in my eyes. The devil's blood in my mouth.

They kept checking Marnie's posts, and the followers' comments, and the whole world wanted me home safe and sound; the whole world sent its thoughts and prayers. Then one evening – I knew it was evening because the TV played the tune for the news – I heard my name.

The man on the TV said *And now, a story that has the internet in a bit of a flap. Tama, a tame magpie with an astonishing vocabulary, has disappeared from his high-country home. His owners say they haven't seen him since Thursday morning. They're concerned, and so are Tama's five hundred thousand Twitter followers. Yolanda Costas picks up this magpie tale.*

Life can be harsh in rugged Central Otago, said a woman in a cowboy hat. *The driest part of New Zealand, it serves up icy temperatures in winter and months of drought in summer and autumn. Still, it's here that internet star Tama found a home, with sheep farmers Robert and Marnie Veldman. I understand you took him under your wing when he was just a chick . . .?*

And there she was – Marnie, my Marnie, sitting with Rob on the front steps of the yolk-yellow house, Smoke at their feet. *That's right*, she said. *He fell from the nest and wouldn't have survived – shouldn't have survived – but I kept him in the hot-water cupboard and fed him by hand, and he decided to stay.*

How beautiful she was, how luminous in the blazing high-country sun. Her black hair shining against her white shoulders, her white neck. One of my moulted feathers in her hand.

And he lives inside with you? said the woman in the cowboy hat.

Yes, said Marnie. *He has his own bedroom, and his own seat at the kitchen table. He comes and goes as he pleases through the cat door.*

Sounds like he rules the roost.

Marnie nodded, gave a sad smile. Smoke panted in the heat.

Most farmers treat magpies as pests, Robert. What did you think when your wife wanted to save one?

That it would go the same way as all the others, he said.

Tama turned out to be pretty special, though.

Yep, he said.

A bit different from your average magpie.

Yep, he said.

A very talented bird.

Yep, he said.

Marnie, tell me about his extraordinary talent.

Well, he can talk, she said. *He reels off full sentences, just like a human. We only have to say something once and he remembers it.* She stopped, bit her lip. Looked at the sky.

And now he's gone missing, said the woman in the cowboy hat. *How does that make you feel?*

Marnie let out a sob.

What do you think might have happened to Tama?

Someone's stolen him, said Marnie. *I know it.*

Is that what you think, Robert?

Seems likely, said Rob. *He's a valuable bird.*

If you know something, said Marnie, *please get in touch. We're @TamaMagpie on Twitter.*

And there's a reward for his safe return?

Ten thousand dollars, said Rob.

No questions asked, said Marnie.

And what's your message to anyone who might have taken Tama?

Smoke sat up, yawned, and Rob scratched her between the ears. Then, exactly like the worried parents on his crime show, he looked straight through the TV screen and into the hotel room and said *We just want our little boy home again. That would be the best Christmas present. Even though Christmas was last week. We're his family, and this is where he belongs.*

Back to you, Henare, said the woman in the cowboy hat.

Thanks, Yolanda. Looks like fowl play to me. Now here's Hobbsy with sport.

My abductors posted the clip that night. Marnie saw it almost straight away, and I knew that she must have been waiting there on her phone, hunting through the comments for any clues about me, because she loved me. I huddled down into my paper nest and dreamed of the rain. It fell on the hot farm, and the ground was so hard that the water began to pool and spread, and it rose and rose until it drowned the yolk-yellow house.

They were starting to stink.

'Tama, my darling,' said Renatard, crouching in front of the shower, 'if you wouldn't mind just letting us have a quick wash. Just a couple of minutes each. We'll put everything back for you afterwards. We'll leave it nice and dry.'

I was not her darling. I began to shriek *We are here and this is our tree and we're staying and it is ours and you need to leave and now*. She was holding up her hands, backing away, but I kept going. *We are here and this is our tree and we're staying and it is ours and you need to leave and now. We are here and this is . . .*

'All right,' she said. 'All right. I can see you're not comfortable with that, which is fine. Shh. Shhhh.'

At the vanity she wet a face cloth, looked around for a cake of soap. Eyed the ones in my nest.

'I don't suppose . . .' she said, slowly reaching in a hand.

I snapped at it.

Tasted her blood.

Snappity snap.

Delicious, delicious.

After that they both just used shampoo, rubbing at themselves – armpit, armpit, groin – and watching me the whole time. Perverts.

And maybe it was the TV story or the clip or both, but I gained more and more followers. 'Well over half a million,' said Renatard. 'We've handed them free advertising, basically.'

'All the more publicity for the cause,' said Brian Holmes.

'And I looked, and behold, a white horse!' I said, tearing into a bag of chips from the basket on top of the fridge. Salt and vinegar. Disgusting. I pushed them to the floor, opened another bag. Sour cream and chives. Also disgusting. To the floor with them.

'I think God's telling us it's time,' said Renatard.

The muesli bar had coconut in it, which I didn't care for. Floor. The crackers tasted a bit stale. Floor. 'Fuck fuck fuck,' I muttered.

'It's definitely time,' said Brian Holmes. 'The problem being, we can't get him to the forest because we can't get him to the car because we can't get him in the cage.'

'I'm aware of that,' said Renatard, examining the gash on her hand. 'He's got to go, though. He deserves his freedom.'

'Absolutely,' said Brian Holmes. 'And he deserves it today.'

They were already pushing back the curtains, unlocking the sliding glass door that led to the concrete patio.

'It's not exactly the forest,' said Renatard.

'There's a geranium,' said Brian Holmes. 'But don't get that in shot. Nothing that can be traced back to us.'

'Okay. I'll do a close-up of you saying we're about to liberate him, and then I'll put my hand over the lens, and then we open the door and release him into nature and I show him flying free against the sky.'

'Shall I still do the script?'

'Of course. I spent ages on that.'

'Only it talks about the kauri forests. There aren't any kauri forests down here. You should have checked that.'

'No one's going to know where we are. That's the point.'

Brian Holmes checked his masked reflection in the mirror, then Renatard started videoing him with her phone.

'We are free as a bird,' he said. 'We come to you today from the quiet of the forest, where the great kauri trees cast their shade and the ferns unfurl their fronds as a symbol of new life.'

'Fucking *theatresports*,' I said, but he kept going.

'And it's new life for Tama the magpie, too, as we release him into the wild, where he belongs. We do not own God's creatures of the air. They are not ours to imprison and abuse.'

'Can I get two orders of spicy wings and a tiramisu?' I said.

Renatard motioned for him to carry on.

'Tama, it is time for you to leave our care,' he said. 'It has been our privilege to save you from a life of degradation. Sing your magpie songs once more, Tama. Reclaim your magpie voice.'

I bit my tongue.

Then Brian Holmes slid open the door and I felt the gush of warm summer air.

'We'd like to pause here to consider—' he began, but I could see a strip of sky beyond the concrete patio, and I launched myself off the shelf above the fridge, shat on the fish-pink bed and flew outside.

'Where is he?' I heard Renatard saying as I sped away. 'God, it's bright out here. Did I miss him?'

My left eye saw the town and my right eye saw the town. I looked for the squad cars veering around corners on two wheels, and I looked for the perps fleeing on foot, armed and dangerous, upsetting stands of oranges and flocks of pigeons. I looked for the hotdog stands, the men in blue aprons saying *You want mustard with that?* I looked for the hookers chewing their gum, leaning against brick walls and calling everyone honey. I looked for the skyscrapers, glassy and hot and as tall as forever. I looked for traffic backed up all the way to Sunset. I looked for blind beggars. I looked for ambulances and I looked for wrecking yards and I looked for dumpsters where naked dead women lay on beds of trash, coffee grounds in their hair and clues in their fists. But this town was not like the towns on TV. This town had beds of flowers, women pushing prams. Men in no particular hurry. This town huddled low beneath the lustrous sky. This town had only a scattering of shops, their windows filled with mattresses and vases and couches, sunhats, televisions, cakes. One window contained pictures of houses and pictures of the rooms inside the houses. Another showed headless white figures in the shape of women, some dressed in gowns, some dressed in casualwear – and there were empty windows too, windows into dark places with nothing for sale. This town had cars that growled and prowled, looking for something to hit. This town had a statue of a man leaning on the tip of a rifle. This town had a fake pine tree ten times the size of the one at home. It fluttered with tinsel and baubles, icicles that wouldn't melt, lacquered apples, tongue-less bells. The streets stopped short at the water that held the town in its silvery arms; somewhere down deep, the drowned farms, the drowned bridges. The powerlines buzzed like flies. I perched on the shoulder of the man with the rifle to feel which way the wind was blowing. Then I headed for high country.

I listened for God to guide me, but as usual he was no help. So was it my flock calling me home, or was it Marnie? I still can't say, but I know that I followed something in my blood. I passed above the houses where men cooked meat in their withered gardens and children screamed *I shot you, lie down, you're dead*. Beyond the edge of town the orchards began, most of the trees covered with nets, though here and there the fruit hung unprotected and sweet. I did not stop. Through the wide world I flew, over the damn dam that held back all the water though they built it on a faultline, the bloody idiots, the bloody mongrels, over the farms where the animals kicked up dust as they crossed the cracked earth. Dry, dry, dry, and from the flat sky no hint of rain to come. Only the gorse bushes flourished, their yellow flowers shining among the riotous green thorns. I came to the place of the dead, the stones laid out in their rows, those at the bottom of the hill squat and glossy and lettered in gold. There were brown stalks rotting in mucky jars and plastic flowers faded and brittle from the sun. There were windmills and booties, a motorbike helmet, a bear slumped in on itself. And over in the corner a fresh hole, deeper than anything Help could dig, deep enough to hold death. The mound of soil next to it must have been bursting with beetles and worms and grubs, but I did not stop. Further up the slope the stones were older, larger. Tilted and toppled, the words eaten away. Stone wreaths and stone urns and a stone child with stone wings, too heavy to fly. No burial of a beautiful victim in a beautiful box that day; no strong-jawed men shouldering her towards the hole, her family stunned dumb. No priest saying *dust to dust*, no detectives watching to see if the perp gave himself away with crocodile tears or an unexplained limp or a certain flower kissed and dropped into the grave – a flower only the killer knew she loved. Dry here too, the dirt shrinking, sinking into every pit. A stand of eucalyptus trees like the ones on the farm, shedding their bark in great dead strips, the leaves pushing perfume into the parched air. I heard other birds as I flew – starlings and blackbirds, sparrows and fantails, and flocks of magpies who watched me pass above their territories and threw back their heads to warn me away.

The land began to look more familiar, and then, in the distance, I made out the pine trees cutting their black shapes from the air, and at last I reached Wilderness Road. As I drew near to our gate I saw piles of flowers and windmills and bears stretching right out to the street, as if it were one big grave, as if I had died and they'd buried me there for all the cars to drive over. I saw the yolk-yellow house, and the pine trees on the hillside that spread their branches like a mother's wings, and both looked like home to me, but the house was the home where Marnie lived. I let myself in through the cat door – meow – and there she was at the kitchen table, Marnie, my Marnie, opening her arms to me and saying my name over and over like a word she wanted to learn.

CHAPTER TWENTY-FIVE

The woman in the cowboy hat said, 'How does it feel to have him home with you?'

'We couldn't be happier,' said Marnie. 'We thought we'd lost him.'

'Robert, how about you?'

'Yeah, just relief,' said Rob, stroking my back. He was wearing a pale-pink shirt I hadn't seen before, and he'd combed his hair flat with water.

'You've installed security cameras at the gate, I see.'

'Can't be too careful.'

'Any ideas where he might have been? Or how far he's travelled?'

Marnie shook her head. 'He's well fed. No injuries. The people who took him haven't posted again. It's a mystery.'

'Tama's not talking, eh?'

'Oh he's been coming out with all sorts, but no real clues.'

'What's he been saying?'

Marnie smiled, looked at Rob. 'He was talking about the Famous Five, wasn't he? And Japanese girls . . . cashews . . . a pet shop in Hamilton . . . a geranium . . . what else?'

'Something about Iceland,' said Rob. 'And Cheezels.'

'That's right, Cheezels. And bits of the Bible, it sounded like.'

'Tama, any comment from you?' said the woman in the cowboy hat. She held the microphone up to me and waited.

I looked at it with my left eye. Looked at it with my right eye. I said, 'You must be scared. Are you scared?'

She laughed. 'And we'll leave it there! Henare, back to you.'

She wasn't the only one who wanted to speak to me, who wanted me to speak. For days they came with their microphones and their cameras and their questions. What was the best thing about being home again? Would I consider entering politics? Was farming still a viable career? Did I think we were in for another drought? If Rob and Marnie had a family, how would I handle being a big brother? Did I have any advice for other pet birds who wanted to become celebrities?

I said, 'You're getting all bent out of shape.'

I said, 'You saw how he wept when he IDed the remains.'

I said, 'There's a geranium.'

I said, 'Be my fucking guest,' and they said, 'We'll bleep that out. It'll be hilarious.'

They loved me no matter what I said.

And then, one day, I said, 'Brian Holmes here, Room 33. Can I get two orders of spicy wings and a tiramisu?'

The followers seized on it, tracking down dozens of Brian Holmeses. Marnie read their comments to me: 'We will bring you to justice, Brian. How are you sleeping, Brian? Guys, look: this one campaigned against a new cell-phone tower. This one voted for the Greens. OMG, this one's wearing a rubber mask! That's because it was Halloween, Sherlock. This one has lots of tattoos. So? I have lots of tattoos and I don't kidnap birds. We need to consider Bryans as well as Brians, remember. This one's eyes are too close together. He lives in Montreal – unlikely. Well, he could have travelled to New Zealand. No, the guy on the video was a Kiwi. Maybe he was doing an accent to throw us off the scent. This one has three DUI convictions. This one quotes the Bible. This one's wearing a parrot T-shirt. I bet he's reading our posts LOL. Brian, turn yourself in, you piece of shit.'

They found him, though – the followers found him. Marnie showed me his picture on her phone: the same narrow chin and high forehead as Renatard, and the same thin mouth I'd seen when he was cleaning his teeth. The police arrested the pair of them a few days later, and they were even on TV for a few short moments.

'Hands where I can see them, asshole,' I said. 'Don't try anything funny.'

But there was no car chase. No shootout. No locking them up and throwing away the key. Only a fine, which was only money, which was only a slap on the wrist.

I gave even more interviews after that, and I was sure I saw my father watching one of them from the roof of the yolk-yellow house.

The interviewer said, 'Tama, do you have any words for your abductors?'

Keeping an eye on the shape of my father, I said, 'We couldn't be happier.'

I wanted him to know how Rob and Marnie loved me, how they adored me, but when I looked again he was heading for the cherry orchard.

As soon as the interview was over I followed him – the first time I'd ventured there since the day I turned my back on my sister. I found him sitting on top of her cage, laying down the law while she listened with bowed head.

'Never have I felt such shame,' he said. 'A child of mine turned call-bird, luring her own family to the traps. Ensnaring her own blood. Oh the disgrace. Oh the infinite sorrow.' He fluttered to the ground, fixed her with his left eye. 'Shall I tear out my feathers one by one?' he said.

'No, Father,' she murmured.

'Shall I peck my own breast till it bleeds?'

'No, Father.'

'Then what do you suggest I try to stifle the pain of a child's betrayal?'

She picked up a morsel from her dish and poked it through the bars. 'Bacon?'

His right eye had seen me, I knew, but he kept on talking to my sister as if I were invisible.

'You are no daughter of mine,' he said. 'You are not even a memory. My new children are better children; they are loyal children. You are not even a ghost.'

'But you're talking to me,' she said.

'Silence! You are nothing.' He stalked back and forth, breast puffed, feathers tufted above and below his red eyes. 'You are to stop calling magpies to the orchard. Stop luring them to the traps. We have lost too many.'

My sister nibbled at a bit of zucchini.

'Well? Nothing to say for yourself?'

'Silence. I am nothing.'

'Nothing,' he said.

She noticed me then. 'You took your time,' she said. 'Bacon?'

'You do not speak to other nothings!' said my father.

'To be fair,' she said, 'this is all his fault.'

'Do you know what happens to the birds in the traps?' he said, and did not wait for an answer. 'They are taken away and killed. Twist, snap, and out with the rubbish – or cooked and eaten. Their bones sucked clean.'

'Stories, Father, stories,' she said.

'I see, I see. A daughter knows better than her father. Although you are no longer my daughter. Tell me, then – what happens to the birds in the traps?'

'They become pets. They live a life of luxury with slaves and adoration. Like him.' She cocked her head at me.

'Or humane release,' I said. 'They're driven out to the bush and let go.'

'There you are, then,' said my sister.

'And I've never seen a magpie cooked and eaten,' I said.

'What is that annoying noise?' said my father.

'It's your son,' I said.

'It's my brother,' she said.

'Far away, so far away,' he said. 'I can hardly hear it at all.'

'I'm right behind you,' I said.

'Right behind you,' she said.

'No,' he said, 'it's just a pebble tumbling down the hillside. A tiny traitorous pebble rattling along. I do not speak to pebbles.'

'Am I a pebble?' said my sister.

'You are nothing. You have betrayed your blood. You are not even a memory, not even a ghost.'

'Not even a pebble?'

My father was about to answer her when something caught his eye – something out on Wilderness Road. He huddled low to the ground, hunched his head into his body, feathers sleeked flat, and I realised he was afraid.

'What is it?' said my sister. 'What what what?'

Rob's car.

My father was making a low warbling sound: 'Oh my love, my love, my love . . .'

Rob's car, beetle-black, and Rob behind the wheel.

I had a bad feeling.

'That is the car that killed her,' said my father. 'I have kept it from you, but that is the car. And that is the man.'

'Killed who? Killed who?' said my sister.

At the end of the row of trees we saw it pass by on its way up the gravel.

'He aimed for her. He saw her and he swerved to hit her, and he hit her. Your mother.'

'No no no,' I said. 'That's Rob.'

'He aimed for her?' said my sister.

'That is the car. That is the man.'

'It must have been an accident,' I said.

'Tell the traitorous pebble it was no accident,' said my father.

'It was no accident,' said my sister. She peered at the morsel of bacon she'd poked through the bars to him. 'If you don't want that, can I have it back?'

He ignored her.

We listened to the engine grow quieter and quieter and stop.

'You can't trust them,' he said then. 'Perhaps they bring you delicious food. Perhaps you think they are your slaves. Perhaps you think they love you. But they will turn on you. One day, they will aim for you.'

My sister examined her empty dish, refusing to meet his eye.

'The calling and the luring stop today,' he said. 'Consider this your first and final warning.'

After he'd gone, she said, 'That's not true, is it?'

'What's not true?'

'The twisting, the snapping. The out with the rubbish.'

'I don't know.'

'The cooking and eating? The sucking of the bones?'

'I don't think so. I've never seen it.'

'Just stories, then,' she said.

Behind us something squeaked.

'Not you again,' said my sister.

'Fat?' said the fantail. 'Fat?'

Before I could say anything he hopped into the trap – but the door remained open. Calmly he pecked at the bait, then fluttered out again.

'How did he do that?' I said.

'He's too light to set it off,' said my sister. 'That's right!' she called after him. 'Keep on stuffing yourself!'

'Do you think it's true about Rob?' I said.

'Who?'

'About the car that killed our mother.'

'Could be, could be. Our father saw it.'

'I think it was an accident.'

'If you say so.'

'I do. I do say so.' Next to me the open trap. For one short moment I thought: I could just walk inside. A few steps and the door would snap shut. And then . . . what? Humane release?

'I'll keep an eye out,' I said. 'Next time you trap someone, call me so I know. I'll find out what happens to the trapped birds.'

'All right,' said my sister. 'But I don't trap them – they trap themselves.'

That night, after lights out, the ghost of my mother came. She settled on my yellow blanket and together we gazed up at the Eye that could see in the dark. I knew it was watching us, listening to us, sending our voices and our pictures out into the wide world.

I said, 'Tell me the car was not beetle-black.'

She said *I do not remember a car.*

I said, 'Tell me his hair was not dirty yellow.'

She said *I do not remember his hair.*

I said, 'Tell me he was a small man, a weak man.'

She said *I do not remember his size, his strength.*

I said, 'Tell me his eyes were not riverstone eyes and his arms were not an axeman's arms.'

She said *I do not remember his eyes and I do not remember his arms.*

I said, 'Tell me he did not aim for you. Tell me it was an accident.'

She said *Go to sleep, little one. It's late.*

I said, 'We never forget a face. Did you see his face?'

She said *It's far too late, and I am only bones*.

She refused to speak of her death.

Because the Eye was watching, listening.

And if she implicated Rob, the followers would see him punished.

And clearly she did not want him punished.

Because it was an accident.

And because he loved me.

His woolshed wall stacked high with my likeness.

'You'll be sick of the sound of your own voice,' said Ange.

'We're talking to Portugal tonight,' said Marnie. 'Then Germany, then India. Or is it India, then Germany? I've lost track.' She was pulling the decorations off the fake pine tree, wrapping each tinkly bauble in tissue. The silver pine cones, the golden birds.

'World famous,' said Ange. 'Who would've thought?'

'It's a bit much,' said Rob. 'I've got a hundred things to take care of, but Lakshmi wants me sitting around in a polo shirt like a dickhead.'

'Can't you say no? Just let Marnie do the interviews? She must know all the answers by now.'

'People need to see the family unit,' said Marnie, lifting the star from the top of the tree. 'That's the narrative. That's the hook.'

'Meanwhile I have thousands of lambs that won't crutch themselves,' said Rob. 'There's a limit.' He began wrenching out the branches, reducing the tree to sticks.

'The thing is,' said Marnie, 'we can't buy publicity like this, and we have to ride the wave. Our engagements are through the roof.'

'You sound just like Lakshmi,' said Rob.

'She really does,' said Ange.

Stick by stick Marnie packed away the dismantled tree.

'Actually, I need to call her,' she said. 'Ask about a distributor for the merchandise.'

'Isn't it slacking off?' said Ange. 'Now we're past Christmas?'

'Not with all the publicity. I can't do it any more.'

'Hallefuckinglujah,' said Rob. 'Maybe I'll get my wife back.'

'Language,' said Marnie. 'We're going live.'

She pressed the button on the black box to turn on the Eye, and the three of them disappeared to the kitchen for lunch. I was a good boy, the best boy: I grabbed at a length of tinsel and trailed it round the room, then climbed up inside the floor lamp and poked my head out the top of the pleated shade. The followers loved it when I did that. I rolled around in front of the Eye for a while too, playing with a silver pinecone that smelled all wrong.

Then I got bored and went outside. I lay in a sun-trance. I preened myself. I whistled Rob's whistles to confuse the dogs. Smoke ran round in circles looking for his master, and Night and Dutchie whined while Help began to scratch at an old hole. Something scuttled past me, tiny, earth-brown. A mouse. I remember thinking: I don't have to hunt any more.

But I wanted to.

I took off after it. First it raced towards the compost pile, then it changed direction and made for the coppery chickens that could not sing. I swooped, and it panicked, dashing for open ground and zigzagging about before finally scrambling into Help's hole. Easy pickings.

I took it inside to eat. It was still wriggling in my beak when I passed through the cat door, and I had to mumble my meow so as not to drop it. Next to Rob's TV chair I tore it open and started with the stomach – grainy, greasy – then pulled out the guts and gulped them down, a warm worm.

I was digging for the little nut of brain when Marnie burst into the room and snatched at the black box behind the Eye, pressed the button.

'I've turned it off,' she said to her phone, and I saw Lakshmi's face frozen on the screen, open-mouthed, about to bite. 'Are you there?' said Marnie. 'Hello? Can you hear me?' She glanced down at my meal and let out a whimper. I set aside the tail for her.

'. . . of them were watching!' yelled Lakshmi. 'They're already posting!'

Rob and Ange were in the living room then too. 'What's going on?' said Rob.

Marnie pointed at my lunch. I swallowed a bit of neck.

'So?'

'So the followers have seen it!' yelled Lakshmi.

'He's a wild creature,' said Ange. 'What do they expect?'

'Cuddles with lambs is what they fucking expect! Tiny costumes! Playing with clothes pegs!'

'You can fix it, though,' said Marnie.

Lakshmi sighed. 'Post this, straight away – are you listening?'

'I'm listening.'

'Tama apologises unreservedly for the upsetting footage that some of you and your children may have just witnessed. He realises he has overstepped the mark and he takes full responsibility for his behaviour. Tama acted rashly, in a moment of weakness, and it won't happen again. He has a special message for anyone thinking about unfollowing him . . . don't you dare!'

'Wait, what comes after a moment of weakness?' said Marnie.

'It won't happen again,' said Rob.

'It won't happen again,' I said.

'That is one beautiful piece of damage control,' said Ange. 'Told you she was sharp.'

In the evening Rob and Marnie stood side by side in front of the bathroom mirror, getting ready to talk to Portugal.

'Have you seen my chapstick?' he said.

'Nope,' she said.

'It's been missing for ages.' He examined his lips in the mirror, dabbed on a bit of Marnie's moisturiser. 'What?' he said. 'It's not gay.'

'I never said it was.'

'Is that what you're wearing?'

Marnie untwisted a ribbon-thin shoulder strap. 'Why?'

'Pretty revealing, isn't it?'

Something scratched and scraped in the roof above.

'I don't think so,' said Marnie. 'It's the fashion.' She smoothed down the collar of Rob's polo shirt, coloured her lips dark red.

While we waited for Portugal to call, Rob honed an axe with his honing stone, rubbing away the last of the feather edge with the palm of his hand, hush, hush, hush. He ran the blade through the hair on his forearm to test the sharpness, and we watched his crime show about shapely murdered women with torn-off clothes who'd let their attackers in their front doors. *We have a DNA match, Trent. Let's nail the lowlife scum and release the remains.* We didn't see the end, though. We never saw them catch the perp.

I don't remember what I said to Portugal.

CHAPTER TWENTY-SIX

B rother! Brother! A bird has trapped himself!'
When my sister called me to the orchard I flew straight
there and found a young magpie in the cage next to
hers, his feathers still mottled grey.

'From their own mouths,' she was telling him. 'Bits of apricot. Bits of apple. Grapes and nuts and cherries.'

'Do you belong to the flock in the pines?' I said.

'He's our cousin,' said my sister. 'Imagine that!'

'Didn't your parents tell you to avoid the traps?'

'I wanted to see for myself,' he said.

'He didn't listen,' said my sister. 'He ignored the warnings.'

'I followed her voice,' he said. 'She kept calling.'

'Well, but also you ignored the warnings,' she said.

'What happens now?'

'They'll come in the evening and take you to your new home.'

I waited in one of the trees a little way off. I could not bring
myself to speak to him, but my sister chattered non-stop. Oh
yes, she said, certainly there would be walnuts, whole piles of
walnuts already cracked open. Almonds too, and pistachios,
which were tiny and sweet and bright green. A bed softer and
safer than any nest. Fresh mice every morning, probably. And
he would be given a name, which was a sound belonging only
to him, and the sound would mean something like *strong* or
hope or *love*. And fire, there would be fire, and he could lie in
front of it, belly to the flames, back to the flames. Fire? Well,
fire was like his own private sun, close enough to touch.

On she went until twilight filled the orchard, turned the air to gold, and he hung on her every word, breathless with the thrill of his future. I watched the followers coming and going at the gate so I would not have to watch him. Some of them pointed and waved at the new Eyes that looked in both directions up and down Wilderness Road. In the distance they called for me, begged for me, while my sister talked and talked. I wanted to tell her to be quiet, that if she was quiet she might not draw attention to the bird she had trapped. But it was evening, and I knew what happened to trapped birds in the evening. And who was that approaching through the trees now, black hair falling over white shoulders? Who was that drawing near and nearer, like Marnie but not Marnie? Pale skin all aglow in the twilight. Gloves covering her hands.

Ange was quick about it: she threw some seeds into my sister's cage, then picked up the trap and carried it away. I skulked along behind her, keeping to the next row of trees so she wouldn't see me. I knew I had to follow, but my feet felt like stone and I wanted nothing more than to fly home to Marnie and let her zip me inside her jacket the way she had when I was little. Up the gentle slope Ange walked, deeper into the orchard where the cherries hung so heavy and full I thought they would split their skins. When we could not see the gate and could not see my sister and could not see the houses or even the pines, she stopped. Slid open the hatch. Grabbed and twisted. Done.

She peeled away her gloves and shoved them in her pocket – she knew not to leave them at the scene – and then she took out her phone. 'Hey,' she said, 'sorry to bother you, but I've got another one. Would you mind?'

A few moments later I heard the motorbike, and then Rob appeared.

'You're racking up quite a tally,' he said, pulling a cherry off the nearest tree and throwing it in his mouth. 'Used to it now, eh?'

'Turns out it was easier than I thought,' said Ange.

He lifted the remains from the trap. The head swung like a dirty sock. Eyes dull as bottletops. 'Watch out,' he said. 'You'll be getting a taste for it.'

He'd left the bike running, and I remember I could feel it growling up through my feet. I remember, too, the way he rolled the cherry stone around in his mouth, stripping off every bit of flesh. Then he rode away, taking the remains with him.

I followed him up the gravel and past the house, the bike raising dust plumes, great mottled feathers that swelled and trembled and sank back to earth. A eucalyptus tree clattered in the breeze, the strips of bark hanging like dead skin. Rob walked to the edge of the gut hole where the air was rank and rotten, and when he threw in the remains I traced their broken-necked flight and knew I was to blame.

'Please stop calling,' I said to my sister. 'As a favour to me, your blood. Please stop.'

'Why?' she said. 'What did you see?'

'I saw . . .' I said. 'I saw . . .'

'What what what?'

I didn't know how to tell her. 'He was our cousin,' I said. 'Our blood.'

'Was?' she said. 'Was?'

I couldn't answer her.

'He'll be back to thank me.'

'Is that how it works? Have the others come back?'

She considered me with her right eye. 'Actually, no. It's very rude of them.'

'Why do you think they never come back?'

'Too busy with the pistachios and the mice, I expect.'

276 - CATHERINE CHIDGEY

I pushed at the latch on her cage with all my might, but I wasn't strong enough; it wouldn't move.

'What are you doing?' she said.

'Trying to let you go,' I said.

'You're just jealous. I call and they come.'

I forced myself to voice it then: the walk to the heart of the orchard where no one could see. The gloved hands around the neck. The head swinging like a dirty sock. The bottletop eyes.

'Socks?' she said. 'Bottletops? I have no idea what you're talking about. You're making up stories.'

'Why would I make up a story like that? Why?'

'Why? Why?' she echoed – and then, as I turned to leave, she said, 'All right. I'll stop.'

Later, at home on the couch, I heard the cries of my flock as they gathered at the gut hole. I pushed my head into the crook of Marnie's arm and whistled Blame It on the Rain, but she said, 'That won't shift the half-price calendars,' and carried me over to the Eye. Then, pressing the button on the black box, she turned it on.

CHAPTER TWENTY-SEVEN

The axeman's carnival was only a week away and Rob still needed to shave off the seconds: despite what his teammates said when they came around to practise, he wasn't a sure thing. It wasn't a foregone bloody conclusion. There were plenty of other axemen itching to get their hands on his trophy, his prize money, and he couldn't afford to let up.

'No more interviews,' he told Marnie. 'You're on your own – I'm under too much pressure.'

One hot morning, I watched him sharpen a practice axe on his father's grinder in the woolshed. The singing of the blade, the bright sparking seeds. The water to stop the edge from losing its temper. After he'd filed and stoned it – the strokes rasping like the breaths of the possums that crept across the roof at night – he set up the pine blocks in the back yard and began to chop, and I felt the blows slam through the air, displacing something. The bits of wood flew, a blizzard in midsummer, and he was a machine, a bloody machine, though he swore when the axe got stuck in a knot and he had to wrench it free, and he swore when one of his climbing boards fell out when he tried to ram it into the trunk, and when Marnie called him to come inside for morning tea he yelled that he had no time, that he was never fast enough, never good enough.

'Have you got anywhere else?' said the interviewer. 'Just that everyone's seen the front porch a few times now.' He was already motioning for his cameraman to follow him round the back of the house.

Marnie and I ran along behind.

'This'll work,' he said when he saw the coppery chickens that could not sing. 'If we can have you feeding them, with the bird sitting on your shoulder, yeah?'

'Okay,' said Marnie.

'Okay,' I said.

In the far corner of the yard Rob was swinging his axe, shaving off the seconds. Starting his climb up the side of his practice trunk, the board bowing under his weight.

'He'll need to stop that while we're filming,' said the interviewer. 'Although –' he glanced at the cameraman – 'yeah, let's get some footage of him too. Something for everyone.'

'He doesn't want to do interviews,' said Marnie. 'The carnival's next week. He's pretty busy training.'

'Oh he doesn't have to talk.'

The interviewer jogged over to Rob while the cameraman gave Marnie a tiny microphone to attach to her clothes.

'Here?' she said, pointing at her neckline.

'Your hair might be a problem,' said the cameraman. 'Probably best just in the middle there, but first you'll need to thread the cord down your top and – do you have a pocket?'

'No, sorry. Sorry, I'm getting all tangled up here.'

'Shall I . . . ?'

'Okay.'

He searched under her clothes for the cord, and plugged it into a small black box which he began to tuck inside her waistband, and my right eye saw his hands all over her and my left eye saw Rob red-fisted and furious and coming our way.

'Do you mind, mate?' he called as he strode across the yard, the hot nor'wester blowing, the axe head blazing in the sun.

I froze. Marnie froze. The interviewer waved his hands, ran a finger across his throat.

'Do you mind not groping my wife, mate?'

'It was my fault,' said Marnie. 'I got tangled up. He was just doing his job.'

'Some job.'

'I think there's been a misunderstanding, mate, yeah?' said the interviewer, but Rob said, 'You need to leave.'

'We won't take five minutes of your time. Be a shame to disappoint the fans.'

'I said you need to leave.'

Marnie pulled off the black box and the cord. 'Sorry,' she said. 'We're under a bit of pressure.'

'Don't fucking apologise to them,' said Rob.

'No, sorry,' she said, her hands shaking as she smoothed her top back down.

'Is everything okay?' the cameraman asked her.

Rob blew a sliver of pine from the blade of the axe. 'You need to get the fuck off my property,' he said. 'Mate.'

My right eye saw them leaving and my left eye saw the stumps all hacked to pieces.

Rob said, 'Go and put some proper clothes on. You'll get burnt.'

I should have noticed the edge in his voice. The sparks bursting and falling.

That night, when Marnie tucked me into bed, she said, 'It's fine, all right? Everything's fine.'

She wound up my ferris wheel and went to her own bedroom, the master bedroom, and as I lay listening to the music I thought I heard the old sounds coming through the wall. The raised voices. The thuds. Old Rob back again.

It's fine, all right? said the ghost of my mother. *Everything's fine.* She sang along to the ferris wheel, though I did not know how she had learned the tune. I closed my eyes and dreamed of Rob and Marnie in rubber bird masks, and when they pulled the masks away they were real birds underneath, and I knew that they loved me.

In the morning I slipped out through the cat door – meow – and watched the red sky: the Sun-Woman kindling her campfire and my flock singing to greet her. And I warbled a few small notes myself in the long shadows of the mountains.

I heard nothing from the orchard for three days. I thought my father would be pleased with me, proud of me, if he knew I was the one who'd silenced my sister. I decided to go to the pines to tell him: perhaps, I thought, he might even forgive me for leaving the flock.

I found him teaching his new children how to rub the sting from a wasp.

'What could happen if you ate it?' he said.

'It could stab us in our mouths,' they chorused.

'Who eats the sting?'

'Stupid birds who don't listen to their parents.'

'Do they deserve to suffer?'

'Yes, yes, they deserve to suffer.'

He gave no sign he had seen me watching from the border.

'Father,' I called, 'I asked my sister to stop luring birds and she has stopped luring birds.'

'Do you hear someone?' he said, and his new children said no, they heard nothing.

'Perhaps just a tumbling pebble,' said the first.

'Or a cicada,' said the second.

'Or a branch chafing another branch,' said the third.

'I saw what happened to my cousin,' I said. 'You were right, Father.'

He puffed his breast. 'If someone were here – someone who didn't belong, who thought he might win favour by admitting I was right – I would tell him I was not so easily bought.'

'I convinced her to be quiet,' I said. 'She has not called for three days.'

'Children,' he said, 'why do humans use call-birds?'

'To lure us, to trap us, to kill us,' they said.

'Why does the call-bird call?'

'For the food, the food.'

'What happens to a call-bird if she stops calling?'

'They kill her.'

'What?' I said.

'They kill her,' they repeated.

'Children,' said my father. 'Let me remind you: we do not speak to pebbles or cicadas or branches chafing other branches.'

'You told her to stop calling,' I said. 'Why didn't you mention the consequences? The cost?' I could hear my voice rising.

'If an outsider were here on our border,' he said, 'blabbering about a sister who was also an outsider, I would tell him she'd made her own bad choices.'

'She's your child,' I said.

'See how I have removed the sting entirely?' he said, nudging at the dead wasp. 'Now it is safe.'

'You're a monster,' I said.

'Do you know, children,' he said, 'I heard a story once. A bird who went to live with humans returned to his flock all high and mighty. Started accusing other birds, decent birds, of monstrousness – but he was the one living with the killers. Lying in the crooks of their arms. Accepting food from their very mouths.'

'Rob's no killer,' I said. 'He saves every single lamb he can. Plenty of farmers don't even bother; they just let them die. And if he hit my mother with his car – *if* he hit her – it was an accident, because accidents happen. And did he dispose of my cousin or did he grant him a burial, which is the human way?'

My father cackled. 'Oh the excuses he made, this high and mighty bird, when he had already seen inside the killing house. The blade, the blood. And still he stayed with the killers. Spoke to them in their own ugly tongue. Sat on their shoulders while they sang their primitive songs and danced their gawky dances.'

'You should see Marnie with the motherless lambs,' I said. 'She makes them beds in her own house and feeds them milk with her own hands.'

'Oh the tricky justifications this bird spouted!' he said. 'He was as blind as a hatchling. He watched them saving the lambs, fattening the lambs, and never thought to ask what they were saving them for. What they were fattening them for. Nor wonder, indeed, why they had saved him and why they were fattening him.'

'They love me,' I said. 'And I earn them money. And they love me.'

But my father was turning away, retreating into his territory, where I did not belong, and his children were following him.

My heart a cherry about to split.

'I've changed my mind, that's all,' said Marnie. 'I don't want to do it any more.'

'But we've been rehearsing for months,' said Ange. 'The costumes, the dance routine. The whole act.'

Marnie shrugged. 'Sorry.'

'You made a bandanna for a bird.'

'Sorry. It's Rob's big day. I've decided I shouldn't take that away from him.'

'You wouldn't be. I don't get it, Mar.'

She shrugged again, shoved a pair of Tama underpants into a mailer bag.

'You used to love singing. Performing. I was always jealous of your voice, if I'm honest. You could have really made it.'

Marnie stuck the address label to the bag and started on the next order.

'Has something happened?' said Ange.

The woman needed to leave us alone. Nothing had happened. Marnie had changed her mind and did not want to sing the song – that was all. Nothing had happened.

Ange began to cry then, but I knew they were crocodile tears. Snappity snap.

'It's just . . .' she sobbed. 'It's just . . .' She reached for Marnie with the hand that had killed in the evening, the hand that had wrung the neck with a sharp twist.

'Ange? What's the matter?'

A big shuddery breath. 'Nick barely touches me. I don't think he finds me attractive any more, after the baby . . .'

'You're gorgeous! Look at you!'

'I think I disgust him.'

'Don't say that.'

'It's true. I can see it in his eyes.'

More crocodile tears. Snappity snappity snap.

'So I thought . . .' she gulped, 'I thought if he could see me up on stage, in my sexy dress, doing my sexy moves . . .' Her fingers were digging into Marnie's forearm, refusing to let her go.

'Calm your tits,' I said.

Marnie gave one of her sad little smiles. 'I always thought you were the perfect couple. New house, new baby, making a go of the orchard.'

'You're not doing too badly yourselves,' said Ange, nodding at the stockroom's packed shelves.

'Lakshmi's organising a distributor. I shouldn't have taken it on. And all the people coming to the house . . .'

'But those are good things,' said Ange. 'Signs of your success. To be honest, I think Nick's a bit jealous.' She was still holding Marnie's arm, digging in, digging in. 'Anyway, he never looks at me the way Rob looks at you.'

'Which way is that?'

'Hungry.'

As if Marnie were live feed. As if Rob might gobble her up.

The ghosts of my brothers settled next to me on the shelf. *Wreck the room*, they sang. *Rip it apart. They are not your blood.*

I pushed a box of Tama keyrings to the floor.

More, they sang. *More more more.*

But Marnie was already picking up the keyrings, saying, 'Who's a clumsy boy?' and I was already throwing myself on my back, warbling *I'm sorry, I'm sorry.*

Are you one of us? sang my brothers. *Or are you one of them?*

'It's all accidental,' said Marnie. 'Our success. Tama's success. And who knows how long it'll last?'

'But the song can help,' said Ange. 'Footage like that – it'll still be getting hits years down the track. Like that husky saying I love you.' She threw back her head and howled at the cracked ceiling: 'I love yooou! I love yooooou!'

'I just feel uncomfortable about it,' said Marnie.

Tell her the sister is a killer, sang my brothers.

'Pre-show jitters,' said Ange. 'You'll be right as rain once we're out there.'

'Hmm. I don't know what Rob will say.'

'Go on. Go on.' She nudged Marnie's shoulder with her own.

'He's just been a bit irritable lately. He's giving up smoking.'

'Trust me, when he sees you up there, he'll know how lucky he is. Please?'

'You think he'll approve?'

'He'll bloody love it. A beautiful song, dedicated to him? What guy wouldn't love that?'

'What do you say, Tama? Shall we still do the act?'

Tell her the sister is a killer, sang my brothers.

I said, 'You're racking up quite a tally.'
Did you tell her? Did you tell her?
I said, 'Used to it now, eh?'
I said, 'Turns out it was easier than I thought.'
I said, 'Watch out. You'll be getting a taste for it.'
'Sounds like a yes to me,' said Ange.
'We *are* sounding good . . .'
'You know you want to.'
'If I say yes, will you let me get on with my work?'
'Cross my heart and hope to die.'
Tell her tell her tell her.
'All right, all right, yes. I surrender.'
My fault.

Marnie sighed to herself, scrolled through the pages of orders on the computer screen.

'Why did I think I could cope with all this, Tama?' she said. 'Why did I bring it into the house? I wanted my own little shop, but it's far too much for one person.'

She sat back in her chair, raised her arms above her head, stretched. Winced. And there on her bare trunk, where her T-shirt rode up, a patch of blue-black that spread like a thundercloud. I looked and she saw me looking. She said, 'Just a stupid accident – corner of the kitchen table. Ange is right about the song – it'll earn us money for years. As long as you play your part, Tama. We missed you so much when you were away. I used to come in here and press the wings on the Tama toys just to hear your voice, but Rob kept saying you'd come back, you had to come back. He'd go and stand on the porch every morning and call for you, and I saw him looking at the sky when he was out with the sheep, watching for you the way he watches for rain. I *know* it wasn't just the money. He hates the attention but he loves you, Tama. He adores you. We just need to ignore his bad moods – cut him a bit of slack. He's under a lot of pressure with all the interviews, and giving up smoking, and the carnival coming up too. Things will settle down again once he's won his trophy, I promise.'

And I believed her. Despite the blue-black at her white waist, despite the thuds through the wall of the master bedroom, despite the remains flung into the gut hole, I chose to believe her.

What use is a call-bird who doesn't call? If I let my sister remain silent, Ange would do away with her. If I told her to start calling again, Ange would keep killing our flock.

I went down to the gate on my own the next morning to perform for the followers, posing for their pictures while the Eyes watched us from the left and the right. I hung upside down; I lay on my back and passed a man's keys from foot to foot. I nibbled at a raisin offered on a child's sticky palm. I copied their voices. Then I began to move along the fence.

'Hey,' I said, edging my way towards the orchard.

The followers followed.

'Sorry to bother you,' I said, sidling further along the fence, 'but I've got another one.'

The followers followed.

'Would you mind?'

I took a few more steps and so did they.

And there was the trap in the first row of trees, and wedged up against it my sister's cage.

I flew to her, and the followers saw her then too.

'Oh my God, look!' they said, aiming their phones at us.

'It's not healthy. It's not natural,' I said.

'I haven't been calling,' whispered my sister. 'Who are they? What are you saying to them?'

'Let me do the talking,' I told her.

'Is it trapped?' said a bony woman in a Tama T-shirt. 'Tama, is that your friend?'

'The brother was devastated,' I said. 'You saw how he wept when he IDed the remains.'

'It can hardly move in there,' said the bony woman. 'Tama's asking for help.'

'I think God's telling us it's time,' I said.

'He's definitely asking for help,' said the man who owned the keys. He looked up and down Wilderness Road, then vaulted over the fence.

'We thought we could fix things,' I said.

'It's okay. It's okay,' the man murmured, approaching slowly, hands in the air like a perp giving himself up.

'God's helping us to understand captivity,' I said.

'Sure, that's right,' said the man. 'I'm just going to get a bit closer here . . . and a bit closer . . . and now I'm going to reach for the latch . . .'

Without warning, my sister jabbed her beak through the bars and pecked his fingertip. He snatched his hand away.

'What are you doing?' I said. 'He's trying to help!'

'Careful,' called the bony woman. 'It looks wild.'

'What did she say?' whispered my sister.

'That you look wild.'

'Oh I'm furious,' she whispered. 'They haven't fed me for two days. All the good stuff's going to waste.' She cocked her head at the bait in the trap, and out of nowhere the fantail appeared.

'Fat fat fat,' he said, flitting in and grabbing a chunk of food before darting away again.

In the meantime the man who owned the keys had covered his hand with his shirt and flicked open the latch. The cage door swung open. My sister just looked at it.

'Now what?' she whispered.

'Now you leave,' I said.

She stepped out of the cage. Shook her feathers. Eyed the followers and their food. The sticky-palmed child threw a raisin to her, and she gobbled it down. The followers applauded.

'I think they like me,' she said.

Another raisin. A bit of banana muffin. Gobble.

They were holding out their hands to her, calling to her, and she fluttered to the fence and began to strut back and forth.

'Say something!' said the bony woman.

'What does that mean?' my sister asked me.

'She wants you to talk.'

'I am talking.'

'They can't understand you.'

'They like me, though. They *love* me.'

'You need to get out of here,' I said. 'For your own good.'

'I think they're having a conversation,' said the man with the keys.

'I wonder what they're talking about,' said the bony woman.

'What are they talking about?' said my sister.

'How much meat you have on your bones,' I said.

'What?'

'Whether they'll cook you whole or in pieces.'

'What what?'

'Which of them gets to eat the breast, which is the tenderest.'

'Is that true?'

'About the breast?'

'What they're saying!'

'Why do you think they're trying to fatten you up?'

She backed away then, beginning to call a distress call, but I knew no one from the flock would come to help her. When a follower threw a piece of sausage roll she took to the air, and I watched her disappear down Wilderness Road. She would have to find her own territory; the flock wouldn't take her back.

I never saw her again.

It was for her own good.

I ate the sausage roll.

CHAPTER TWENTY-EIGHT

On the day of the axeman's carnival Rob drank three raw eggs for breakfast. He cracked them open with one hand on the rim of the glass and gulped them down, the yolks disappearing inside him like three glossy suns.

'I feel a bit sick,' said Marnie as his Adam's apple bobbed in his throat.

'I feel a bit sick,' I said.

She put on a long, loose dress that would keep her from burning.

'I'll make my own way there,' she told Rob. 'You'll want to stay later – celebrate your win with the boys.'

'Don't jinx it,' said Rob.

He was pacing back and forth, as restless as Brian Holmes stuck inside his magpie mask.

'Don't forget to keep yourself hydrated.'

'I know I know.'

'Am I allowed to wish you luck?'

'No.'

'Well, I'll be proud of you whatever the outcome.'

'Just stop talking, okay?'

Marnie and I rode to the showgrounds on the motorbike; she knew better than to try the car with me again. I sat on her shoulder as we set off down the stretch of gravel to Wilderness Road and we whooshed along as fast as flying, the wind flooding past my folded wings. From the silent orchard the dummy birds watched with their shining eyes. Not real. A trick.

'See you soon,' she called to Ange, who raised her hand in a friendly wave as if she had never said *Trust me, it's kinder.* As if she meant us no harm.

The showgrounds smelled of trampled dirt and fried food. Children bit at woolly wisps of pink rammed onto sticks and jostled one another for a turn inside a wobbling castle filled with air. They queued to have their faces painted, disguising themselves as wild animals; they watched a man pull coloured scarves from his pocket and coins from behind their ears; they burst from a haunted house, squealing about bodies that rose from the ground and bodies that hung from the ceiling. On a small stage a man with a guitar sang of drinking his baby off his mind; behind him a table stood piled with prize ribbons and the golden axe Rob was there to win. A dog wove through the crowd, trailing its leash, and a woman ground sunscreen into her freckled arms, turning them chalky white. Every so often a voice spoke from nowhere, ringing out metallic and shivery as if it were trapped in a grain silo, and I thought that it must have been God, because it told us what to do. It said *Let's give a big southern welcome to Darren, our very own Johnny Cash.* It said *Just a reminder for everyone: smoking is prohibited anywhere within the showgrounds.* It said *Listen up, folks: we have a lost child. A little girl in a blue T-shirt who doesn't know her name.* It said *Any under sixteens still wanting to enter the Boys' Chop, make sure you sign up in plenty of time.*

At the centre of it all was the arena where the logs, stripped of their bark, peeled to uniform size, shrink-wrapped in plastic to keep the moisture in and the grit out, waited for the axemen. Ange, Nick and Barbara had saved a spot for us just behind the cordon, where the baby kept pulling off its sunhat – and there was Rob, standing over by the competitors' tent with his relay team, each man dressed in his white trousers and black singlet. Arms crossed over their chests, they surveyed the grounds, nodded at other men. One of the shearers – the one with no hair – stopped for a word with Chin Scar, who gestured at the sky, the white-hot sun. I remember seeing the shearer who'd crushed his hand in the wool-press, too; he was eating a hotdog, right as rain, but when he went to lick his fingers I noticed the space where his pinky used to be. He walked right past Rob without a nod, without a glance.

Not long now till the first heat in the Underhand Chop, said the voice that must have been God. *I don't know about you, but I can't wait to hear the bite of the axe on wood. And another friendly reminder, folks: no smoking whatsoever. This place is bone dry.*

The axemen drew lots for their logs, then carried them to their cradles. They unwrapped them, secured them in place. They cut their footholds at either end. Made their chalk marks. Climbing on top, they rolled their shoulders, tilted their heads backwards and forwards and side to side. Took practice swings, stopping just short of the wood.

Axemen, you're in the starter's hands, said God, and I looked around for this starter, these hands. *Axemen, stand to your logs*, God continued. *Oh, one, two, three, four* . . . And there was no starter and there were no hands, just God, and I saw him then, a man with a microphone, standing on the far side of the arena in a towelling hat.

The chips began to fly and the crowd called and cajoled. 'Come on, Hunter! Go hard! You can do it, Manaia! Full power now!'

God said *They're in amongst it! I'd say Shaun Tennant got the jump a little bit there, but Manaia King's not far behind. Watch out! Look out! It's all happening. We've got the TV guys here so I want to hear some noise, folks! And Shaun is round the back now and he's burying that blade in deep. Manaia turns now too, he's opening up the back, he's giving it heaps, but will it be enough? Hunter Buchanan's round as well, and Cody Jankowska, but Shaun's going for it, and yes! He's through, and that's a good chop for Shaun Tennant, and he'll be pleased with that. What you can see now is the referee inspecting the logs to rule out any funny business, and then he'll lock in the result.*

When it was Rob's turn in the Underhand heats he ran his hands over his block's pale surface, then secured it in the cradle and cut his footholds. He marked in red chalk where he would aim, and rubbed the handle of his axe with chalk too. Chin Scar stood poised on a log next to him; Ethan bloody McKay was just in front. God began the count again: *Oh, one, two . . .* The slower, newer axemen started first, while those more experienced waited for him to reach their handicap number. Rob was the last to swing his axe. I could see the force of the blows travelling up his arms, juddering through his neck, his gritted face, but the other men were far ahead of him.

'Pick it up, pick it up,' muttered Marnie.

'Maybe he's saving his strength,' said Ange.

'Come on Rob, ya mongrel!' yelled Barbara. 'Show us what you're made of!'

God said *And the timber's really hurtling now! Watch out! If that doesn't get your blood pumping I don't know what will. Jase Kamo's making a nice clean job of it, but newcomer Ethan McKay's giving him a run for his money, and they've both turned already, followed by Dean Baird. And here comes reigning king Rob Veldman, and he's one of our finest cutters, but it's looking a bit doughy there for him and he's got a lot of work to do with those big arms. Ethan's streaking ahead and he knows he's got to keep up the pressure, and look at him go! The power of these men! You wouldn't want to get on their bad side, that's for sure. And Rob's catching up now, he's on fire, and I can't call it! I can't tell! It looks like he's tied for first place with Ethan McKay, and we'll check the video footage to be sure about that.*

A surprise finish there, folks, but you never know how the wood's going to behave on the day.

Ethan bloody McKay tried to shake hands, I remember, and I thought Rob would rip his arm off.

'Good chop,' called Nick.

Rob walked over to us, still scowling. 'That was an abortion,' he said.

'You're through, though,' said Marnie. 'Don't let it put you off.'

'It's a bad omen.'

'No such thing as bad omens,' said Barbara. 'Just people looking for excuses.'

'Okay, Mum,' said Marnie.

For the Underhand semi-final he entered the arena without even glancing in our direction.

'Goodness,' said Barbara, 'I've never seen him so worked up.'

The count began, and one by one the axemen started to cut. God said *They're all in the game now, ladies and gents, and Shaun Tennant's found some dirty timber. He's not happy about it but that's the luck of the draw. Rob Veldman's into it hard, he's found his rhythm quick smart and he's punching through the block with Isaac Tupuola hot on his heels, but Rob's stretching it out to a reasonable lead, and he's around in ten hits! What's he going to do on the back? The heart's heaving, the lungs are burning, the arms are swinging, and let's hear you yell, folks! Let's make some noise! Ryan Cessford's doing his best to catch up and Shaun's digging deep, he's no slouch, but it's Big Rob thumping away, massive chunks coming out! He's got the run on the others. And he's done it! He's done it!*

'That's more like it!' screamed Barbara.

The referee inspected the logs to rule out any funny business.

'You're hitting your stride now,' said Marnie. 'You'll be fine.'

'Early days,' said Rob. 'I'm up against Ethan bloody McKay

in the final.' He looked at me. 'What's that doing here, by the way?'

'Exactly,' said Barbara.

'Moral support?' said Marnie.

'No such thing as bad omens,' I said.

While we waited for the final I posed for selfies with members of the crowd, and then once again God started the count – and once again Rob lagged behind. Ethan bloody McKay was gouging into his block as if it were butter. From across the arena his wife shouted, 'Oh God Ethan you're incredible. Do it! Oh God! Oh God!'

But God couldn't hear her. He said *And here they come, fighting it out! The timber's flying, folks, and are you ready to shout? Are you ready to scream? They're burying those axes deep as you like, straight into the heart. A little bit of stick in the log for Rob Veldman, and he's neck and neck with twenty-year-old Ethan McKay as they both go round to open up the back. Isaac Tupuola's slamming through, slamming through hard. Mitch Harland and Isaac round now too. Rob and Ethan are demolishing the pine, and look at the power in those blows, the depth, they know exactly what they're doing and they're setting a blistering time. Rob tries to finish with a ferocious swing but the log's not ready, and the veteran axeman can't quite match the speed and strength of the new blood, and it's looking like Ethan – and yes, Ethan McKay takes the Underhand Chop title.*

Rob threw down his axe and yelled, 'His log was fucking rigged!'

The referee strode over to him. 'Let me remind you, Mr. Veldman, of the rules: you must not use crude or abusive language. Another outburst like that and you're disqualified. Do you understand?'

'Yeah,' muttered Rob.

The referee inspected the logs then, as usual, and as usual they weren't fucking rigged.

'So has he lost the trophy?' whispered Nick.

Marnie shook her head. 'It's calculated on points, so as long as he does well in his other events . . .'

Rob came over and grabbed the water bottle she held out to him. Drained it in a few gulps. Headed for the competitors' tent.

Next up is the Single Saw, said God. *While they're getting ready, let's hear from Amber Hailes, just back from the yodelling championships in Tasmania, Australia.*

Tasmania, Australia, where the first magpies came from. The clever magpies who propped up the sky so all the creatures of the earth could stand and walk and fly. And she sounded a bit like a magpie too, Amber Hailes, her voice darting from low to high and back again, seeming to sing two notes at once. Nestled on Marnie's lap, smelling her smell, I closed my eyes and had a little sleep, and I dreamed that I followed the Sun-Woman all the way to the edge of the world.

When I woke, Rob was competing in the Standing Chop final, and Marnie, Barbara, Nick and Ange were cheering him on.

'Watch out!' I yelled. 'Look out!'

'Finish him!' screamed Barbara.

God said *I don't know what Rob had for breakfast, but he's eating up the timber! They're all into it, they're making quick work of it. Look out, folks, we've got champions in the arena and it's a real competition now. Ethan and Rob are round the back, and Manaia and Jase not far behind. Somebody call the fire brigade, these guys are lighting matches! It's going to be a quick race. Will it be Ethan, or reigning champion Rob? They going toe to toe, blow for blow! A little fumble by Ethan, he's a great cutter, he knows what's required to bring him back in the race, but he can't catch up now! And there's a shake and a rattle in the block . . . and yes! Down it comes! And that's a great finish for Rob, and Rob Veldman takes the Standing Chop. Remember we've got the TV guys here filming, so take a look at the box tonight – you might even see yourself.*

As Rob grabbed the water bottle from Marnie, she noticed a nick on the back of his hand. Blood trickling down his forearm.

'You've hurt yourself,' she said.

He peered at it, shrugged. 'It's nothing.'

'You should get it cleaned. Covered up.'

'Can't even feel it.'

Little spots of blood on his white trousers too.

He sat with us to watch the next event: the Jack and Jill. The competitors worked in pairs to saw through a thick log, a man at one end of the saw and a woman at the other, and they pushed and pulled in unison until they'd sliced off a perfect disc, a wooden moon.

And look at those ladies go! said God. *They're keeping up with the men all right, they're giving it heaps, you wouldn't credit it, and there's acres of timber being cut here today, folks.*

'You could have entered that, Mar!' said Ange.

'Don't be silly,' said Barbara, looking the female competitors up and down. Their powerful arms; their singlets and white trousers, the same as the men. 'At any rate, it's nice they involve the lesbians.'

We'll take a break for lunch now, ladies and gents, said God. *Make sure you try one of my wife's legendary mutton pies – last year they sold out in fifteen minutes. Here to entertain us is Jimmy Parata all the way from Gore . . .*

'When are you girls doing your thing?' said Barbara.

'What?' said Nick.

'What?' said Rob.

'Oh, Marnie and I wanted to go through the haunted house,' said Ange.

Nick said, 'I'll get us all some lunch, shall I? My treat.'

Rob was jiggling his leg, tapping his fingers.

'Looks like somebody needs a smoke,' said Barbara. 'It's a bit miserable, isn't it. Soon they won't even let us light up on our own property.'

'I should go see how the boys are doing,' said Rob. 'We need to talk strategy for the relay.'

When he and Nick had left, Ange said, 'Well done, Mum. You just about ruined the surprise.'

'Goodness me, Kaden,' said Barbara, tickling the baby's belly, 'your mummy's in a bit of a grump. Yes she is! Yes she is! Nobody likes a grumpy grump.'

They listened to the man all the way from Gore sing about knowing when to hold 'em and knowing when to fold 'em. Ethan bloody McKay's wife was dancing, eyes closed, hair falling over her face.

'So you're okay to video us, right, Mum?' said Ange. 'You're clear on which button to press?'

'I'm not retarded, Angela,' said Barbara.

'Make sure you start it *before* we come on stage.'

'Shh,' said Marnie. Nick was back.

'Dig in,' he said. 'I got hotdogs, chips and pies. And this is for you, buddy.' He gave the baby a mangled balloon.

'What's that meant to be?' said Ange.

'I asked for a cat,' said Nick.

'Meow,' I said.

'It looks like a haemorrhoid,' said Barbara.

A girl disguised as a tiger dashed past us, chasing a boy disguised as a bear. The man all the way from Gore was singing about knowing when to walk away and knowing when to run. While the others ate their lunch, Marnie fed me some pumpkin seeds and the baby tried to eat the balloon cat.

'No, darling. Dirty. Dirty,' said Barbara. She nudged it with her foot and it bounced along the ground, then lifted into the air.

I looked at it with my right eye, looked at it with my left eye.

Flew at it and popped a leg. Popped another leg. And another. The baby began to cry.

'Tama!' said Marnie. 'Stop that!'

But I didn't want to. It felt even better than popping the roll of bubble wrap in the stockroom.

'Grab him!' said Barbara. 'Do something!'

Pop went the neck. Pop went the bulbous eyes, the sausagey tail.

'Control him!' shouted Barbara.

Too late: the balloon cat was just a rubber rag.

'Awww, it's okay, buddy,' said Nick. 'I'll get you another one, eh?'

'That was amazing,' said Ange.

The baby screamed and screamed. I lay on my back, passed a hot chip from claw to claw.

'Tama, that wasn't very nice,' said Marnie. 'Sorry, guys. I'll replace it.'

'And what if he'd attacked *Kaden*?' said Barbara.

'But he didn't.'

'But he might have. He's completely unpredictable.'

The boy disguised as a bear ran roaring past, chasing the girl disguised as a tiger.

'If you want to do the haunted house, you'd better get cracking,' said Nick. 'Rob's on again at one thirty.'

'Right,' said Marnie. 'The haunted house.' She looked at Ange.

'Good idea,' said Barbara. 'I think we'd appreciate a break from the bird.'

'Come on, then,' said Ange. 'Bit of fun.'

It had a sagging wooden porch just like ours. We sat in a little carriage that moved along a little track – not a car, said Marnie; nothing like a car – and the front door opened and we were inside. It was so dark I couldn't see a thing. 'Too late to turn back now,' a voice boomed, and laughed. To our left the lights flashed on and off, and we saw a bloodied man chained inside a cage, shaking the bars and screaming. Marnie jumped. Another cage to our right held a fleshless woman, also scream- ing, her grey hair blowing across her bony face.

'I don't like this,' said Marnie.

'Too late to turn back now,' said Ange.

Something rattled and clicked above us: a dangling skele- ton, its toes all but touching Marnie's head. She flailed her hands about the way she had when my father attacked her, and Ange took her photo. Gravestones loomed up at us, like the ones I'd seen when I flew home after my abduction. I could feel Marnie trembling. The flashing lights showed a picture on the wall: a framed photograph of a family in old-fashioned clothes. It swung to the side and rats hissed in the hole behind it, their red eyes glowing. Marnie let out a shriek and Ange said, 'I don't know what's more entertaining – you or the ride!' *Whooooooooo*, said the children disguised as wild animals in the carriage behind us. We passed a dining table where skele- tons sat at a decayed feast. The floorboards began to tilt and lift, and a buried man rose up out of the ground, swinging an axe. Marnie shrieked again, and Ange took her photo again. As we headed for the exit a woman's body dropped from the ceil- ing, the chest cut open and the ribs splayed, all her insides on view like the women on Rob's crime show. Then we were back in the daylight.

'Oh my God, look at you!' said Ange. 'Since when have you been so jumpy?'

Marnie crouched down, her breath coming in gulps.

'There's that bird off Twitter,' said a woman in a sundress that was too tight for her. 'Say something. Go on.'

'It's not a good time,' said Ange.

'Well excuse *me*,' said the woman. 'Just making conversation.' Her son, who was disguised as a shark, showed me all his teeth.

'Mar. Mar,' said Ange. She touched her on the shoulder, and Marnie jumped again. 'Hey – newsflash. None of that stuff was real.'

'Stupid idea,' said Marnie. 'Stupid. Stupid.'

God announced the start of the Tree Felling Event then, so we went back to the arena to cheer Rob on. He made it through the heats and the semi-finals, just, and when he returned for the final he stood at the base of the trunk he had to climb, his riverstone eyes fixed on the table of prizes waiting on the stage, the blood on his forearm dried to a dark vein.

'You can do it,' shouted Barbara. 'Can he do it?' she asked Marnie.

'I hope so.'

We watched him scaling the tree, balancing on the flexing board as he swung his axe.

'Makes your heart stop,' said Barbara.

The entire crowd was on its feet and yelling, so I yelled too: 'I'm not retarded! Nobody likes a grumpy grump! It looks like a haemorrhoid!'

The TV camera followed Rob's climb and God said *Always a crowd pleaser, this event, with the element of danger adding to the excitement, and I've seen a few men fall, ladies and gents. And look at those boards bending under the competitors' feet: one false move and it's all over, and Rob knows that, he's the heaviest of the finalists. Ethan makes it to the top first, and that guy's got some guts, every hit he's flinging the timber out and the tree's rocking round all over the show. Rob's at the top now too, and he's going after Ethan, he's making some aggressive moves here. I tell you what, he's hungry for timber! He's eating it. He's aggressive. And look at his face, he's got his game face on. But the newcomer's not going to be beaten easily. And down they come to start on the other side just as Shaun and Manaia make it to the top. It looks like a two-man race now, folks, and there's almost nothing in it. Ethan and Rob are cutting those wedges and climbing those trees as if their lives depended on it. Up they go, the twenty-year-old still in front, but Rob's chasing him hard. If you've got a scream in you, give it up right now for these guys. They're on the home stretch and it looks like Ethan's going to take it, and here comes the wobble on the block – and it's down! And oh boy did those guys go head to head, but young Ethan McKay has eclipsed the competition to win the Tree Felling. Good chop.*

Rob strode out of the arena.

'Shit,' said Marnie.

'Is that it, then?' said Ange, pushing the baby's sunhat back on its head.

Marnie twisted and untwisted her fingers. 'If he wins the Hard Hit, he should still win the trophy. Relay points don't count. If he loses the Hard Hit, it's all over. Shit.'

'I think it's sweet you care so much about it,' said Ange. 'Hey, can you show me where the toilets are?'

Their secret code: it was time to get ready for our act.

In the ladies' room Marnie and Ange zipped each other up and stood side by side in front of the mirror, their costumes glittering.

'I don't know why I'm doing this,' said Marnie.

'Because you love me?' said Ange. 'Because it's fun?'

'I don't know how I let you convince me. I feel sick.'

'You'll be fine once we're out there.'

Marnie stuffed her sunhat and her long, loose dress into her bag. She and Ange pinned up their hair and began to apply their makeup, colouring in their faces with face-coloured paste. They drew on their lips and eyes, made their bones stand out.

Ange reached inside her costume and pushed up her breasts. 'You never used to get nervous when we were little.'

'Didn't I?' Marnie draped my bandanna around my neck and fastened it at the back.

'Don't you remember? You couldn't wait to sing for people.'

'I suppose so. But Rob—' She held a hand to her mouth.

'Are you okay?'

Marnie rushed into one of the cubicles and vomited.

'Hey, are you okay? It's just a song, Mar. Just one song.'

Outside, God had started the team relay. I could hear the crowd shouting, the blows beginning to fall.

'I think I'm pregnant,' said Marnie.

By the time we'd made our way to the wings at the side of the stage, Rob's team had won the relay. I inched forward and peered out at the crowd: I could see him sitting next to Nick, gulping a bottle of water. *Now we're going to hear from two of our prettiest songbirds*, said God – and there he was, the man with a microphone, standing next to the table of ribbons. He peered at a clipboard. *Let's welcome Ange and Marnie to the stage, and special guest Tommy the magpie!*

'Thanks, Mar,' whispered Ange. 'I need this.'

The crowd began to cheer as we walked out; some of the men whistled, and Ange did a little shimmy.

'Niiiiiiice,' shouted a man near the front.

'Smokin' hot,' shouted another.

'Hi everyone,' said Ange. 'We wanted to surprise—'

But the men were in full voice now, calling, carolling. 'I like your dresses – they'd look awesome on my bedroom floor. Wanna see my baby elephant? Wanna see my hairy canary? I've got some wood for you, girls. Hey! I said I've got some wood for you! My name's Justin – remember that so you can scream it later. How do you like your meat? Hey girls! *Girls!* What's your favourite – standing or underhand? Nice legs, what time do they open? Are you free tonight, or will it cost me?'

I could see Rob sitting up. Slowly wiping his mouth with the back of his hand.

All right, all right, settle down, said God.

'Thanks everyone,' said Ange. 'We wanted to surprise our husbands with a bit of an act we've been working on. This is for you, Nick and Rob.'

She and Marnie started to sing, and I played my part like a good boy, pecking Marnie's cheek on cue just as I was supposed to. *I love you, a bushel and a peck* (peck)*, a bushel and a peck* (peck) *and a hug around the neck . . .*

Barbara was videoing us on Ange's phone, mouthing every word of the song, *a barrel and a heap and I'm talking in my sleep . . . yes a mess of happiness . . . it beats me all to heck how I'll ever tend the farm*, and the TV camera was pointed at us too, and Nick was punching Rob on the shoulder: 'Yeah! That's my girl!' The other men kept up their calls too, even after we'd finished: 'Those are some awesome oral talents! Take a bow! Lower! Lower!'

I could see Nick clapping, cupping his hands round his lips to let out a howl. Rob was clapping too, but I didn't like the look on his face. Hard eyes, hard mouth. I didn't like it at all.

When we came off stage and wove back through the crowd to him, the women grabbed at me but the men grabbed at Marnie and Ange, pressing up against them, snatching at thigh and buttock and breast so fleetingly it seemed accidental.

'Well?' said Ange, doing her little shimmy for Nick. 'What did you think?'

'You were incredible,' he said. 'God, look at you both. We're lucky men, eh Rob?'

'Lucky all right,' said Rob. Hard eyes. Hard mouth.

The TV camera found us again and watched us with its blank black eye.

'Did you like it?' said Marnie, searching Rob's face.

'Sure,' he said.

'Really?'

'Loved it.' He kissed her cheek.

'Oh go on, give her a proper kiss,' said Barbara, still video-ing us on Marnie's phone, but Rob glanced at the TV camera and the phone and said, 'Yeah, I'd rather keep that private.'

'Look out tonight then, Mar!' said Ange.

Well folks, said God, *it's almost time for the last event of the carnival: the Hard Hitting Contest. Competitors, kindly make your way to the arena.*

Off Rob went without a word.

'He's just nervous,' said Marnie. 'He has to win this.'

And I should have said something. I should have warned her about Rob's eyes, Rob's mouth. How could she not have noticed?

'Told you he'd love it,' said Ange, and Marnie smiled, nod-ded.

Then she took her phone from Barbara and tweeted the video of our act.

Eight men were competing in the Hard Hit, and one by one they took their turns.

This event's a little bit different, said God. *Each man has two minutes to cut through his block, underhand, and the man who can do it in the least number of blows is the winner. A real test of strength, folks. First up is Jase Kamo.*

Chin Scar climbed onto his log, and as he chopped, the crowd counted the blows along with God. *One, two, three, four . . .*

Rob didn't count. He wasn't even watching Chin Scar: he was watching Marnie. Hard eyes. Hard mouth.

Twenty-two! said God. *Based on his other events he won't claim the Golden Axe, but will he claim the Hard Hit title? Let's see what the other competitors have in them.*

'I think I'm burning,' said Marnie, squinting at the sky. 'I need to change.'

'No time,' said Barbara. 'You might miss Rob.'

Marnie took her long, loose dress from her bag and pulled it on over her costume. Ange pushed the baby's sunhat back on its head. The children disguised as wild animals were lolling on their parents' laps, their face paint smeared and flaking away.

Next up is Ethan McKay, said God, *and at the moment he is the man to beat. If he wins this event, he takes home the Golden Axe – the youngest competitor to win it in the history of the carnival.*

Still Rob kept his eyes on Marnie.

Ethan bloody McKay needed only eighteen hits to break his log in two; when it split between his feet he stepped off as lightly as a dancer.

He's annihilated it, said God, *and would you look at the carnage? Timber all over the show. This is poplar they're cutting, folks, which can be a trickier wood than pine – the roots draw silt up into the heart of the tree, making it abrasive on the axe, taking the edge off, but clearly that was no problem for young Ethan.*

Rob had to wait until last, and as he walked to his log he looked away from Marnie and up at the hot bright sky.

Our reigning champion, folks, said God. *Rob Veldman, the proud owner of nine consecutive Golden Axes. Yes, you heard me correctly: no one has beaten this man in nine years, and he's on a mission to make it ten. He'll be gunning for it now. No doubt that he's a fearsome opponent, but he's been a bit off form today, so let's see what he's got left in the tank.*

'Come on, Rob!' shouted Ange.

'Make us proud,' shouted Barbara.

'Nice legs!' I shouted. 'What time do they open?'

Rob glanced over at me.

'Wanna see my baby elephant?' I shouted. 'Wanna see my hairy canary?'

Rob shot another look at me. Gripped the chalky handle of his axe. Hard eyes. Hard mouth.

Then the count began, and everyone was calling out the number of blows – everyone but me.

'How do you like your meat?' I yelled. 'Are you free tonight, or will it cost me?'

I knew he could hear me; he lifted the axe and plunged it down deep into the wood, lifted it and smashed it down. Slashed through all the silt in the heart, blunting the blade with every hit, but that didn't stop him, nothing could stop him, and he would have chopped with the handle if he had to. In eight blows he had turned to start on the other side, and in sixteen blows he was through.

And what a comeback from Rob Veldman! said God. *He buried that axe! He set it alight! The aggression! The power! I don't know what got into him, but he brought his A-game. He's broken his own record, he's broken the local record, and he's left everyone else for dead.*

'Oh thank God,' said Marnie. 'Thank God.'

'Do you want a lift home?' said Nick. 'We can pick the bike up tomorrow.'

'Tama won't get in the car,' said Marnie. 'I'll be fine.'

Barbara was holding the Golden Axe, making little practice swings. 'I could get the hang of this,' she said. 'Rob, you'll have to give me some lessons.'

'Yep,' he said.

'So I'll see you at home later?' said Marnie. 'We're all so proud of you. But give me a ring if you need me to come and get you – if you end up celebrating a bit too much. Or get a ride with Jase. Okay?'

'Yep,' he said.

Do make sure you take all your belongings with you, said God. *Let's be tidy Kiwis.*

People were folding picnic blankets, picking up their rubbish. A boy yawned and slumped over his mother's shoulder. Rubbed away his wolf eyes. The children were turning back into children, and God was just a man with a microphone.

CHAPTER TWENTY-NINE

I should have known when I saw Rob's car swerve through the gate on Wilderness Road. It wove across the gravel, all over the show, and then he was stumbling up the front steps to the open door. In his fist the tenth Golden Axe.

'What are you, the fucking butler?' he said as he pushed his way past me and inside the house. 'Where is she?' The drink hot and bitter on his breath. All the prize ribbons trembling on the walls.

Marnie came running when she heard the door. She'd taken off the long, loose dress but she still wore her costume for him and she threw her arms around his neck, kissed him on the cheek. 'You did it!' she said. 'I'm so proud of you! Can I have another look?' And she held out her hand for the axe.

Get out get out get out, sang the ghosts of my brothers.

Rob slammed the front door and shoved at her, and she fell into the living room, and I should have swooped him, I should have flown into the small gap between them. I should have tried to catch her – tried at least to cushion her fall. All those things I should have done. Instead I flew to the couch. Flew to the mantelpiece. Flew to the coffee table where Marnie's phone lay, the followers still talking about our act. *Get out get out get out.*

'Rob, please, I don't—' Marnie started to say, but he grabbed at her costume, hauled her to her feet. The shoulder seam ripped open.

'What are you even meant to be?' he said. 'Because you look like a whore.'

'A cowgirl,' said Marnie, her voice shaking. 'We were cowgirls.'

I crept towards the black box on the bookshelves in the corner of the room.

'Oh right,' he said. 'Cowgirls always have their tits out. Just like the cows.' He laughed, staggered. Grabbed at her costume again to steady himself, tearing a hole at the waist. 'Didn't even know it was you at first, walking onto the stage. Didn't even recognise you. Hair up, tits out. I thought, who are these sluts? Then I realise it's my wife. And it's not just the locals who can see her tits – she wants to show the whole fucking world.'

I crept closer to the black box.

'Ange and Mum came up with the dresses,' Marnie said all in a rush. 'I told Mum not to make them so short. So low-cut. I tried, Rob, I really tried—' Her fingertips on his chest as if she might be able to push him away, but he'd had a skinful, a gutsful, and he was stronger than ever.

'They didn't hold a gun to your head.' He flicked her hand away. 'But someone should.'

'You're scaring me, Rob. Don't talk like that.'

The ghosts of my brothers sat in the fireplace and sang fit to burst, and in the small hard space they sounded louder than a whole flock. *Leave her, leave her behind, return to your blood, get out.* I pressed the button on the black box. Turned on the Eye.

Rob waved the Golden Axe in Marnie's face. 'Know what this means now?'

She shook her head.

'Nothing. Zero. Might as well chuck it in the gut hole.' He staggered again.

On Marnie's phone screen the faces started to pile up. All the followers. All the faces of the followers, talking their heads off.

'That's not true, Rob! You won, you won, you got what you wanted—'

He knocked her into the wall and roared like an animal, and the entire house rattled as if it might collapse. All the rotten wood giving way at last.

Marnie held her hands over head. 'I wanted to tell you something,' she said. 'I think I'm pregnant.'

'Yeah right,' he said. 'How convenient.'

And yes: one of the women on his crime show had told her perp she was having his baby but he found out it was a lie, a dirty lie, and she got what was coming to her.

Rob fell silent. Swayed from foot to foot. In the corner on the bookshelves the Eye watched, and on the phone the faces multiplied. The ghosts of my brothers held their breath.

I shook my feathers. Opened my mouth. 'What are you even meant to be?' I said.

Rob roared again, flung the Golden Axe at me. 'That fucking bird,' he yelled as I skittered out of the way. 'It's all gone to shit since you let that thing in the house.'

He had no idea the Eye was on, open. No idea everyone could see. He lunged for me, grabbed me round the neck, but I twisted free and left him holding only my bandanna. The little square of cloth in his hand enraged him still more, and he seized the coal shovel from beside the fireplace and started swatting at me. 'Who dresses a fucking magpie up, anyway?' *Smash.* 'It's a wild animal.' *Smash.* 'And a fucking curse.' *Smash.* 'Nothing but bad luck.' *Smash.* Cracks in the coffee table. Cracks in the floorboards. Cracks in the walls.

'Leave him, Rob, please, please,' Marnie begged, then lowered her voice to a whisper. 'Think of the money.'

'It's not about the fucking money.' *Smash.*

She tried to stop him; once or twice she even managed to grab the end of the coal shovel, but he wrenched it from her and kept going. 'I'll flatten him,' he yelled, his words all spit and slur. *Smash.* 'I'll flatten the smug fucker.' *Smash.* The ghosts of my brothers jumped at every blow, little grey puffs that rose and fell in the fireplace and sang *Why don't you leave? Why don't you leave leave leave?*

I flew to the curtain rail, too high for him to reach, and he went for Marnie then, ripping her costume apart, his fists finding all her softnesses. Her nose bled and her mouth bled and I remember her calling, 'Tama! Tama!' and I knew she wanted me to save her, was begging me to save her, but I was too small; I was no match for him and his axeman's arms full of blood from his win. And I watched from above as if from the branch of a tree, and his hands were around her neck, her pretty neck, trapping her voice in her throat. When he let go, she fell to the floor and her nose bled and her mouth bled and she lay there in her torn dress like one of the beautiful dead women on his crime show. Then he started kicking her in the ribs, and she rolled herself up tight, as tight as a chick in an egg, and cried for me.

All I had was my voice. 'Licence and registration, please, sir,' I said, but it made no difference. 'Step out of the car please, sir. Open the trunk please, sir. Open the trunk. Open the trunk.'

'Shut up!' Rob yelled, and kept kicking, and he would crack her, I knew he would crack her.

Why don't you leave? sang the ghosts of my brothers as if their lives depended on it.

'The suspect is heading east on foot,' I said. 'Do not approach. Over.'

'Jesus, shut up!' he yelled again. Marnie had stopped moving, and he prodded her with his toe. 'Nothing to say for yourself?' he slurred.

'Male Caucasian, mid-thirties,' I said. 'Armed and dangerous. Over.'

'I wasn't talking to you!'

'Over. Over. Over.'

'Shut the fuck up!'

I looked at Rob with my right eye, looked at him with my left eye. Edged along to the far end of the rail. Then I said, 'We have a two-four-five in progress, corner of Lincoln and Maple. Request backup. Repeat, request backup. Do you copy?'

In three strides he was at the window. He grasped the curtains and began to tug on them, and I felt my claws juddering on the rail, then slipping. 'Do you copy?' I said. 'Do you copy? Over.' The fabric made a snapping sound with every tug: tiny bones breaking. The ghosts of my brothers hovered in the doorway to the hall, leaving without me. Marnie lay still as a stone, and on her phone the faces piled up. 'Do you copy? Do you copy?' My claws slipped a little more, nowhere to dig in, and the rail groaned, and with one last powerful tug Rob tore it from the wall. As it plunged to the floor, plaster dust spreading like smoke, the curtains sinking into soft mounds, I fled the room.

The front door was shut. The kitchen door was shut. No way out, and Rob thundering down the hall, roaring a wordless roar. Herding me straight into the bathroom. I landed on the windowsill to catch my breath, but he was right behind me, slamming the door, shutting us both inside. I flew to the top of the mirror, then to the rail above the bath, then to the rusty heater – all within his thrashing reach. He snatched at the tip of my tail, and as I pulled myself free I saw a long black feather whirling away, caught in the updraughts of our bodies. I flew high, higher; I had no choice but to keep circling that cramped room, my wings brushing the speckled ceiling. Down below, Rob was watching, waiting for me to tire. I caught glimpses of myself in the mirror: my soft black belly; the flashes of white just like my father's. Rob sat panting on the lip of the bath, his breaths marking time with my wingbeats. Perhaps he would pass out. That happened when he drank; it happened. Perhaps he would fall backwards into the bath, or forwards onto the broken tiles. Crack his head, snap his neck. Over. But he just kept watching me trace my orbit around and around the lightshade that looked like the moon if the moon were filled with moths.

'I've got all night,' he said. 'Nowhere to go.'

Nowhere to go. Nowhere to go.

He stared up at the mould. 'Fuck that's filthy.'

In the distance I could hear my flock carolling, singing their wild songs, the notes tumbling one over the other. Little bright pebbles, little bright coins. The Sun-Woman was almost at the edge of the world, and soon she would snuff out her blazing bark torch, and soon every magpie would return home to the pines, settle down with their family for the night. The song grew and spread until it was pouring from one vast throat, one vast bird, a bird so immense it could snatch up a man in the gorge of its beak and devour him.

Then I heard a much smaller sound.

A much closer sound.

Something scurrying above me.

Something scuttling and scuffling.

Eating through the wood and the wires.

Not a bird.

Above the vanity I saw the place where Rob had climbed into the roof to lay the poison, and I aimed straight for it, shoved myself against the trapdoor. It jolted in its frame. I circled the room once more and tried again, and this time it lifted the width of a handspan, then fell shut. Down on the lip of the bath, Rob was laughing. 'Knock yourself out,' he slurred. Over and over I pushed against the door, but I could feel myself weakening. I listened to my flock. One vast bird. Their blood my blood. On my final try I approached from as far away as possible, from the corner of the room. I was my father's son, my father who knew no fear and swooped like a gale, like a god. With a strength I didn't know I had, I smashed my body into the trapdoor – and it opened. And it stayed open. A hole in the mouldy sky. Up I went.

The space was close and airless, all the heat of the day trapped there, and the stench trapped too: old straw, something unburied. Blotches of evening light fell through the rusty iron roof, but to begin with I couldn't see much. Then the scuffling started up again, and soft shapes whipped past me. The shine of little eyes. Slowly I made out the rotten rafters, the borer-beetle dust piled in great powdery drifts. The rats going about their stealthy business. Here and there a rat skeleton, its skull the size of a thumb, its tail bones as tiny as grains of rice.

Rob was shouting at the hole: 'Yeah, you belong with the vermin. Stay up there and starve.' He opened the bathroom door and stumbled along the hall, and I followed above him, tracing his steps, listening, listening, head tilted to the side, the way my sister had taught me to listen for the grubs under the earth. I heard the kitchen door open, the clink of a bottle. The unscrewing of a cap. More stumbling back to the living room, and the click and creak of the footstool on his TV chair. Then his voice, chopping its way up through the eggshell-thin ceiling, rattling the nibbled wires: 'Are you just going to lie there? Stupid bitch. Stupid fucking whore. I should slit your fucking throat.'

I could not move. I could not breathe. Head tilted, I strained my ears for any sound from Marnie. A whimper. A plea.

Nothing.

Rob started flicking through the TV channels: people laughing too hard; people talking about incredible prices that wouldn't last, and a vacuum cleaner that could handle anything you threw at it, and an SUV that wasn't your average SUV. A man sang about pasta. A woman said *Finally tonight*, and another woman said *How did it feel when you knew you'd lost the leg?* Then came a story I knew. A man was saying . . . *for the whole family at today's Axeman's Carnival.*

Internet sensation Tama the talking magpie was the star of the show, performing with his owner and her sister. Marnie and Ange started to sing, and though it was only their voices, and not the real Marnie and the real Ange, I pecked at the empty air right on cue. *Tama was saved*— the man started to say, but Rob yelled, 'Fuck off!' and the TV fell silent. A moment later I heard the back door open and then slam shut.

Over in the corner, above the master bedroom, something caught my eye. It looked like the bear from my bed. I edged closer. Light from a rust hole showed brown fur, whiskers, a tail. No, half a dozen tails knotted together, and half a dozen heads too, and countless little claws. Not a bear but a tangle of rats, a rat king rotting away to pelts, each animal bound to the other by its own tail – and, I saw, by strands of long black hair. As I shrank from it I sensed movement, a subtle displacing of the foetid air. Was the terrible creature rousing itself? Was it about to speak, many-mouthed, in some terrible voice? But instead I heard the ghost of my mother as she landed next to me, the click-click of her bones, and she said *You can't stay here forever, you need to return home.* And I knew she was right. She led me back through the gloom of the roof to the trapdoor, and I stood at its edge and listened. *Nothing*, she said, pushing me closer to the hole. *Nothing nothing.* Down I went.

In the living room Marnie still lay on the floor. I didn't know where to touch her; everything seemed hurt. Blood on her face. Blood on her arms and legs. Her left hand swollen red. Softly, softly, I nudged at her swollen cheek – and she opened her eyes.

'Tama,' she whispered. 'My Tama. Shhh. I'm playing dead.'

I nudged at her again, and she looked around the room. Then, flinching, she sat up. 'Has he gone?' She pressed her right hand to her ribs as if to hold herself together.

In front of us on the coffee table, her phone glowed.

'Oh my God, it's on,' she said, looking over at the Eye as the followers kept appearing on the phone screen. Face after face after face, each with something to say. Bracing her elbows against the cracked glass tabletop, she pushed herself to her feet and tried to take a deep breath, but the air caught in her throat. She crossed the room to the black box, step by slow step. Turned it off. Sank onto the couch. 'Where is he?' she said. 'The woolshed?' We both looked out the cracked window that bent the hillside in two. Then she reached for her phone and started to scroll through the comments. She said, 'Listen to this. Listen. Holy shit, are you watching the live feed? Is that Tama's dad? He's really laying into her. Is anyone watching? I think she said she's pregnant! OMG is Tama OK? Did he hurt him? What about her? Someone should do something. This guy needs help. Can he still fly? @Pamorama you have to see this! Please Jesus help our friend Tama at this time. What about his mum? Someone should ring the police. Why doesn't he fly away? @SmudgyBudgie are you watching? Tama, get out of there now! He's attacking him, he's attacking Tama. And Tama's mum, right? Sending thoughts and prayers to you Tama. Someone should stop him. He's got him round the neck! He's going to wring his neck! He's breaking his neck! @Jessie99 WTF are we watching LOL. @MikeCorbett pass the popcorn. OMG OMG poor Tama! Hello, people – there's a woman there too! Someone should call the SPCA. Dear Lord Jesus protect our precious Tama who is without sin. Why doesn't she fight back? Is that a coal shovel? I can't look I can't look. He'll crush his skull. Who's watching? @Sherrywithacherry this is the talking bird I told you about. Someone should go round there. The man's a maniac. Does anyone know the address? We need to uplift Tama! AND HIS MUM!!!! Where did he go? I can't see him? @BlackYoda I can't see him either. Tama, Tama, where are you? Say something Tama! Let us know you're OK! I'm crying here, crying.

I can't look away. KICK HIM IN THE NUTS, LOVE. Shit is she OK? Someone should intervene. Everyone pray for Tama as hard as you can so God hears us. I think he's up above the curtains? I hear him now! Haha he thinks he's a cop. He's above the window. Oh please not Tama our special boy. A WOMAN IS BEING ATTACKED WHAT IS WRONG WITH YOU??? He's talking like a cop LOL. @KlausInHamburg Das ist doch deine neuseeländische Elster, oder? Sweet Lord our Saviour lower your loving hand to keep Tama safe. Wilderness Road. It's Wilderness Road. Where's that? Middle of fucking nowhere, mate. Who's the slut?'

Marnie dropped the phone back on the coffee table and began shivering. 'I'm leaving,' she said, but she stayed where she was. 'You too, Tama. We need to leave.' Still she stayed where she was, cradling her swollen red hand.

Go home, said the ghost of my mother. *Home. He will kill her. He will kill her just as he killed me. And then he will kill you.*

I looked through the window again, up past the woolshed to the pines that cut black shapes from the air.

Go home. It's not safe here.

Marnie made her way to the bathroom, trying to hurry now, leaning against the walls with her good hand. She dabbed herself clean – as clean as she could – and stripped off the remains of her costume. I could see the contours of his fists on her, the furious blotches. The marks at her neck. That was how houses worked. I thought again of all the clues I'd collected about Rob to stay one step ahead, to figure out his MO. To beat him at his own game. All the evidence I'd stored under the bath, right at the back, against the gurgling pipe that vanished into the ground. His beer-bottle top, cool and dull and bitter. His headache pills that rattled behind their silver foil. His page of newspaper twisted into a twig. His pile of plastic lighters with fire in their hearts.

'What's that smell?' Marnie said, and sniffed at her own forearm. Then she saw the trapdoor open in the ceiling, and I half expected the rat king to appear at the hole and launch itself at us, all claws and tails and shrivelled snouts bound with long black hair. 'Come on,' she said. 'We need to get out of here.'

In the master bedroom she pulled on a fresh dress, wincing as she raised her arms, then dragged the suitcase from the wardrobe.

I knew what that meant.

The car.

When she saw me backing away she said, 'It's fine, Tama. Just a little drive. We have to go. We have to.' Her voice a whisper, a gasp.

She disappeared to the laundry and when she returned she was carrying a cage. 'Look,' she said. 'Your own private quarters. It won't be like last time. You won't be scared.' She opened the door to show me. 'We'll put my nice soft jersey in here for you. See? It's not a trap, I promise.'

I poked my head inside. It looked like a trap. No mirror, no morsels of fat, no call-bird luring her own family to their deaths: just Marnie, my Marnie, stroking my back, speaking to me in her softest voice. But it looked like a trap.

'This was Snow's carrier,' she said. 'Our old white cat. You know how to be a cat, Tama, don't you. Meow? Meow?' She waved her good hand inside the cage door, tried to push me towards it. I fluttered a few steps back. 'Okay. Okay. I'll just leave it here so you can have a bit of a poke around, all right? But then we really will have to go.'

She started packing clothes in the suitcase, pausing every few seconds to catch her breath. Fingertips fluttering over her kicked ribs.

It looked like a trap.

When her back was turned, I stole from the room.

I had no idea what I was going to do, but I knew I had to find Rob.

I said nothing as I passed through the cat door.

Over the paddocks I flew, over the dusty sheep gnawing at the last of the grass, the gold miners' water race cutting its way through the dry earth, though there was no gold these days. The shelterbelts whispered and sighed, and high on the hillside ahead of me the sweet-scented pines, the susurrous pines, where my mother warmed me in my egg and spoke to me of the parching sun and the pummelling wind so I would know how the wild worked.

In the woolshed Rob stood at the grinder, sharpening his practice axe. The sparks burst and fell, bright seeds, and the blade sang its keen song. He tested the edge on his thumb, then stumbled over to sit on the broken couch, its guts spilling out around him. A cigarette burned between his teeth, and in his hands the honing stone. He dragged it across the blade, his movements all haywire and wild, the glittering specks of steel catching in his clothes, shining in the grain of his skin as if they had always been part of him, and surely he would slip, surely he would slice himself open. He stropped the axe across his palm to take off the last of the feather edge. Hush, hush, hush.

He didn't see me. In the darkness I was only moonlight and shadows.

A bottle lay at his feet, and he paused to gulp down the last of its burnt-brown contents. 'Fuck,' he mumbled when he realised he'd dropped his cigarette. He tried to light another, but the flame kept dying in the breeze from the open door, so he turned his body towards the shelter of the shed. Puffed out a great wing of smoke. Then he stood, raised his arms and buried the blade of the axe into the belly of the couch. He yanked it towards him, the old upholstery creaking as it split. 'Bitch,' he said. 'Stupid bitch.' I said nothing. Not a word.

Piled in cartons against the wall, all the toy Tamas. Rob's eyes drooped shut for a second or two, then he snatched up the empty bottle, trying to drink from it before hurling it at the wall. 'Bitch,' he said again, chopping the couch. 'Bitch. Bitch. Bitch.' Chop. Chop. Chop. The blade stuck in one of the arms. I remained silent. Not a word, not a word. He sucked at his cigarette and then he wrenched the axe from the arm and rested it on his shoulder the way he rested his rifle on his shoulder when he went to shoot pests in the pines, the way the perps on TV rested their rifles and their swords and their lengths of blunt-force steel on their shoulders – *He will kill her*, cried the ghost of my mother, rattling at my side, *he will kill you* – only his legs wouldn't hold him, and he slumped onto the couch. In a moment his eyes closed, and the cigarette tumbled from his mouth, and those things would kill him. It came to rest on the wrecked upholstery. The bone-dry, wrecked upholstery.

Not a word.

Other birds knew how to build nests, but I knew how to build a fire. Pinecones and paper and kindling, crisscross, crisscross, and gaps for the air to get in. What a clever boy. What clever thinking.

I stole over to a box of toy Tamas and sliced open the tape the way I'd seen Marnie and Rob slice it open. Not a word. On the couch the cigarette shone like a father's eye. *Quick quick*, said the ghost of my mother, so I pulled strips of packing paper from the box and lay them across the smouldering couch, and in the cobwebby corners of the woolshed I found some dry leaves and strips of straw, and I wove those in as well. Crisscross, crisscross. The breeze from the open door did the rest, forcing its airy fingers into all the gaps. Stroking the tiny twitch of flame.

And it rose up around him, that fiery nest, as red as my red eyes, as red as the devil's blood, and he did not wake. So much hotter than the fire in our hearth. So much louder. Things cracked and smashed. Things collapsed. And I stood at the door and watched, and my right eye saw Rob cast on the couch, and my left eye saw my father landing on the mound of stones from the dry riverbed. Hopping to the grassless ground. Drawing near. Nearer. He did not call to me, though I knew he had seen me. He began to preen himself, his feathers iridescent in the strange light. The woolshed was filling with smoke, a thick grey fleece that rubbed at the rafters, and I turned to look at the fire with both eyes, to take in its every barb and twist. Soon enough it reached the boxes of toys and tore away the cardboard, and then their wings were on fire and their heads were on fire and they started to speak.

'Good morning and welcome,' they said. 'I'm Tama . . . I'm Tama . . . I'm Tama . . .'

One after the other they opened their throats and I heard myself copied many times over, a chorus of selves, a babble of Tamas offering up their flimsy repertoire. 'I would like to gobble you up . . . yum yum yum . . . good morning and welcome . . . welcome . . . that's not funny . . . I'm Tama . . . gobble you up . . . you up . . . I'm Tama . . . Tama . . . Tama . . . meow . . .'

And then, above the roaring voice of the fire, Rob's voice faking my voice faking Rob's voice: 'Don't you dare . . . Don't you dare . . . dare . . . dare . . .'

When I looked back again my father had gone, his black-and-white body vanished into moonlight and shadows.

CHAPTER THIRTY

While Marnie was in hospital, Ange came to the house to feed the dogs. She put food in my dish too, but I wouldn't touch it; I still remembered how to fend for myself. Chin Scar fed out to the sheep, and he tried to get the dogs to obey him, but he didn't know Rob's whistles and calls and couldn't do Rob's voice, so they ignored him.

There was little left of the woolshed. Men arrived and scrutinised its remains, took photos of the burnt wiring, the steel bones of the wool press, the stumps that had held up the floor. They poked at the panels of corrugated iron all buckled and crushed. They examined the black guts of the couch. It looked like an accident, they said. Conditions couldn't have been better: the weeks without rain, the old timber. All the lanolin in the wood.

For a few days Rob's shirts still clung to the clothesline by their cuffs, not a breath of breeze to stir them. Then Barbara and Ange came in their rubber gloves, and they ripped down the shirts and shoved them into rubbish bags, followed by the rest of Rob's things still in the house. His jeans and socks and jumpers, his underpants, his shoes, his boots that stood dusty at the back door. His hairbrush, his toothbrush, his sunglasses, his wallet. His ten golden axes. His balaclava. His cigarettes. Away it all went. Rubbish.

'Jase rang me,' said Barbara. 'Offered to help with the funeral. I told him that was nothing to do with us and he could contact the undertaker himself if he wanted to. Goodness me, what is the man thinking? That we're sitting around deciding between Amazing Grace and Nearer My God to Thee?' She tore another rubbish bag from her endless roll.

'I'll feel much happier once he's in the ground,' said Ange. 'Or is it a cremation? I mean, it's half done already.'

'Burial,' said Barbara. 'At the local cemetery, where his parents are. Only one more day to wait.'

'Do you think she'll stay on here?'

'She says she will. The bloody bird, I suppose.'

'Language.'

That night I dreamed of a man-sized box made from planks of pine. It started to shake and splinter, and an axehead tore through the side and the lid split in two – and there was Rob chopping his way out, his hands on fire.

In the morning I flew to the place of the dead: the graveyard I'd passed on the way home from my abduction. I saw a fresh hole near the bottom of the hill, deeper than anything Help could dig, deep enough to hold death. I waited in the eucalypts that were shedding their skins. To either side of me, just beyond the fenceline, the gorse was taking over the hot hills, the black pods popping, spreading their seeds. On the graves the little windmills started to flutter: something was coming.

The long black car crept along the road with barely a sound, and stopped not far from the hole. The mourners followed in their own cars: men wearing crooked ties round their necks, women in their best casualwear smartened up with pearls. The axemen wore their team uniforms – white trousers, black singlets – and with their axemen's arms they bore the box to the hole. Then I heard it: wingbeats disrupting the hot thick air. I looked up and saw the sky full of birds, full of magpies – my own flock, my own blood, landing all around me in the scraggy eucalypts. The mourners looked up too, and the axemen set the box down on the planks that straddled the hole, and Chin Scar said, 'I wonder what that means.' I thought I should say something, but I did not know whether to speak or sing. And then, as the axemen took up the ropes and started to lower the box, my father threw back his head and opened his throat and began to call *This is my son, my own boy, who has killed the man who killed his mother. Rejoice, rejoice at the work of my child!* And the rest of the flock joined in: *See what our boy has done, our precious boy born in the pines. He has killed the killer of magpies, the chopper of trees. Rejoice, rejoice! The man with the gun is dead, the man with the beetle-black car is dead, the man with the axe is dead.* On and on they carolled, and I sat at the centre of the song and felt their every note buzz in my blood.

Barbara wanted to stay with Marnie when she came home from the hospital, but Marnie said she'd prefer to be alone. That first evening, I remember, she and I sat on the back porch and watched the sky change colour. Up on the hillside the remains of the woolshed were nothing more than a smudge of soot. I thought of the night it happened: how quickly the fire had grown from Rob's dropped cigarette. The shock of the heat. The noise of it. The flames surrendering themselves to the sky. My father drawing near to see. And then, after he'd gone, someone else drawing near too: someone walking up the hill, slowly, gingerly, every step an effort. Marnie, my Marnie, coming to find me. Standing beside me while everything burned and collapsed. 'I suppose we should call the fire brigade,' she'd said. 'I suppose we should call an ambulance.' But there we'd stood, she and I, watching the flames cast their beautiful light, as if we had found the source of the Sun-Woman's fire.

On that first evening home, as we sat on the porch, she took a photo of me silhouetted against the twilight and a photo of me perched on her cast. When the sky was black-black we went inside, where the only reminders of Rob were the clues I'd stored under the bath, against the gurgling pipe that vanished into the ground. And he too had vanished into the ground, and he would stay under the ground, a great white root, and one day I would return to the graveyard and tilt my head to listen for the corpse grubs, deep, down deep and chewing. And in a little while, after Marnie's belly had swelled to an egg, and the baby had begun to flutter in the soft close dark, held in that membranous press, we'd be a family.

Marnie cleaned her teeth in the speckled bathroom, and I watched her in the mirror as she brushed and spat and brushed and spat and rinsed, and she watched me watching her, and the sooty mould crept across the ceiling and around the lightshade that looked like the moon if the moon were filled with moths, and it crept down the walls and over the window and along the skirting boards, and there was no stopping it.

In the master bedroom Marnie lifted the cushions from the master bed: the cushion with the sheepswool sheep and the cushion with the dead lavender and all the satiny heart-shaped cushions. Then she folded back the blankets and climbed in, and I climbed in too. The rain began to patter on the roof.

'Good night, Tama,' she said.

'Good night, Tama,' I said.

And then we slept.

ACKNOWLEDGEMENTS

I am grateful for the use of diaries written by my late mother-in-law, Beryl Bekhuis, who lived on a high-country sheep station. Likewise, the publications of Gisela Kaplan, an expert on the Australian magpie, proved invaluable. For their help with my research, thank you to Hinemoana Baker, veterinarian Dave Bergen, Neale Blaymires (TrapWorks), Suz and Campbell Bremner, Kate Cocks (Mt Nicholas Station), Neil Gillespie (Contact Energy), Paul Hersey, Marcus Hobson, Tamara Izhar-Larsen, Michael Mathieson, Davida Mead (Dingleburn Station), ornithologist Colin Miskelly (Te Papa), Officer Cho (Los Angeles Police Department), champion woodchoppers Bradley Pako and Mikhayla Tainui-McLean, John Perriam (Bendigo Station), Jayne Rive (Cloudy Peak Station), Kylie Ryan and Mudjar Aboriginal Corporation, Diane Ruwhiu, Suz Sainty, Dan Salmon, Marty Smith and her resident magpie Pecky Sharp, Oliver Stewart, woodchopping commentator Peter Templeton, and Peter Young.

Thank you to my publishers Fergus Barrowman and Christopher Potter, and to everyone at Te Herenga Waka University Press and Europa Editions. For their editorial guidance, thank you to Jane Parkin and Sarah Ream. Thank you to my agent Caroline Dawnay and her assistant Kat Aitken. Thank you, Sue Orr, Tracey Slaughter and my colleagues at the University of Waikato. And thank you, as ever and ever, to Alan Bekhuis, Alice Chidgey and Pat Chidgey.

NOTE

Throughout the book, Tama refers to his 'flock.' Strictly speaking, this is not the correct term for a territorial group like his – it applies to larger, less cohesive groups with no defined territory. However, since Tama uses whichever words he pleases, I left the decision up to him.

ABOUT THE AUTHOR

Catherine Chidgey's novels have been published to international acclaim. *The Axeman's Carnival* was a number one bestseller in the author's native New Zealand, as was her previous novel *Pet* (Europa, 2023), which Ruth Franklin in the *New York Times* called 'a lingering, haunting book.' Chidgey's many awards include the Prize in Modern Letters, the Katherine Mansfield Award, the Janet Frame Fiction Prize, and the Jann Medlicott Acorn Prize for Fiction. She lives in Ngāruawāhia and lectures in Creative Writing at the University of Waikato.